MARBLED MARVELS

Where the Magic Happens

Katie Simpkins

Katie Simpkins is the pseudonym of Duncan Brockwell. This is his second book, after the heart-warming romance, The Southern Belles.

Duncan Brockwell is also the author of critically acclaimed crime thriller series, *The Met Murder Investigations (No Way Out, Bird of Prey and Bad Blood), and psychological thriller, Mr Invisible.*

Coming Soon:

The Hard Way – Crime Thriller – April 19th 2021

Oakwood Falls – Supernatural Fantasy – 1st July 2021

Hellingly – Supernatural Horror – October Date TBC

Follow Duncan here:

Instagram: @dcbrockwell

Facebook Page: DCBrockwell Author

Twitter: DCBrockwell

Published by Fusion Press
Printed in the United Kingdom

Cover design and layout by Emmy Ellis

THURSDAY, JANUARY 10TH 2019

1

"Excuse me, dear," an elderly lady on table fifteen said, her hand raised.

Francesca Darby left the tea towel behind the bar, picked up her pad of paper and walked with purpose over to the table of two. Taking her pen out of her black shirt pocket, she smiled at the woman. "Hi! Is everything alright with your meals? Is there anything else I can do for you?"

The white-haired lady slid her plate to the edge of the table. "No, I'm afraid not. This shepherd's pie is too dry, and my husband's chips are overdone."

"They're fine, really. A bit dark maybe, but perfectly edible. Please don't trouble yourself on my account. I like my fries crispy."

"Darling, do shush," the lady said, apologising to Francesca with a roll of her eyes.

Cursing to herself silently, Francesca could do without complaint handling this afternoon. "Oh, I'm so sorry it's not to your liking. I'll take these back to the kitchen, bring you new meals. I'll pour you a tea or coffee for your troubles as well."

Stooping to pick up both heavy plates, Francesca apologised once again, turned, and walked the dishes through the swing door. In the kitchen, Aidan Marble leaned against the stainless-steel counter, his mobile in hand. She guessed he was playing some game or other. "The pie's dry, and chips over-fried."

Guessing that he would moan about having to provide two new dishes, Francesca walked out before he could start.

Back out in the restaurant, she stepped up to the table of six, asked them if everything was to their satisfaction. The business owner who booked the reservation nodded, not that he cared. "Brilliant! I'll be back later with dessert menus."

Behind the bar, the safest place to be that afternoon, she made herself look busy. Over the last couple of years, Francesca had made a habit of making herself look like she was hard at work. Two years earlier, Marble's Marvels would have been packed to the rafters every lunch and dinnertime. Before the accident, Aidan and Kate Marble loved the restaurant.

They used to love Bishops Drake, too. Sometimes she wished she had moved somewhere bigger, a town like Basingstoke or Winchester, maybe. Or a city like Southampton, or Portsmouth.

Her daddy bought her the three-bedroom house off the High Street for her and a friend. He tried to palm it off as a gift, but Francesca knew he wanted to keep her in Bishops Drake. She could have fought him on the issue, asked for a place in Basingstoke, but she fell in love with her white house with black beams.

Francesca sauntered back into the kitchen when the bell rang.

Two steaming plates sat under the lights waiting to be consumed, hopefully by a happier elderly couple this time. "Thanks."

He muttered something, not that she cared what. Francesca was trying to please his customers. She tried to forget her negative thoughts. Aidan was a lovely guy, or at least he had been before...No, she had to take the plates to table fifteen with a smile.

"Shepherd's Pie for you, and Scampi and Chips for you." Placing the dishes in front of their respective owners, Francesca stood and smiled, before bowing. "Enjoy!"

"I hope to, dear." The lady prodded and poked her meal with her fork.

Having taken a step back towards the bar, Francesca stopped.

"Do you mind if I ask what happened to this place? It used to be full every time we came, didn't it, Henry? The last time we came here was for Henry's seventy-fifth birthday a couple of years ago, and I have never seen a busier restaurant."

Back at the table, Francesca listened to her story.

"Every table in here was taken. That night, they even had to bring out extra seats. And the kitchen, don't ask me how, but they kept up with the orders. Food came flying out of those doors. And the proprietors, they were lovely. A couple-"

"Aidan and Kate Marble, yes, the current owners."

"You mean? They're still here? I thought someone else must have taken over, or something? For it to be this quiet during lunch, even in January; it would have been unheard of a couple of years ago. We have friends in Robertsbridge who used to drive over an hour and a half just to come here. What happened?"

Francesca glanced around the large open-plan room, looking for Kate, who was around somewhere. Happy the coast was clear, she knelt so that she was on the same level as the lady. "I shouldn't say this, but things have changed a bit around here."

"I can see that dear. Changed how?"

Checking for Kate again, Francesca needed to explain the average food. "Their son, Vincent died in a car accident." Before the woman asked for details, she headed her off. "He was driving with friends when their car was hit by a drink driver. Out of five people in the collision, only one survived. He's never going to walk again and suffers from mild brain damage."

The woman's face changed, from nosey to horrified. "Oh, that's just awful. My heart goes out to them, darling." She looked to her husband for support.

"Aidan took it hard. He's never healed. The business took a hit, only it never bounced back. Aidan's love of cooking never returned either. The restaurant across the road mopped up the customers who would have come here, the locals and walk-ins. There's a two-week waiting list at Elio's now." She stood, regarded the shepherd's pie. "I shouldn't say this, but if you go now, you might be lucky and grab a table there."

"Thank you, but that would be rude," the lady ruled. "Oh, how awful for them."

Francesca nodded her agreement. "Ooh, here's Kate now. Please don't let on I told you their personal business; it's more than my job's worth." When the woman reassured her that her secret was safe, Francesca relaxed a little. "Thank you! Enjoy your meals. If there is anything else you need, I'll be by the bar."

"These chips are delicious, by the way," the husband said, spearing one with his fork.

"I'm going to mention you to my son, dear," the woman said, as Francesca went to leave. The woman smiled up at her.

Standing at the table, Francesca's brow furrowed. "Really? Why?"

"He's a Michelin star chef," the woman confessed. "He's opening a restaurant here in Bishops Drake. When he told us he has a meeting lined up with the owner of this wonderful place, we had to come and take one last look."

Francesca glared over at Kate Marble, who was standing behind the bar, tapping away on the till screen, oblivious to her staring. "What? No, there must be some kind of mistake. Are you sure?"

"Oh yes, dear, he's meeting with her in a couple of weeks, apparently. I'll put a good word in for you. You seem like a hard worker; you're polite to customers. I'm sure he'll snap you up. I'll speak to him."

Annoyed, and trying to hide the fact, Francesca thanked the lady, who introduced herself as Margaret, and her husband as Henry. Finally free, she sauntered over to the bar, where Kate tapped on the screen. "That couple over there, they're interesting people."

Her employer didn't look up, continuing to tap. "Hmm? Yeah, that's nice, Fran."

For years, Francesca had admired Kate Marble. Everything about her screamed stylish, from her trendy hairstyles, clothing, and jewellery, to her down-to-Earth outlook on life. With fabulous glossy brown hair, a pretty smile, and slim figure, Kate was a catch. Francesca didn't think she looked forty-nine. Thirty-nine maybe. "Yeah, interesting."

"I'm a bit busy here, love." Her boss stopped typing for a second, regarded her. "I'm inputting a big party's pre-order. Can this wait?"

Apologising, Francesca loitered, anger bubbling inside her. "When were you going to tell me you're putting this place up for sale, huh?" She couldn't believe the words came out.

Kate shot her a warning glare, gesturing for Francesca to follow her over to the coffee machine, away from the few customers. "Keep your voice down! No one's selling this place."

Not believing her, Francesca folded her arms. "Oh? That woman's lying, is she? You're not meeting some Michelin star chef to discuss him taking the lease on this place?" She could tell Kate wanted to be anywhere but here, squirming.

Kate's face changed, from defensive to apologetic; her demeanour softened. "Look, I'm meeting him to talk through his plans. It's all preliminary at this stage, and I haven't even told Aidan yet, so Lord only knows what he's going to say."

"If he has any sense, he'll try and stop you." Francesca felt choked up.

Kate put her hand on Francesca's shoulder. "You know better than anyone that this place is dying, Fran. Marble's Marvels is on her last legs, and it's going to take a miracle to get her on her feet again, especially with Elio over the road with his two-for-ones, and all you can eat for a tenner meal deals. We can't compete with that."

"Maybe if you got a decent chef in people might start coming back?" She regretted speaking out of turn when she received a glare. "I'm sorry! I didn't mean that. It's just that Aidan's head's not in it anymore, Kate. This place needs the old Aidan. He had heart and dedication. He was a laugh, too."

With a sigh, Kate agreed. "He was. This place used to be fun. Packed every lunch and dinner, tables turning over twice, sometimes three times of an evening."

Being the two-year anniversary of the crash tomorrow, Francesca felt guilty adding pressure on Kate. "I didn't mean to bring back old memories."

"It's fine. Don't you think I reminisce about the glory days? I do. I would give anything to take this place back to the way it was a couple of years ago, anything. But reality has different plans for this restaurant. And like I said, without some sort of miracle, we're probably going to be closing the doors soon. I'm sorry you're finding out like this."

Maybe having Margaret put in a good word for her with her son was not such a bad idea. Francesca had known about the financial strain, but not the extent. She should have seen the situation coming months earlier, with lunches all but dead, and dinner services erratic.

Walking over to the front windows, Francesca thought she might enquire about vacancies at Elio's. She had waited busy restaurants before - well, one, here - and it didn't matter if she took out Italian dishes, or British fare.

2

Kate Marble wanted to cry. Although she was inputting a pre-order for thirty starters, mains and desserts, the large bill wouldn't help much. Her beloved restaurant was gasping her last few breaths.

The hardest thing about their situation was remembering how Marble's Marvels used to be. On the night of the crash, she and Aidan had seen their thirty tables turn over twice, some three times. So, while she had been behind the bar getting drinks orders ready, and while her husband had been on the line in the kitchen, her son Vinnie was being cut out of his Vauxhall Astra, along with two of his friends. The two in the other car died as well.

Printing the bill off, Kate saved the tab on the till. Looking at her place now depressed her. With only two tables in use, the amount they made from lunch didn't cover the wages, much less the bills. Kate didn't want to start down the path of closing if she was empty, knowing it was a short step away from shutting her for good. If people couldn't rely on Marble's to be open when they needed them to be, her customers would go elsewhere.

Taking her laptop to table thirty, at the far end on the right, Kate sat down, her clipboard in front of her. She and Aidan were expecting a notification of their credit application from The Roderick's Foundation, a small charity offering loans to businesses unable to secure finance from more traditional channels such as banks.

Lord knew she had attempted securing investment from every bank possible. Every executive she spoke to considered investing in Marble's Marvels a huge risk; they couldn't foresee that miracle she needed happening. One manager suggested they compete with Elio's on two-for-one meal deals, which they tried. It didn't make a dent.

The biggest problem she had was her husband. Or rather the shell of her husband, who resided in the kitchen, producing average food at best. Since Vinnie died two years earlier almost to the day, Aidan had lost his passion for the job. If they had a full restaurant now, she would be offering free drinks to every table in compensation for their lacklustre experience of dining at Marble's. It was no way to run a business.

She only wished she could talk to him about it. Before the crash, Aidan was wonderful, a devoted father, loving hubby, magnificent chef, and loyal friend. Kate couldn't have been happier with her choice of partner. They had everything going for them. For fifteen years they owned a successful business that brought in a great income, enough to put Vinnie through private school, and for three family holidays a year. Then there was the house, a five-bedroom palace on the outskirts of Bishops Drake. And the cars. While he drove a top-of-the-line Range Rover, Kate owned a red MG convertible, her baby.

Their lives so different now, she and Aidan still lived in the same house. Now up to its neck in mortgages, they had to re-mortgage it twice to keep the restaurant afloat. What counted for their savings amounted to a few thousand, which alarmed her. If they didn't come up with a new line of credit soon, she would be forced to close Marble's doors forever, and file for bankruptcy. Kate would do anything to prevent that.

It wouldn't have been so bad if Aidan talked to her, but he didn't. Her husband bottled his feelings, letting them build up until they exploded, which they had on a couple of occasions since losing Vinnie. She would have left him by now, except that she knew he was a good man, and in spite of his flaws she still loved him so. It was this attitude that had caused most of the other staff to leave, although they would have had to let them go eventually anyway.

The only thing keeping them together was Aidan's occasional displays of affection. He could be a blank piece of wood for weeks, hardly saying a word, and then one night, he would want sex. Desperate for a bit of normality, Kate would oblige, clinging on to those moments, hoping he might open up, let her in.

It never happened, though. Aidan couldn't mourn Vinnie's death, it seemed. He never confided in her his true feelings, but Kate didn't need psychic abilities to realise that he carried a lot of guilt over Vinnie's death. They both did, but she unloaded on her sister. Kate cried often, wondering what would have happened if she and Aidan had let Vinnie quit university? Would he have been in his car at that time?

Vinnie and Aidan had argued so intensely that afternoon about their son leaving his architects course at the University of Southampton. Kate had joined in, backing her husband; she didn't want to see him throwing it all away over a silly notion to go travelling for a year. "Go abroad after," she'd said. "Take two years out if you need to but finish your degree first."

Her words were ignored. Aidan and Vinnie kept arguing until she thought her husband would explode. At the height of their row their son flounced out, like he always did when losing an argument. Kate ran after him. Outside, on their driveway, she tried to stop him driving angry, but he closed the Astra door too quickly. "Wait! Don't go like this, Vin, please."

Those were the last words she said to her son. Why couldn't she have told him she loved him? Still, it could have been worse. Aidan's last words to Vinnie were, "You're a bloody fool, do you know that?"

Francesca approached the elderly couple's table with the card reader. Kate watched the couple prepare to leave when her waitress apologised for their first meals. She overheard the woman tell Francesca the replacements were fine. Not great, not wonderful, just fine.

They had eight customers over lunch, and two were unhappy. Kate shook her head. "Unbelievable!" After the couple had left the premises, she beckoned Francesca over. "What was all that about?"

Her best waitress attempted to cover for Aidan. "Come on, Fran, I heard you apologising over there. Tell me what happened, please."

"A small complaint, honest, nothing big. The woman complained her shepherd's pie was dry, and the man's chips were overdone."

Kate's temper rose. "You're kidding me! We're getting chips returned to us now? I don't believe this."

"They were a bit brown, sure, but there was nothing wrong with them, Kate," Francesca tried to reassure her. "She complained for him; he was happy with them."

Standing, Kate regarded Francesca. "I appreciate you're covering for my husband, I do, but you shouldn't. He's probably not changed the oil in the fryer. I keep telling him to keep up with the cleaning. You watch, I'll go in there only to find him on his mobile playing some stupid game."

Why had she let it go on like this for so long? For months he'd neglected his duties, preferring to play games on his phone. Marching into the kitchen, she caught him leaning against the stainless-steel salad counter, phone in hand, thumbs poised in some stupid game, usually Angry Birds. "What's this I hear about two complaints, Aidan?" She stood in front of him, her arms crossed.

He looked up. "I dealt with them." He went back to his game.

Grabbing his mobile, Kate's eyes narrowed, her face growing redder by the second. "Those two customers represented twenty-five percent of today's lunch trade; did you know that? We've served eight mains all day, and a quarter of those sent their food back."

Aidan leaned against the salad bar, his face blank.

"Well? What have you got to say?"

He had the ability to make her so mad she wanted to punch something, anything, just to relieve herself of the anger and frustration. He stood in front of her, not caring one bit. "Do you want this place to close?" He shook his head. "So why are we having so many complaints, huh? Talk to me!"

Aidan walked towards the double sink. "What can I say? She found the pie dry. I made it yesterday; it's been in the fridge overnight. You know how food dries up in there. I prefer my shepherd's pie to be dryer myself. There was nothing wrong with it."

Kate strolled over to the double deep-fat fryer. "What about the brown chips you sent out?" She inspected the fryers. "When was the last time you changed the oil? It's disgusting in there."

Meeting her at the fryers, Aidan threw his marigolds at the basins behind him. "Monday. And what's the matter with you anyway? You're acting like we receive complaints every service."

She stopped staring at the oil. "How can we when we don't have any customers? You chased them all away with your less than average cooking." Her husband walked back to the sink, putting his yellow gloves on. "That sign out front, the one that says, 'Where the Magic Happens,' should be changed to, 'Where the Shit Happens,' because that's how you're running this kitchen now."

He turned to her, a yellow finger pointing at her. "Oh, it's my average cooking, is it? Rather than customers coming in to find you with a long face every day. If I were greeted at the door by you, I think I'd turn on round and go across the road to Elio's as well."

How dare he? Kate was the strong one in this relationship; at least that was what her sister kept telling her. "Me? I've done all I can to build this place back up again. I couldn't have put more effort in if I tried."

Francesca burst through the double hinged door. "Will you two stop fighting, please. It's not helping any, is it? We need to bring this place back before it's too late. Now, stop blaming each other, and don your thinking caps, will you?"

After receiving Francesca's mouthful, Kate stared at the dirty floor. "What's that?" She pointed at the red, grease proof lino. "It's filthy, Aidan. Look at it. No wonder we've only got a hygiene rating of three from the FSA."

"Don't even try and bring that up." He turned the hot tap off, placing plates in the soapy water. "You know as well as I do my kitchen got passed last time. It was the building's structural integrity that brought our stars down. If customers research us, they'll find my food hygiene in here is impeccable. Go ahead, honey, check my day dotting, temperature charts, the works. It's all there, look at the logs."

Kate couldn't argue with him. The important stuff he was fanatical about; her husband did everything the way it should be done. There was no chance of any of their customers getting poisoned from Marble's food, Aidan personally probed every piece of meat he sent out. If it wasn't at seventy-five degrees or higher, it didn't go. "It's fine, I believe you. Please clean this floor, though. It is disgusting."

"Yes, boss." He saluted her.

Back out in the restaurant, Kate thanked the table of six suits. She picked up the remainder of their plates and carried them through to the kitchen, where Aidan took them from her, sinking them in hot bubbly water. "I wish Roderick's would contact us. I'm sick of all this waiting."

3

Aidan Marble muttered to himself when his wife left him washing up the eight plates and four cups. Who the hell did she think she was? Ordering him about like he was her lackey. They were partners, and if he wanted to, he could be brutally honest.

The majority of the capital they put into the restaurant came from his parents, not hers. If anything, it made Marble's Marvels more his, especially given that he cooked the food, without which there wouldn't even be a business. She drove him mental sometimes.

Looking around his once magnificent kitchen, Aidan wanted it to go back to the way it was before the crash, with his teams running around, trying to get their starters, mains or desserts out, nearly bumping into each other in the process. Not many people knew how much blood, sweat and tears went into keeping a busy kitchen.

He took pride in knowing that in all seventeen years, fifteen of which were successful, not one customer had ever waited for over thirty minutes for their meals. Nowadays, he scoffed at pub owners giving warnings of more than forty-five minutes wait on service when the building was all but empty.

Back when he had staff to manage, Aidan split his team into three. He had two chefs on starters, three including himself on Mains, and a further two on desserts. When the starter and dessert teams ran out of orders, they helped with the mains. He found this system worked better than giving each member of staff a specific section, although it did add to near accidents.

Behind the line, Aidan started wiping the steel surfaces, spraying them with cleaner, because contrary to Kate's assertion, he took health and hygiene seriously, as he should. When the Food Standards Agency inspected his kitchen, they had not brought up one area of concern. All issues were to do with the building's upkeep, and their landlords were responsible for that.

His mobile buzzed in his blue and white checked trouser pocket. Checking it, an email appeared from Roderick's Foundation, the charity they applied to for a medium sized loan. He and Kate spent days filling out the relevant forms.

"Oh no!" He hung his head at the words, *'We regret to inform you.'* That was it, over. There was no more money coming their way. He slammed his phone down, the steel making a loud metallic echo.

Kate was going to be devastated; she had scoured the internet for loan opportunities, having visited numerous bank managers, all to no avail. The Roderick's Foundation counted as their last chance at breathing life into Marble's Marvels.

He couldn't tell Kate, not yet. Aidan had to wrestle with the idea himself first. Squatting, he wiped the front of the salad bar down, making it spotless for tonight's service, such as it was. Four tables, twenty customers in total, all staggered.

Unable to put it off any longer, he picked up his phone and strolled out to the restaurant to find Kate at table thirty. Pulling out a chair opposite her, he sat down, placing the mobile with the email open in front of her. "This came through just now."

After reading it, Kate put it back down, her elbows on the wood, her fingers massaging her temples. "So that's it? We're done? We don't have any more money?"

"It looks that way, unless you found somewhere else to apply?" He would do anything to take away Kate's look of desperation. She shook her head. "We've still got enough in the bank for a few months, haven-"

"One month, tops." She stared at the wood. Kate looked up, regarding him for a second. "Well, that's that. The last resort it is then. You need to suck it up, pick up that phone and ask your parents for help."

"I'm going to be off now, Kate," Francesca said from across the restaurant. "I'll see you both this evening." She waved, walked to the front door, and left.

Aidan stood, staring at his wife. "Forget it! I'm not asking him for a penny." His wife knew how he felt about begging his parents for financial assistance in his business. "You don't want dad as a silent partner, trust me."

"No, you're right, I don't, but these are desperate times." Kate stood; her eyes unblinking. "We have a few thousand left in our account. We need a cash injection if we're going to keep her doors open." Her eyes softened. "Please, love, for me?"

Ordinarily, he would do anything for Kate. "I can't. I won't. He'll want a percentage, like Alan Sugar on steroids. If we accept more money from him, he'll be interfering and causing mayhem before you can say, 'Bill, please.' I would rather close than have dad as a partner. And you know this. Why are you asking?"

"Because I'm desperate here, Aidan, that's why." Her voice wobbled. Wiping her welling eyes, her chin crumpling, Kate stared at the wood again. "I don't want to lose her." She looked up at him. "This place is all we have left of-"

He put his hand out, squeezed her arm. "Alright, I'll phone him. Please don't say it." His wife was about to say this restaurant was the only thing they had left of their life before the crash. Before Vinnie died. If they lost this place, it would be like losing him for a second time. And he would do anything to not let that happen. "I'll phone him later. But don't be expecting miracles; he's still an arsehole. And if he accepts, don't come running to me when he starts meddling in this place. Agreed?"

Kate nodded, wiping her face. "Agreed. Thank you!"

Aidan smiled. "Anytime."

"What about now?" Kate stared at him, awaiting his reply.

"What about now, what?" He tried to seem confused.

"What about ringing your dad now? We really need this money, love. Without it, we're finished; we'll be closing her doors by the end of February at this rate."

Aidan took out his mobile, put the phone to his ear, and pretended to call his old man. "It's going through to his answerphone," he mouthed to her. "Yeah, dad, hi, it's me. Long time no speak. Erm, listen, I need to talk to you about something important. Could you give me a call back when you get this? Thanks."

"Oh, thank you for doing this," she said after he hung up. "I know you don't want to involve your parents, but we need them." She kissed him on his cheek.

"You're welcome!" He slipped his phone in his pocket, guilt rising at lying to her. She would be on his case from now on. '*Has he called yet*?' She would pester him until he relented. Now all he had to do was pretend to have a row with his dad, and that would be the end of it. Aidan would prefer to close the restaurant than have *him* sticking his oar in.

While he pretended to be in communication with his dad, Aidan started looking into possible revenue streams himself. Instead of playing Angry Birds during service, he would put the time to good use. There had to be more small charities out there like Roderick's.

After wiping the surfaces and mopping the floor, he went into the restaurant, waiting for Kate to finish the paperwork.

After five minutes, he stood when she picked up her laptop. "Are you ready?"

At five to three, Aidan let his wife out of the restaurant, stepped outside. He closed the front door behind him and locked it. "Let's go home!"

Their Range Rover was parked behind the restaurant, but to get there they had to walk past four shops. A florist, *Flo's Flowers*, run by the charming Florence; an actual greengrocer that every resident of Bishops Drake bought from - it was the hub of the community and the owner, Albert, was also vice mayor of the village. Next to the grocers was a little convenience store with a tiny post office, and lastly a small model shop.

He and Kate said good afternoon to a couple of residents as they walked past.

It made him sad to think of how Bishops Drake used to be before the crash. They'd talked to everyone. It split their home in two; there were those on his side, who believed his Vinnie was killed by a drink driver; then there were those who somehow suspected his son steered into the wrong side of the road, causing the fatal collision.

The father of the lad who crashed into Vinnie, Christian 'Chris' Ashcroft went around telling the locals that Vinnie went into his son. Aidan had nearly punched Chris in the King's Head for that slur. Ashcroft's son, Liam had been found to be over the legal drink driving limit.

Up ahead was the village church, an imposing figure that sat judging everyone. Aidan had not been to a service for over a year.

4

Elio Cappelli caught Aidan and Kate locking up. While his rivals across the road hosted for a measly eight diners, his restaurant had all twenty-five tables taken, a huge ninety-six diners leaving satisfied, with full bellies.

"How is that place still going? They only had eight customers all lunch," Martin, his assistant manager said behind him. "We're creaming them."

"Don't gloat, Martin. Don't forget how we got this busy." Elio turned away from the window. "I wouldn't wish that on my worst enemy. And Aidan and Kate are far from that." Martin nodded an apology.

Martin had worked for him for long enough to remember Marble's Marvels for the beast it once was, catering for a hundred to a hundred and fifty guests, depending on the night of the week. Aidan had that kitchen running so smoothly, Elio often wondered how he did it. Cooking fresh from scratch at that capacity was no mean feat. His team had trouble keeping up with pre-cooked produce. "Let's clean up thi
s place."

The restaurant looked like someone had thrown a grenade in it, with every table littered with plates, bowls, cutlery, and glasses. It would take his six waiters half an hour to clear away, moving around the remaining stragglers, who were finishing off their coffees and digestifs.

While he helped stack dishes from one table, he remembered how difficult setting up Elio's was four years earlier. His rival had such a huge reputation for providing home cooked British food that diners flocked from surrounding villages and towns.

As he carried the plates to the kitchen, he recalled days when his restaurant only catered for eight customers at lunchtimes. They were dull, scary times, when he wondered if he had done the right thing opening across the road from such a well-established business, where all the locals knew and liked the owners.

Aidan and Kate had been gracious when he opened the doors, offering help where it was needed. So confident were they of their business' success that they could afford some humility. Elio had taken them up on their offer, sometimes popping over there to ask for produce his chefs had run out of or needing change. They accommodated him as much as they could.

Those first two years were the toughest, most gruelling of Elio's life, the constant worry of never knowing from one month to the next if his restaurant would turnover enough capital to pay the mortgage. Luckily, he always found a way. Elio put his hair loss down to stress caused by this place, even though every male in his family had lost their hair. Hereditary factors didn't even come into it; it was the restaurant's fault.

The transformation happened shortly after the crash. Elio had lived above the restaurant for two years by this point and knew some of the locals. Vinnie's collision split the village apart, creating a crack dividing the two halves. It proved fortunate for Elio's, as Christian Ashcroft, the father of the drink driver boycotted Marble's Marvels, taking his friends with him, setting up in Elio's. Almost overnight, he had half the locals eating his food. Elio had befriended Chris Ashcroft.

It was a hard time to live in Bishops Drake. Being friendly with Chris meant he had to be careful not to be seen talking to Aidan and Kate. That was the hardest part; he liked his rivals. They were good, decent people.

The division between the Ashcrofts and Marbles went further than the restaurants. The two pubs in town took sides as well. The King's Head, owned by Aidan's best friend, threw out Ashcroft and his lot. The Red Lion's owner - a good mate of Ashcroft's - barred Aidan and Kate in response.

While Elio hated the conflict, the wound-up energy, he began making some decent money, the restaurant coming into its own, competing with Marble's Marvels.

After the funerals, he started receiving diners from across the road, locals loyal to the Marbles, who informed him that standards had dropped considerably over there. They told him that Aidan was falling to pieces, that the business was flailing.

At around the time of the first anniversary, Aidan and Ashcroft almost came to blows in the King's Head. When villagers saw Aidan cracking up, they started eating at Elio's, leaving Marble's Marvels to its self-pity.

Aidan Marble managed to alienate a significant portion of the village with his attitude, which only went to help Elio. He hated seeing his rival in pain, but every outburst brought with it more customers for his restaurant. Aidan was chasing them in.

Placing the stack of plates next to the sink, where the pot wash tried keeping up, Elio went back out to pick up more. They had a huge night ahead of them: a party of thirty-five and a booking of twelve, plus numerous other reservations. Wednesdays could be up and down. Some were frantic, others quiet; there was no reason for it.

At fifty-six, Elio tried to do less of the physical work these days, opting to manage the restaurant from behind the bar, or in front of the line in the kitchen. He left the heavy lifting to his staff, most of whom were Bishops Drake residents.

"I'll take those, Elio," his assistant manager said, picking up another stack.

It was sweet, Martin looked out for him like that. "Thanks. I'll bring the cutlery in." He didn't need to help. Elio should be counting the tills, making sure the float was ready for dinner service. The rest of the staff could set up tables for the evening. True to his word, he carried the silverware to the kitchen.

Behind the bar, he did a till read, ripping the paper, and checking the day's takings so far. Just shy of fifteen hundred was excellent for a lunch service. Elio thought of the profit margins, which were considerable for food, but not the drink.

Feeling a siesta coming on, he sat back in his office chair upstairs on the first floor, stretched and yawned. His wife would have loved how much money the restaurant took now, had she stuck around long enough to find out. Bitch! He was in this for himself, his baby, his beloved eatery was all he had.

5

Francesca Darby walked along Kings Road towards her gorgeous cottage, its white walls a shining beacon, even with the grey, dreary clouds overhead. It was small, with two bedrooms, a lounge, kitchen, and bathroom, but it had a big plot of land around it, which she and her husband, Paul planned to extend on.

Reaching her drive, the first thing she noted was Paul's car missing.

Curious, she tried shrugging it off, knowing that sometimes he liked taking long drives away from the house. Working from home had its pitfalls. She enjoyed going for long walks herself. Being so close to acres of fields at the back of her house helped.

Upon opening the front door, the coat hooks seemed emptier than usual. "Strange."

Two of Paul's jackets were missing.

Closing the door, she told herself that he might be dropping them off at the launderette; they had not been cleaned in months.

When she left him at his desk earlier in the morning, Francesca had kissed him goodbye as she did every day.

Taking off her coat, she hung it up. Cold outside, she shivered in the warmth of the cottage, thinking she might put the gas log fire on. She had three hours before she was due back at Marble's.

In the lounge, her attention focused on Paul's armchair, or rather the book cabinet next to it. Her husband used it to store DVDs. The shelves were bare. "What the-" She marched over to it, noticing only her movies remained.

Francesca scratched her head, trying to put the pieces together in her head. What would Paul do with his collection of gory and brutal movies? Would he have taken them to a charity shop? Sold them to a store? What? And what about his coats?

Struggling to focus, she trudged upstairs to their bedroom. She gasped when she saw his bedside cabinet had been emptied. His pants, socks, T shirts and jumpers were all gone, the only thing left were empty drawers. "No! You bastard!"

Forcing tears back, she checked the rest of the house.

In the bathroom, his toothbrush and toiletries were gone, along with his guitars and amp from the spare room. All that remained in the house was hers.

Pacing her lounge, Francesca wondered what she'd done, trying to piece together any evidence he might have left regarding his disappearance.

In the kitchen, she found a white envelope on the work surface with her name written on it. Not wanting to, she picked it up, ripping the sealed flap open, and taking out the A4 plain paper.

Reading his words again, drawing it out, poring over every syllable, she couldn't match them up with his actions. It said, in his handwriting, that he had met someone new, someone he had a lot in common with. "But we have lots in common." Her hands shook.

None of it made sense. She read about how they had been in a rut for over a year. He blamed her for not getting pregnant, suggesting they would still be together had she borne him a child, like that would have changed everything.

Every word he wrote stung. Francesca had herself checked out after failing to conceive. Paul knew it wasn't her fault, but he had been too afraid to have himself tested.

For two years they tried to conceive a child, two whole years. In the end he blamed her for it, saying she was barren. He apologised almost straight away, although the insult stayed with her for months after. To show him she wasn't 'barren', Francesca took herself off to see the doctor.

After a trip to the hospital for tests via a referral from her G.P, Francesca showed them to Paul. His reaction annoyed her; he shrugged it off, like he didn't care. His sperm count was the problem, not her being 'barren', and he couldn't bring himself to acknowledge it.

"Bastard!"

Standing by the kitchen counter, she wondered if maybe that was when he began the affair? Paul started being nice. His attitude had improved, too. Sex after that became more recreational, rather than at the desired times of her menstrual cycle. It all fit together now she was in full receipt of the facts.

"You utter bastard!" Her hands were fists.

The doorbell rang.

Francesca glanced at the clock on the wall: 15:30. With Paul's declaration, she completely forgot about Declan bringing over the wardrobe. "Shoot!"

She bashed the counter with her right fist, wanting nothing more than to open the cupboards and throw the contents of china plates on to the lino; she wanted to smash them to pieces, to hear the noise of them breaking. Paul's mum bought them as a wedding gift. Bitch!

The doorbell rang again.

She organised for Declan to deliver her wardrobe; she couldn't pretend to be out. He worked hard making her teak furniture. Every piece she now had in the house was hand-carved by Declan, the wardrobe being the final bit.

"I'm coming."

Francesca raced to the front door, trying to keep tears at bay, which seemed impossible.

Opening it, Declan's smile had the opposite effect on her than intended. Francesca's throat strangled the words she tried to relay.

"Fran? What's wrong?" He stepped forward, wrapping his muscular arms around her. "Let it out, honey. Let it out."

After burying her face in his neck, Francesca sobbed, still trying to comprehend the fact that her husband had left her all alone in the cottage. Declan's embrace was comforting and welcome. Between sobs she heard him quietly order his helper to go back to the truck and wait for him.

"Let's get you inside." Declan helped her into the lounge, easing her on to the sofa.

Sat on the comfy cushions, Declan joined Francesca, his arm around her, as she leaned on him, her cheek on his shoulder. "Thank you," she sniffled.

"Do you want to tell me what's wrong? I'm a great listener."

"Paul's gone," she informed him between sobs. "He's packed up all his gear and left me for some woman he's met." She found it difficult to see through the tears. "He waited until I went to work, then got his stuff together. He wrote me a note in the kitchen."

Declan stroked her arm. "What did it say?" His voice was quiet, deliberate. "Sorry! I shouldn't pry. You don't have to answer that."

She stared up at him, through teary eyes. "He's had enough of me, that's what it said." Her words were loaded with scorn. "Paul's found another woman, someone he has lots in common with." She sobbed again. "And I thought we had loads of things we liked doing together."

"What a bastard!" Declan put his hand over his mouth. "Oh Fran, I'm sorry! I shouldn't have said that. It's not my place to judge." Francesca sat up, wiped her face. "No, you're right. There's no need to apologise for calling him on it. He is. And a total one at that."

An uncomfortable silence wedged itself between them.

She had known Declan since primary school. They had been friends all the way through secondary and college, neither having moved from Bishops Drake. Or rather Declan came back after moving to London for a few years.

He returned three years earlier to look after the family business when his father died. If she were honest with herself, Francesca was relieved when he took on his parents' farm, opting to turn the barn into his new carpentry company.

Scratching his head, awkward, Declan stood. "Right, I really should bring this wardrobe inside now, Fran. Are you going to be okay here by yourself?"

Francesca rose. "Sure, the wardrobe. I almost forgot." After wiping her face with a tissue from her pocket, she walked with him to the front door, not answering his question on purpose.

While the boys were doing the heavy lifting, Francesca went to the bathroom to make herself more presentable. When she came out, Declan was walking upstairs backwards, trying to carry most of the weight himself, his helper a tall, lanky teenager. "Careful!"

"It's alright, I know what I'm doing."

Knowing she'd overstepped, Francesca stood back, letting the boys heave it through to her bedroom. Everything would change now. This was her house, her wardrobe. How would she get used to saying 'hers' instead of 'ours'? It took her months to learn to say 'ours' when she agreed for Paul to move in. "Thanks, both of you. I appreciate this."

Declan asked where she wanted it. Francesca told him, and her saviour offered to take the existing wardrobe away and chop it up for leftover wood. He was her hero, twice.

6

Kate opened the front door to the restaurant, letting Aidan in before closing and locking it again. Having rushed their own dinner of macaroni and cheese, she wanted time to sit and let it rest, but she had to open for their first customers, who were due at half-six.

Being a Thursday night, anything could happen; they might only have their reserved diners, or a big group might descend on them.

Benjamin Babcock, an eighteen-year-old local lad was starting at six, helping set up the kitchen with Aidan. From Thursday onwards each week, Kate liked to have two out front and two in the kitchen. The reason they taught Ben waiting was so that he could help out front when the kitchen rush ended.

"I'll get started in the kitchen," her husband said, carrying his chef whites.

"You won't forget, will you?" She knew pestering him might annoy him but securing capital for this place was always at the forefront of her mind.

Aidan turned to her. "Forget what?"

When he failed to smile, Kate tutted. "To try your dad again. Do I have to do everything? Phone him now, will you? We need that money, love."

“I knew that." He grinned, taking his mobile out of his jeans pocket. "I'll phone him now, but don't get your hopes up."

"Thank you!" She called after him, as he put the mobile to his ear. "Be nice to him, or he won't want to help."

Kate didn't want to rely on Aidan's difficult dad, yet she had no choice. Over the past six months she had exhausted every avenue of cashflow she could think of. Banks, building societies. Online it was a minefield, full of them. The problem: most of them wanted interest in the thousands of percent. Kate had no intention of getting in bed with a loan shark.

Having received the email from Roderick's Foundation earlier, Kate was far less hopeful of the restaurant's doors remaining open past next month. She crossed her fingers walking behind the bar.

After switching the till on, she heard voices outside. Looking up at the clock on the wall, it was ten to six. They increased in volume. Laughter. The glass in the door rattled. "Benjamin! What are you doing?"

She couldn't see them, but Kate could hear their taunting. Every so often the local teenagers liked to gang together and bully Benjamin. He knocked on the window, scared. With the keys in hand, she rushed over and unlocked the door.

Four young lads in their late teens stood leering at her.

"Leave him alone, you nasty yobs. Go on! And don't think I don't know who you are, Finlay Ealing. If your mum and dad find out you're a bully-"

They turned and walked away, grumbling. "We'll see you later, Bab*cock*."

Three of them laughed at Ealing's use of the word 'cock'.

"Grow up, the lot of you," she barked after them, closing the door and locking it again. "Lovely bunch of boys you hang out with, Benjamin."

The slight, effeminate Benjamin leaned against a chair. "They're not my friends, Mrs Marble. They were in my class at school, but I don't like them."

"I know they're not your mates. Are you okay? You're shaking. Would you like a drink of water before you start?" He shook his head. "Very well! Aidan's in the kitchen waiting for you."

Kate had a soft spot for Ben, who preferred his long name, Benjamin. He was at the awkward age of eighteen and gay. He told her in confidence once that he longed to tell his parents of his sexuality, but he couldn't tell his tyrant dad, or break his mum's heart.

Such a lovely boy, she thought, watching him walk away. "Wait!" She ran and caught up with him, arriving at the kitchen door. As soon as it opened, Aidan turned away, the phone against his ear.

"Look, I need this, Dad," he said, his voice stern yet pleading. "You don't know what this place means to me, or Kate. Please, won't you at least think about it?" He took the mobile away from his face. "Using you? I'm asking you for a favour. And I told you just now we'll give you a percentage of the profits and pay you back eventually." He stared at her while he spoke. "Yeah? If that's the way you feel, fine. No, I just said, don't bother, I'm not interested." He hung up by jabbing a finger at the screen.

Kate didn't need to be psychic. "That went well."

"I don't know what you expected." Aidan walked over to the stand-up fridge, opening the door, and taking out a tray of small dishes. "He thinks I'm using him, and he's right, isn't he? I haven't spoken to him in months, and I ring him up one day asking him for money. He's old; he's not stupid."

"I know he's not stupid. I guess I thought I would never see the day when your dad saw one of you go without, that's all. I thought he would always help, no matter what."

Benjamin stood next to her in the doorway. "What's going on? Is this place closing? Please don't tell me that; I love this job."

Kate squeezed his shoulder. "I hate to say this, but it's a possibility. If we don't get a cash injection soon, those doors will be closing. So, Benjamin, if you want to help, tell your friends at those clubs you go to about this place, tell them to book a table, or something, we need lots of bums in seats if she's going to survive."

Aidan walked over to her. "You never know, mum might talk dad round. I'll call her separately. How's that? See if I can't persuade her to help."

Relief poured out of her in that moment.
Aidan's mum would help. If there were ever a mother devoted to her children, Celia Marble was that woman. "Would you do that?" When he nodded, she smiled, stroking his cheek.

Walking back to the bar, Kate made a mental note to keep on at him to phone Celia, when a knock at the door made her jump. Francesca stood outside. By the look of her red eyes, Kate could tell she'd been crying. "Fran, honey, what's wrong?"

Her waitress stepped inside. "Oh, damn it! I said I wouldn't cry." She walked with purpose over to the bar, went behind and picked up a pint glass.

"What's he done now?" Guaranteed it would be something to do with Paul, her shit of a husband, who blamed poor Francesca for not conceiving a child. Francesca looked awful, with red puffy eyes.

"He left me," Francesca answered with a sardonic laugh. "For a younger model he has more in common with." She poured water from the sink behind the bar into her glass, took a big swallow. "He waited until I was here this morning to pack his things. Now all I have is the house, and my car."

Kate wished she could act more surprised. Having never warmed to Paul Darby, she always imagined him flirting with whichever lady fell for his good-looking charm. "I'm so sorry, Fran," she said, taking her employee into an embrace.

"He blamed me for not getting pregnant," her waitress wailed. "And this whole time it was his fault, his low sperm count. When I told him the doctor gave me the all-clear, he just shrugged, like it was nothing."

Breaking the embrace, Kate glanced at the clock: opening time. "Listen, I would love to talk this through with you, honey, but I need to open up. Are you staying tonight? If not, I'll muddle through. Benjamin can help me out front."

Francesca stood up straight, wiped her eyes with a tissue from her handbag. "No, I'm fine. I'm strong. He's not going to affect me, not this time. I've cried enough over him." She took out a compact, checked her face in it. "Oh, I look awful. Give me five minutes to sort myself out, and I'll be right with you."

With a sigh, Kate walked to the front doors, bent over to unlock the bottom bolt, then reached up for the top lock. She smiled at her first guests, who were stood outside waiting. "Mr and Mrs Spencer, good evening." They were well-to-do, so she adopted her Queen's best accent. "Please, come in. Make yourselves comfortable."

They weren't part of the two bookings they had in the diary. Marble's Marvels needed walk-ins like these, only lots more of them.

7

"The last ticket." Aidan took the receipt from the rack, held it out in front of him. "Two shepherd's pie, mash, peas and sweetcorn; one Hunter's chicken with chips and a side salad, two liver and bacon on mash with peas; three scampi, chips and mushy peas; three gammon steaks, chips and peas, one with egg, two with pineapple, and finally one steak and ale pie, mash and mushy peas." He pierced the pastry with a temperature probe. "Eighty-three degrees, go, go, go!"

"I need some help over here, Aidan," Benjamin said, getting flustered with desserts.

Aidan threw the tea towel on the counter, celebratory style. He and Benjamin had just served thirty-three happy guests. He'd at least expected one complaint. With mainly him cooking, he'd survived the busiest evening service in over a year. "Benjamin, give Fran a hand with taking out the mains, will you? I'll take over desserts."

As per usual, the largest table, the booking of twelve were the last to order, choosing their meals at quarter to ten. He shut the kitchen to new orders at ten sharp, giving him enough time to clean down. "Let's see where we're at," he said to himself. "Two knickerbocker glories, one treacle tart and a chocolate fudge cake."

Benjamin had heated the fudge cake through. The dessert counter looked like a bomb site. The vanilla ice cream was out, melting. "Great! That's two quid going right there." He often found himself moaning.

His frown evaporated, though, when he told himself how many customers he'd cooked for. Like the good old days, before the...Enough of that. He needed to focus on getting the puddings ready. As he picked up two tall knickerbocker glory glasses, Fran and Benjamin returned for more plates.

Mixing the vanilla ice cream with raspberry coulis, pieces of tinned peach, pineapple, and mango, and topping it off with chopped pistachio nuts, Aidan almost slapped his forehead, forgetting the blueberries. This was the busiest night in over a year; of course, he was rushing and forgetting things.

He scooped two balls of vanilla ice cream on the side of the fudge cake. It smelled fantastic, sweet. Salivating, he then put the treacle tart in the microwave, while he went about finishing off the knickerbocker glories.

By the time Francesca and Benjamin had taken out the last plates for the table of twelve, Kate started bringing dirty dishes in to be washed. He asked his wife to take the fudge cake out before the ice cream fully melted.

Kate picked up a knickerbocker glory and the bowl containing the fudge cake and took them out to the dining room without saying a word. No smiles, nothing. Aidan continued with the treacle tart, smothering it in custard, as most of his customers preferred.

When Francesca came in carrying a stack of dirty dinner plates, he strolled over to the sink and dunked them in the hot bubbly water. "Hey, is Kate alright? She's been very quiet."

He turned round to find an empty kitchen; Francesca had gone without replying. Or maybe she hadn't heard him? Shrugging it off, he continued washing up, until his mobile vibrated in his trouser pocket.

Not being able to pick up straight away, Aidan dried his hands using a tea towel before answering. He frowned at the caller ID: Mum. "What the hell?" He turned to face the kitchen door, leaning on the sink. "Hi! What are you doing ringing so late? It's after ten."

"Just what do you think you were playing at?"
His mum sounded angrier than he had heard her in a long time.

"Excuse me?"

"Why would you pretend to be phoning your dad when you're not? And if you're in queer streets, why didn't you come to us? I had to find out from Kate that the restaurant's in danger of closing? How do you think that makes me feel, hmm? It should be you coming to us for a bail-out, not her. Lord knows, she's got enough to deal with." Her voice grew louder, more intense with the conversation.

Aidan rubbed his hair, understanding Kate's silence earlier, and probably why Francesca left without saying anything to him. The two had spoken about it. He didn't know what to say to his mum. "I didn't mean to involve you. I apologise. Kate asked me to call dad, but I didn't want to. This isn't your problem, so I pretended to phone him. I told her you guys couldn't help, and that's fine. We'll find another way of keeping the restaurant going."

"How?" Her accusatory voice hurt his eardrum. "How do you expect to keep her going, Aidan? With what? Kate tells me you've sunk your savings into Marble's. When were you going to come to us with this, hmm?"

"Never!" He walked into the dry storeroom when Kate came in with more dirty plates.

After closing the store door, he leaned against shelving. "I'm never coming to you for financial support. I know Kate doesn't mind taking your money, but I do. I'm a grown-up. I'm not going back to you for handouts."

His mum sighed. "You're so stubborn, just like your dad. We want to help you, darling, but your dad doesn't want to throw good money away, so I'll tell you what he told Kate. If you have a good, workable plan of what you're going to do with the restaurant, with costings, your dad and I will invest fifty thousand in the business. Consider it a loan, but you only need pay us back when you have the capital. How does that sound?"

Awful, he thought, wanting to punch the dry goods. "What does he expect in return for the investment? What percentage?"

His mum's silence said it all."

"Twenty...Five percent."

"A quarter?" He kicked a bag of potatoes. "He sticks in fifty and expects that much? Forget it! No deal. Marble's Marvels is mine and Kate's. Dad's not going to come in here and start lording it over us. I would rather close than have him involved here."

"Be careful what you wish for, Aidan." His mum's tone was as cautious as the warning itself. "Kate says you're about a month away from closing. Don't be stupid now. And besides, Kate's your business partner, and she's accepted our offer."

"Thanks a lot," he said to her, hanging up abruptly.

After kicking the sacks of potatoes a few times, Aidan took long deep breaths, trying to calm himself. He had to face reality with Kate.

8

What a rollercoaster of emotions! On the one hand, Kate was livid at Aidan's lies. He stood in the kitchen pretending to be begging his dad for financial support. What kind of person did that? Certainly not the good, kind-hearted man she married.

On the other, she had never felt such relief before. Aidan's mum, Celia had assured her that they would help with finance if she and Aidan put together a decent proposal showing growth plans and means of paying them back. "Good night all," she said, waving to the last of her customers with a smile so easily served because of her chat with Celia. "Come back again, and don't forget to tell your friends."

Once the doors were locked, Kate had the tills to count, leaving Francesca and Benjamin to set up the tables with cloths, cutlery, and glasses.

She felt lucky having such great staff.

Dreading Francesca crying on her shoulder all night, the lovely waitress couldn't have been stronger. She never once mentioned the break-up.

She couldn't have asked for more. Even Benjamin had been worthy tonight, helping in the kitchen with starters, then mains, and finally desserts. On top of that, he'd helped Kate and Francesca with waiting on tables. Kate felt guilty only paying him minimum wage for his age. If they had more money in the bank, she would increase his earnings.

Upstairs in the tiny office she counted the day's takings, including the card reader receipts. She would have smiled, had they not needed lots more days like today. Having the odd one brilliant service wouldn't cut it. Kate studied the bookings list on the PC monitor. Two, an eight and six.

Being the two-year anniversary of Vinnie's death tomorrow, Kate wanted it to be quiet. She needed time to herself. They were closing for lunch, and only opening in the evening for dinner service. The two tables were close friends of theirs.

"If it's alright with you, Kate, Benji and me, we'll be off now?"

With her back to the door, Francesca's voice made her jump. "Jesus! Don't do that to me, Fran." She turned to face Francesca in her chair, patting her chest. "I need to calm myself now. Of course you can go. Thanks for tonight, and I'll talk to you soon about the whole Paul thing."

"Thanks. I get to go home to an empty house now. But, on a more positive note, Declan brought the wardrobe over this afternoon. It's fabulous, Kate. You should come over one night. We'll open a bottle of vino, make a night of it."

"I'd love that." She glanced up at the calendar on the wall. "But I don't know when. You're the only one who can cover for me. I'm glued to this place."

Francesca smiled. "Great news about Aidan's parents coming through, though, right?"

In spite of her relief, doubts invaded her mind. "That remains to be seen. Aidan doesn't want his dad anywhere near this place. If I had another option, I would take it."

"Oh! I thought our troubles were over." Francesca dropped her gaze.

"I wish! They've given us an extra life, let's put it that way. If they invest, we limp on for a few more months."

Leaning against the doorframe, Francesca lifted her head. "You don't sound hopeful, Kate. Do you not see this place taking off again?"

"I wish I could. But with how things are between Aidan and Chris, I can't see the village mending bridges, can you? If they made up, put the past behind them, then I could see everyone coming together. Without it, we're stuck being outsiders in our own home."

"Then we focus on getting word out to neighbouring villages and towns?"

"With respect, Fran, that's not the problem," she said quietly, in almost a whisper. "You've seen this place at its best and worst. Aidan's heart's just not in it anymore."

Francesca stepped towards her. "So, hire a new chef. Someone with heart; someone with a flair for this, who wants to actually cook."

Kate stood from her chair, her mouth by Francesca's ear. "I would if I could, but this is as much his place as mine. I can't fire him, can I?"

"So, don't. You hire someone to 'help' him, only you employ the best damn chef you have ever seen in your life. Make Aidan think he's in charge, but take on a far better cook than him, someone he can learn from. He might just get his mojo back."

"When did you become so wise, huh?" Kate hugged her, then held her shoulders. "I think that's a brilliant idea. I'm going to have to run it past him first, but I have leverage now. I think I might be able to pull this off."

Excited, she kissed Francesca on the cheek, and watched her walk away. "Oh, and Fran, don't worry about all this. You can always fall back on your signing qualification. Schools must be clamouring for signers, mustn't they?"

Francesca shrugged. "They are, but Paul doesn't want me to...What am I saying? I'm single now. He can't tell me what to do. I can do whatever I want. I'll start looking straight away." Francesca skipped down the stairs.

Kate smiled when she turned back to the tills. Expecting a long and teary break-up between Francesca and Paul, she would be delighted if her waitress and friend rose to the challenge. Working with children with special educational needs was Francesca's dream, one she would be fantastic at.

"We need to talk, love," Aidan said from behind her.

Without turning to him, she stood, picked up the tills and placed them inside the open safe. Closing the thick metal door, and locking it, she put the long key in her bag without saying a word to him.

"Come on, are you going to give me the silent treatment all night? I'm sorry, alright? It was stupid to think I could fool you like that. I'll make it up to you, I swear."

Standing up straight, Kate put her phone in her handbag. "It's too late for all that, Aidan. You lied to me. You had an argument with yourself, for pity's sake. You actually stood there pretending to be arguing with your dad. I can't tell you how disturbing I found that when I called your mum tonight to argue our case. When she told me your dad hadn't spoken to you, I almost dropped my phone. How could you?"

"I told you, I made a mistake." he sighed. "Look, I apologise for lying, but I only did it because I love this place so much. I don't want him involved in any of it. He'll take over, and before you know it, we'll be working for him. We'll come here and resent it because my dad will make it feel like a job, or a chore. Please, don't let the Captain win. I beg you."

Captain Marble. Joseph 'Joe' Marble, Aidan's dad even made his wife call him Captain. Kate laughed in Aidan's face the day he told her that. *'When you meet him, call him Captain; he'll love you forever, trust me,'* Aidan said all those years earlier. "Don't 'love' me, Aidan! You're in no position to be asking favours from me, are you? You lied to my face. No, you have some making up to do-"

"I'll do anything you want, if you promise to refuse dad's offer, please," he begged.

"Even hire an extra chef?" She had his attention; she could see the anger in his eyes. "And I'm not talking a cook here, Aidan. I want this place to fill up again. I want to be rushed off my feet every day, while the tills bleep away, and the diners put money in our bank account the way they used to."

Aidan's eyes changed, from angry to hurt. "And you think hiring a new chef will do that for us? You don't think I'm good enough?"

Why she felt guilty, she didn't know. "Of course I do, honey, but you've lost your way recently. I hate to be the one to say it, but Marble's Marvels needs an excellent chef, darling. She needs some passion in her kitchen. You don't have that fire in your belly now, do you? If she's going to survive, you need help in there."

Anger took over. "Forget it! We can't even afford one, can we? And I'm not about to let some upstart take over my kitchen. I'll do anything else you want."

Kate had been here before. His stubbornness was legendary. "Fine! I can't talk to you anymore. I think it's time we took a break from each other. I spoke to my sister earlier, and she's letting me crash at hers for a few weeks. You can look after yourself, can't you?" She left him standing by the bar, speechless.

9

"Wait! Kate, please don't go!" Aidan started walking towards her. "We can work through this, like we always do." The anger in her eyes told him not to push too hard. "Come on, we can talk through this; I'm open to negotiation."

"I'm not negotiating here. I told you what this restaurant needs, and you said no. That's your prerogative, of course, but when I submit my proposal to your dad, and he accepts, it will be two versus one, won't it? The Captain being a twenty-five percent owner, and me being equal to you, it will swing in my favour. So, either agree to hiring a decent chef, or we take a vote, and I get my way regardless."

When did his wife become such a conniving bitch? "But what will happen to me? It's my kitchen. I've been managing it here since we opened, and now all of a sudden you want to bring in someone new? You want them to teach me? It's insulting."

"And look where it's got us. You haven't had passion in your cooking since Vinnie died, have you? I know we all grieve in our own ways, but the world keeps spinning, Aidan. This place has been going downhill for ages. A couple of months I can understand, but it's been two years."

When Kate went to unbolt the front door, Aidan stopped her. "You know what the date is tomorrow, and you announce you're breaking up with me tonight?"

"Don't you dare bring Vinnie into this! You might blame yourself, but it's not your fault, Aidan. This isn't about our son anymore. This is about us getting on with our lives." She yanked on the top bolt. "I hoped and prayed we could come through this together, and come out stronger, but you make it impossible because you're not grieving. You're not going through the process, and until you do there can't be an us. I'm sorry!"

Aidan went to her and stepped into the lit High Street. "Where are you going now? We came in the same car."

"I'm calling a cab." She took her mobile out of her bag. "You take the Range Rover home. I'll call a taxi in the morning to collect my car from the house when I'll pick up a few personal things. Night, Aidan. I'll see you at the house."

He went to touch her again, to try and pull her into his arms. Kate balked. "So, this is it? It's over? I made a mistake, Kate.

Let's go home and talk about it, like we always do. I'm sorry I lied to you, okay? It won't happen again."

Kate walked backwards into the road. "I'm not going home with you; not this time. I need some space. I need time to think things through."

The more he chased her, the more she backed away. When she dug her heels in there was no talking her round.

With the phone to her ear, Kate called for a taxi. Hanging up, she caught his attention. "Lock up and go home, Aidan. You can't talk me down. My sister's waiting up for me, and I need to sort my head out."

His head hung, Aidan turned and walked back into the empty restaurant. The clock on the wall said it was almost half eleven.

Kate's taxi pulled up outside within five minutes.

Sat on a high stool in front of the bar, the only sound the gentle humming of the fridges to keep him company, he decided to go to the King's Head for last orders.

After locking up, Aidan strolled across and down the road, the lights of the pub a shining beacon in his hour of need. A couple of his customers stood outside the front door smoking. He said hello, walked past them into the busy main bar.

"An Old Speckled Hen and a whisky, please." He found a stool to sit on.

Both pool tables were in use. Aidan saw the trays of food spread out on cloths. It was league night. "Who are we playing tonight?"

The barmaid looked at him. "The Red Lion."

10

Christian Ashcroft inhaled on his electronic cigarette while sat watching one of his teammates taking a beating by one of the Kings Head players. He reached across the table next to him and picked up a warm sausage roll, putting the whole thing in his mouth.

In the distance, Aidan Marble entered, sitting on a stool while he ordered a drink.

One of Chris' 'Lions' sat next to him. "We don't want any trouble tonight, Chris. You said if you see Aidan, you're going to rise above it, right?"

He had known there was a possibility he might bump into Marble. In truth, it was why he agreed to play. "You don't have anything to worry about from me, mate." He clapped at his friend's potting two reds in one shot. "Nicely played, Nigel." He was a little too exuberant as he stood and continued clapping.

The friend who warned him placed his hand on Chris' shoulder. "Sit back down where I can see you. You've had, must be, six pints tonight."

Around the pool table his friends and the Kings Head players were uneasy. Chris felt the stares from the pub's locals, residents of Bishops Drake he grew up with, who sided with Aidan and Kate, believing his son, Liam to be drunk when he drove into Vinnie's car.

"Let's finish this game off, and get the hell out of this dump, shall we? I hate this pub so much," his teammate said, encouraging him to sit down.

Not putting up any resistance, his team could try and stop him having a go at Aidan, but they couldn't prevent him staring.

Aidan sat on his own with his pint in front of him. He knocked back a whisky and ordered another. The landlord of the pub went and joined Aidan. Chris could tell the owner was talking about him; he kept glancing over.

Instead of looking away, Chris remained focused until Nigel stood obscuring his view. He leaned over and kept staring.

Tomorrow was the two-year anniversary of his son's death. Whoever planned the league fixtures was not local, Chris had taken the offer to play tonight, having to reassure his wife, Edith that he would behave himself if he happened across Aidan.

He lived a very different life now to the one before the crash. His once happy marriage was anything but. Prior to the collision, he'd led a relatively content life, tending to his small holding on the outskirts of the village while tinkering with friends' cars.

Since Liam's sudden and horrific death, his small farm was nothing more than a shell of its former glory. To meet his mortgage requirements, he turned his barn into a workshop. His car hobby became a full-time gig.

To deal with her loss, his wife Edie threw herself into the local church. She had her faith to rely on, but he couldn't bring himself to join her anymore. He didn't believe in God, never had really. His lack of faith had never bothered Edie, she knew he was joining her to keep her company, until their son was killed.

How could he not have faith that God would look after their Liam now? She would ask him these questions. His rebuttal: Why would God let their Liam die in a car crash? Why would He make him suffer for thirty-eight minutes, being cut out of the twisted and contorted metal chassis before dying on route to the hospital? Edie never answered him.

When the coroner's report confirmed that Liam's test results showed his blood-alcohol level was double the legal limit, he couldn't commit to being an atheist.

He preferred to think of himself as an agnostic, which meant he could curse God. Liam knew about the dangers of drink driving, which was why Chris took the news so badly.

The report threw him into a deep cycle of drinking. Every night he would take himself out of the house and walk over to his workshop, where he would sink bottles of beer and down tumblers of whisky until he was so drunk, he couldn't think straight. Most mornings he awoke to find he'd fallen asleep at his desk, the barn door open, the lights on.

Covered in stubble, his eyes grainy, breath vile, Chris had driven out to the crash site one morning. Parking on the side of the road, a few miles outside of Bishops Drake, near Dead Man's Corner, he exited his vehicle and started examining the street. It didn't take him long to find what he was looking for: skid marks on Vinnie's side of the road, heading away from the village. "I got you now," he said to himself, cursing Vincent Marble.

It took him months to prove to his friends that Liam was the victim, and that Aidan's son lost control of his car and killed his son. When the only survivor of the crash, Wyatt Newall awoke from his coma, the truth came out, not that it mattered to Aidan Marble; he would never concede that his Vinnie was to blame.

His marriage took more of a hit than his career. He barely spoke to his wife these days. They slept in separate bedrooms when he actually slept in the house that was. Then, one afternoon four months earlier Edie was diagnosed with terminal breast cancer.

Having been there for her during her chemotherapy sessions, while they both grieved the loss of their son, Chris and Edie had been informed by the oncologist that the cancer had spread from her breasts to her lungs, and brain.

Chris watched the landlord whispering in Aidan's ear.

He continued staring when Aidan glanced over at him. Chris needed Aidan to make a move. He didn't want to be the bad guy; he wanted Vinnie's dad to be the monster, so he would be justified in attacking him.

"That's it, match over." Nigel put his hand on Chris' shoulder. "How about the Lion for last orders, Chris?"

Picking up his pint, Chris necked the last third in one gulp, burped and inhaled on his e cigarette, waiting for his teammates to drink up. He kept his eye on Aidan, who chugged another whisky before taking a slurp on his ale. "Ready, boys?"

"Let's leave this way, Chris." Nigel pointed at the fire exit leading to the car park, which was in the opposite direction to the Red Lion.

"Why? I'm not going to cause any shit, guys," he assured them. "I'm more than capable of walking past Aidan Marble without starting something."

Chris led their way towards the bar.

All conversations near them stopped.

He felt eyes on him. Before he reached Aidan, three of his friends put themselves in between them.

"Jill Noble's over there, mate. Don't start anything," Nigel whispered in his ear. "We don't want to spend another night in a cell, do we?"

The local police officer, Jillian Noble was the local uniformed cop. She arrested Aidan and Chris last time. A good friend of Kate Marble's, she went above and beyond for Aidan and Chris, trying to reconcile them while booking them both.

"I keep telling you I'm alright."

Tension increased in the King's Head as Chris walked past Aidan.

"Good riddance." Aidan sat facing the bar, his pint glass in hand.

With a couple of his teammates in front of him, Chris went for the father of his son's killer. "You just couldn't leave it, could you?" He reached out for the restaurant owner, trying to grab at him.

Aidan stood up straight, turned to him with half a glass of ale in his hand. He threw the remaining contents of the Old Speckled Hen in Chris' face.

Half-blind, the rage inside Chris grew. He didn't have the words to use; he was incensed, grabbing at Aidan, who looked cool and collected. "I'm going to get you!"

When his teammates saw the ale splash in his face, they were with him, against the Kings Head lot, who all protected Aidan. The fracas lasted mere seconds, until Jillian Noble stood on a table and whistled using two fingers.

"Aidan Marble and Christian Ashcroft, outside, now," she yelled, pointing at the door.

As he walked into the cold night air, Chris heard Jillian on her phone calling for assistance. When he was on the pavement, he waited for Aidan to emerge, surrounded by his cronies.

Wasting no time, Chris rushed at Aidan, cracking him in the mouth before the off-duty police officer came out of the pub. "Oops, my fault." He put his hands up. "Won't happen again." But he wanted it to. The satisfaction he felt from hitting Aidan dwarfed any regret.

It took five minutes for two panda cars to arrive. When they did, Jillian made Chris place his hands behind his back. "Hey? You're arresting me? He started it!"

"No, you're both being taken in," Jillian answered. "You're drying out in our one-star hotel cell for the night. Both of you have had far too much to drink."

"I've only been here for fifteen minutes," Aidan moaned, cuffs around his wrists.

"Yeah, well, you both should've thought of that before you decided to disturb the peace, eh!" Jillian walked Chris over to the first panda, helping him inside. "Mind your head, Chris. I've got more than enough paperwork to fill out because of you."

FRIDAY,
JANUARY 11TH

11

"Oh dear lord, how long's he been in there?" Kate stared at her sister, Liz, horrified. "Since midnight? And Chris is locked up, too?" She listened to Jillian describe the situation in The Kings Head, her mobile to her ear. "Who let Chris play? Of course it will kick off; neither of them have accepted what happened yet."

The police officer, her long-term friend and squash partner went on to explain that the pool league wasn't run by locals. It was county wide, so the organisers wouldn't have local knowledge, or care about such issues. "Then it was the players for the Lion. They shouldn't have brought Chris along. They should've benched him, is that the right word?"

It didn't matter. The result was the same: her husband was locked up, sleeping off a hangover no doubt. When Jillian hung up, Kate sighed, her mug of tea going cold. "I don't believe it! He's been arrested, again. Jill's going to keep him in if this keeps happening."

Her sister, Elizabeth, Liz, shook her head. "I'm surprised you stuck with him this long. I keep telling you to ditch him, don't I? He's bringing you down with him, and you let him every time. Maybe this will show you what he's like."

Every word her sister spoke was true. "I should've listened to you before. You're so right, though. He is dragging me down with him."

"So, what are you going to do?" Liz stood in her dressing gown, took her mug over to the sink and started washing it up. "Are you going to leave him? Because if you are, I heard a rumour about Graham Winston the other day."

Hearing her ex-boyfriend's name piqued her interest. "I need to clear my head." She got up, walked over to the basin with her empty cup, put it in the water and leaned against the counter next to her little sister. "And what about Graham?"

The one who got away, Graham Winston. Kate smarted every time his name was mentioned. Tall, dark hair, handsome face. she fell hard for him in the fifth year. They were inseparable for two years, into the first term of college, when without warning his family moved to the States. They gave him no hint it was on the horizon, nothing. When she went to the airport to wave him off, they agreed to make a go of it, long distance, but it didn't end up lasting.

Three months in, pining for him, Graham confessed to Kate that he'd met a girl. In the second year of college, she started going out with Aidan, and the rest was history. "Come on, spill. I need to go bail him out soon."

"Oh, leave him in there for the morning, serves him right," Liz said.

"Serves who right?"

Kate was in awe of her sister's girlfriend, Rae. Desirae always looked immaculate, with shiny straight black hair, milk chocolate skin and a smile to melt a million hearts. "Aidan's." She loved Rae in her grey two-piece suit. "You always look amazing in whatever you wear, doesn't she, Liz?"

Her sister turned, accepted Rae's kiss, and went back to washing up the breakfast things. "I have always said, give her a sack to model, and everyone would start wearing one."

"Why thank you!" Rae curtsied. "What's he done now?"

"Oh, it doesn't matter." Kate didn't want to waste time talking about Aidan when she could be discussing Graham. "Tell me what you heard about my ex-boyfriend? Come on, out with it, Liz."

"Alright, fine, he's divorced, and he's moving back to Basingstoke," Liz confessed, a broad grin stretched the width of her face. "He has no kids, and he's bought a house in Cliddesden, over on Woods Lane. What do you make of them apples?"

Kate stood with her mouth open.

Rae snuck in, kissed her on her cheek. "You might want to close it, honey, you don't want to catch flies, do you?"

"Oh my! He's moving back home? To Basingstoke?" Kate couldn't think straight. "When? Don't hold back on me."

"Soon, I think." Liz seemed pleased with herself. "What I do for you! I listen out on your behalf, but I must admit, I'll be interested to find out what he looks like now."

"He could've put on weight, don't forget," Rae said, blowing her cheeks out, her mouth comically small.

Kate laughed. "It won't bother me if he has." Her sister and Rae grinned across from her. "Because I'm married, to Aidan. Nothing's going to change that."

"Yeah, right!" Liz went back to washing up.

"Ooh, Kate, what time are we getting to the cemetery for?" Rae had her phone out.

"Three at the church, so come back here in time to get ready, I guess." She glanced up at the clock. Almost nine. Kate kissed Liz and Rae on their cheeks, ran upstairs to her bedroom, flung some jeans and a jumper on, and flew downstairs, having ordered a taxi back home.

Once she had her convertible MG, she was independent again. The red sporty car was her pride and joy, after the restaurant naturally. As soon as she sat in the leather seat, behind the steering wheel, she knew it was the car for her. Four years old, and it had not given her one bit of trouble.

On the way over to her house, thinking about Graham on the anniversary of Vinnie's death, Kate wondered what would her son think of her now if he were looking down on her from heaven? What would he think of Aidan? Vinnie would be shaking his head.

Paying the driver, Kate let herself inside her house, collected a few personal effects, clothes, makeup, toiletries, passport, and put them in a small suitcase she bought herself last year. Aware that it was nearly ten, she jumped in her car, started the engine, and drove out of their driveway. "You're such a pain," she mumbled to herself.

Bishops Drake had no police station. The nearest one with cells was in Basingstoke, so she had to drive fifteen minutes there to pick Aidan up. Outside the building, she parked and headed for reception.

"You must be kidding me!" She glanced through the glass only to find Edith Ashcroft standing in front of the desk. Kate wanted to hide, but Edie turned, saw her, and looked away. "Come on, Kate, you can do this."

Holding her breath, she opened the door. "You're here picking up Chris I assume?" She smiled as sweetly as she could. Edith nodded, the merest whiff of a smile. "Why can't our boys play nicely, huh?"

It was a silly and crass thing to say. They all knew why, Aidan and Chris both believed the other's son had killed theirs. Kate was nervous in front of Edie, though. She and Edie had been good friends before the crash. Even Aidan and Chris used to get on, playing pool and darts together at the Kings Head.

"I'm here to pick up my husband, Aidan Marble," she said to the desk sergeant, who gave her some paperwork to fill out, and a charge of a hundred pounds to pay. It was standard for drunk tank inmates to incur such fines. "How are you holding up, Edie?"

Up close, Kate thought her old friend looked awful. Thin and gaunt, with bags under her eyes, Edie was a shell of her former self every bit as much as Chris and Aidan were. Edith Ashcroft had aged suddenly. Only four years Kate's senior, she looked to be in her sixties.

Edie told her she was fine, before coughing so hard Kate thought she would faint.

"Can I fetch you some water?"

Pitched over, Edie coughed until blood appeared on her handkerchief.

Holding her hand up, Edie reassured Kate she was okay.

Kate tried not to notice how out of breath her old friend was, or the spots of blood, both of which were not good signs. Coupled with the stifling, debilitating cough, they made for a probable grim diagnosis. She thought it such a shame. Edie in her golden years outshone most women in looks alone. A true beauty prior to the crash, Kate had admired her poise and elegance. "Here, let me help you to a seat."

She helped Edie into a plastic chair in front of the window. When Kate sat down next to her ex-friend, the doors behind reception opened. Aidan walked through the security gate, followed closely by Chris, both of whom had their heads hung in shame.

12

Francesca took a deep breath, pushed open the door to her old school, Bishops Down Primary, and strolled towards reception. She recalled it being bigger, but guessed it was because she was eleven when she left. Everything seemed small now.

"Francesca Hayward? What are you doing here?"

Mrs Freeman stood from her chair, a friendly smile forming. She approached the desk. "Come over here, you. Let me look at you. You've not changed a bit, I tell you."

Her former teacher jested. "I'm Francesca Darby now, and I am about two feet taller now, Mrs Freeman. I hope I'm at least a bit different." She couldn't work out why her favourite tutor greeted her from behind the reception desk. "Why aren't you in one of the classrooms?"

"Oh, I gave up teaching a couple of years ago, my darling. When I left, a position opened in the admin department. I couldn't leave this place, could I? Anyway, enough about me, what have you been doing since leaving, hmm?"

Wondering why the area's grapevine had not extended as far as Mrs Freeman, Francesca thought of what she could tell her former teacher. "Well, I, er, I got married, and I work over at Marble's Marvels waiting. And I..." She couldn't think of a single noteworthy thing she had done that would make Mrs Freeman proud.

A sudden thought made her smile. "I learned to sign."

Her ex-teacher grinned. "You sign? Wonderful! What made you learn?"

Francesca shrugged. "It's something I've always wanted to do. Paul, my husband, didn't want me working. Well, nothing more than waiting on tables, I should say. I had to beg him to let me study signing. I think he thought there was no harm in it. What could I do?"

"Uh, sounds like a right charmer." Mrs Freeman made an unimpressed face. "And where's your delightful hubby now? I'm getting that you got rid of him, am I right?"

Wanting to confirm Mrs Freeman's guess, Francesca couldn't lie. "Well, he dumped me is more accurate, I would say." She noted the sorrow in her teacher's eyes. "Oh, it's alright, I'm fine about it. I can do whatever I want now. Which brings me to why I'm here."

Mrs Freeman stood; her face serious. "If you're here looking for a job working with hard of hearing children, I'm afraid you've come at the wrong time of year. You need to be applying in the summer for a place starting in September, my darling."

"Oh!" She tried not to let her disappointment show.

Her old teacher leaned on the counter. "But Cherry Tree Lodge are always looking for teaching assistants. They're over on Farleigh Wallop, near Broadmere."

"What is it? A school for the hard of hearing?" Having studied signing, she should be familiar with the places local to her that specialised in sign language. "I'm sorry!"

"Don't be. Cherry Tree hasn't been around for long, but they're always looking for signers." Mrs Freeman picked up a pen and piece of paper. "Here, I'll give you the address and directions. And I'll put in a good word with the headteacher for you. How's that?" She handed Francesca the note.

"Oh, thank you, Mrs Freeman, so much" she said, excitement in her voice.

"In fact, I can do better than that."

Francesca tried to object when her ex-teacher picked up the desk phone. "Please, you don't need to go to all this bother."

"It's no trouble. Oh, it's ringing." Mrs Freeman turned away; her voice quiet.

Scanning the room while she waited, Francesca read all the leaflets hung on pin boards around the room. She was in her old primary school no less. Odd being here now, she thought.

"Don't say I never do anything for you, Francesca Darby," the senior lady said, getting up from her leather swivel chair. "I just spoke to the headteacher. She can meet you this afternoon. Here's the school's number. She's lovely, by the way, you can do a lot worse than work at Cherry Tree Lodge."

Wanting to jump over the counter and give Mrs Freeman a kiss, Francesca instead opted for a hug over the desk. "Oh, thank you so much! I have no words."

"Give over, you daft woman." Her ex-teacher joked. She straightened up. "You'll be tested while you're there. There's no point even going for a TA position if you're not proficient at signing, eh?"

"You don't need to worry about that," Francesca reassured her. "I have been learning on and off for years. I taught myself a lot before I married Paul. I'll pass a test."

With directions to the lodge in her bag, Francesca said goodbye to her old teacher.

Still excited, she wondered who she should tell first: Declan. He was the first person she thought about. He would be pleased for her, so much more than Paul would, even back when they were in love.

Jumping in her car, she drove the quarter of an hour back to Bishops Drake, turning left into Declan's dead-end road. Francesca imagined herself in front of a room full of children, signing her lessons.

Pulling up outside Declan's farmhouse, she turned the engine off and sat in her car. No sign of Declan, except his truck was in the driveway. "Where are you?"

Out of her car, she walked up to the door, knocked, waited.

Nothing.

Snooping round the back, a saw buzzed in the distance. "There you are," she said to herself, strolling in the direction of the barn.

Before she reached it, Declan stood in the doorway, waiting for her. "Hello you! What brings you out here?" He leaned against the frame in jeans, boots, an old T shirt and sawdust covered brown overalls.

A smile stretched across her face. She handed him the piece of paper. "Guess who's got an interview this afternoon at Cherry Tree Lodge? I'm finally going to use my signing."

Declan's confusion turned to joy. "Oh my! Well done, honey."

His embrace was her reason for visiting. After finding out Paul had left her, she needed the warmth and love of a good friend. Kate was one thing, Declan quite another. "Thank you!" She stood looking up at his beautiful face, his hair dusty. "I had to come and tell you; I hope you don't mind."

"Of course I don't." He brushed himself down. "Sorry! I wasn't expecting company. Come in, I'll make you a cuppa."

Never one to give up a cup of tea, Francesca accepted his offer, following him inside the rear of the farmhouse. She took off her shoes like any polite person would. She loved Declan's family home; it was like going back in time to her childhood.

In the kitchen, looking out of the window at the back garden, she could remember playing on the swings when she and Declan were about eight. They were simpler times. She often wished she could regress.

"Here! Tea, just how you like it."

He had known her so long; he knew how she liked her hot beverages. The best thing about being with Declan was how comfortable he made her feel. "Thanks for this. Just what I need."

"No bother." He gestured the table and chairs. "Come and sit down. There are biscuits in the pantry. Only boring old digestives, I'm afraid."

Nodding her approval, Francesca scanned the familiar room. Nothing had changed in forever; the same pictures hung on the wall of the farm back in the day. Declan's family's small holding had evolved, in as much as it was merely land now. "It has been so long. I can remember us swinging out the back. Can you?"

"I recall jumping off and twisting my ankle." He offered her a biscuit, sat down next to her. "You came with me to the hospital, scared I was going to die, or something." He chuckled to himself. When he stared for more than a couple of seconds, he averted his gaze.

For some reason, Francesca couldn't think of anything to say. It had never happened before with Declan. After a lengthy awkward silence, she laughed.

"What's so funny?" Declan smiled, waiting.

She shrugged. "Nothing. It's just weird being here, I guess. Brings back so many memories. I'm sorry I should've come and said hi sooner."

Declan leaned back in his chair. "I understand, Fran, you were with Paul. He wouldn't have wanted you skipping over here, would he? And he's right. If I was in a relationship with you, I wouldn't want you visiting him at his house either."

Francesca smiled at the thought of being Declan's girlfriend. If she were, sitting here like this, enjoying a cuppa at the kitchen table would be a daily joy to look forward to. "I guess you're right." When he blushed, she looked away out of respect.

She forgot how shy Declan could be. They had some fantastic times together growing up in boring old Bishops Drake. When they were about fourteen, she recalled him having a massive crush on one of the girls at school: Melanie. He confided in her walking home from class one day, and she could still recall the heartbreak at hearing those words.

So many years ago, or was it decades? Yeah, twenty-two years.

Only five more years and getting pregnant would be considered dangerous.

"What time's your interview?" He finished his cup of tea.

"I need to phone and firm up a time, but not until after school hours." She drank the remains of her tea. "I only hope I get back in time for work. It's the anniversary today; Aidan and Kate are going to the cemetery this afternoon."

"I heard about last night, the bust up between Aidan and Chris." Declan helped her up and let her thread her arms through. "It sounds nasty."

It was the first she heard of it. "What? What bust-up?"

"Jill arrested Aidan and Chris last night, didn't you hear? The Lions and the Headers played pool. Aidan showed up at the Head after work, sunk a few drinks and had a pop at Chris. Jill was there off-duty, arrested them, and held them overnight. I'm surprised you didn't hear this yourself?"

"Poor Kate; she'll be so upset." She searched for her keys in her coat pocket. "I need to know if she's alright." Turning to him, she stood on tiptoes, kissed him on his cheek. "Thank you so much for the tea. We'll have to do it again sometime." She loved the way he blushed when he agreed. "Maybe you can come over to mine for dinner one night?"

"I would like that." He smiled, as he let her out.

13

St John's Anglican Church at the top of the High Street was the oldest building in Bishops Drake. The village was built around it, and its vast cemetery. Aidan had not set foot on the grounds for exactly a year, since the first anniversary of his son's fatal road traffic accident.

Being back at the site he and Kate had picked to lay Vinnie to rest brought back that day. They chose a lovely plot to bury their only child, surrounded by bulb flowers in the springtime. All around the perimeter of Vinnie's grave were hyacinths, crocus and daffodils of varying colours.

Holding a bouquet of assorted blooms, he bought from the florist next door to the restaurant, he bent down and placed them at the foot of the gravestone. "I hope they're not too girly for you, Vin," he said, standing up straight, taking Kate's hand. "I asked for neutral colours; no pinks." His wife squeezed his hand.

Although he was out of favour with Kate, Aidan knew she would let him off for the rest of the day at least. When she picked him up from the Basingstoke police station, she barely spoke to him on the way back to the house. Aidan dared not start her off, so he sat quietly in the passenger seat.

Kate had probably spent time bashing him to Liz and Rae. Before Vinnie's death, he and Liz were friends, but over the past couple of years they'd drifted apart. His sister-in-law rarely visited the house these days, and only came by when she knew Kate was home alone. Shame. He and Liz used to laugh together, a lot.

"We're all here for you, Vin," Kate said. "We miss you, so much. Every day hurts without you." She stared at the ground.

He squeezed Kate's hand as a tear fell on the grass. A lump strangled his will to speak, leaving it up to Vinnie's auntie to take over.

"Hey, Vinnie, it's Aunt Liz and Aunt Rae." His sister-in-law held Rae's hand. "We went and did it. Look, isn't the ring beautiful? We had such a happy day. I only wish you could have been a part of it."

Aidan looked up from the perimeter of the grave, Liz's sad face forcing the lump further. "It was a lovely day." His voice sounded strained, even to him. Tears welled up. He rubbed his nose, a habit he acquired to prevent him from crying.

Kate spoke about Liz and Rae's wedding next, telling Vinnie the particulars of the ceremony, where it took place, where the reception was held. She kept her voice in check, unlike him. "I so wish you were here."

After standing around the grave for half an hour, Kate called time. "Are you coming, or not?" She stood waiting for him, as Liz and Rae walked on ahead.

"You go, love, I'll catch you up," he said, turning back to the grave. "I need to talk to Vinnie about something. I'll meet you back at the restaurant." His voice wouldn't hold for long. All he wanted to do since arriving at the ceremony was speak to him.

"Are you sure?" She nodded her understanding, turned, and shouted for Liz and Rae to wait for her. She walked after them, leaving him alone at their son's grave.

He waited until she disappeared from view. Reaching inside his jacket, Aidan took out a hipflask. "I hope you don't mind. It's your favourite whisky. I thought we'd have a drink together." He took a sip, tears forming. He fought them. "It's been too long, son. I should come here more often, being on our doorstep and all."

After pouring a shot's worth at the head of the grave, he took another sip, only bigger this time. "I'm glad we have this time together, Vin. There is something I've been meaning to say to you, since-" He cut off from his speech, taking the time to look behind him, before turning back to his son. "Well, I don't need to tell you when."

Fighting the tears, his vision deteriorating, he took a swig from the hipflask. "I'm so sorry, mate. It's all my fault, the crash, the four of you dying. All on me. If I hadn't argued with you that day; if I had just listened to you for once you would all still be here. Chris' son would still be here. If I had let you take a year out from uni this village would still be a happy place to live."

14

"Why are we hiding like this?" Rae peeped over the tall gravestone.

Kate rose to eye level, her forehead above the top of the grave. "Because I can feel a change in him. I think he might finally be grieving. He's never stayed behind before. I just want to make sure he's alright."

"Jesus, Kate, it's been two years now, to the day, and you don't think he's been grieving?" Her sister sat on the outer rim of an old grave. "What's he been doing? I mean, apart from being a royal pain in everyone's bum?"

In the distance, Aidan took a swig of his hipflask, continuing to talk to their son. "He's been in denial this whole time, Liz. I told you before how he hasn't once cried since the crash." It was not uncommon to not cry, but Kate understood Aidan; she knew her husband almost as well as he knew her.

"Just because he doesn't ball his eyes out doesn't mean he's not grieving. You know what they say: everyone grieves in their own way, Kate."

Kate hid behind the gravestone, turning to her sister. "I was slagging him off last night. Now I feel like a right bitch. I still love him, Liz, no matter what he's done. You used to get on so well. I still remember how you both used to gang up on me."

Liz smiled. "You're right. We did get on, mostly at your expense. Don't blame yourself for sounding off about him. He was really out of order yesterday."

Going back to spying on her husband, Kate almost ran out from behind the gravestone when Aidan's legs buckled from beneath him. Rae pulled her back.

"Don't! He asked you to go back to the restaurant, right?" Rae had forceful hands. "He might not thank you for spying on him."

Thinking about Rae's comment, Kate stepped back behind the gravestone, keeping vigil on Aidan. He sat on the grass, his head hung, his shoulders going up and down. "I can't leave him like this. I'm sorry!"

With her head down, she ran to the next tombstone along, ducked behind it. Then the next, continuing until she hid behind the gravestone in front of her son's. She sat with her back to it, listening to her husband.

"I'll do anything to take it back, Vin," he said between sobs. "Please forgive me."

Kate had never heard him cry before. She wanted to go and comfort him. Having been through the process of grieving herself, reaching acceptance maybe a year and a half after the accident, she was strong enough to help Aidan start his steps.

When she came out from behind the stone, he was sat on the grass still, his back to her, his head hung, shoulders bucking. "Aidan?"

He held his hand up to stop her, turned his body even further away from her.

Instead of standing back, Kate went to him, squatting, engulfing him in a tight hug.

He buried his face in her jacket, his sobs muffled.

"I'm so sorry, this is all my fault." She made out his sob-filled words, just. "If I'd listened to you, Vinnie wouldn't have driven angry. He would still be here today. If I let him quit uni, he wouldn't have been in the car to hit Liam."

She pulled him in even tighter. "Shh! It's not your fault. No one's to blame." She rocked him back and forth, his face still buried in her jacket.

These past two years she believed he blamed himself for the crash. Every time they argued, she would bring up that the only reason he was being such an arsehole was because he hated himself, that he thought he caused the fatal collision.

Aidan clung to her, the uncontrollable sobs subsiding.

"Let it all out," she said, in a soothing, calm voice. "That was in God's hands. You can't blame yourself for the crash. It was a freak accident, a terrible, cruel act of nature."

In that moment, she would have done anything to take his pain away. Behind her, footsteps, two sets. She craned her neck. "Give us a couple of minutes, would you?"

Liz and Rae obeyed. Liz mouthed, 'Sorry!' before they headed for the restaurant. "We'll be waiting outside your place."

15

Francesca pulled up in front of the administration building of Cherry Tree Lodge. Bigger than she expected, the 'Lodge' consisted of three huge red brick buildings. There were also pre-fabs on site, in addition to a couple of other large halls, maybe gymnasiums, she couldn't be sure. Switching the engine off, she took deep breaths before exiting her car.

Through the glass reception doors, she entered a well-maintained, orderly institution of learning. Walking along a hall, she smiled at the framed pictures of varying ages and ability adorning the walls. Some of the students were exceptionally gifted.

"Can I help you?" A curious woman, tall and thin stood behind her desk in reception.

Explaining who she was, along with the reason for her visit, Francesca thought the support staff at the school might be hearing impaired too. The name on the badge said, 'Ingrid Kirk'. After the initial confusion, the receptionist asked her to take a seat.

Sat waiting for the headteacher was akin to hanging about for the dentist. Francesca had not been for a job interview since fluffing hers with Kate and Aidan. She smiled at the memory of her waffling on at them at the restaurant.

"Mrs Redmond will see you now, Miss Darby."

Not especially taken with Ingrid's version of customer service, Francesca followed the receptionist's directions to the headteacher's office on the ground floor and knocked on the door. Butterflies fluttered in her belly.

The door opened.

Greeted by the loveliest of smiles, the headteacher stood about five feet six inches tall, with a perm of dark hair, round glasses, and of portly shape. Francesca held her hand out. "Mrs Redmond, I'm pleased to meet you."

The headteacher had a strong grip. Francesca liked that in a person; there was nothing worse than a limp handshake in her opinion.

Inside Mrs Redmond's spacious and newly decorated office, Francesca took a seat in front of her interviewer, her nerves at their peak. "I love this room." She surveyed the room while her hopefully soon-to-be employer got her paperwork together. "So warm, inviting."

"Thank you, Francesca!"

"Oh, please call me Fran," she insisted. "It reminds me so much of being scorned by my mum when anyone calls me by my full name." When she waffled, she dived into her bag, taking out a white envelope. "Sorry! Here's my resume."

Taking it from her, Mrs Redmond opened it, slid out the piece of A4 paper. She fiddled with it, expecting another page, maybe? "Thank you for this, Fran. I'll photocopy it for our files." She read through it briefly. "Shame about what happened to Marble's Marvels. I understand they're going through tough times at the moment. Is that why you're here?"

"Partly. I'll level with you, Mrs Redmond. I haven't done much with my life, except marry a controlling man, who wouldn't let me work. I had to beg him to let me study signing at evening classes. That's why my CV is so sparse in experience. And you're right about it being a shame. I worked there at the height of its popularity. It used to be such a vibrant and exciting place to work. The owners are trying new ideas."

"I remember how busy it was." Mrs Redmond sat back in her seat, regarded Francesca. "Let's see how good you are, shall we?"

The headteacher asked Francesca how long she had been signing for.

Using British Sign Language (BSL), she replied that she started six years earlier. She went further, stipulating where she learned it, spelling the name of the adult education centre with her fingers.

Impressed, Mrs Redmond put her through her paces, asking her longer and more complicated questions about her past. Francesca loved the challenge, finding she could answer them all with ease. Having not used her signing for a year, since leaving the adult learning centre, she thought she might be rusty.

"Marvellous, Fran." Reaching across the desk, Mrs Redmond shook her hand. "You're more than qualified to join our team. As a teaching assistant, you'll be shadowing one of our more experienced teachers. We have a class still here if you would like to meet them?"

Francesca smiled. "Oh yes please."

"It's not a class as such, more a club. Some of the parents can't pick their kids up at the normal time so we keep those students together until the last one leaves."

Following Mrs Redmond out of the administration building, along covered corridors to the first red brick unit, Francesca chatted some more with the head teacher. Nerves kicked in when they stopped outside a door.

"Don't be nervous, they'll love you. Ready?"

Francesca nodded, letting out a long-held breath.

The room was silent. Her ears couldn't marry up with her eyes. It was chaos, with children busy chatting away to one another, drawing pictures, playing board games. It should have been loud, an abuse to the senses, she thought, stepping inside.

Joining Mrs Redmond at the front of the classroom, the headteacher managed to catch their attention. Francesca waved hello, before introducing herself, spelling each letter of her name. Telling them a little about herself, she received a mixed welcome. Some of the children were excited, others not so.

"Let me introduce you to Naomi. She's lovely, and she's in Rachel's class, the teacher you'll be shadowing. If I were you, I would use the time you spend here working out if teaching is something you want to do. There is only a short window of opportunity to apply. Don't be alarmed, staying a T.A. is always an option if not."

"I can't wait to meet Naomi," she said, standing aside to let Mrs Redmond through.

She followed Mrs Redmond to the back of the room. Approaching a girl in a wheelchair, Francesca stood waiting to be introduced. The head teacher explained to Naomi that Francesca was new here and needed a friend.

Naomi smiled up at her. '*I want to be your friend*,' she signed.

'*I would like that*,' Francesca signed in response.

16

Kate couldn't speak. Since Francesca's interview at Cherry Tree Lodge, her waitress wouldn't stop talking about Mrs Redmond, or a little girl called Naomi, who Francesca explained had cerebral palsy. "How are the Bedfords enjoying their meals?" She had to cut Francesca off mid-sentence.

"They're fine," Francesca confirmed. "So, as I was saying."

Her hint fell on deaf ears, but Kate needed Francesca to focus on the customers. Eventually Francesca's words became a noise. Stood behind the bar, she kept thinking about earlier at the cemetery.

Aidan broke down in her arms. Kate had waited for that moment for months, at one point giving up hope. He needed to break that barrier down, if he were to ever accept the death of their gorgeous son. She wanted to survive this with him, not in spite of him. Maybe this afternoon was the beginning of his grieving process? She hoped.

"Are you listening to me? Kate?" Francesca nudged her.

"I'm sorry, I'm miles away," she said, turning away from the customers.

"Oh no, I'm sorry. Here I am prattling on about my day, I didn't even ask you how it went at the cemetery."

Leaning into Francesca's ear, Kate made sure no one was listening. "Aidan collapsed at Vinnie's graveside. It's the first time he's shown any emotion other than anger or apathy. I swear, Fran, I think this might be the breakthrough we've been waiting for."

"What? That's great!" Francesca frowned. "That sounded wrong. You know what I mean. He needs to grieve properly."

When Kate turned to face the dining room, a hand was up on the Stringer table, the only other table in use. "What now?" Putting on a fake smile, she sauntered over to Mrs Stringer. "Is everything to your satisfaction over here?"

"I'm so sorry to do this, Kate, but everything was either dry, or chewy." She rattled off what was wrong with every meal. There were eight family members sat around the table. "I managed to eat mine, but I don't think we should pay full price for this. Just my opinion."

The husband hardly touched his steak and kidney pudding. The two young sons ate their scampi, but left their brown, over fried chips, and mushy peas. The two elder daughters tried to eat their gammon, but the meat was fatty, not very appealing.

Scratching her head, she decided to call it quits. "I'm terribly sorry about this," she said, wanting to cry. They needed well-fed, happy customers, not complaints. Francesca started taking plates away, leaving Kate to deal with the fallout. "I won't charge you. Please accept my sincerest apologies, Mrs Stringer."

"Please, Kate, I don't want to make a fuss."

"No, I insist." She accepted Mrs Stringer's nod as confirmation, turned and walked back to the bar.

The front door opened.

Wandering past the Bedford party of six, grateful that they had not complained about their meals, she smiled at the matriarch, who overheard her conversation with Mrs Stringer, giving her a sympathetic glance.

Behind the bar, she met a small man in his mid to late fifties, who had white hair, and tanned skin. Kate thought he looked Greek. "Can I help you?"

Mrs Stringer and her family left. Kate let Francesca clear the table, while she studied the small man in front of her. "I'm sorry! Do you have a reservation?"

The dainty man shook his head, pointing at his mouth. He held a finger up, took out a pad of paper and a pen from his coat and used the bar to write on. '*I'm profoundly deaf. I can lip read. I understand you're looking for a new chef?*'

He had the kindest eyes she had ever seen. Kate couldn't turn him away.

"You're a chef?"

'*Among other things, yes,*' he wrote, turning the pad round for her to read.

Speaking slowly and clearly, Kate mouthed the words carefully. "We're looking for a sous chef, not a kitchen manager. Are you still interested? And if you are, I can't promise we'll be open in a month's time, I'm afraid. If you're willing to give it a go, I'll fetch my husband, introduce you?"

The Greek wrote, '*I am very interested. Thank you!*' on his pad of paper.

Kate smiled, left the bar unattended and rushed to the kitchen, where Aidan had his hands in marigolds soaking the Stringer party's plates. "You won't believe what's just happened, love." He glanced at her, interested. "A tiny Greek guy has just walked in asking for a job in the kitchen."

Her husband stopped washing the dishes and gripped the sink. "Not this again, Kate. Look, we don't need a new chef; I don't have enough to do as it is, much less adding someone else to the mix. Please, drop this, will you?"

"You told me last night you'll give it some thought. Come out to the dining room and meet him. Please?"

With a huff, Aidan peeled the marigolds off, threw them on the draining board. "Come on, then. What's his name?"

In her excitement, Kate forgot to ask. "I don't remember." She led their way out to the restaurant, where Francesca stood behind the bar signing with Greek guy. "Oh, you're familiar with Francesca, Mr..?"

"Call me chef," Francesca said, a smile forming.

"You're kidding, right? My wife asked you a question. What's your name?" Aidan's tone, while not hostile, created an atmosphere around the bar.

"Aidan, you're being rude to our guest." Kate scalded him. "Let me introduce you to Chef. Aidan, this is Chef, Chef, Aidan."

Francesca made herself useful by translating Chef's answers, while relaying hers and Aidan's questions. When she spoke to him, she couldn't take her eyes away from him. He was mesmerising. "Chef can see that Mr Marble isn't convinced about his credentials." Francesca translated Chef's signing. "Give me the kitchen for the next hour and I'll cook you all the best meals you've ever eaten."

Checking Aidan's response, Chef nodded.

"If it's not the most delicious meal, I'll leave and never come back again. None of us lose anything. If I succeed, you give me the sous chef job. Deal?"

Kate smiled when Chef held his hand out for Aidan to shake. The Greek knew to ask her husband, his potential new boss. "What do you say, love? It can't hurt. You can wash up all the other plates. We'll leave Chef in peace to work his magic."

Slowly, her husband's face changed from confrontational to agreeable. "Deal! But when it's not the best meal I've ever had, you're out of here."

"It will still be tastier than yours," Francesca muttered.

It was loud enough for Aidan to hear. Kate shot Francesca a warning glare. "So, it's a deal. Aidan, show Chef the kitchen, would you? And when you're done washing up, come out and join me. This is our first dinner date in months; I don't want to waste a minute." She shooed her husband, keeping Francesca by her side behind the bar.

"Where did he come from?" Francesca asked.

"He said he heard we're looking for a sous chef, but I haven't told anyone yet, or posted an ad anywhere." She had to admit it was suspicious. "I have such a good feeling about him. I can't explain it."

Francesca dug her in the ribs. "Hey, what about my interview? Did you get that feeling then, too?"

Kate pulled a face. "Yeah! We gave you the job out of pity, Fran. Your interview was terrible." She laughed. She was only half-joking. "I can't wait to see what he cooks up."

17

Christian Ashcroft tilted the dregs of his can of Fosters in his mouth, scrunched up the can and threw it in the large plastic bin in the corner of his workshop.

His mobile, connected to his radio, was playing a country song: The Good Stuff by Kenny Chesney. Chris loved country music. If he had the money, he would fly over to Nashville during a festival. The song was perfect for how he felt about Edie, his wife. Not least because the lyrics had a character die of cancer.

Sitting on his swivel chair in front of his large mahogany desk, Chris thought how cruel life was, taking his son from him two years before diagnosing Edith with breast cancer, which had metastasized into the lungs. She underwent all the treatment possible, chemo and radiotherapy, starting with attempting to cut the tumours out. It all failed.

"Chris, I'm going to bed," Edie yelled from the back door.

Two seconds later the rattling cough took to the airwaves, telling him how poorly his wife was. "I'm on my way," he said, getting up from his chair, switching the lights off in the barn-turned-garage, and locking up.

Having drunk eight cans already, it was only nine o'clock, and he would probably sink another four by the time he passed out on the sofa. Now Edie was sick, Chris didn't like waking her up getting into bed. "Wait up, I'm coming," he shouted, heading for the house.

The cough grew in intensity and volume, causing him to run towards the house. "Edie?" He rushed into the kitchen, where his wife clung to the table, her knuckles white. "Edie!" She wouldn't stop coughing.

Her eyes rolled back.

Chris held her, easing her on to her back on the floor. "Talk to me, honey. Please." She couldn't catch her breath. He suddenly thought about the cannister of oxygen upstairs in her bedroom. "I'm going to fetch help. Hold on!"

Fearing the worst, he raced up to the bedroom, grabbed the oxygen, turned, and ran back downstairs as fast as he could, all the while listening to her cough up bloody phlegm. "Here! Take this."

Fixing the face mask over her mouth and nose, Chris twisted the dial on top, the hissing sound of air flowing the loudest noise in the room. The plastic mask started getting condensation inside it. "Good! You lie there, take as much as you need, Edie."

He stroked her hair, as she stared up at him with fearful eyes. Wanting nothing more than a healthy wife, Chris would do anything to swap with her. Why was God doing this to them? He went to church with Edie every Sunday; he prayed regularly. Why was he being punished? What would the vicar tell him if he asked?

Edie's breathing returning to normal, the rattling abated. Chris unstrapped the oxygen mask, sat her up. Her breaths were still laboured. "Put your arms around my neck," he said, picking her up so easily it scared him how much weight she'd lost. "Let's get you to bed, shall we?" She nodded, half asleep.

Easing her on to the bed, Chris pulled the duvet back for Edie, then gently covered her in it. "Sleep, my love." He kissed her forehead. Sweat from her attack made him go into the bathroom for a flannel.

He washed her face with it, seeing the gratitude in her smile.

Sat on the bed, Chris saw her struggling to raise her hand to stroke his cheek. He helped her, kissing her hand in return, holding the tears back. He had to be strong, for her.

He thought about putting a complaint in to the Basingstoke Police station. When he arrived, he told the holding cell officer that his wife was too sick to come and pick him up. That officer went and phoned her anyway. "I'm so sorry you had to come collect me." His voice strained, he tried to hide his pain from her with a smile.

"Come...Here." His wife beckoned him.
"You're...My...Good...Man."

His chin crumpled, tears forming. "I'm not good." He fell on to her, burying his face in her shoulder, as sobs wracked his body.

18

"What's he doing in there?" Aidan went to stand. Kate stopped him by putting her hand on his. He scanned the room. The Bedford party, having finished their mains, remained at their table without ordering desserts. He itched to enter the kitchen. "Oh, come on, Kate, just let me go in there."

Kate took her hand away from his. "Go if you want," she said, annoyed.

He went to stand.

"I thought this was our first date night in a while, but it doesn't matter. I can sit here by myself. You go and chase Chef out of our kitchen."

Remaining seated, Kate confused him. "I thought we were having time apart?" He knew in an instant he'd said the wrong thing. He held his palms out. "Whoa! I didn't mean anything by it."

"You can be such an arse at times," she said, folding her arms.

"I can, I'm sorry!" When she looked away from him, he tried to attract her attention. "You're empty over there." He raised his hand. Their waitress arrived. "A bottle of the 92 Sancerre please, Fran."

"Scratch that, honey, make it the house red. Don't waste the Sancerre on this table, Fran." She glared at him.

"Right you are, Kate." Francesca went to fetch her order.

Not knowing what to say, Aidan sat back in his seat, arms folded. Kate wasn't joking when she said it had been months since their last date. He tried to think of something to talk about.

"Well, this is fun, isn't it?" Kate avoided eye contact.

The bell rang, meaning their food was ready. Aidan gestured with his hands for Francesca to bring their meals out. She obeyed, almost running to the kitchen. "Here it is," he said, hungry and eager to clap his eyes on what 'Chef' had cooked him.

He picked up his knife and fork, held them ready. As Francesca approached the table, he saw she was carrying two bowls. "I wonder what we've got."

She arrived, placing Kate's bowl on her mat first, followed by his. The steam coming from the spaghetti Bolognese blew his way. Aidan inhaled, taking in the sweet aroma. "Italy." He visited Rome several times during his childhood, loved Italy. When he opened his eyes, Kate smirked. "What? Doesn't mean it will be the best thing I ever tasted."

Kate leaned forward. "Keep an open mind."

"I'm nothing if not open minded, honey." Chef had broken the raw spaghetti into smaller pieces, which were mixed in with the meaty sauce. Aidan used his fork to pick up his first bite, waiting for Kate to join him. "Ready?"

The taste hit him almost the moment the meat touched his tongue. Smooth, succulent, delicious, just like Chef said it would be. "Mmm, that is so good." He smiled at Kate. "Excellent even."

It was the best thing he'd eaten in a long, long time. He tried a few more divine mouthfuls, salivating at the thought of the next bite. Before he knew it, he had polished off his bowl.

Kate finished hers shortly after he did. "We have to ask Chef out here."

She asked Francesca to fetch him.

With food this good, the restaurant couldn't fail. Aidan wanted to believe Chef might be the answer to their prayers. "Come on over here." He stood and clapped the short Greek over. "Well done! That was delicious, Chef. A real masterpiece of magic. The best Bolognese I've tasted in years."

Sitting back down, Aidan poured himself a glass of house red. "It melts in your mouth; I'll give it that. Only one problem: it wasn't the best ever. My parents took me to Rome a few times when I was growing up. Their Bolognese was to die for. I mean, this was lovely and all, but nothing on their authentic blends."

Kate shot him a warning glare. Looking up at Chef, she smiled. "I for one thought it was divine. You didn't disappoint." She looked across the table at him again.

"Well? Does he have the sous chef job?" Francesca stood, eager, her eyes wide. "Please say yes, Aidan. Please say yes. His food will pack this place, I promise you."

Food like that would bring in the customers. "Fine, I concede that his Bolognese is out of this world, but what else can you cook, Chef? Having a speciality is one thing, being able to make loads of other dishes as terrific as this is quite another."

"He says give him a recipe; he can make it. And I believe him, Aidan."

"It's up to you, love. You know my opinion." Kate sat back in her seat, waiting.

For dramatic effect, Aidan made them all wait. "Fine! You can start tomorrow morning at 08:30. But you're my sous chef, understood? It's still my kitchen, my baby. You're here to help me. If you agree to this, welcome to Marble's Marvels."

Aidan didn't need to be a signer to recognise Chef thanking him, bowing, with palms together. "Is there any left out there?" Francesca told him there was. "What are you waiting for? Dish it out to the Bedfords. Let's get word of mouth going."

Francesca ran to the kitchen. Aidan smiled at his wife; whose glare had softened. "Let's get some personal details from you, Chef. Where are you living? Our previous sous chef lived upstairs. We have accommodation if you need it."

Chef nodded his approval.

SATURDAY, JANUARY 12TH

19

Kate let herself inside the restaurant. Tired after the excitement of testing Chef's divine cuisine, she lay awake most of the night imagining Marble's Marvels brimming with diners again, like it used to before the crash.

The one problem they had was the rift between Aidan and Chris Ashcroft. If she could find a way to bring the two together, Chris' half of the village would end their boycott of her restaurant. She locked the door behind her.

As she turned to face the dining room, the lights were on in the kitchen. It couldn't be Aidan, his car was not in the car park. Forgetting for a moment that Chef had access to the whole place now, she rushed over to the kitchen door.

"Oh my!" Kate stood in the doorway watching Chef stir a pan of Bolognese sauce. Her nostrils were assaulted with competing succulent aromas. It made her salivate. "Morning!"

When he failed to turn round, she wanted to slap her forehead with the palm of her hand. "He's deaf. Of course!" *No harm done*, she thought.

Chef had four pans on the go. "Morning, Chef!" She moved her mouth deliberately, speaking slower than normal. He smiled, bowed with his palms together, like he did last night when thanking her for the job. "What's in these?"

Picking up a pad of paper, Chef started writing.
'*Chili, chicken casserole, chicken tikka masala, and Bolognese.*' Four of the restaurant's staples, in batches that they could freeze if necessary. He continued scribbling.
'*I thought we could put a table outside the restaurant with samples, hand them out to the villagers as they walk by?*'

How could her neighbours not be drawn in by these delightful aromas? All it would take was for the residents of Bishops Drake to have one mouthful. Taking a wooden spoon, Kate sampled some of Chef's tikka masala, closing her eyes as it touched her tongue. "Mmm! That is amazing!"

She had tried so many different tikka masalas in her life. Chef's topped them all. Every ingredient within leapt out at her palate. "How do you do it?"

'*Cook by rote, season with love. It's all in the seasoning.*' Chef picked up an ornate wooden pepper grinder, twisted the top, sprinkling pepper in the chili.

"Well, whatever you do, keep doing it, please." Kate's attention turned to the door when it opened, and Aidan walked in, his mouth open, anger in his eyes.

"What the hell's going on in here?" He scanned the room, his face growing redder.

"Chef made an early start this morning." She put her arm round Chef's shoulder. "He's cooked off a batch of Bolognese, chili, chicken casserole, and a divine tikka masala. You need to try this, Aidan."

"I don't believe this!" Her husband stepped closer.

"Will you just try it, please," she said, her tone growing as angry as his face grew red. "Stop being so negative. Chef had a fantastic idea." She picked up the pad of paper and showed it to Aidan.

"We're doing what now?"

"We don't have any bookings, do we?" He shook his head. "So, we're going to set up a trestle table on the pavement and give away free samples of all these dishes. It's amazing advertising. And I think we might encourage some diners through the doors. Trust me, as soon as they try these, they're going to want more."

When he went to say something, she shot him one of her warning glares. "Please don't be a pain in my bum about this, Aidan. This is the best way to entice our diners back in."

Aidan put his hands up in surrender. "Alright! Anything you say. If you think this will work, we'll give it a try. But don't raise your hopes, you can't expect miracles, Kate."

"A miracle's exactly what we have in Chef."

20

"I don't believe you!" Francesca transferred her mobile from her left to her right hand. She stood in front of her full-length mirror inspecting her uniform. She cursed an ugly spot on the back of her skirt. "I don't have time for this, Paul. I'm late for work. And now that you're gone, I need every penny I can earn."

Her husband scoffed, implying she could always call on the bank of mummy and daddy. "I'm not like you. I don't go sponging off people...How dare you! I work hard for my money...Why did you even call me? Is it just to wind me up? Oh, go and have a nice life with your tart. Bastard!" She hung up with a jab at the screen.

Speaking to Paul right before work was not a wise move. All she had now was resentment, bitterness at him leaving her. When he called, she should have ignored it. He would be at that tart's house laughing now. "No! Deep breaths, Fran. In...Out."

Her mobile vibrated on her dresser. Expecting it to be her husband back for round two, Francesca scowled at the display, her expression changing at the caller ID: Declan. Holding her phone to her chest, a smile spread over her face. "Declan! Hi! How are you?"

Taking a moment to reply, Declan coughed. "Yeah, hi, Fran."

Another silence made her look at the clock on her dresser. "What can I do for you? Sorry to rush you, but I'm late for work." She could tell how nervous he was.

"Um, sorry for disturbing you, I'll go-"

"No! You don't have to leave. What did you want to say?" She closed her eyes, hoping, no praying, he would ask her out. She barely slept last night thinking about him alone in that old farmhouse. The coffee they shared kept rolling over in her mind.

"I, um, was wondering if you would like to come over for dinner sometime? We mentioned it yesterday but didn't set a date or anything."

If she had been able to, Francesca would have whooped. She had to settle for an air fist of victory instead. "Oh, I'd love to. When?"

"You have Saturday nights off, how about mine tonight for seven?"

How did he know her work schedule? Had he been watching her? For some women that might have set off alarm bells. Not with her Declan, though. "Tonight, at seven, round yours it is. Until then?" About to hang up, she added, "Oh, do I need to bring anything?"

"Just yourself. I have everything else covered."

Francesca hung up with a grin. "Yes!" She punched the air again. "Yes, yes, yes!"

She was so late for work, not that Kate would mind all that much, they were so quiet. Even so, she didn't want to push her luck. How had she gone from fuming to walking on clouds in the space of five minutes? Declan. "What am I doing standing around?"

Shrugging at the ugly spot on the bum of her skirt, Francesca went to the kitchen, picked up her coat, keys, handbag, and wandered over to the front door. She wanted to walk to work, but being so late, she jumped in her red Mini Cooper with a white roof instead.

The drive through her village was what she needed. Waving at some of her fellow Drakes, the mood Paul put her in evaporated. It was Declan mostly, although the sun shining down on her helped as well. Parking round the back of the restaurant, next to Kate's MG, she locked up and walked while humming as she strolled to the front of the building.

"What the-" She stopped in the centre of the pavement when she saw Kate and Chef stood behind a trestle table, setting it up with plastic cups, and cardboard boxes. She stepped in front of the table. "Morning!" She signed as well as spoke. "What's all this?"

Kate let Chef speak for her, while Francesca observed his signs.

"Wow! We're giving away free samples? Can I come out here, too? I can take some around the village if you'd like?"

"No, we'll settle for passers-by, but I might take you up on that later. For now, though, can you take over for me? Everyone in the village loves you, Fran. Try and encourage them to come in and have lunch.

Excited, Francesca took an apron from Kate, tied the belt around her waist.

21

"What are they doing?" Martin stared out of Elio's window.

Elio Capelli stood beside his assistant manager. In front of Marble's Marvels, Francesca tried to tempt passers-by, while standing next to a short, Greek looking guy. "What are they up to?" He straightened his tie, watching as Mr. and Mrs Singh approached Francesca.

The waitress handed them both cups. Elio couldn't believe it when Kate opened the doors to the restaurant, and the elderly Asian couple walked in. "Did they just get Mr and Mrs Singh inside by touting?

"They sure did." Martin glanced at him. "You're not worried about this, are you? We've got this market covered, Elio. They're just trying a gimmick. The locals won't fall for this, trust me."

"Never believe a man who says trust me, Martin," he said, making sure he looked respectable before he pulled on the door handle.

Outside, the sun shining on a beautiful crisp morning, Elio shivered in only a white shirt and dark waistcoat. He waited for a car to pass before crossing the road, his breath visible as he walked. "Morning, Fran," he said, stopping in front of the trestle table. "What's going on over here then?" He studied the short Greek man stood next to her.

"Elio, let me introduce you to Chef," Francesca said, smiling. "Kate and Aidan hired him as a sous chef. Here, try one of our signature dishes." She pointed at four plastic cups, explaining what each one was.

"So, you're giving away free samples, to what, tempt villagers inside?"

"Uh-huh! Would you like to test one?"

"Chef, is that your first or last name?" He smiled, expecting a laugh from one or both of them. "Come on, Fran, introduce us properly. What's your real name?"

The short man in his chef whites pointed at his throat, explaining in universal signing that he couldn't talk. He covered his ears with his hands too.

Elio glanced at Francesca. "He's deaf?" She nodded. "That suits you, I guess, having learned sign language. Where did you find him?" He intentionally turned away from 'Chef'.

"He just walked in off the street last night asking for a job." She held up a cup. "Here, try this spaghetti Bolognese, Elio. You're Italian, see how it compares to yours."

Taking the cup from her, and picking up a fork, he dug around in the receptacle, speared a forkful, and popped it in his mouth. Determined to not like it, he salivated at the old-style flavour. "Oh, my Lord!"

"Huh? You see? Stunning, isn't it?" Francesca picked up another cup.

Placing the Bolognese down, he took the second container from her. "Tikka masala," he said, taking a sniff, looking forward to tasting it.

As he was about to enjoy a sample, Kate walked out and joined Francesca and Chef behind the table. "I'm sampling your wares, Kate. And I must say that Bolognese is to die for; it'll be a winner for sure."

"Morning, Elio, I think you might be right. Mr and Mrs Singh just ordered a bowl each after trying some." Her smile was broad, genuine.

He popped the fork in his mouth, the masala making him close his eyes again. "What are you putting in this, Chef? Again, beautiful. Your customers are going to love this, too."

Wanting to try all four dishes, Elio stopped himself. If they were all as divine as the Bolognese, and especially the tikka masala, his place was in trouble. He prided himself on producing quality cuisine, but even he conceded it could be beaten by other traditional Italian restaurants.

"Won't you come inside, Elio? I'll ask Chef to make you whatever you want from our menu." Kate held the door open for him.

"Tempting, but I can't," he said, placing the cup back down. "I need to run back to my place. We have a fully booked restaurant this lunch and dinnertime."

He didn't need to panic yet. Kate may have a new, amazing chef, but it would take more than that to fill Marble's Marvels with diners, certainly from Bishops Drake. Half the residents had boycotted Kate's place because of her husband's insistence that Liam Ashcroft caused the crash. "Great job, Chef. How much will it cost to ask you cook over at my place?"

Kate laughed at Elio's joke. "Go on. You wouldn't try and poach my staff, would you, Elio?" She waved him off.

After waiting for a car to pass, Elio ran across the road to his restaurant, where guests were starting to arrive for their lunches.

Martin busied himself behind the bar, while the two waiters he had on duty lingered, as diners seated themselves.

"And? How is it over there? What did Fran say?"

"It's nothing to worry about. Kate's hired a new chef, and he's quite something," he said, going behind the bar and picking up a white envelope. "When did this arrive?" He read the writing on the back. A solicitor's firm.

"While you were chatting to Kate and Fran, why?" Martin reached for a bottle of red next to the till, opening it with a corkscrew.

Tearing the envelope, he slid the A4 piece of paper out, unfolded it. "Oh shit!" His wife had hired solicitors to apply for a divorce. Their separation was final. His assistant manager asked if he was alright?

Strange question, that. The woman he once loved wanted more than half of everything he owned, including her share of the profits of Elio's Restaurant. It was clear from the lawyer's tone that his wife wouldn't haggle with him. These solicitors meant business.

"Elio, are you alright?" Martin grabbed his arms, stabilising him.

Light-headed, Elio found himself sitting on a chair behind the bar. One of his waiters rushed it over. "Thank you!" He accepted a glass of orange juice from his assistant.

"Low blood sugar again?" Martin stood judging him. "You really should take better care of yourself. If you want some time, I can take over this lunchtime."

His hands shaking, Elio nodded. "I would appreciate that." He needed to sort his head out about his wife's demands for settlement.

22

Chris could tell by the grave expression on Dr Bryson's face the news was going to be devastating. The elderly doctor took his stethoscope away from Edie's chest, as she buttoned up her blouse. Sat next to her bed, Chris stroked her clammy forehead, and smiled. "Well?"

Dr Bryson stood from the chair. "It's like we talked about. The most I can do is keep her pain medication topped up, Christian. We've exhausted all other avenues. I'm so sorry, Edith. If there were more options available, I would use them, believe me."

He didn't need the quack's opinion to know his wife would die soon; he awoke to her coughing her lungs up this morning, which had prompted his call to the surgery. He was desperate now, his eyes beseeching the medical man. "Please, I'll do anything you ask. There must be more you can do."

Edie held his hand, squeezed it. "It's my time, Chris."

The effort of talking brought on another coughing fit that sounded like her lungs had collapsed. Sweat poured down her temples.

"Don't just sit there, do something!" He stood, staring down at Edie in so much pain. He would do anything to swap places with her.

Bryson placed the oxygen mask over her nose and mouth, giving her the air to breathe normally. She levelled off. "There. When she has another spell of coughing, make sure you put the mask on. And try not to let her talk too much." He stood and met Chris' stare. "I'm sorry about this, Christian. It's hard, but Edie refused hospice care. This is going to be the hardest thing you'll ever do."

"I can't believe it's happening so fast," he said, watching the condensation appear and disappear from her oxygen mask. "She drove over to the Basingstoke police station yesterday. How can she be so bad so quick?"

"The lung cancer is secondary, Christian. It spread from her breasts to her lungs and brain. It's in advanced stages now."

Edie pulled the mask off, her eyes drowsy. "It's okay...Doctor...It's...Fine."

Chris thought about calling his daughter, Amy home from university. "Thank you for your time, Doctor. It's appreciated."

"You have all the pain medication you need," Bryson said, using his walking stick to make it to the bedroom door. "Afternoon Edith. Christian. I'll see myself out."

Not the most sympathetic doctor in the world, Bryson's seventy-eight years had de-sensitised him to the sadness of death, Chris thought, following the old codger into the hallway. "I didn't want to ask in front of Edie, but how long do you think she can carry on like this? What I mean is-"

"In my experience, with how she is, I would say six to eight weeks." Dr Bryson put his hand on Chris' shoulder. "I am sorry!"

"I was going to phone Amy, ask her back here to say goodbye."

"Not yet, Christian. Trust me, you'll know when the time's right."

The doctor disappeared down the stairs.

Chris took a couple of deep breaths, turned, and walked back into the bedroom. His wife beckoned him with a crook of her finger. "What is it, my love?" He sat on the bed and used a flannel to wipe her forehead.

Edie pulled the mask off. "I need to...Speak to...Kate...Marble."

"Kate?" Surprised by the mention of her name, Chris shuffled. "Why? What can you possibly want to talk to her about?" He wanted to forbid her talking to Aidan Bloody Marble's wife. "Explain it to me."

"I need to...Tell her something." She pleaded with him to make it happen. "Her...Number's in...My phone." She clambered to put the mask back on, her breathing deteriorating.

He couldn't say no to his dying wife. The last person he wanted visiting Edie was Kate. They were close friends before the crash, sure, but not now. Reaching across her, Chris picked up Edie's mobile from her bedside cabinet.

23

Aidan could not understand how Chef did it. He asked his sous chef what ingredients he used in the Bolognese from last night. His deaf, mute cook showed him by collecting everything together. The only outcome he could think of was that Chef lied to him; he had a secret ingredient.

He expected a quiet Saturday lunchtime. Chef's four samples went down well with passers-by. Instead of zero tables, they cooked for six. All he did was heat Chef's dishes, as they all chose his testers from outside. Kate came back in with empty bowls and plates wearing a big grin.

Standing in front of the sink, he placed a stack of dishes in the soapy water, making sure they were clean before he ran them through the machine. He would never admit it, but he enjoyed washing up, found it therapeutic. "Did they enjoy it?"

Behind him, Kate added more crockery to his dirty pile. "Loved it. They couldn't have been any more complimentary if they tried. Four tables we managed to pull in from outside, and three of those booked evening meals for next week. I asked them all to tell their friends, and they all said they would."

"Even Mrs Singh?"

"We can do worse than having Mrs Singh telling her friends," Kate said, happy. "it's like the Marble's Marvels of old out there, I swear."

Continuing to wash up, Aidan mumbled to himself. Everyone was so confident about Chef's abilities, but not his. He ran this kitchen back when the dining room was full, getting hundreds of dishes out every day.

"There's such a fantastic atmosphere out there," Francesca said, adding to his washing up. "You should put in an appearance. They're loving Chef out there. He's a huge hit. I'm regaling them with his stories. Chef's so funny."

"I need to finish this, Fran. I'll be out after. Thanks." He would do no such thing. A cook's place was in the kitchen, not out front in the dining room.

He was being grouchy, having slept so badly last night.

After his busy day, he should have been out when his head hit the pillow, only he couldn't stop thinking about Vinnie. He hadn't cried once since the crash. Why now? Maybe it was the added pressure of Kate moving out?

Fetching another load of dishes, Aidan turned his focus to Chef finally showing his face. He waved to grab Chef's attention. "This isn't going to work out."

He spoke slowly, using his hands to express himself. "If you don't tell us your real name, we can't put you through our system. We need your national insurance number. We need to tax you-"

Kate entered. She was about to ask him something when her brow furrowed. "I was going to ask if you two have thought about specials for tomorrow. What did you say to him, Aidan? Why does Chef look so sad?"

"What? Nothing." He scratched his head. "I just told him it's not working. We need his details for tax purposes, and to be honest, I would like to know his real name. What has he told us about himself?"

"Here you go again, trying to sabotage us." Kate's eyes flared. "Do you want this restaurant to fail? Is that it?"

He stood back, shocked. "What? Of course not! How can you say that?"

"Easily. You've done nothing to contribute to our success." She pointed at him. "And now you want rid of our best shot at getting our customers back?"

"We need his national insurance number and P45, don't we?" He knew he was right on this. Every member of staff had to hand them these documents before they started working for them. The last thing he wanted was for Marble's Marvels to be hit with a huge tax bill.

"Sure, in an ideal world, but I'm sure we can come up with a solution." Her tone cooled when she realised he was right.

Chef put his finger up, signalling he had an idea.

"What's going on in here?" Francesca brought dessert plates in.

"Translate for us, would you?" He signalled for his waitress to watch.

Chef signed for Francesca.

"He says he'll stay here for home and board. He has a rich family, a full bank account. He's not here for money. He says he's here to help you two build the restaurant back up. He's here as long as you need him."

What could he say to that? "You'll work for room and board?"

"We don't need to declare him as working for us, do we, love?" Kate approached him, took his hand in hers. "I think of him as our secret weapon. With food like this we'll have a packed dining room in no time. Think about it, Aidan, it will be like before. You'll be managing a full contingent of kitchen staff, I'll be running the floor, like old times."

Kate had a way of getting around him. Was it her soft skin? He squeezed her hand. "I guess not, if he's volunteering. But I still feel like we're taking advantage of you. Why are you doing this for us?"

"He says he goes where he's needed," Francesca explained. "How do you know? I don't understand."

Chef shrugged his shoulders.

Aidan waited for Francesca's translation.

"He gets a feeling, he says." Francesca smiled at her new friend, making some signs of her own. "I'm glad you're here with us, Chef."

Aidan didn't believe Chef's reason for being here, but he had to admit to needing him.

"Well? What do you say?" Kate squeezed his hand this time.

"I say," he paused for dramatic effect, "welcome to Marble's Marvels. For real this time." He shook Chef's hand. His sous chef reciprocated with both hands, a broad smile stretching across his face. "I guess I need to learn some signing, don't I."

Francesca clapped, said, "Yay!" like a child might. "I can teach you. It will be a little project for me. Oh, I can't wait! I'll bring some books in for you."

Aidan smiled. "Thanks."

Kate let go of his hand when her mobile rang. "Chris? Hi! This is a surprise." She turned away from him. "Oh my! Of course! I'll be there as soon as I can."

His wife hung up, her back still to him.

"Chris? Ashcroft? What did he want?" He tried to hide his disdain.

Kate turned to him, tears forming. "Edie's dying. She's asked to see me." Grabbing him, she cried into his chef's whites. "I saw her in the police station. She looked awful, thin, gaunt, pale. Her hair was all wispy."

Had he known, Aidan would have kept his mouth shut at the pub. How could he and Kate not know she was dying? They lived in a village. "That's terrible. Go and make peace with her, please."

After she finished making his whites wet, Aidan told Kate that he would set-up the restaurant for dinner service. "Come on, Chef, let's sort out a menu for the week. I want to see how capable you are at some traditional British cuisine."

While he leaned on the stainless-steel counter, going through the options with his newest 'employee', he couldn't help but think about Christian Ashcroft. The poor guy had already been through the wars, from losing his farm to dealing with the death of Liam. There were big similarities between himself and Chris: neither could face the truth. He knew he had to grieve, to accept the fact Vinnie was gone.

24

Kate had mixed feelings as she pulled into the Ashcroft driveway. On the one hand she was excited about the future, about Aidan's sudden interest in Chef. On the other, she was burdened with such guilt, she would need to unload on the vicar. Why had she let Aidan and Chris' feud come between her and Edie's friendship?

Parking outside the farmhouse, she exited her little MG, stood staring at the dilapidated house, with its tiles hanging off the roof, cracking white paintwork, and dirty windows. Chris had let the homestead go as much as himself. "Such a pity," she mumbled.

She and Aidan used to visit the Ashcrofts quite regularly for dinners together. They used to play cards after. Their son, Liam was gorgeous. And Amy, how could she forget the lovely Amy? Almost as beautiful as her mother. "Here goes."

The door opened before she arrived. Edie's husband stood in the doorway. "Chris, I'm so terribly sorry. If there is anything I can do for you?"

"I'm doing this for my Edie, do you understand? I don't want you or your husband in here, but she needs you for some reason. Now go in there, make it up with my wife and leave!" He stood aside.

It broke her heart to find Edie lying in bed with an oxygen mask covering her mouth and nose. Kate didn't believe it possible, but her friend seemed weaker and smaller than she had at the Basingstoke police station. She sat on a chair next to the bed. Why had Edie driven there in her condition? Didn't she have carers looking after her? She reached out, holding Edie's hand.

"I'll leave you ladies to it." Chris closed the door.

What should she say to a dying woman? With how thin, how slight Edie was, it wouldn't be long until the cancer took her. Edie's eyes drooped. "If you need to sleep, Edie, I can come back later? Or tomorrow morning?"

Her eyes suddenly wide, Edie tried to sit up. "No! I need...To talk to you."

Once Edie lay comfortably, Kate held her hand again. "Anything. You can tell me anything." And sitting there, staring at the shell that was once Edith Ashcroft, she prayed for her old friend to recover. Edie and Chris had already been through enough. "Why didn't we keep in touch? It's not fair!"

Having difficulty keeping her eyes open, Edie squeezed her hand. "It was out...Of our hands...Kate. It was...Between our...Husbands." Sweat trickled down her cheeks.

Concerned, Kate reached under Edie's chin, placing the mask over her face. "Here, use this for a bit. I'm here until we're finished." The hardest part was seeing how weak Edie was. For years, Kate had admired Edie's poise and elegance. With beautiful cheekbones, lovely voluptuous lips and sharp dark eyes, Chris' wife could have had her pick of men.

Kate found it hard to keep the tears back.

To see the difference in Chris broke her heart. Back when they were friends, Chris knew how to make her laugh. He had the best sense of humour, and it didn't hurt that he was a good-looking man either. On those evenings playing cards, Kate and Chris always ganged up on Aidan. Edie was too lovely to bully. They were such fun-filled, glorious days.

"Don't be...Sad, Kate." Edie put her palm on Kate's cheek. "I'm going...To a better...Place." The energy it took to talk almost overwhelmed her. "It's my time."

"I'm so sorry! I never meant to lose contact with you. You're one of my best friends." Her voice broke, bringing with it tears. Kate tried to fight them, but they wouldn't hold back. She wiped her eyes. "I said I wouldn't cry."

"I have a...Favour to ask," Edie said, her eyes still full of life.

"Anything you need, I'm right here." Kate leaned forwards, still holding Edie's hand.

"When I'm gone...Look in…On Chris."

Kate gasped. "Me? But why? We haven't been close for well over a year. You have lots of friends you could ask this of. Why me? I don't understand."

"You were my...Best friend…Kate." Edie struggled to swallow. "I want that...To continue." She tried to pull herself up.

Trying to help her, Kate stood, fussing with the duvet, not knowing what she was doing. Finally she sat back down. "You're giving me this important role?"

"It won't be...Easy." Edie looked up at her. "Chris is a…Stubborn man. He won't take...Me leaving him...Well. Please be...There for him...I beg of you."

Before Edie injured herself, Kate agreed to keep a vigil over her friend's husband. Chris spelled out his feelings to her clearly enough. How could she keep an eye on him? "I'll do what you ask. Of course I will." Kate paused for effect. "But don't you think you should ask one of your sisters this? Chris doesn't even speak to me anymore."

"I have...Already." Edie put the mask back on briefly. Taking it off, she smiled at Kate. "I am asking...People to look...In on him...From time...To time."

It made sense to her now. Kate was not the only person being asked to keep an eye out for her husband. Which probably meant half a dozen women were asked, including Edie's two younger sisters. She squeezed Edie's hand. "In that case, how can I refuse? I'll gladly check in on him."

Edie rolled on to her side, starting to splutter. The cough was deep, angry, and made her lungs sound hollow. Kate stood, bent over her friend. "What can I do, Edie?" The door opened.

"I think that's enough now, Kate. You need to leave," Chris said, striding up to the bed, placing the oxygen mask over his wife's face, barging her. "Well? What are you waiting for?"

Kate tried to smile at Edie. Her friend had her eyes closed. "I'll speak to you soon, Edie." Taking Chris' advice, she left the Ashcroft house, climbing into her MG.

Behind the wheel, she slammed her fists on it, tears flowing freely.

25

Aidan stirred the beef stew, inhaling the aroma, salivating at the thought of spooning some into his mouth to test it. The meat so tender and moist it melted on the tongue, he was a master at making dumplings to place on top. Back when Marble's Marvels had customers, his beef stew was a firm favourite with his regulars.

Scooping a dollop on the wooden spoon, he blew it first.

Chef stared up at him. The beef stew was his first attempt.

"I don't understand how you do it, but that is to die for," he said, stirring the pan with a separate spoon. "You certainly have the knack, I'll say that." He asked Chef how to sign the word 'beautiful'. Using his right hand, he copied his cook. "How was that?"

Chef tried to seem impressed, giving him a thumbs up.

"You wouldn't be humouring me, would you?" He grinned, knowing he had a lot to learn. Chef had shown him some basics. 'I love you' he would use on Kate later, although she wouldn't understand what it meant until he told her. "Whatever! I'll improve. When Fran brings in a book, I'll start studying."

Bending over, writing something on a pad of paper, Chef picked it up, showed him. '*You're doing so well. Signing isn't easy.*' He smiled warmly.

Universal sign language he knew. Putting both palms together, looking like he was praying, Aidan bowed, saying '*Thanks.*'

He had not enjoyed a day in the kitchen this much in well over a year, probably more. Tonight, his favourite waitress was working Bonnie Fowler. He glanced up at the clock on the wall: 17:56. Kate was still at the Ashcrofts, which meant he would have to open, but at least he had Chef in the kitchen. He could help Bonnie out front for a bit.

The doorbell rang. Aidan took his apron off, went into the dining room and walked over to the front doors. Bonnie was on time, as always.

His server stood waiting to be let in, wearing a pair of huge sunglasses. He wouldn't think it strange, except for the time of year and it being dark out.

As he opened up, Aidan could see how nervous she was. "Come in." He closed the door behind her, not ready to open to the public yet.

She gave him a weak smile.

"Is everything alright? You're acting strange." He walked over to the bar, went behind it and faced her, expecting her to at least take her coat off. "What's wrong?"

With reluctance, Bonnie took her shades off, revealing a nasty bruise around her left eye. It was new, given the colouring. "Don't go getting upset, Aidan, like you do. I walked into a cupboard; it's so embarrassing."

Aidan almost bit his hand he was so angry. "I'll kill him!"

Her hands shaking, Bonnie tried to placate him. "Don't blame Tate. I walked into a cupboard; I just told you. I was going to call in sick, but we need the money."

The front door opened. Kate strolled up to the bar, but Bonnie turned away from her.

"Show her! Go on, Bonnie, show Kate 'what your cupboard did to you.'" He didn't even try hiding his disbelief.

Bonnie revealed her shiner. "Can I still work tonight? Please, Kate, I need the money. I'll put some cover-up makeup on, how's that?"

Unlike him, his wife didn't gasp. In fact, she showed very little emotion. Aidan thought it odd that Kate would take Bonnie by the hand and pull her in the direction of the ladies.

Tate Fowler. What a bastard! He thought Tate a pretty cool bloke until about two minutes earlier. If the restaurant didn't need him, Aidan would have driven over to Tate and Bonnie's house, and served him up a fist sandwich.

While Kate and Bonnie were in the ladies' room, their first customers arrived. Aidan, in pristine whites, sauntered over and let them in, knowing the Tenant family well enough to have a bit of banter with the father.

"Please, take a seat." He made himself busy behind the bar for a couple of minutes. The girls didn't come back, so Aidan went over and took the Tenant party's drinks order.

Sometimes he forgot how much he missed running a bar. By the time he made the order for all eight of the Tenant family, Kate came back with Bonnie. Makeup won the day. He could still see the bruising, but Kate's professional application hid the majority of it.

"What do you think? Am I a master, or what?" Kate wanted his adoration.

He bowed in jest. "We're not worthy. Now, be a dear and take this lot over to the Tenants, would you?" He winked at his wife.

"Cheeky!" Kate let Bonnie take over. "Mind how you go, honey."

As Bonnie carried the tray of eight drinks over, Aidan took Kate by her hand and pulled her into the kitchen, where Chef made himself busy. "What the hell's going on? Did she tell you? Was it Tate? Because this cupboard story doesn't hold up if you ask me."

Kate tried to calm him. "Of course it was Tate. She told me in confidence." Checking Bonnie was nowhere near, she lowered her voice. "He's home twenty-four-seven now. He got laid off at the factory a few weeks ago. It's the first time he's ever not worked. She got annoyed with him being a slob around the house, and during the fight he hit her. She says he apologised profusely straight after."

"And that's supposed to make it all better, is it? The fact he's sorry?" Kate shook her head. "Because if he does anything like that again, I swear I'll make him sorry."

"Who's this?" Bonnie appeared. She walked straight up to Chef behind the line.

"Oh right, I need to introduce you to Chef." Kate stepped up to them both. "Bonnie, this is Chef. He's helping us out for a while. Chef, this is Bonnie. She's a part of the family, been with us for years."

Aidan found watching the way Chef interacted with people fascinating.

Chef held out his hand, as Bonnie shook it. Then, he placed his other hand on top. His smile couldn't have been any broader.

"You can let go now, Bonnie."

He interrupted her. Bonnie jolted awake, pulled her hand away from Chef's. "I'm very pleased to meet you, Chef. Is that your real name?" She chuckled.

"Funny you should ask that. It is. He's my new sous chef. You should try his food. It's off the charts delicious."

Instead of following him over to the stove where the beef stew awaited her, Bonnie kept staring at Chef, a flicker of a smile forming. "Bonnie! Wake up!"

"Huh? Oh, right. You want me to taste something." She met him at the hobs.

Bonnie glanced over at Chef, who remained in front of the line.

"Here." Aidan scooped some beef stew on to a silver spoon, holding it for her.

The expression she gave him said it all, her eyes closed, the joyous, 'Mmm' a clear indication of a culinary triumph. "Tasty, huh? Hell, who am I kidding? This is to die for."

"You made this, Chef?" Bonnie wandered back over to him.

Bonnie and Chef didn't say much; they stared at one another until Aidan felt awkward. He clapped, waking Bonnie up again. "Right, now that the introductions are over, go and help Kate, would you, please?"

"Sure thing, Aidan." Bonnie stared at Chef until she disappeared into the dining room. She poked her head back in. "Oh, thanks for letting me stay." Before she backed out, Bonnie caught one more stare of Chef.

The first orders of the night came through the ticket machine. Five starters, and eight mains. Aidan had everything in stock and started to take everything out of fridges. "What's going on with you and Bonnie?" He mouthed clearly between fridge raids.

Chef shrugged. He wrote, '*She's a lovely girl.*'

For the first time, Aidan thought he might need to watch Chef. "She's a bit young for you, don't you think? And she's married."

With a coy smile, Chef put his mind at ease without signing a word. He had a way about him; he could articulate without speech. "Oh! Well, I'm just saying. Bonnie's special to Kate and myself, so no funny stuff."

26

Excited, Francesca put on her lipstick in front of her dresser mirror. She wondered what culinary delights Declan had prepared for her tonight.

He texted earlier confirming their date, ending it with four kisses. Behind the bar at the restaurant, she'd sent him a reply saying how much she was looking forward to it, finishing hers with the same number of kisses.

Sat on her dresser chair, she smiled while applying the lipstick, her mind wandering. Francesca daydreamed about their first farewell kiss. Would it be tonight? Or was Declan a true gentleman? Would he wait until the second date? Either way, so long as she got to kiss him, she didn't care.

The doorbell rang.

Pressing her lips together, she smiled at her own reflection before getting up and rushing for the front door, wondering who it could be.

"I've come to pick up the rest of my stuff." Paul made to step inside.

Anger enveloped Francesca when she saw a woman standing behind him on her doorstep. She tried to slam the door on her husband, who put his foot in the way.

"Don't be like that, Fran." He pushed the door - and Francesca - back enough to make it inside. "This hurts, honey, I get it, but it has to be done. The sooner all my stuff's gone, the sooner you'll be rid of me."

Standing with her back against the hallway wall, Francesca stared at Paul, then at her replacement. The woman, or rather girl in front of her looked eighteen with long blonde hair, kissable lips, and a size six figure. Francesca couldn't decide whether to scratch her eyes out or feed her. *How dare he bring her here?*

"Are you going to introduce us, Paul?" The waif asked.

"Yeah, Paul, I really want to meet the girl you dumped me for, in my own hallway," Francesca added, glaring at Blondie. "Please, I would love to hear everything about her. How and where did you meet? Don't hold anything back, will you?" The sarcasm oozed over every word. "Just take whatever you need and go!"

"I told you to stay in the car, didn't I? In fact, go and wait outside while I talk to my wife. I'll be out as soon as I can. Go on!"

What had she seen in him? Condescending, arrogant, great-looking, fantastic in bed. Some of it was coming back to her. The physical side of their relationship she never had a problem with. Paul was the issue, or rather his personality. He was a prize-winning arsehole. "Go on then, get your stuff and go!"

Her husband chuckled. He took her advice, walked through to the lounge. "Are you going anywhere nice?"

Her husband was lucky she couldn't reach him from the hallway; she would have punched him in his perfect face for that remark. "Grab your shit and leave, please. I'm not wasting my breath on you."

"No, you're right, it's my fault," he said from the lounge. "Me and Tegan are going to that new Mexican place in Basingstoke tonight. I'll text you how it is later."

Tegan? That was her name? "Do whatever you want, Paul. I won't be reading it. Please hurry up, or you're going to make me late." Or maybe that was his intention?

When he emerged from the lounge carrying some CDs and records he had missed, he opened the cupboard in the hallway and took out a box. "You are dressed up. Who's the lucky guy?" The smile he wore infuriated her.

She sighed. "Just grab your stuff and go, would you! I'm not talking to you about it."

"Now let me guess: It wouldn't be that wet carpenter, would it? Declan?"

Her face gave it away. "What? No! I'm going out with a couple of girlfriends. Not that it's any business of yours who I see."

"It is." Paul laughed. "You'll have a right time with that drip. He's been after you for years. Shit, he'll bore you to death spending a whole evening with him."

Having had enough, Francesca grabbed Paul's shirt collar, dragging him along the hallway carrying his box of belongings. "I told you to get out! And Declan's twice the man you are. Now, get out! You are such an arsehole!"

After the door closed, she heard Paul complaining that he still had bits to collect, although he was enjoying himself too much. Francesca could hear it in his voice.

Leaning against the door, Francesca slid down it. She didn't want to cry, not after applying all her makeup. The more she fought it, the more her chin crumpled. With her face in her lap, she sobbed gently.

Enough! She told herself to wipe her eyes, get up and make herself presentable again.

She wouldn't let him win. He would be off somewhere with his eighteen-year-old trophy girlfriend.

Having texted Declan that she would be twenty minutes late, she reapplied her makeup, making sure her mascara didn't run. "You and Tegan deserve each other," she told an imaginary Paul.

In her car, she put on some cheerful songs to help lift her spirits. By the time she arrived at Declan's old farm, her mood had lifted considerably. As she parked outside the farmhouse, Francesca told herself that she was about to have dinner with her oldest school friend, Declan.

"Come on in," Declan said, standing in the doorway.

With butterflies fluttering like crazy in her belly, she exited her car. "Sorry I'm late. Paul came over uninvited to pick up some bits." He nodded his understanding, stood out of her way, letting her inside. "It smells divine in here."

While she wore a sophisticated black dinner dress, low-cut, short, Declan sported white shirt and black trousers. So dashing, she thought. "Are you going to be my waiter for the evening?"

He grinned, placing a dishcloth over his forearm. "If you'll follow me, ma'am, I'll show you to your seat."

Going along with it, Francesca took his arm and walked with him to the kitchen, where Declan had prepared a banquet. The table was laid out, covered in an ornate cloth, complete with silverware, sparkling wine glasses, and candles.

27

Kate had not seen a Saturday night like this in over a year. The compliments she received from her customers couldn't have been more glowing. Everyone had fallen in love with Chef's cooking, telling her they were going to tell all their friends and families about their fantastic experiences.

"I swear this is like the Marble's of old, Kate," Bonnie said, opening another bottle of red for the Tenant party. "I've actually had to work tonight." She chuckled. "And not one complaint either."

Crossing her fingers, Kate put the tray on the back bar for Bonnie. "I can't tell you how positive I am about Chef. He just popped in here looking for a job on the off-chance, and bam, here we are serving up the best food we ever have."

"Don't let Aidan hear you say that." Bonnie bounced her bum into Kate's jovially. "He'll have you cleaning out the grease trap."

"Which is why I said it quietly."

Four tables had booked off the back of the testers outside earlier. Having expected a relatively busy Friday night, a further eight parties of varying sizes arrived on her doorstep. Upon greeting them, she didn't need to ask why they chose Marble's. They all told her they had heard praise from neighbours and friends about the new menu.

About ready to take a table of four's order for desserts, Kate spotted the village mayor, Kendall Gaines and his wife, Harriet stood inside the doors waiting to be seated. "Mr and Mrs Gaines, how lovely to see you this evening," she said, welcoming them in.

Showing them to a table for two by their fire, Kate handed them both menus, reeling off the day's specials, and recommending the beef stew and dumplings.

She never liked Kendall Gaines. An arrogant and self-serving whatsit, the only reason he remained mayor after voting every four years was because no one else wanted the meaningless title, except old Kendall. "Can I get you some wine to start you off?"

After rattling off the list that was burned into her memory for time immemorial, Kate went over to the bar, where she made up their order of a bottle of Châteauneuf Du Pape, and two glasses of water.

Kendall Gaines always tried talking like he knew everything. Tonight, he was the authority on red wines, their regions, bouquets, and everything in between. Carrying their drinks over, she deposited the tall wine glasses in front of them, pouring a mouthful into the mayor's glass. "Is it to your liking?"

"Oaky. Excellent." The mayor picked up his menu. "And while you're here, you might as well take our order, Kate. We will have two prawn cocktails to start and two of your special beef stews with dumplings, please. I have been hearing nothing but glowing reports about your new menu all day."

Kate didn't gasp when the mayor ordered for his wife. It was the kind of controlling behaviour she expected from men like Kendall Gaines, men who thought they were born better and more important than other mere mortals. "Right away, Mr Gaines. The beef stew is particularly delicious, I must say." She gave Harriet a little smile, picked up the menus and walked their order to the kitchen.

"Was that old Kendall I saw out there just now?" Aidan watched through the door.

"Here's his order, Aidan." She handed him the slip. "I don't need to tell you how important he is, do I? He knows everyone and their dog." She caught Chef's attention, mouthing her words as well as she could.

She forgot how nerve wracking having influential guests could be. Marble's Marvels needed positive, glowing publicity; they couldn't afford complaints. Taking the prawn cocktails out to the Gaines table, Kate received thanks.

"Can you imagine being married to that? Horrible, patronising git that he is." Bonnie whispered when she returned to the bar.

Wanting to laugh, but too nervous, Kate spoke in Bonnie's ear, "He is, you're right, but we need him. He eats out regularly, plus he speaks to so many people. And you're right about poor Harriet as well. I would love to see her with a decent man."

Only a minute after finishing their starters, Kate took the dirty glass bowls away, carrying them into the kitchen. "The mayor's ready for his mains now."

Chef ladled out two fair portions of beef stew and dumplings into two bowls, wiping away the drips of gravy on the sides with a napkin. Then he scooped the veg and put it in a separate side dish. Carrots, peas, and cauliflower steamed away under the lights. Chef bowed, telling her that the order was ready to go.

"Wish me luck," she said, backing out of the kitchen with a bowl in each hand.

At the table, Kate placed the bowls in front of their owners. The stew was still steaming when she left them. She asked if they required anything else? Kendall asked for another bottle of red. "Right away." She did a little bow, turned, and walked back to the bar.

"Don't you just love the way he puts a bib on? Very sophisticated," Bonnie said, smiling at Kendall about to spoon his first mouthful.

Kate watched Harriet eat her first bit. "Thank God! Why was I so worried? She loves it. Look at the expression on her face. Anyone would be forgiven for thinking it's an aphrodisiac." Now she knew Kendall's wife was happy, Kate only had one to go.

It took the best part of a couple of minutes for Kendall to pick up his fork and spoon. Kate grew impatient, watching him play with his food first. "Just eat the damn thing."

"I didn't think you church folk liked swearing, Kate?" Bonnie asked.

"We don't, but I'm stressed. The Lord will forgive me."

Finally, Kendall dipped his fork in his bowl, lifting the first of his beef stew into his mouth. Gravy dripped on to his bib.

Kendall closed his mouth, pulled the fork out, and his eyes grew fierce.

He reached into his trouser pocket and took out a handkerchief. Disgust.

What happened? Kate stood behind the bar in shock as the mayor of the village, one of the most influential faces in their small piece of the world spat the stew into his hanky.

"Oh, my Lord! Vile," he shouted. "Kate Marble, get over here!" He got up and frowned at her, wiping his mouth with his handkerchief. He picked up his glass of water, taking a large gulp.

Hurrying over, Kate arrived at the mayor's table. "What's wrong, Mr Gaines?"

"Are you trying to poison me, or something? This is vile. Go ahead and try it," he ordered, sliding the bowl towards her. "Go on! Have a bit. Has your new chef used tainted meat, or something? I can't believe I almost swallowed some."

Harriet glanced up at her with apologies. "Mine's divine, Kate. Compliments to the-"

"Oh, do be quiet, Harriet!" Kendall glared at her. "Well?"

Kate couldn't understand how two bowls of the same batch of stew could be so different. Harriet was more than happy with hers. "Sure, Mr Gaines." She picked up a spoon from a vacant table next door and scooped up some stew.

It melted in her mouth. She closed her eyes while chewing, savouring every flavour. "Oh my! That is excellent," she said, scooping up more. "I'm sorry Mr. Mayor, but this is exquisite. I don't know what to say."

Kendall Gaines snatched his bowl back, trying some more. "It's vile!" He spat it into his already soiled handkerchief. "What the hell kind of game are you playing here, Kate? I wanted a delicious meal with my wife, and I receive this?"

Before she could argue with him that there was nothing wrong with his food, the mayor dragged his wife out of the restaurant. "Please wait!"

"I was going to suggest this place as our venue for the U3A General meeting next month, but you can forget that now." He turned from her, held his head up, and walked away.

"Mine was divine, Kate," Harriet said, being dragged away.

"Shit!" Kate stamped her foot in frustration. Turning back to the dining room, all eyes were on her. "I'm at a loss for words. Was everyone else's food excellent?"

She received nothing but nods. Kate couldn't understand it. How could two people have such vastly differing experiences of the same meal? Obviously, some people loved cauliflower, and some hated it, but this was something else. Kendall spat his out, saying it was off, twice. No, something was going on. She picked up the bowls, knowing where to go to get answers.

28

"How is it?" Declan forked some steak into his mouth, waiting for her reply.

Why couldn't she just enjoy the company? Francesca had to go thinking about her bastard of a husband. Here she was with a gorgeous specimen of a guy, Declan, and what was she doing? Thinking about Paul and that waif, Tegan. She doubted Paul was daydreaming about her. No, he was probably seeing to Tegan's eighteen-year-old needs while she played with her food. "Huh?"

"I asked you how it is?" He tried not to show his hurt. "I can make you something else if you want? Or maybe it's not the food. Maybe it's the company?"

The last thing she wanted was Declan thinking he was the problem. "Oh no! Please don't think it's you. You're great. And you've gone to so much trouble tonight." Francesca put her cutlery down.

He leaned forward. "What is it, Fran? You can tell me."

"I don't want to burden you with all this, Declan. You deserve a decent guest who isn't thinking about her bastard of an ex-husband. I'm so sorry! I should have rung and cancelled tonight."

"Hey, don't apologise." He placed his cutlery together. "It's not your fault he turned up on your doorstep. If anyone should be apologising, it should be Paul." He lowered his voice. "What an arsehole."

Declan rarely had a bad word to say about anyone. He'd said something bad about Paul twice now. He really meant it. Even as far back as secondary school she couldn't recall him ever saying anything nasty about even the worst bullies. He rose above it. Hearing him call Paul an arsehole was a big deal. "Well, I'm sorry anyway."

"Let's give dinner a miss and go through to the lounge for drinks," he suggested, getting up, bringing his glass of wine with him. "Come on, let's try and salvage some of tonight, shall we?"

No use, Francesca wouldn't be attractive company. Taking her coat off the backrest of her chair, she started putting her arm through the right sleeve. "Thank you so much, Declan, but I'm going to go home, take a long hot bath, and wallow by myself. I have no intention of making your life miserable, just because mine is."

Stepping towards him, she put her arms around his neck, pulling him down to kiss him on the cheek. "You're so sweet. You deserve better. Let's try this when I'm not still hung up on Paul?"

Declan stood with the door open, disappointed.

As she drove away, Francesca was flooded with guilt. What had she been thinking? Who arranges to go on a date a couple days after their husband dumps them? It was her through and through, just the kind of hair-brained thing she would do.

Why was she feeling such loss? Paul was the worst husband ever. He didn't love her. Hell, the only person Paul was capable of loving was himself. It didn't make sense, her grieving their relationship.

Pulling into her driveway, Francesca parked outside her garage. She exited her car and locked it. With a sigh, she opened her front door, stepped inside, and hid herself away from the world.

In the bathroom, she turned on the hot tap first before turning on the cold water. In the mirror she saw a sad, lonely thirty-something woman whose chance of having a baby was slowly drifting away from her. In four or five years she would be classed as high-risk.
Taking her dress and knickers off, Francesca left them on the toilet seat all neat and tidy, as she eased herself in the hot bubbly water. Once submerged she lay back, allowing the bubbles to massage her skin. Fighting back the tears, she lathered her legs with bath soak. "A complete waste of time shaving you earlier."

Without Declan on the horizon, the only thing in her life worth anything was her new job starting Monday. Everything else was knackered. To think, only last week she had a husband. This week, it didn't bear thinking about.

29

"What are you talking about? How can Harriet love it and Kendall throw it up? It doesn't make any sense. They're from the same batch made fresh today. It hasn't even been frozen yet." Aidan took the bowl in question from her. "This is his?"

"Yes, I tried it," she replied, handing him a spoon. "It's exquisite. And so is Harriet's. Every meal we served tonight has been heavenly. Everyone loves Chef's cooking, except it seems the one person we need on side."

Aidan put the spoonful in his mouth. "Just as tasty as earlier, if not better."

"The mayor was going to hire our dining room for a U3A meeting next month, he said. I've never heard of them, but they sound important, and could have brought us a lot of new customers I'm guessing. And now Kendall's going to be going around slating us."

He noticed Chef staring at the floor. Aidan tapped him on the shoulder. "You served up their food. Have you got something to add? Why would the mayor spit it out?"

Chef found his pad of paper, leaned over the stainless-steel counter. '*Old bones?*'

Aidan sniggered. "There you go, honey. That about sums Kendall Gaines up. He has old tastebuds. That's why it was delicious to us, and rancid to him."

"Is that supposed to be funny?" Kate took the bowl over to the washing up area, scraping the leftovers into the bin and leaving the empty with the stack of dirty plates. "Because it's not. We're trying to keep this business afloat, and if you two keep sending VIPs away complaining, those doors will close, I promise you that."

After his wife stormed out, Aidan let out a big lungful of air. Chef turned to him, wiped his forehead as though saying, 'Phew!' He had to laugh at his sous chef's expression. "You're right, she can be tough. But don't worry, she'll get over it. Plus, everyone else loved our cooking tonight, so she can't be too pissed off about that."

When Kate marched back in, Aidan grinned. "Look who's back. My gorgeous wife."

She stayed in front of the line, talking to him over the food prep counter. "I'm glad you're in such a great mood, Aidan. Tate's just arrived. Bonnie's bringing him through to introduce him to Chef, so please behave." She stared at Chef. "Be polite to Tate. We don't want to make Bonnie's home life any worse, do we?"

Aidan turned away from Kate, cursed to himself, then turned back. "You want us to play happy families? He punched her, for Christ...Crying out loud."

"I mean it, Aidan, be nice to him, or we're going to fall out."

Promising to go along with it, nodding his agreement, Bonnie walked through the door holding hands with a happy-looking Tate. Aidan took to Tate as soon as Bonnie introduced him; it was hard to see him beating his wife up. "Tate!" He couldn't bring himself to be any friendlier, wanting to lay into him, verbally and physically.

Bonnie brought Tate behind the line. "Honey, let me introduce you to Chef. Chef, this is my husband, Tate. Chef's deaf and mute, so speak in a clear voice."

Aidan waited for his sous chef to shake Bonnie's husband's hand. They didn't break the shake for longer than was normal. Chef kept smiling, the way he had with Bonnie earlier. He had the same hypnotic, broad smile.

"Right, enough!" He broke their concentration. "This is a kitchen. If you want to carry this on, take it out to the dining room, please."

"It was nice meeting you, Chef," Tate said, walking backwards towards the door.

Chef signed something to Bonnie's husband.

"Hey, what's wrong with you? You know what he did to her," he said to Chef, a scowl forming. Aidan ignored Kate when she tried to intervene. "If he believes there are no repercussions, he'll think it's fine to punch Bonnie."

With a shake of his head, a scowl of his own, and a stamp of his foot, Chef hunted around for his pad of paper. Kate found it, handing it to him. He bent over the counter. '*He's a good man beneath it all. He has a full and loving heart. He's lost his way; we must help him find it.*'

"Good man, my arse." Aidan could not believe what he was hearing. "Good men don't go punching their wives, Chef. Why would you say that?"

'*Because I'm a very reliable judge of character. Tate needs a helping hand.*'

"He needs a fist in the face more like," he said, Chef turning away from him. He took a deep breath, anger getting the best of him. After a pause, he tapped Chef on the shoulder. "Hey, I'm sorry! I didn't mean that. If you say he's a good person, I believe you."

'You're a good man. It takes one to recognise one. Your mayor, he's not.'

Aidan read Chef's message, checking Kate's response. "Hang about, you don't know the mayor. Or Tate for that matter. All you've done is shake his hand." Being called a good person himself didn't sit right with him. He wasn't a good man, far from it. "You're full of shit, Chef."

'You know the mayor better than I do. Am I right? Is he an honourable man?'

Kate shook her head. "No, you're right, Chef. He's an egotistical, self-serving, womanising windbag. He doesn't possess a decent bone in his body."

'And you want him eating here?' Chef glanced up at Kate. *'Why?'*

"He's got you there, love," he said, wanting to pat Chef on the back.

"Because he knows lots of people, Chef, that's why. We're a business. If anyone could persuade the half on Chris' side to try us again, he could. Do you understand? We can't bar customers we believe aren't 'good' people."

Chef nodded his agreement. *'I apologise for mayor's food.'*

Aidan regarded Kate. "Is all forgiven now, my darling?" He placed his hands around Kate's waist, pulling her in for a kiss. To his surprise, it looked like she might reciprocate, until she put her palm over his mouth.

"We're not there yet." She took his hands off. "Not even close. If you think I'm just dropping everything and coming back home, forget it. I still need time."

THURSDAY,
MARCH 21ST

30

Francesca enjoyed her first couple of months at Cherry Tree Lodge, helping the teacher with the kids, getting familiar with them, and above all signing.

The first day was terrifying, being introduced to her students by Mrs Jones, the experienced teacher Mrs Redmond assigned her to. Francesca stood in front of the fifteen inquisitive children, spelling out her name with her fingers. Once the initial introduction was over, the nerves in her belly stopped fluttering, and she found herself conversing with them.

Cherry Tree prided itself on having high expectations of its students, and by extension teachers, which included teaching assistants. Mrs Redmond highlighted the school rules to Francesca on her first day. She hoped she could live up to them.

As with mainstream schools, the lodge stuck to a rigid curriculum, teaching the hearing-impaired children mathematics, English literature, and language, along with all three sciences. History, geography, religious studies, Information technology, and everything in between.

It surprised Francesca; she thought the curriculum would be watered down. Every child at Cherry Tree had the same opportunities to achieve great GCSEs as students attending state schools. Mrs Redmond went further in saying that these children sat in smaller classes, so they had even higher chances of passing the exams with decent grades.

After her first week, Francesca felt she was making a difference with these students, helping them. On her first Friday there, Naomi brought her an apple, giving her a huge smile. She went to Marble's the following night glowing, boring Kate with how her first few days went.

She wished the rest of her life were as successful as her new job. After leaving Declan's house without eating any of his food, texts and phone calls stopped. She had not seen him in passing, which she thought odd.

One good thing had happened elsewhere. The restaurant was heading in the right direction. Kate's positive attitude at Marble's shone through, along with Chef's cooking. Bookings, instead of dribbling through, were coming in droves. The phone needed answering regularly for reservations. To top it off, Kate didn't need to offer special discounts, it seemed, unlike Elio's across the road.

"Are you alright, Fran? You look pale this morning," Mrs Jones asked, putting her hand on Francesca's forehead. "You're clammy."

Francesca had only just taken her coat off. She felt queasy in the car on her way to the school. Sat on a chair next to Naomi, she suddenly felt sick, holding her belly. "Excuse me a moment."

Without waiting for permission, Francesca got to her feet and ran for the door. Luckily, there were staff toilets next door to her classroom. She burst through the door, dashing for the nearest cubicle, and locking the door behind her.

Having thrown up twice, she rested her cheek on the toilet seat waiting for round three. This was the second morning she had been sick. When she told herself that, a pang of fear swept over her. "No way! It can't be."

Trying to ignore the obvious, Francesca picked herself up, went over to the middle basin, and splashed her face with water. Staring at her reflection, she pulled a serious face. "You can't be. No, that's ridiculous."

Mrs Jones poked her head inside. "Fran? What's wrong?"

Flicking water over her face again, Francesca wiped her forehead, cheeks, and chin with paper towels. "I'm fine. Must have been something I ate."

"Two mornings in a row?" Mrs Jones stepped up to her. "Do you want me here when you do it? I'll give you time to run down to a chemist. It's better to know one way or another. Or you can tell me to back off. It's your call."

"I can't be pregnant. Paul was the last guy I slept with, and that was...On Christmas Day?" It dawned on her. "Oh, it could be that. Bugger! Why now? I tried for two years. Why now?"

"Maybe because you're not trying? Sod's law works like that."

31

Kate had twelve reservations for Thursday's lunch. Having set them all up with cloths, cutlery, glasses, and candleholders, she stood back, surveying her handiwork.

The tables were spread out, making the restaurant appear more in use. If she had walk-ins, she would seat them at the front, in between the bookings, and pack the dining room out. Word was spreading fast about their 'new menu', which was nothing of the sort.

With Francesca working at Cherry Tree Monday to Friday daytimes, and with how much busier they were, she had to hire two new members of staff. Being the eternal pragmatist, Kate hired a kitchen hand, who Aidan was training to be a starter and dessert chef, and an all-rounder, someone she could use both front and back of house.

While conducting a routine stock take on spirits, a knocking on the entrance door caught her attention. Wondering who it could be, Kate dropped what she was doing, walked out from behind the bar. "What the-?"

To her surprise, Harriet Gaines stood outside, her demeanour suspicious, as she had a hood up. "Hi! Won't you come in?" She closed the door, locked it. "What can I do for you?"

"Oh Kate, I simply had to apologise for my husband's behaviour." Harriet's eyes urged forgiveness. "I know it's been a while. I was too humiliated before."

Giving the mayor's wife a genuine smile, she offered Harriet a drink. "I can make you a tea or coffee? A bottle of water. Or maybe something stronger?"

"I'm meeting friends for lunch. I could murder a glass of wine." Harriet followed her over to the bar. "I meant what I said before, you know, the beef stew was exquisite. I've never had anything that tasty in my life."

Kate poured a large house red, sliding the drink over to Harriet. "We've been getting a lot of that lately. Our new sous chef is amazing. I don't know what he does, but whatever it is, he's done this place the world of good."

"He's putting love into it, Kate, has to be." Harriet smiled. "Which brings me to my reason for popping by like this."

"Oh? It wasn't to apologise?" She let Harriet know she was joking.

"I told you I'm meeting friends for lunch." Harriet leaned in. "I don't suppose I could book a table for five at midday, could I? They simply must try your chef's cuisine. I know it's an ask in light of Kendall's outburst."

"Don't be silly, Harriet, of course you can. You're welcome here as often as you like." Kate opened the bookings folder.

"Could we sit at a table at the back?" Harriet shushed her, like she was doing something naughty. "I don't want him knowing I'm here, or I'll get an earful."

Wanting to laugh, Kate used the till to start Harriet a tab. "Discretion's our middle name. Although, this is a village, don't forget. He will find out, plus he's the mayor."

"If he finds out, so be it, but the longer I keep it a secret the better, Kate. The food here is infinitely superior to Elio's. You know, it's strange how this place picks up, and his starts emptying. I guess it goes like that."

Pouring herself a bottle of water into a glass, Kate listened. She had not seen a dip in trade across the road. "Oh? Is Elio having troubles?" She took a sip.

Harriet leaned closer to her again. "His wife's divorcing him; she's taking him to the cleaner's apparently. She's demanding half of everything, including the restaurant. The poor man; he's so lovely. I never took to her."

It was news to Kate. He might be the local competition, but she wouldn't wish his soon-to-be-ex-wife on anyone. Horrible woman. "I'll go over soon, find out how he's doing. He's been kind to us over the past couple of years."

"Would you? I would be ever so grateful." Harriet sipped from her glass. "I'd visit him myself, except he and Kendall don't get on. There seems to be a lot of that going about when it comes to my delightful husband."

Kate checked the time. "Oh bums, I need to open up. Excuse my language, Harriet. I'll be right back." She hurried out from behind the bar, keys in hand.

"Will I be seeing you at the funeral tomorrow?" Harriet turned in her seat.

"I'll be there." She unlocked the door as Benjamin arrived. "Afternoon. Come on in. You're working the floor with me this lunchtime."

Leaving Benjamin to it, Kate showed Harriet to her table, handing her five menus. She asked the mayor's wife if she needed anything else.

"I'll be bringing a lot of custom your way, Kate," Harriet promised. "Here's to the new and improved Marble's Marvels."

Music to her ears. Having a heavy hitter like Harriet promising to send lots of her friends their way was like winning a sweepstake. After the fiasco of last time, she needed to make sure Harriet's table's food was perfect. Walking through the swing door, Kate found Aidan and Chef hard at work. "We have another VIP out there."

Aidan looked up from his chopped lettuce. "Oh? Who is it this time?"

"Harriet Gaines, by herself. She's promised to bring in lots of ladies for lunches and dinners." Kate made sure she caught Chef's attention. "This needs to be amazing." Relief swept over her when Chef smiled, bowed, before going back to slicing tomatoes. "Thank you! I knew I could count on you both."

"Have you checked with Chris about the food?" Aidan looked hopeful.

"It's a no-go, love," she told him. "He decided to use the Red Lion's caterers instead. And before you say anything, I told him how superb our food is. To be honest I'm surprised I'm even invited to the funeral, so I didn't want to push it."

Her husband backed off and went back to chopping up the salad for lunch service.

Kate left them to it, walking over to the bar where Benjamin was talking to Harriet.

A group of four arrived. "Ladies, welcome to Marble's Marvels. Have you booked?"

"I'm afraid not," the tallest woman asked. "Can you squeeze us in? We've all heard so much about your food, we had to try it for ourselves."

"I'm sure we can accommodate you. Follow me to your table." She led the way to a table of four sandwiched between two reserved tables of six. The front of the restaurant would appear busy soon enough. It might encourage more walk-ins.

32

Chris Ashcroft had so much to do he didn't know where to start. The funeral arrangements were all taken care of; the flowers; the hearse; the burial; invitations, everything. He went through a list of hymns and prayers with the vicar and his daughter, Amy, who was home from university. She was a Godsend. He didn't know how he would have coped without her.

In his oily overalls, he tried to unscrew a bolt while lying on his back beneath a pickup truck he promised to fix by the end of the day. Why he made such promises, he didn't know. "Bloody thing. Why won't you come off?"

Frustration pushing him, anger boiled up from inside him, releasing itself in a torrent of rage aimed at the bolt. He hit it with the spanner several times.

"Dad! Stop!" Amy's voice gave him pause. "Please, you're going to break it. Come out from under there. The post's arrived. There's a letter here for you. It looks important."

Shimmying his way out from beneath the truck, Chris studied his beautiful daughter. A vision in black, Amy was going through a goth phase, wearing nothing but dark tops. With her hair dyed black, she even had black lipstick on. Despite the harsh appearance, she could never makeover her kind, genuine eyes. "Thank you!"

Amy held her hands out, helped him up. "I might need to hire some carers for you, make sure you climb out of the bath at night."

"Ha bloody ha!" He stood for a second, stars in his peripheral vision. He had polished off eight cans of lager last night. Amy had begged him not to drink them all. The evidence was in the bin behind him. "What do we have here?" He took the letter from her.

The day before his wife's funeral, he received the correspondence he knew was coming, and the one he didn't want to read. From the bank. His mortgage payment had not gone through. "Erm thanks for bringing this out, Ames." He kissed her cheek. "Go on back in the house. I'll be through in a minute."

"What is it?"

"Oh, nothing for you to worry about. Go on! Let me know when lunch is ready. I'll be by in a sec." He was not concentrating on what he was saying, his mind firing a thousand different scenarios at him, most of which pointed to him losing everything.

With his son's death, his wife's illness and subsequent passing, Chris had let everything else go. He swapped the hardship of farming for fixing cars, which at the time seemed like a smart move. Upon reflection, he needed to be repairing more motors.

"Oh shit!" He would have to phone the number on the letter to arrange a meeting with the bank manager. He meant to call before his mortgage was due to organise a payment holiday.

Taking out his mobile, he keyed in his password for online banking. "You idiot!" He had under fifty pounds left in the account, and only a couple of hundred in the savings account. "How could you let it go so low?"

He could kick himself for being so careless. Giving himself time to think, Chris went over to his desk, sat on his swivel chair. There was an itch he couldn't scratch.

In the desk a bottle of whisky beckoned him.

Turning away from it, he forced himself to think about his problem. "Focus!"

No use, he would think better with a slug of whisky inside him.

Checking for Amy, Chris pulled out the drawer, picked up the bottle of Macallan whisky, unscrewed the cap and took a mouthful.

Ashamed the second he swallowed, Chris screwed the cap back on, threw it back in the drawer and slammed it shut. Now he had hard liquor inside him, he needed to fix the problem. "Let's do this."

The number on the letter said it would take him through to the arrears department, where he would speak to an advisor specialising in helping customers with their finances. Dialling the number, he sighed, putting the phone to his ear.

While he was on hold, as happened with every big company he dealt with, Chris thought about outstanding payments. He had two jobs he had yet to send invoices for worth three and a half grand. He chided himself for not being on the ball with invoicing.

Pressing five, he had to endure more God awful 'hold music'. He switched his computer on, waiting for it to boot up. He suddenly thought of a third job he needed to invoice, taking his outstanding payments to over six thousand pounds.

What was the matter with him? He yanked the drawer out, unscrewed the cap and took another slug of whisky, this time keeping hold of the bottle on his lap.

"Dad? It's lunchtime," Amy said.

Chris turned his chair away from her before she saw the bottle in his hand. "Um, yeah, thanks honey. I'll be in." He tried to replace the cap, screw it on, and hide the bottle.

"Are you drinking? It's not even one o'clock yet."

Chris recognised the fear and anguish in her voice. When he turned to her, Amy's chin crumpled, tears fell down her cheeks. "It was only a taste, honey."

He couldn't have said anything more stupid if he tried.

Regretting it straight away, he got to his feet as she ran for the house crying.

Angry, he grabbed the front of his desk, upending it in a demonstration of brute strength, as the glass in the PC monitor shattered. "Shit!"

He needed to assure his daughter that he did not have a drinking problem. Chris might have stayed there smashing his workshop up if Amy were away; instead, he took the grown-up route. He took a couple of deep breaths, steadying himself. "Honey, I'm sorry!"

Running over to the house, he expected her to be sat at the kitchen table. Inside, lunch was waiting for him, but no Amy. At the foot of the stairs, he heard her crying. "Please don't cry." He climbed them, her cries growing in volume.

"We're burying mum tomorrow, and you're out there killing yourself. First Liam, now Mum. Am I going to be saying goodbye to you as well?"

A lump formed in his throat. He fought back the tears. "I'm not trying to kill myself, sweetheart, I promise. I'll stop drinking, I swear."

33

Francesca sat on the toilet seat with her knickers around her ankles. Reading the pregnancy test, she hoped for one stripe, not two. Placing the testing stick in her urine stream, she waited for a few seconds, and brought it back out. "Five minutes. Please be negative."

"Fran, honey, have you done it yet?" Mrs Jones asked outside her cubicle.

"Uh-huh! I'm on it." She pulled her knickers up.

Stepping outside, she carried the test to the sinks, washed her hands, thinking she had been waiting for a full minute now. Using the provided soap, she took thirty seconds lathering her hands. "Please be negative."

"I know it's hard to think about, but what are you going to do if it's positive?" Mrs Jones sneaked a peek at the test. "Have you thought about keeping it?"

Those words cut through her. "Of course, I'm keeping it! What kind of question is that?" With a frown she whipped the test away.

Mrs Jones placated her, putting her palms out in a calming manner. "I'm sorry, Fran, I didn't know you had such strong opinions on abortion. I apologise. Had I known I wouldn't have asked."

Francesca's expression softened. "No, I'm sorry! I shouldn't have snapped. I'm so nervous about this. I don't want to be pregnant. Not now. I don't want to be a single mum."

With a comforting embrace, Mrs Jones took away her fear for a moment. Over her mentor's shoulder Francesca's attention turned to the test waiting to be read. "Thank you so much for being here. I'm so grateful for the support."

"This is what I'm here for, Fran."

"I think it's ready," she said, breaking the embrace.

"Would you like me to check it first?"

With a nod, Francesca picked up the plastic test, and without peeking handed it to her senior, who took her time reading it. "And? Don't keep me in suspense over here, please."

"Um, I think you need to see for yourself."

Francesca opened her eyes, glanced down at the test, taking it from Mrs Jones. Two stripes. "Damn it!" She shook it, desperately trying to shake one of the stripes away. When she studied it again, they were still both there. "No! I can't be pregnant. I can't." She leaned on the edge of the basin.

"At the risk of offending you, there are options, Fran." Mrs Jones put her hand on her shoulder. "It's not just keep or abort these days. There are thousands of couples out there who want a baby but can't have any. If you don't want to keep him or her, couldn't you ask someone to adopt?"

"It's food for thought," she conceded. "Look at the time. Lunch is almost over."

Thanking Mrs Jones for her support, Francesca binned the test, making herself presentable in front of the mirror. She went inside her classroom, where Naomi beamed at her from across the room. Such a beautiful girl, she thought, thinking about the baby growing inside her. She would need to book a doctor's appointment, to be sure.

What was she going to do now? The father was Paul, her bastard of a husband, who had yet to file for a divorce. While she should have been helping the children with their reading, Francesca's mind kept wandering.

"Go home, Fran! I'll cover for you."

Waving goodbye to Naomi, Francesca thanked Mrs Jones for her help.

Outside, she sat behind the wheel of her Mini Cooper. "What am I going to do?"

Twisting the key, she started the engine, wanting to talk it through with Declan, her friend. She couldn't do that to him, though. Who else? Paul? No way! She didn't want the scorn from her mum until she decided on her best course of action.

Reversing out of her space, Francesca drove towards Marble's Marvels, hoping Kate had some words of wisdom for her.

34

Kate had tried to give Francesca the time she needed. Her friend arrived during the first rush, which a few months earlier wouldn't have mattered. This lunch, however, she was rushed off her feet. She understood the gist of Francesca's problem: she was pregnant with her soon-to-be-ex-husband's child. Kate had to agree, Francesca was in a pickle.

She didn't know if she'd helped, or not. Francesca left happily enough. Poor Benjamin had been running food and helping in the kitchen with starters and mains. Kate thought she might need to start bringing in more staff.

"How was everything? I hope it was to your liking." She leaned over Harriet Gaines' table, picking up the dirty dessert plates and bowls, stacking them neatly on the edge. "Is there anything else I can bring you? Tea or coffee? A digestif, perhaps?"

"Oh, we couldn't, Kate, but thanks." Harriet put her hand on Kate's. "This was all superb, by the way. The food sublime as always. I make sausage casserole myself, but that was beyond beautiful. Is your chef for hire?" The ladies around the table laughed.

Kate smiled with them. "I'm so glad you enjoyed it, Harriet. Don't forget to tell your friends about us."

One of Harriet's lunch guests beckoned her over. "While you're here, could I book some tables for lunches and dinners I'm organising? This restaurant is perfect, and I would like to throw you some custom, and impress my family and friends with your heavenly food."

As she walked the plates away, Kate grinned to herself, knowing she'd hit the motherlode with Harriet's guests. She was sure the other ladies would be booking tables at the same time.
"We've hit the big time out there. Harriet's lot love us."

Only Aidan reacted, Chef deep in concentration, with his back to her. "I'm pencilling in reservations for them now. This is crazy. Fifty-five covers we've done this lunch, with two of us out front."

"And not one complaint, don't forget," Aidan added.

Back in the dining room, Kate went around the table individually to each of Harriet's friends with her diary. She squatted, writing events down, until she arrived back at Harriet. She booked in a table for lunch tomorrow. "Thank you, ladies. When you're ready for your bill, put your hand up, I'll bring it over."

Happier than she had been for a long time, Kate made herself busy on the till.

"Ahem." A guy cleared his throat.

"Just a second," she said without looking up. "I'll be right with you."

"Kate?" He was persistent, whoever he was.

"That is my name." She took her attention away from the till, glancing up at him, her jaw dropping the moment she saw him. "Graham!"

She couldn't believe he was standing in front of her, in the flesh.

With her mouth open, she stood there, glued to her spot.

"How are you? It's been a while." He stared at her, a strange smirk forming.

"I'm grand." She shook herself out of the shock. "What are you doing here?"

He rubbed his hair. "I would like to book a table for Saturday night, please."

She chuckled, feeling foolish. "Right, of course! I'm sorry! It's just been so long. My sister said you're back, but I never thought you would come here." Kate couldn't stop staring at his beautiful face, the tan, the dark hair greying at the sides.

"I hear you're doing well," he said, looking around the restaurant. "I mean, better than before. I heard you had a family tragedy. I'm sorry!"

Vinnie. "Right, yeah, thank you! Our son died two years ago, but my husband and I, we're muddling through. We were on the verge of folding the business recently when we hired a new chef. He's wonderful. He's given this place a new lease of life."

"Wow! One man did all that?"

He didn't believe her. "If you tasted his food, you would understand how it saved us." Stop staring! She told herself, stepping out from behind the bar. Kate joined Graham. "Would you like to meet him?"

"Hmm, meet who? Sorry!"

"Our new sous chef, and my husband, of course," she said, remembering Aidan was in the kitchen, almost cursing to herself. "They'll be cooking for you on Saturday. Come on, I'll introduce you to them."

He was reluctant at first, as she grabbed his hand, pulled him along.

Unable to believe she was holding Graham's lovely hand, Kate opened the door, waiting for her ex-boyfriend to join her. "Aidan, I

want to you to say hello to someone. Come and
meet Graham Winston."

Her husband stopped wiping down the doors of the counter, stood with a cloth in his hand. She despaired when he wiped his hands on his checked trousers. "Graham, hi, I'm Aidan, Kate's husband." He shook Graham's hand.

Graham wiped his hand on his jeans after touching her husband's. "Graham's just popped in to say hello and book a table for Saturday evening." She had the biggest smile. "And this is Chef."

"Is Chef his first or last name?" Graham joked.

Looking up at him, or rather swooning, Kate shook her head. "No, it's Chef. He volunteers here. And he's done a magnificent job." She beckoned Chef over.

Chef stepped up to her. Kate said, "Say hello to Graham, an old friend of mine from my school days. You'll be cooking for him on Saturday."

Her ex-boyfriend, and new sous chef shook hands.

An electric shock between the two hands made them all jump, including Kate, who laughed at being surprised. Chef stared at his hand, his usual joyful demeanour gone. "Are you okay, Chef? You're not hurt, are you?"

When he shook his head, Kate breathed out, relieved. "Be thankful for small mercies."

Graham stared at his hand. He then made his excuses, saying cheerio.

Walking out to the dining room, Kate hooked her arm in his. "What are you doing now? Tell me what you've been up to since you left me here all by myself."

35

Aidan watched his wife and 'Graham' through the window in the kitchen door. They sure were cosy with one another, sat on a table by the fireplace, his Kate opposite Graham.

Why had she not mentioned a Graham before? He recalled Kate telling him one time about an old boyfriend called Graham, who left her and moved to California. Nah, it couldn't be, could it? Would she be brazen enough to introduce him to her ex? No!

He tried to tear himself away from the door. The more Kate flirted with Graham the worse his mood became. Chef was washing up the last of the plates, pots, and pans. "What was all that about, Chef?" He signed the question.

Since Kate and Graham left the kitchen, Chef's mood had changed. On any normal day, his sous chef wore a big old smile, but not this afternoon. "What's wrong with you?"

Chef winced at his hand, not getting it wet. Signing, 'Nothing,'

Tapping Chef on his shoulder, Aidan held his stare. "No way come on. Tell me! What happened when you shook hands with Graham?"

As Chef hunted for his pad of paper, Aidan found a pen and handed it over.

'*He's not a good man.*' Chef glanced up at him, then back down at the paper. '*He's not what he says he is. We need to warn Kate that he's deceiving her.*'

Aidan leaned against the counter, expecting a punchline, although Chef had yet to tell an actual joke. "What are you saying? I could have told *you* he's an arsehole. You only need look at him." He folded his arms when Chef wrote some more.

'*I knew you wouldn't believe me. I don't want Kate hurt, do you?*'

He wanted to laugh. "Believe what? That you can tell all that about 'Graham' just by shaking his hand? Of course I don't buy it. What you're talking about is mumbo jumbo, Chef. People can't do that kind of thing."

'*I knew about the mayor, didn't I?*'

Those words grabbed his attention. "Yeah, you'd better fill me in on that. What was all that about? He ate the same food from the same batch as his wife. How come his was rancid?" His face was serious. "Don't hold back."

With reluctance, Chef started writing. '*I don't know how, but the food knows who is good and who's bad. Don't ask me how it happens, it just does*."

He had to admit it was a terrific joke. "So, it's Santa's food? It knows who's been good, or bad?" He refused to sing the bloody song.

'*No, but I can tell who is good and who is bad myself.*'

Rolling his eyes, Aidan unfolded his arms. "Let me guess: you shake their hand."

Chef nodded. '*I'm sensitive to it.*'

"Yeah, right! Whatever. I was only asking; you don't need to make up crap. Just say it's a gut feeling. Hell, even I can understand them." He wandered back over to the line to finish his cleaning. "I'm sensitive to it," he mumbled, chuckling to himself.

While wiping down the counters, curiosity overcame him.

Getting up, he went over to the kitchen door again. Rage built up in his chest when he saw 'Graham' cover Kate's hand with his. "That piece of-"

A hand touched his shoulder. Looking over it, Chef stood behind him.

The rage evaporated. "What was I doing?" He lost his train of thought.

Chef walked him back to the line, put the cloth in his hand. "Oh yeah, thanks Chef." He bent down and started wiping the doors of the stainless-steel storage cupboards. A tune came into his head.
He started whistling as he went from left to right with the cloth.

36

By nine in the evening the dining room was three-quarters full, with over seventy diners all at different stages of their meals. Francesca remembered it being as busy before. For a Thursday, it was unheard of with only the three of them out front, two when Benjamin helped in the kitchen.

All afternoon Francesca sat at home moping, mulling over it in her mind. At one point she picked up her phone, Paul's number ready to dial, when she gave up. What good would involving him at this early stage do?

"Can I take your order?" She eyed a lady in her seventies.

With professionalism, Francesca went around the table asking each of the six diners what they would like for starters, and mains. She had to lean in closer on a couple of occasions, the din of voices and laughter in the background muffling their answers.

"Thank you, ladies. Your drinks will be with you shortly." With a slight curtsy, she took her pad of paper behind the bar, input their orders on the till, and sent the order into the kitchen, where Aidan and Chef would collect the ticket.

"I can't believe how busy it is tonight." Kate took over at the till. "Now this is like the Marble's Marvels of old. Except we had more floor staff back then."

"It might be an idea to bring some more on board?" She took six glasses from the wine glass shelf, placed them on the back bar. "We don't want to be victims of our own success, do we?" She poured six small glasses of red, placed them on a tray, and carried them over to the table. "Here you are, ladies. Six small glasses of house red."

The kitchen bell rang. Carrying the empty tray back to the bar, Francesca left it on the counter, told Kate she would answer it, and walked to the kitchen, where Aidan and Chef had six plates waiting to go out. "Table eighteen. Two scampi, two sausage and mash, a cod and chips, and a steak and ale pie."

Reading it back to herself was habit. Picking up the four plates on her arms, she left the bowls until last, picking them up and backing out of the swing door with six orders.

As she walked through the dining room, she smiled at Benjamin, who was carrying dirty plates back to the kitchen. Stopping at table eighteen, she placed the plates in front of their owners, remembering who had ordered which dish. "Is there anything else you need?" They all shook their heads. "Enjoy your meals."

The bell rang again. On her way back, she opened the swing door for Benjamin, who held four plates for table fifteen. "I'll bring the rest."

Francesca took the remaining four plates to the door, waiting for Benjamin to walk through. "It's alright, I'll take them." On her way out, Aidan asked Benjamin to take the bin bag out to the garden wheelie bin. Grateful Aidan had not asked her, she walked the plates over to the right table. "Enjoy your meals."

As any worthy waiter did, she cleared three tables of dirty plates on her way back to the kitchen, where she scraped leftovers into the bin by the sink. She promised dessert menus to the three tables. The first drop of sweat rolled down her temple arriving at the bar.

Taking the stack of dirty plates, Francesca dunked them in soapy water, put the yellow marigolds on, and started washing up. Building a tower of plates, she placed them in a plastic tray, before sliding it into the dishwasher, closing the door and pressing the green 'Start' button. "One load's going through, Aidan."

"Have you seen Benjamin?" Aidan stood in front of her holding a ticket.

"You sent him out with the bin bag, remember?" She peeled the marigolds off.

"That was five minutes ago," Aidan complained. "Can you go and find him, please? I need to make these desserts."

With a huff, Francesca agreed, not thinking it her job. The fire exit door open, she stepped outside, where the wheelie bin sat the bottom of the garden on the other side of the fence.

The sound of shouting made her stop. Francesca turned round, ran back to the kitchen door. "Aidan, Benji needs you out here. I think someone's beating him up."

Waiting for Aidan and Chef, she ran after them, relieved that the men were there to sort everything. Francesca had never been a fighter, even at school. The closer she came to the gate, the louder the shouting grew.

"Oi! Take your hands off Ben," Aidan bellowed. "It takes four of you to beat on one kid, does it? Cowards! The lot of you." He stepped towards the yobs. "How about me and Chef here even things up a bit?"

Both excited and afraid, Francesca stood behind Chef. "Come here, Benji," she said, holding her hand out. "Finlay Ealing, you should be ashamed of yourself. Wait until your parents find out about this. They're going to skin you alive."

"Over a poof like him?" Ealing pushed Benjamin away. "I doubt it."

Benjamin ran over to her. She held on to him like his life depended on it, then made him stand behind her. "We'll see about that."

Although only eighteen, the four youngsters were tall. Francesca was certain they would be a handful for Aidan and Chef, given Chef's lack of height, and age.

"Come on, then, old boys," Ealing said, ready for a fight.

Francesca kept Benjamin back.

Chef put his hand on Aidan's shoulder, then pointed at Ealing's crotch.

She wondered what Chef was doing, before she realised he was laughing.

No sound came out. His head went back, his shoulders rocked up and down.

"Oh no! Not again." Ealing looked down at his crotch.

Francesca burst out laughing when she saw a dark patch in his jeans growing. She pulled Benjamin into a hug, pointing at his tormentor. "He's pissed himself!"

The boy next to Ealing glanced down at his friend's jeans. He pointed, laughing.

Chef pointed at the tall boy's crotch, laughing silently, yet harder.

Unable to control her own laughter, Francesca stood cuddling Benjamin, tears streaming down her cheeks. Her belly hurt.

Ealing held his groin, his knees bent. "You're all dead!"

Aidan and Chef might as well have been rolling on the floor. They pointed and laughed as Ealing took his bullies out of the restaurant car park.

"What's going on out here? There's no one in the kitchen cooking." Kate had her authoritative voice on. "Aidan? What's going on?"

"That horrible Ealing boy was beating on Benji." Francesca checked he wasn't beaten too badly. "You're fine," she said, pulling him in for a hug. He was like her little brother.

Aidan ruffled his hair. "Come on, let's go back to work." He strolled back to the restaurant next to Chef. "I don't know how you did it, but you scared the piss out of them." He chuckled to himself.

Francesca followed with Benjamin. Unsure of what she just witnessed, she thought about it for a second. How could Chef have made two adult males piss themselves? From where she stood it looked like Chef pointed at Ealing's crotch, making his bladder burst.

Dismissing her thoughts, she stepped inside the kitchen, closing the fire escape door behind her. "Right, back to it," she said, ruffling Benjamin's hair, something she knew he hated. "And as for you, there's a dessert order with your name on it."

37

"Man, that was a brutal dinner service." Aidan sat on a chair in front of Kate, who was busy counting the tills. "How much did we take?" She handed him the End of Day report in the form of a till receipt. He whistled. "That much? I guess we did have a blinding lunch and dinner service. You know this isn't far off our old daily takings."

With a bundle of twenties in her hand, Kate started counting them, flicking through four, and wrapping the fifth around them on each batch of a hundred. "I'm counting here, love. Give me ten minutes and I'll be with you."

Pulling himself up, Aidan went over to the bar, poured himself a lager from the tap.

Francesca and Benjamin finished setting the tables up for lunch service the next day. "We'll be going now. Everything's ready for lunch tomorrow, Aidan. I'm off tomorrow, and I will be going to the funeral, but if you need me, I can be around for dinner service, but only if you're stuck, mind."

"Chef's finishing up in the kitchen. He said I can go, Aidan."

"Off you go, peeps." He took a big gulp of his lager. "And don't worry, Fran. We're covered for tomorrow. Benjamin, and Bonnie are out front with the three of us back of house. Thanks for the offer, though."

"I'll meet you at the church at three, Fran." Kate stood, carrying both tills. "Are you coming to the Red Lion after?"

Francesca told Kate she planned on it. Then she offered to give Benjamin a lift home, leaving via the front door.

While Kate was locking the tills in the safe upstairs in the office, Aidan sat at table 30 with his beer. Images of Kate and Graham flashed in his mind, anger rising. Why he had not gone out and said something earlier, he couldn't say.

"Are you all done, love?" Kate had her handbag ready.

"Come and sit with me for a bit, Kate." He sensed her reluctance. "Please? It's been ages since we had a chat. I miss it."

She wandered over to the bar, poured herself a small house red. "You didn't miss it during our last date night, did you? From what I recall, you couldn't wait to run away from me." Kate walked back over to his table, sat in her usual spot.

"What? When?" He thought back. "I can't even remember our last date night."

"The night we met Chef, remember? You made out it wasn't a date night, and all you wanted to do was shadow Chef. Anything to avoid talking to me." She knocked half of the wine back in one. "It hurt, you know. We used to talk, all the time. It was the one truly great thing about us; we were on the same wavelength on most things. I miss that."

"We can get it back." He reached across, took her hand in his.

Baulking, Kate whipped her hand away, and picked up the wine glass.

"What? Are we not allowed to hold hands now?"

Finishing her drink, Kate stood, staring down at him.

"You didn't snatch your hand away from Graham, though, did you?" Her surprised expression made him stand.

"What are you talking about? I did no such thing. Graham's an old friend."

"There's no point lying about it, Kate. I saw you both sat over there." He pointed at the guilty table. "I saw him hold your hand. And you didn't object."

Aidan thought his wife wanted to say something.

Instead, she put her handbag on her shoulder. "I don't have to listen to this. We're having time apart, remember? I can visit as many friends as I like, do you understand?"

Angry, he followed her through the dining room. "You're kidding, right? Friends. Is that supposed be a joke? Graham's a friend, is he?"

Kate stopped, turning to him. "I introduced you to him as a friend, didn't I?"

He wanted to launch his pint of lager across the room. "He's a friend? And not your ex-boyfriend?" He had her on the ropes, her eyes darting in every direction. "I remember you mentioned a Graham when we got together. Is that him?"

Kate hung her head. "Yeah, he's my Graham. He's the one that got away."

Hearing it from her mouth made him feel worse. "I don't believe this. Do you have to rub my nose in it? You're over there holding his hand. Do you know how disrespectful that is? Wars have started for far less."

Kate reached out to him. "We're just friends, love. Nothing more. I was catching up with him over there. I'm sorry if he held my hand. I didn't notice; I was too busy listening to his stories. It won't happen again."

Aidan sighed. "Look, he held your hand. It's not your fault. I guess I'm jealous."

"Jealous of what? I'm still your wife. I would never cheat on you." She held his hand. "I still love you. I just need more time to straighten my head out."

"You've already had two months." He squeezed her hand. "How much longer do you need? I miss you. I need you back home."

Kate stared at the floor. "I don't know. My sister said I can stay for as long as I need. I'm sorry, but I'm not ready to come home yet."

"Why? Because of Graham? You want to find out where things go with him, is that it?" He regretted saying it the second he saw her wounded eyes.

"Is that what you think of me? Is it?" She stared into him. "You really think I'm that sort of person?" She flung her bag behind her. "Thanks. Thanks a lot."

Making to run after her, he stopped himself when he heard her shout, "Bastard!" before she left the restaurant, slamming the front door behind her. His hands back on top of his head, Aidan stamped his foot. "Oh shit!"

Aidan caught sight of Chef in the doorway of the kitchen. "Shit!" He strolled over to hi sous chef. "I'm going to make a move home."

Making his hands look like a pillow, Chef told him he was tired.

"Me too, mate. Me too." He placed his empty pint glass on the bar. Remembering he left an out-of-date chocolate fudge cake in the fridge for himself, Aidan went and retrieved it.
Chef said he was going upstairs to bed.

"Wait a sec, I'll walk out with you." He closed the refrigerator door, noticing that Chef had carried on walking. No point in calling after him, Aidan took one last glance around the kitchen, making sure everything was off, when he followed Chef out to the dining room.

Pushing through the swing door, he stopped when he couldn't find Chef. "What the?" His sous chef should have been a few feet in front of him. "Chef?" The man was deaf. Why was he calling out his name?

A man couldn't disappear like that.

Unnerved, Aidan went back into the dimly lit kitchen. "Chef?" Still, he called out for him. Why?

Chef disappearing, while not the only weird thing to happen, it was the creepiest. Placing the fudge cake on a table, he decided to take a look upstairs. Maybe Chef ran from the kitchen up those stairs?

No luck in the office, or in the flat, Aidan found himself back downstairs in the dining room. He bent down to pick up the fudge cake.

He jumped.

When he turned to leave the restaurant, Chef stood in front of him.

Aidan leaned forwards, catching his breath after such a shock. "Oh my God! You scared the shit out of me." Now he knew Chef was around, Aidan decided to leave, to go home, finish off the chocolate fudge cake, and open a fresh bottle of Glenfiddich.

FRIDAY, MARCH 22ND

38

Aidan and Chef spent the Friday lunch shift twiddling their thumbs, or in Aidan's case, playing Angry Birds on his phone. Kate predicted a quiet lunch, due to most of the village attending Edith Ashcroft's funeral at three.

They had a couple of tables in, Bonnie and Benjamin fussing over the guests. Bonnie reported back that both tables loved their food so much they were going to recommend Marble's Marvels to their friends.

"Better still, ask them to review us on Trip Advisor," he suggested to her.

Later, Bonnie told him that two of their customers had submitted reviews. Determined to raise his restaurant from a three-point five rating to a five out of five, he was confident with Chef's food their ranking would rise dramatically soon.

Glancing at his watch, Aidan decided to nip next door to the florist. He threw his tea towel down, put a jacket over his chef whites, and left via the fire escape door into the back garden. He didn't like walking through the dining room.

After saying hello to Flo, the owner, he told her what he was looking for.

Florence was busy with orders from Edith's funeral. She apologised for not having the best in stock. "It's fine, Flo. Whatever you have left."

Happy with the bouquet of lilies, gladioli and carnations, Aidan paid for them with his credit card. He took the long route back to the kitchen via the car park and garden. Chef took the flowers from him, placing them in a glass vase. He signed 'Thank you!' which he thought looked like he was blowing Chef a kiss.

Three o'clock, the kitchen was clean, clear, ready for the dinner service. "You can go now, Chef. All I have to do is lock up."

Leaning on the counter, Chef wrote something in his pad of paper. "*Can I go with you to the funeral? I want to pay my respects to Mrs Ashcroft.*"

With a shake of his head, he dropped Chef's hopes. "I'm not going to the burial. I'm going to put the flowers on her grave after everyone's gone."

Chef wrote, '*Why didn't you go with Kate and Francesca?*'

"Like you don't know already," he muttered to himself. "We don't like each other anymore. Me and Chris Ashcroft, I mean." Chef asked why without saying as much. "It's a long story. But it has to do with our sons dying in the crash."

Signing, 'Sorry!', Chef put his hand on Aidan's shoulder. '*You don't have to tell me what happened if it's too upsetting.*'

As Aidan was about to unload on his sous chef, Bonnie entered carrying the last of the dirty dessert plates. "This is it for definite. Oh, and there's some guy outside asking lots of questions about this place. He's a bit suss if you ask me."

Checking the customer out, Aidan stared out of the glass in the door. "Which one?"

"The handsome one in the suit, table fifteen."

"*Graham.*" He recognised the man's profile from yesterday. "What the hell does he want? What was he asking?"

Bonnie kept vigil at the same time. "I don't know. He's only bought a coffee, but keeps trying to talk to me, asking me over to his table. He asked how busy it gets here, things like that. He's a bit creepy if you ask me."

Buttoning his whites right up, his mobile in his trousers pocket, Aidan went into the dining room for the first time since opening. He headed straight for table fifteen, where Graham sat talking to some bloke in a suit. "Can I help you? You've been asking my waiter questions about the restaurant. I'm the owner, I'm sure I can answer your queries."

Graham stood, holding his hand out. "Aidan, it's Graham, remember? I came in the kitchen yesterday with Kate?"

Aidan slapped his forehead, making out he'd forgotten. "Oh Graham, of course. I'm so sorry, I didn't recognise you without Kate. My apologies, I thought you were some weirdo hitting on my waitress." He left Graham's hand out in the cold.

"Cold!" The suit, remaining seated, chuckled to himself.

Aidan sensed Chef behind him.

Graham seemed nervous at the arrival of his sous chef, rubbing his right palm with his left fingers. "Here he is, the Man. Hi Chef, remember me?"

The pain in Graham's hand grew in intensity it seemed. Aidan noticed him flexing his right hand. "Are you okay there, mate?" He tried not to smile. "Something wrong with your hand?" Chef stood next to him.

"Yeah, it's been sore since I shook Chef's hand, actually."

The suit laughed. "Was his shake too tight for you, mate? I always said you have delicate lady hands." He got to his feet, stood next to Graham.

"No, mate, I shook his hand, and we had some sort of electric shock, didn't we?" Graham grew uneasy when Chef remained silent. "Does your hand hurt?"

Chef shook his head, his face blank.

Wanting nothing more than to punch him in his 'traditionally good-looking' face, Aidan knew it would be more than his life was worth with Kate. He needed to be on his best behaviour, or he might end up pushing her into Graham's open arms. "What is this? A business meeting, or something?"

"Or something." Graham pulled his chair out, sat down, staring up at him.

"I haven't seen Kate much since yesterday afternoon." Aidan changed the subject. "She never told me what you do."

The suit grinned. "He's in acquisitions, aren't you, mate?"

Aidan didn't like the way Suit was grinning. "Acquisitions, huh? Is that business acquisitions?" Suit nodded; his expression cocky. "And what are you looking to acquire now?"

"All will be revealed." Suit smiled up at him until Graham kicked him under the table. "Ouch! That hurt, you arsehole!"

"Honestly, Aidan, if I explained what I do, you would be standing there snoring, trust me. It's very dull." Graham was trying not to grin. "I can put my parents to sleep like that."

Without trying to be rude, Aidan sighed, checked his watch. "As fun as this has been, gentlemen, I'm afraid I need to ask you to drink up. I need to lock up and get to the church."

"Ah, the funeral," Graham said, staring up at him with apologetic eyes. "I was sorry to hear about your friend passing. I know Kate was upset. I'm meeting her at the Red Lion later, so I'll pass my condolences on then."

"You? You're going to the Lion?" Anger swelled up inside him. Aidan had to swallow to keep it coming out in a bile-filled foul-mouthed tirade. Chef put his hand on his shoulder.

"Didn't she tell you? She invited me over last night." Graham smiled up at him, the tone of his voice cocky. "I met her at her sisters for a nightcap after she finished here."

The words didn't seem real. Aidan should have sent Graham flying over the table. Instead, he nodded. "Good for you." Even his words sounded hollow, like someone else said them. He should be flying at the smug git.

He turned and headed back to the kitchen, Chef by his side. Why did he feel so calm? Kate invited Graham back to hers for a drink after here, for Christ's sake. "Tell me why I didn't punch his lights out!"

Chef picked up his pen, leaned on the counter. "*Because you're better than him. In every way possible, you're a better man.*"

"Yeah, sure, only he's with Kate, and I'm not, so how does that work?" He should be throwing things about by now, yet he had no desire to.

'*Give Kate time. She'll realise what she's missing.*'

Out in the dining room, Graham and his suit friend left, both appraising Bonnie before she locked them out. Aidan joined her and Benjamin. "All done? Ready for dinner?"

"Uh-huh! That guy was a proper sleaze. They both kept checking me out."

"I know he is. Shame we're stuck with him for the foreseeable." He forgot she didn't know what was going on. "The taller, better-looking one is Kate's ex-boyfriend from way back when. She calls him 'the one that got away'."

"That guy?" Bonnie pulled a less than impressed face. "Well, she must value him as a friend, Aidan. I'm sure there's nothing going on. Kate's not like that."

At half three, Aidan locked up, said thanks to Bonnie and Benjamin. With Chef by his side, he strolled towards the church.

39

"It's nice of your husband to show his face," Chris murmured.

Kate leaned into Chris. "You're joking, right? He wanted to come, but you made it more than clear he's not welcome. You need to make your mind up." She hoped her face didn't betray her.

Standing around the grave, the pallbearers lowered Edith Ashcroft's coffin into the grave using the straps. Four of Chris' big, burly rugby friends had agreed to carry her. Kate was the only one from her half of the village present, with the exception of Francesca, who knew Chris' daughter, Amy well. "You and Aidan need to sort things out."

"Kate's right, Dad," Amy whispered on the other side of Chris, dabbing her eyes with a tissue. "This has gone on for too long now. Mum's made amends with Kate. It's time you did the same with Aiden."

"I might have done, had he turned up today." He glared straight ahead. "Since he couldn't be bothered, how can I forgive him for that?"

Kate bent forwards, gazed over at Amy, and rolled her eyes. She stood up straight. "Don't try that trick with me. You had no intention of forgiving him today. Whatever he does, you'll take it the wrong way. He doesn't turn up he doesn't care; he turns up, you have a go at him." One of the guests glared at her for talking.

"That's not how it is," he countered.

"Please! That's so how it is," Amy argued. "We need to heal this community; don't you see that? I hate coming back here mostly because it's so frosty."

Kate shot the nosy woman a glare in return. "Shh, the vicar's about to start."

"Whose side are you on anyway?" He ignored the vicar.

"Yours, Dad, I'm always on your side. You know that." Amy dabbed her eyes with the tissue. "But Aidan's not your enemy. What happened was a tragic accident, why can't you both understand that? Liam and Vinnie are both gone. They wouldn't want you at each other's throats like this."

The vicar, in traditional dress, proceeded with the chosen readings from the bible. Having had the church funeral service already, the readings were short. Quinn, the vicar asked Chris to sprinkle earth over the casket.

Kate had a hard time keeping the tears back, thinking of poor Edie withering away over those final weeks. She went to visit her friend as often as Chris allowed. His wife needed vast amounts of rest, speaking taking its toll on her energy levels. A fortnight before she passed Edie stopped talking altogether.

Watching her friend die put life into perspective. She did nothing but think about her and Aidan's relationship, how meaningless it was. Memories flashed in front of her of how strong it had been prior to the crash. They used to live and work together as one almighty, unstoppable unit. Now they barely talked to one another.

"Kate, your turn." Chris stood next to her.

Scooping up some soil after Amy sprinkled hers, Kate waited in turn, finally staring down at Edie's resting place. Fighting the lump in her throat, she dropped the soil a bit at a time. "I love you!"

"Thanks for your help organising this." Chris continued staring ahead when she was back in line, waiting for the rest of the guests to sprinkle their soil.

Kate had to catch her breath, surprised at the gratitude.

"And that concludes our service. Christian would like to invite you all to join him for food and drinks at the Red Lion pub. If you are visiting our lovely village, and don't know where it is, follow the congregation. It's only a five-minute walk."

When Kate went to follow Chris and Amy, he stopped her. "Not you, Kate, I'm sorry. I want this send-off to be friends and family only. I thank you for your help, but please respect my wishes. I need to say goodbye to Edie in my own way."

Amy apologised to her with a glance.

"No, it's fine. You go on." With relatives and friends of the Ashcrofts staring at her as she stood still, watching them leave the cemetery, Kate never felt so alone. She welled up, as the last of the group walked out of sight.

"Aren't you going with them?"

Kate recognised the voice immediately. She turned to find Aidan holding a bouquet of flowers flanked by Chef. She rushed into his arms, wanting nothing more than to feel his warmth. He held her, while she sobbed into his chest.

"I'm here for you, always." Aidan enveloped her in a protective shield.

Breaking the embrace, pulling away from her husband, Chef signed, *'I'm sorry!'* Kate had learned a fair bit from Francesca over the years to know the sorry sign. She smiled, wiping away the tears.

Collecting herself, Kate stood by the graveside. "Are you going to put those down?"

Aidan placed the bouquet at the foot of the grave. "I'm so sorry, Edie. For everything. I'm sorry for blaming Liam for so long."

Stood by his side, Kate glanced over to find Chef's hand on her husband's shoulder.

It was unlike Aidan to show emotion. Apart from a few weeks earlier, she had never seen him cry, not once. Not even at the funeral. Tears rolling down his cheeks now rung alarm bells. She held his hand, hoping this marked the start of his grieving process.

"What the hell is that?" A voice from a distance yelled.

"Daddy, no wait!"

Kate nudged Aidan. Chris and Amy ran over to them, the anger in Chris' eyes obvious the closer he came. "Oh shit!" She turned to face the enraged husband of the deceased, standing in front of Aidan for protection.

"It's alright, Chris, we're just leaving," Aidan said over her shoulder. "We came to pay our respects to Edie. Now we'll go." He put his hands out in a placating manner.

"You have some nerve showing your face here, Marble!" Chris pushed Kate out of the way, leaving a small gap between himself and Aidan.

"Daddy don't!" Amy tried to step between them.

Trying as hard as she could to get between them, Chris kept pushing her, brushing her away like an irritating fly. "Don't fight here, boys. Edie wouldn't want this. Please."

Chris pulled his arm back. Before she could intercept, he punched Aidan in the mouth.

"Chris, no!"

Aidan staggered backwards, his lip cut, his gum bleeding. He wiped his mouth. "If this is what you want, come on, then!" His eyes grew into spiteful slits.

Kate had to intervene, but Chris kept her at bay.

Chef stepped behind Chris, placing his hand on his shoulder.

The anger and fight left Chris' body. He seemed to relax, facing Aidan.

"Chris? Are you alright?" Kate waited for him to say something.

With Chef's hand still on his shoulder, Chris' face changed. It crumpled in front of her and Aidan. His legs wobbled beneath him. To Kate, it looked like the weight of his grief swept over him in a single second.

Chris fell to his knees, his eyes filled with tears. "I'm so sorry!" His head slumped. "I don't mean to."

"Daddy!" Amy rushed to her dad, wrapping her comforting arms around him. "Shh! I'm here. We'll make it through this together." Her voice broke mid-sentence.

Kate stared up at Aidan, the anger in his face had changed to pity. "Why don't you take Chef back to the restaurant? Start setting up for tonight. I'll help Amy with her dad."

Her husband nodded, collected Chef, and left the cemetery.

Chris sobbed for the next ten minutes, guilt, compounded with sorrow and self-loathing wracking his body in the form of huge sobs. His daughter kept him wrapped in her love. Kate fought the need to cry, needing to be strong for the Ashcrofts, who had more sorrow to follow after today.

After Chris stopped sobbing, Kate helped him to his feet. While walking with him towards the Red Lion, Kate thought about Chef, about how he prevented a fight between Chris and Aidan, just by putting his hand on Chris' shoulder.

Yesterday, Chef made those bullies wet themselves, or at least that was how it appeared to her waitress. Aidan spoke to her about Chef disappearing into thin air, although her husband admitted Chef said he ran up the stairs. She would start watching him closely.

With an arm around Chris' shoulder, Kate walked with the Ashcrofts until they reached the pub, at which point she backed away.

"Come and join us, Kate, please? I was wrong earlier. Edie wants you here."

"Please, Kate. Mum loved you. You were sisters."

40

Francesca picked up her bag, slung the strap over her shoulder. "I'll buy these."

The Red Lion was packed with mourners, with friends and family of Edie Ashcroft saying their last goodbyes to 'the loveliest woman they ever met'.

At the bar, Francesca had to wait in line.

She said hello to a lot of villagers, a couple of whom she'd known since childhood, while most had moved here much later. Having worked for Marble's Marvels for so long, she knew about every face in the village, if not by name, then definitely by face.

At the bar, she ordered a lemonade, a Pepsi for Amy, and a big glass of red wine for Kate, who she was keeping an eye on. Since Kate brought Chris and Amy in, she had not said much. "Thanks. Don't worry about the change."

Back at her table, she placed the drinks in front of Kate and Amy. Sat down, she tried to make conversation with Kate, but every thirty seconds or so a relative or friend of the Ashcrofts kept coming up to Amy. "What's wrong?" She reached out for Kate's hand.

"Hmm? Oh nothing." Kate kept evading her questions.

Over in the corner of the open plan pub, Declan queued for the buffet with a long line of hungry guests. Francesca went to get up. "How about some food? Shall I get you a plate, Kate? Ooh, I'm a poet and I didn't know it."

Her boss thanked her, saying anything from the buffet is fine with her.

With Amy in tow, Francesca joined the back of the queue. It didn't take long to reach the plates. Amy was too busy chatting to guests, who all gave her sympathetic smiles and squeezes of her shoulder. "The spread looks fantastic by the way," she managed to tell Amy.

"Yeah, the caterer's a friend of dads." Amy kissed yet another relative on their cheeks. "Can you put an assortment of sandwiches on a plate for me, please."

Still queuing, Francesca spotted Declan returning from the far end of the buffet with a plate loaded with food. She managed to catch his eye. He stopped in front of her. "Hi! I was wondering if I would find you here."

"I had to pay my respects." He smiled warmly. "Edie was my babysitter years ago. It's so sad." He stopped and gave Amy a hug and kiss. "I'm so sorry she's gone, Ames. I loved your mum to bits, but you know that. How's your dad holding up?"

"I wish I could say well, but I think he's cracking up," Amy confessed.

Declan hugged her again. "I'll keep an eye on him when you go back to uni."

"Oh, I'm quitting uni." Amy looked at Declan as though he were absurd suggesting she return. "I'm not leaving dad here like this. I need to be around for him, not living it up in Manchester while he falls apart back home."

It was the first Francesca had heard of it. "Whoa! Hold it! You can't make a decision like this without discussing it with your dad first. Have you even told him?"

"Well, no, but-"

"Fran's right, Amy, you can't make a snap decision like ditching university without at least asking your dad what he wants. Your mum was so proud of you getting a place in Manchester. I know she wouldn't want you to ditch it like this."

Francesca couldn't stop staring at Declan's rugged face.

He cared about Amy, cared about the village, and many of its residents.

She listened to them go back and forth, Amy arguing her point, Declan countering. She could tell how much Amy respected Declan's opinion, probably because Amy fancied him, and had since she was a little girl, when Declan used to babysit for her.

One of Amy's relatives stopped for a chat.

"While she's away, can we talk in a bit?"

Declan invited her to sit with him. Francesca told him she had a table with Kate and Amy. She invited him to join them. "Go and sit with Kate, and I'll be right with you."

While she was putting sandwiches, sausage rolls, a slice of quiche, and cold pizza on a plate for Kate, she loaded hers with bread and cheese, dips, and a couple of sandwiches. She was eating for two now. Having taken another test this morning, the reality had hit her in the shower, when she burst into tears.

"I always thought you two would make a gorgeous couple." Amy placed an assortment of sandwiches on her plate, along with some potato salad.

Trying to laugh the comment off, Francesca finished piling up hers and Kate's plates. "Don't be silly. We're friends. Always have been, always will be."

"Oh, come off it, I've seen the way he looks at you," Amy whispered in her ear. "He's liked you for years, everyone knows it."

Francesca picked up both plates and ignored Amy's comment by walking away.

Was it that obvious? Had she missed the signs for years? "Here you go, Kate. A mix of everything." She slid Kate's plate along, before sitting down next to her boss and opposite Declan, who was tucking into his loaded plate. "Steady on, save some for other people."

She wanted to speak with him in private, to explain to him what happened. With Kate and Amy there, she couldn't say or do anything, other than make small talk.

After she finished her plate of food, seizing a quiet moment when Kate was visiting the ladies, and Amy was talking with a relative by the buffet, Francesca glanced around her. "Do you fancy going outside for a bit? There's something I need to say to you, but it's too crowded and noisy in here."

"Sure." He got up. "Let's go!"

The sun was shining outside in the courtyard. Groups of guests loitered on the paving, some smoking, while others joined their smoker friends. Francesca and Declan both said hello to people as they made their way to a quiet spot at the outer edge of the courtyard.

"You know you don't need to explain, don't you?
What happened before, shouldn't have happened, Fran. We're friends. We shouldn't throw that away on a whim."

"No, I know I don't." She sat on a low perimeter wall, patted the bricks next to her. "I need you to know I wanted to enjoy that night with you, I did. But after Paul and that baby came over, my mood deteriorated, I'm so sorry! I know how much effort you went to as well. I have felt so bad about it since. Will you forgive me?"
"There's no need, Fran. You're making a mountain again." He almost laughed, but she could tell he didn't mean it. She hurt him. "It's fine. You leaving like that stopped anything happening. We're friends, and that's the way I want to keep it. Are you okay with that?"

Francesca nodded, almost imperceptibly. "Uh-
huh! Friends is fine." She wanted her words to sound genuine, only they weren't. Taking a sip of her lemonade, an uncomfortable silence fell over her. "I'm glad we sorted that."

"Me too." Declan took a sip of his ale.

A noisy car pulled up outside the pub. Francesca rolled her eyes, spotting Paul inside his orange 1974 Porsche 911 Carrera. Her husband loved his classic car. Bless him, he always wanted a Porsche, and now he had one, only it was a dirty orange colour. She almost laughed when he brought it home. "He's such a poser."

"Be cool," Declan said, not turning. "If he says anything, ignore him. It's the best policy in situations like this."

At least he was not with that schoolgirl. Francesca tried not to watch Paul, yet found her eyes wandering over to his stupid car. And to her irritation, he was wearing his dark suit, the one she bought for him. He looked so handsome in it, too. "Here he comes. Laugh!"

Declan eyed her. "What? I'm not playing silly games, Fran."

Paul spotted her from his car. Instead of walking through the pub door, her husband walked along the courtyard, through groups of mourners, actively seeking her. "Hi Fran. Declan, how are you doing?"

"Paul!" Declan left it at an acknowledgement that he knew Paul's name.

"There's something I need to talk to you about."

"If you need to come and collect the rest of your stuff, it's fine. Ring ahead first, though, is all I ask." Francesca noted his genuine expression, or was it sorrowful? Gone was the cockiness.

"It's not about that, I promise." Paul stared at Declan for ten seconds.

"I need another drink anyway." Declan stood from the wall, checked she was allowing him to leave. "Do you want another lemonade, Fran?"

Francesca smiled, shook her head, as Declan walked back to the pub. She patted the bricks where Declan had been sitting. "So? What did you want to say?"

Paul sat next to her, but turned slightly, facing her more. "I made a huge, monumental mistake, Fran. I'm so sorry! The way I behaved, the way I treated you, I'm so ashamed. Please forgive me?"

Stunned. Francesca sat on the wall; her mouth open.

"Are you going to say something? I'm apologising to you for treating you like shit."

"I don't know what to say." She closed her mouth, shuffling. "She dumped you, didn't she? I don't believe it, your schoolgirl dumped you for a college lad." With a little chuckle, she stood and stared down at him. "Who would have thought you, with your Porsche, and your fancy clothes, that gifted gob of yours, you were dumped by a little girl."

"Ah wait now, that's not what happened." He stood. "I dumped her. I realised what an idiot I'd been, honey. You're who I'm supposed to be with, not her. I dumped her a month ago, you have to believe me."

"Believe you? Why should I believe a word you have to say? You lied to me for months. You were shag-" Heads turned in her direction at their conversation. "You were sleeping with that baby for months behind my back, Paul, so explain to me why I should believe you. Go on! I dare you!"

"You're angry, Fran, I can understand that. I would be, too. Please, though, please hear me out, okay? If you do that, and you still say it's over I'll leave you in peace."

With raised eyebrows, Francesca sat down again. "You expect to win me back that easily? With one conversation? Then you're dumber than I thought. Go ahead, though, say what you came here to say."

"Look, there's no excuse for my behaviour, so I won't even try. You have to admit we were on our way out, though. We never did anything together; we passed each other on our way to work every day, and in the evenings, we sat in different rooms doing different things."

He tried reaching out for her hand. "Then I met Tegan at the gym, and we hit it off straight away. I'm sorry to be saying all this, but it needs to be said. Do you remember how exciting it was when we started seeing each other? I had that excitement in my life again, Fran. I was hooked from day one."

"Good for you!" Why the hell was he telling her all this? How did it help him win her back? It didn't; all it did was make her angry. "I'm glad for you. You got your excitement back, I'm thrilled."

"No, you don't understand." He took her hand in his. "Now I realise the excitement's a passing phase in any relationship. I started seeing holes in my relationship with Tegan straight away, but I loved the thrill of it. With you it was different. Even without the buzz I'm at home with you. I'm not talking about the house either; I'm talking about you being my home, my guiding star and everything in between."

"If I could puke without embarrassing myself I would, all over you." She saw Declan talking to a group by the conservatory doors. "I'm not listening to any more of this crap, Paul. You made your bed, now lie in it. You wanted your fun, now you can have as much as you want. Knock yourself out."

When she turned to walk away, Paul tried to pull her back. "Please Fran, I'll make it up to you, I promise. I don't know how, but I will."

Whipping her wrist away, she carried on walking.

How could she be thinking how gorgeous he was? So rugged yet sophisticated in his suit. Declan nodded at her, beckoning her over. Maybe it was the baby inside her begging her to give its daddy another try?

41

Kate couldn't stop thinking about Chef's intervention in the cemetery. Sitting with Amy, who was busy talking with various relatives and family friends, she munched her way through the assorted party food Francesca placed on her plate, occasionally joining in conversation, but mainly nodding and agreeing.

Francesca and Declan returned.

"Is everything alright, Fran? You look like you're about to mug someone."

"Paul's outside." Francesca leaned in closer, her voice low. "He wants us to get back together, can you believe that? He goes off with some schoolgirl and he thinks he can jump back in my bed?"

Spotting Paul in his dark suit, Kate leaned back in her chair, warning Francesca with a stare. "Hey, it's Paul. It's been a long time." She didn't know what else to say.

Paul smiled at Francesca. "I meant every word I said, Fran, I'm going to make it up to you, I promise." He stood in front of their table, waiting for something.

"You'll have to excuse me if I don't believe you." Francesca turned away from him in her chair, facing Declan. "So, what were you saying, before we were rudely interrupted?"

Kate glanced up at Paul and shrugged. The guy was a sleaze. The girl he ran off with was half his age, a nubile twenty-year-old from what Francesca said. She thought about Aidan then. At least he was not going through some mid-life crisis. No, their relationship was dying for an altogether different reason.

Needing some fresh air, Kate excused herself, taking her glass of wine with her out to the front courtyard, where she spotted space on the perimeter wall. Lovely out, she sat and enjoyed the sun on her face, even closing her eyes and facing it.

"Is this a private party, or can anyone join in?"

Knowing the voice immediately, Kate opened her eyes. "How did I guess it was you?" She smiled up at Graham, who wore a light grey suit and black shirt. With his dark hair and rugged face, she couldn't help patting the bricks next to her. "How long have you been here? I was looking out for you."

He smiled. "Not long. Just got here actually." He put his pint of ale at his feet. After a lengthy silence, he nudged her. "It's so weird seeing you after all this time. I mean it in a good way."

Kate loved his slight American accent. "Goes without saying."

Another moment of quiet sat between them.

"You look deep in thought, Kate. I'll give you a penny for them."

Opening her eyes again, Graham was looking over at her, expecting an answer. "I'm sorry! I had an encounter with my new chef in the cemetery. I can't stop thinking about it, is all." She picked up her glass, taking a sip. "Where are my manners? I asked you here this afternoon, and I'm being rude."

"Don't be daft." He had a swig of his pint. "Do you want to tell me about this encounter? I'm intrigued. What happened?"

She explained the events in the cemetery, how Chef put his hand on Chris' shoulder, and about how she witnessed the anger drain out of him. She couldn't explain it or understand how Chef managed to get Chris on his knees, sobbing. "And this isn't the first encounter we've had with Chef either."

Graham leaned back. "Wow! Quite the story, Kate."

She stared into his green eyes, smiled. "You don't believe me."

"No, I do." He put his pint back down. "After getting that electric shock from him, anything's possible. I think there's more to Chef, too. Tell me what else happened. I'm interested."

With her voice low, making sure no one else heard her, Kate explained what Francesca told her about Chef tackling the bullies. "Fran says he started laughing at Finlay Ealing and the poor lad wet himself. And when one of his friends fell about laughing, Chef pointed at him, and he did the same." The expression on Graham's face said it all. "Now I know you don't believe me. But I swear this is all true. Aidan told me Chef disappeared into thin air one evening."

"How's that?" His eyebrows were raised.

"Aidan told me he was walking behind Chef, stopped to take something out of the fridge, opened the kitchen door, and Chef was nowhere to be found. He hunted everywhere for him, and then Chef reappeared behind him."

Graham looked at the ground. "But you didn't witness this happen, or the kids wetting themselves?"

"Well, no, but I saw him move Chris to tears just now."

"I don't know, Kate. It all sounds a bit hokey to me."

Kate frowned. "I know it does. Maybe I'm cracking up."

"I wouldn't say that, but I'm sure he's not some magician."

Kate shrugged. "He is in the kitchen. The food he cooks is out of this world, except it seems for bad people."

"Come again? What does that mean?" Graham took another mouthful of his beer.

"The mayor of Bishops Drake came in one evening with his wife for dinner," she explained, telling him about how Gaines spat the food out, yet his wife raved about it.

"Yeah, that is weird," he agreed. "So, you think the food knows if someone's naughty or nice? Kind of Santa's grub then?"
He laughed out loud. "I'm sorry! I'm not laughing at you, honest. It's, well, you know, it's a bit-"

"Hokey?" Her cheeks reddened. "I know, but you did ask what I'm thinking about."

She dug him in the ribs with a playful elbow.

"And there's something else, only I don't know if I should tell you or not."

She hit him playfully. "Don't do that. You're teasing."

"He's not very friendly, is he? Your chef, I mean."

It was the first time anyone had said a bad word against Chef. "Excuse me?"

"I popped into your restaurant earlier for a coffee with a colleague. Your husband and Chef came out as we were leaving. Aidan all but threw me out, and Chef spent the whole time glaring at me. I'm sorry to be the one telling you this, but if you think your chef's some kind of Saint, or something, I don't see it."

Her jovial demeanour vanished. "He did what? I'll kill him!"

"Now, don't be rash, Kate. Aidan's probably threatened by me, and your chef adores him. Go easy on him, okay?"

"Threatened by you? What does he think we're going to do? We're two old friends catching up, for crying out loud." She would be in her husband's face if he were here.

"Well, we're a bit more than that, wouldn't you say? We have history."

"Sure, we do," she said, standing up and glaring down at him. "Back when we were kids. Does Aidan think I'm going to jump in your bed? I'm insulted. Does he think that little of me?"

His hands up in surrender, Graham stood. "Hey! I'm the messenger. Don't shoot!"

Kate had to take a couple of deep breaths. She took a glimpse at all the pretty dresses and smart suits for the first time, having been lost in thought for most of the wake. "Anyway, enough of that."

“Huh?" Graham looked around the courtyard, too.

"I was being selfish, talking about Aidan and Chef. I apologise."

Graham bent over, picking up his pint and her glass of wine. "No apology necessary."

"Now that you're here, let me introduce you to a few locals."

SATURDAY, MARCH 23RD

42

Chris Ashcroft opened one eye. Hunched over his desk in the barn-turned garage, the lights still on, he lifted his head with all the strength he could muster. Every movement brought with it pain. "Jesus! What did I do?"

"Nothing good, I can tell you that much." Amy stood in the doorway; her arms crossed.

"What time is it?" He didn't want to physically look up for the agony it would incur. Chris tried to think back to last night. The last thing he remembered was punching Aidan in the mouth.

"Coming up nine in the morning. " Amy glared at him. "You don't even remember, do you?" Her voice came strained, annoyed. "You don't recall being carried by your friends and put in that chair. I'm quitting uni. I can't leave you here like this."

Wanting to comfort his distressed daughter, guilt overwhelming him, Chris tried to stand, only his legs buckled beneath him, sending him back into his desk chair. "It feels like someone died in my head. Amy, go and grab me some paracetamol, would you?"

"That's what you got from what I just said? I'm quitting university, Dad." She stood firm, not moving from her spot. "I can't trust you not to kill yourself on drink, can I?"

The words had not registered in his fragile brain the first time. "You what?" He couldn't shout; his head couldn't withstand the battering. "Don't be so melodramatic. I had one too many last night, no big deal." One too many, what a joke!

"You're joking, right? You couldn't walk by yourself, much less speak. The rugby club boys had to bring you home and plonked you where you sit. I've never been so embarrassed. And you're missing the point, still. I'm quitting university."

By the expression on Amy's face, she meant every word. "And stop saying that. You're not leaving uni. Your Mum was too proud of you getting a place there to throw it away now. I'll quit the booze from now on, okay? You don't need to worry about me, I swear."

On the desk in front of him stood a half-empty bottle of Scotch whisky. His mouth was so dry, the thought of drinking made him want to vomit. "I'll show you." Getting up, his legs wobbly, he picked up the bottle, hobbling with it over to the sink.

He didn't hesitate in unscrewing the cap, urning the bottle upside down and watching the golden contents gurgle as it drained away. "See? Done. No problem."

"You know, I might be impressed," she said, walking over to his desk, "if you didn't have another two back-up bottles."
She yanked the drawer open and pulled out two more, both half full. Amy pointed at them. "Go on! Pour those away as well. Bet you can't."

The whisky was the least of his worries, when it dawned on him what he had in that drawer. "Fine! I can give up the drinking. It's not like I'm an alcoholic."

When he arrived at the desk, Amy's attention was drawn to the letter he left in there. The words 'Final Notice' in bold red writing stood out. Chris pretended he had not seen it. He picked up both bottles, turned and tried to close the drawer with his bum.

"Wait! Let me check that." Amy stopped him closing it on her hand by pushing him away. "Is that a final notice letter?"

There was nothing he could do to stop her; he had whisky in his hands. Before he could plonk them down on the desk, she backed away from him, pulling the note out. "It's not for your eyes, Ames. It's grown-up stuff."

"I don't believe it! It goes from bad to worse," she said, scan reading the letter. "You forgot to pay the mortgage? Oh my God! Dad, how could you!"

"It's not as bad as you think, love, honest." He stepped towards her, desperate to snatch the note from her, not that it made any difference now. She still knew how careless he had been with the family finances. "I'm phoning them this morning to arrange a mortgage holiday. Relax! I let the bills get away from me, but I'm back on it, I promise. You don't have to worry about me."

"But I do, though, don't I? The mortgage hasn't been paid in three months." She held the letter up in front of his face. "It's a wonder the bailiffs aren't at our door now. In fact, why aren't they? Do they know about Mum?"

"I informed them, yeah. I don't know how it got this bad, Ames, but I promise you I'm on it again, okay? I'll call the mortgage people this morning, and I'll explain everything."

Unconvinced, Amy pointed at the bottles. "First, you're going to throw that down the sink, Dad. Then, you're jumping on the phone, and clearing everything with the lender."

"Yes, Ma'am." He was grateful to have such a wonderful daughter. He limped over to the basin and began pouring both bottles of whisky away together. For the briefest of moments, he wanted to stop and take a swig. He stopped himself, turning his head to find Amy watching him with her arms folded. "Easy-peasy."

He remembered leaving a half-drunk bottle out the back one night. He couldn't recall drinking it, so it should still be there, he thought, the anxiety of not having whisky on the premises almost too much to bear. "There! Done."

Amy marched up to him, took the bottles at the same time as handing him the cordless home phone. "Call them! Now! I don't want you losing our home, Dad."

"You think I do?" He took it from her.

When did Amy become so much like his wife? Had Edie been alive, she would be so ashamed of him for everything, but especially missing the mortgage payments. The family home was at stake. "Leave it with me. I'll sort it."

43

Aidan held tissue on his lip and pressed down, hard. Chris Ashcroft split it with his one lucky punch, and since returning from the cemetery it had not stopped bleeding. Every time he spoke, his lip cracked again. "Try it again," he said to himself in the mirror.

Satisfied the bleeding had stopped, he disposed of the tissue in the plastic bin and walked out of the restaurant's gents' toilets to find Kate counting the spirit levels, inputting the results on to a stock print out. "How was the wake?"

"Fine." She held up a litre bottle of vodka, then put it back on the bar. "I'm a bit busy with the stocktake, love. Can we talk about this later?"

Talk? Aidan felt like he wouldn't be talking for a while. At least he learned some signing so he could converse with Chef. Instead of answering, he walked away.

The situation between Kate and himself seemed to be deteriorating day by day. For the life of him, he couldn't work out why, or how to mend it. He wanted to speak to her about Graham, to tell her that Chef didn't trust him.

In the kitchen, Chef was busy cooking batches of four dishes in preparation for lunch and dinner. 'Morning!' He signed. Thinking about it, he used his hands to ask, 'Where do you need me?'

Chef asked him to start prepping a batch of toad in the hole, the only dish in need of starting. Aidan went through the fridges and freezers with Chef last night. Together they established what they needed to prepare for their busy Saturday.

Making enough to serve twelve diners, he took out two baking trays. Putting oil in both, he placed eighteen chipolatas in each 30 x 40 cm tray and stuck them in the oven to cook for quarter of an hour, while he mixed up the batter.

Over the last couple of months his enjoyment of cooking had returned, thanks to Chef and his infectious enthusiasm. Mixing the flour, eggs and milk, and not forgetting the half a teaspoon of salt, he used an electric whisk to mix the batter until it was all bubbly.

Checking the sausages, he heard them sizzling, making sure they were brown, before he poured an equal amount of batter into the trays, and put them back in the oven for twenty-five minutes, setting the timer. 'Be right back,' he signed.

Out in the dining room, with Kate still counting the wet stock, Aidan saw the postman walk past the window. Four letters were posted through the letterbox. Picking them up, he recognised notes from his suppliers, bills no doubt, as well as a leaflet offering them guttering services. One letter caught his attention.

After tearing the envelope, he slid out the A4 piece of paper with their estate agent's name and logo over it. "Kate, we've got a letter from the agent." His lip cracked.

"Bet it's some offer, or something." Kate didn't look up from her paperwork.

"No, it's not." He walked over to the bar while reading it.

He stopped in the middle of the floor when he read the words, *'Lease will not be renewed. The premises need to be vacated, including additional furnishings by October the 31st at the latest.'*

His hands shook as he read and reread the letter no fewer than four times. "Oh no! Just when we were getting somewhere." He didn't care about his broken lip, as he slammed the paper down on the marble surface of the bar. "Did you know our lease was up for renewal?"

Kate looked up from her paperwork. "What? No, it's not. Our renewal date's not for a couple of years. Let me see that."

"I don't believe it! We've been here for seventeen years," he said, pacing back and forth over his own footsteps. "We've never reneged on our obligations. Why would they pull the rug out from under us now?"

With her hands shaking almost as much as his, Kate reread the letter.

Kate's face reddened with each read of the letter. Aidan thought she might explode if she didn't calm down. "It's a mix-up, Kate. We've been excellent tenants, why would they throw that away now, after seventeen years? We'll clear this up with a phone call, you'll see."

"How can they do this to us?" Kate slammed her fist on the bar. "I know we've been through the ringer lately, but we've never missed a payment, not once. We're finally coming out the other side, and they throw this at us?"

Walking behind the bar, Aidan held his wife for the first time in months, excluding his breakdown at the cemetery. "We'll sort it, honey, I promise. Let's check the lease details. They might have sent the wrong letter, you never know."

"I swear it's not due for another couple of years." Kate pulled away from his embrace.

Following her up to the office, Aidan sat behind her desk while Kate opened a filing cabinet drawer. When she took out a folder, he leaned back, letting her open it.

"I know it's in here," she said, flicking through papers, finally pulling one out. "Here!"

Waiting for her to read the lease, she cursed under her breath, handing him the document. Glancing at it, he scanned it for a date. October 2019. "Oh shit!"

Kate took a seat next to him, shocked. "I could've sworn we had a couple of years left. I don't know what happened. I'm supposed to be the organised one."

If he were unkind, he could have made her feel bad about her organisation skills. "Don't blame yourself, love. It's been a horrible couple of years. Let's try and focus on finding a way out of this, yeah?"

"You're right!" Kate picked up the landline phone on the desk. "Um, hi, it's Kate Marble, over at Marble's Marvels. I need to speak to someone regarding the termination of our lease."

Aidan listened as his wife went back and forth with the person on the other end of the line. When she put the phone down in anger, he asked her what happened.

"I'm driving over there now."

44

Having to drive into Basingstoke on a Saturday was not how Kate foresaw her morning heading, not by a long stretch. Pulling up in the small car park devoted to three of Black and Bloom's clients, she parked in the bay next to the white building. Her hands were still shaking, thinking of what she was going to say to Russell Pine, the estate agency's manager.

After locking her MG, Kate walked round to the front door, peered inside, locating Russell sat at a desk near the window. Taking a deep breath, she opened the door, stepped inside, and closed it, as the bell tinkled behind her. "Russell."

"Ah Kate, please take a seat." He stood and motioned for her to sit. "I've been expecting you. Can I get you a drink? A tea, or a coffee?"

Dispensing with the pleasantries, Kate declined. "All I need from you is an explanation. We've been fantastic tenants to you, and the owners. Why throw us out now?"

Russell Pine sat back down, his bald head shining under the light. "Let me start off by saying that I had nothing to do with it, okay? I disagreed with the decision, having been your agent for ten of your seventeen years with us. I tried to stop the deal, but unfortunately, it's not up to me. Mr Bloom calls the shots."

"What deal? What are you talking about?" Kate stared at the fat man who said she knew so well. She hated having to work with a third party, instead of the building's actual owners all these years. The owners were the reason why Marble's Marvels only obtained a four-star award with the FSA. They didn't keep up with maintenance.

"The building's been leased from October the 1st, Kate," he answered. "A private company agreed to take on a ten-year lease, at a higher rate than you pay. Mr. Black and Mr. Bloom made a decision, which regrettably means you need to find alternative premises. I am sorry! Like I said, I fought it, but there's only so much I can do."

Kate sat back in her chair. "What private company?"

"I'm not at liberty to say. You know that."

Kate took a moment to mull it over. "So, Black and Bloom, or rather the building's owners decided to throw us out in favour of another company coming in, is that what you're telling me? And they offered to pay more than we are for the lease?"

Russell nodded. "Yes. I'm sorry!"

"Please don't keep saying that. You don't have anything invested in my restaurant, so do me the courtesy of not acting like you do." She took a breath. "Now, tell me how much this mystery company agreed to pay, and we'll match it."

"I'm afraid-"

"We'll pay more. Please Russell, help us out here. We're finally coming out of our rut. We're on the up. We have two excellent chefs now, and we're turning over a profit again. Please, help us."

"Why? You said it yourself, I'm not invested."

She had a feeling she would regret those words. "I apologise, okay? I'm angry and frustrated. Please help me. Relay my message to the owners, please. Aidan and I are willing to negotiate with them on the lease."

Russell leaned forward, his elbows on the desk. "The thing is, Kate, the negotiation is over. The company sought the owners out themselves. They started the ball rolling, so it's out of our hands now, the lease agreement's been signed."

"Can you at least tell me if it's going to be a restaurant?"

"I can't say that either."

"You can't tell me? Why? Are they turning it into flats?"

"No! They're not converting it into accommodation." He sighed, sitting back. "Fine! It's going to be a restaurant, yes. Are you happy now you know?"

So, the company planned on starting a restaurant in her building. It was a start. If Russell wouldn't tell her who the company was, she would try and find out through other means, other channels. "Yeah, I'm peachy, thanks." Sarcasm oozed over every syllable.

She stood to go, staring down at him. "Thanks for letting me know, Russell. Thanks a lot, for everything."

When she turned to leave, Russell got up also. "I am sorry, Kate."

Kate nodded. "Yeah? Not as sorry as I am."

Outside in the car park, Kate opened up her MG, sat behind the wheel, thinking.

She felt like bursting into tears at the thought of losing her restaurant. No sooner had they started to turn over a profit, then this comes along and kicks the wind out of them, she thought, turning the key.

Hadn't she and Aidan been through enough? What more was life going to throw at them? On her way back to the restaurant, she thought about her evening spent with Graham. He was such a good-looking man, so much so that she couldn't keep her eyes away from him. She had to stop daydreaming about him.

As much as her sister, Liz wanted her to, Kate had no intention of divorcing Aidan. The thought of dating again, at her age, filled her with dread, even with someone as dashing as Graham Winston. All she wanted was Aidan to start grieving the loss of Vinnie, or at least start making forward progress in that direction.

Pulling up in her space behind the restaurant, she glanced at the time: 11:47. Almost time to open up. "You'd better have the tills working, Aidan," she mumbled to herself, as she got out of her car, closed and locked the door.

After using her key to let herself in, Kate found Aidan behind the bar, in front of the till. "Everything alright, love? Is the kitchen ready for service?"

"We're all set, but never mind that," he said, looking up from the screen. "How did it go at Black and Bloom's? Was the letter kosher, or not?"

Taking a seat on a high stool in front of the bar, she nodded. "We've got to be out by October the first. We've got about six months to find new premises, or Marble's Marvels ceases to be."

Aidan came out from behind the bar, put his arm around her. "Shit! After seventeen years. Bastards! Did you find out why now?"

"Some private company signed a ten-year lease with the owners. Russell told me they agreed a higher price than we're paying. When I offered to increase our rent, he shut me down. He said the deal's been negotiated. So, that leaves us high and dry."

Aidan squeezed her shoulder. "Can we try going direct to the owners, and miss out the agent? You never know, they might consider an offer from us directly."

Getting off her stool, Kate shook him off. "No, we can't. We don't have their contact details, remember? We've always gone through the agency, which is the point, I guess."

"Then how did this 'private company' approach them?"

"I don't know, but I'm more interested in finding out more about this company, to be honest. I managed to get Russell to let it slip that it's going to be another restaurant. I wonder if we know anyone who might be in the know?" She went and stood behind the bar, opposite her husband. There had to be someone they could ask.

"Any new company coming to the village needs to submit a planning application."

Kate stood up straight. "Right! And the application must be signed off by the-"

"Mayor!" They both said in unison.

"But there's no reason for Kendall Gaines to give us that information. I bet he's been given a backhander by this company." Aidan hit the bar, frustrated.

"No, you're right, but we've got the next best thing: his wife. And Harriet loves it here. If she can help, she will, I know it. I'll ask her to do a bit of snooping in Kendall's office for us."
She poured herself a glass of water, stood it on the bar. "She'll come through for us."

"I do hope so, but even if she does, what good's knowing the name of the company going to do? It won't change the fact we need to start looking around for premises to rent."

"No, but it might give us some leverage." But thinking about it, Aidan was spot on. It wouldn't change a thing. "I'll start looking for possible premises." After a short silence, she took a sip of water. "I love it here, for crying out loud. I don't want to move!"

45

"Dare I say it, Francesca? Congratulations! You're pregnant." Dr Bryson smiled, then turned to his computer. "You must both be over the moon. How long's it been now? A year?"

"Two actually. Two years of trying." Francesca looked away from him, not wanting to explain that Paul had left her for a twenty-year-old. The embarrassment was almost too much. "And of course, we are. Now we know for definite, we've got choices to make. Colour of bedroom and things like that."

"I bet Paul is delighted," Dr Bryson added, still facing his monitor. "Well, there's no point arranging an ultrasound yet. Let's book you one in week fourteen, shall we?"

"That'll be great, except-"

"You don't want to know your baby's gender, I get it. Let's book it in. It's routine to check everything's going to plan."

Bryson tapped on his keyboard.

"Can you tell me the due date yet, or do I wait for that?"

"September 30th."

Going back over it, the last time she and Paul had sex was on Christmas Day.

In her bag, her mobile rang. Taking it out, Francesca checked the caller: Mrs Redmond. She almost gasped, wondering why her headteacher was calling her on a Saturday? "I'm so sorry, but I need to take this, Dr Bryson. It's a work thing."

"Oh, don't mention it, we're done here. He handed her a card with an appointment for a few weeks' time. "You go on and enjoy the rest of your weekend. I'm all done now anyway."

"And thank you for seeing me on a Saturday; you don't know how appreciative I am," she said, her thumb hovering over the 'answer' button.

When Dr Bryson waved her away in his old, jovial manner, she walked out of his consulting room into a corridor. "Mrs Redmond, is everything alright? You're calling me on a Saturday morning."

"Good morning, Francesca, don't worry it's nothing bad."

Her headteacher sounded upbeat.

"I'm hoping you might be able to help me with a problem."

With her hand on her chest, Francesca controlled her breathing. "Thank Chr... You for not being something serious. For a minute there I was getting worried. What's up?"

"I'm in a bind, and I was hoping you might get me out of it."

"Okay, she replied, confused. "Shoot. If I can help, I will."

"The restaurant we use for the end of year presentations dropped out. They took a double booking apparently. Anyway-"

"You were hoping I'll ask Kate and Aidan if you can host it there?" She didn't need to be a psychic to work that one out.

"Would you? It'll help get me out of a predicament. Tell them it's an end of year do for twenty children and their parents. Sixty in total, plus about five members of staff."

"I can do that for you, sure, although I need to warn you that Aidan's not big on children coming into the restaurant. Don't get me wrong, we have a children's menu, but he expects them to be well-behaved."

"That won't be an issue; our children are little darlings, aren't they?"

"All I can offer is to try, Mrs Redmond, I'm sorry. He's a stubborn man." She waited for a response from her second boss.

"I know you'll try your best, Fran. You always do."

Hanging up, Francesca thanked the receptionist and headed out to her car.

46

Aidan took the ticket from the printer. He hooked it behind the service counter, so he could figure out what he needed to put on the grill and what he needed to put in the oven. Once the mains were heating up, he would focus on the choice of potatoes required, leaving vegetables until last. He had a huge pan of boiling water for the veg.

It was only half past twelve, and he had twelve meals to cook, split between three tables. If it kept on like this, they might even set a record. He tapped Chef on the back. "Can you put on five portions of chips, please." He mouthed it clearly.

Another ticket came in. "Starters, Chef, do you mind?"
He handed the ticket over, taking the bag of chips from Chef, and weighing out five lots. Then he poured them in the fryer, listening to them hiss as they hit the oil.

He quickly raided the fridges and freezers, placing all the main courses in the oven. Using the red tongs, he slapped three steaks on the grill, along with a chicken breast on a separate grill plate. "Everything's on."

Francesca and Kate entered. "It's official, Aidan, I'm pregnant. Dr Bryson confirmed it. I'm due at the end of September."

Stepping out from behind the line, he went to hug her. "I don't know what I'm supposed to be doing. Is it congratulations?"
He hugged her. "Does Paul know yet?"

"No, and don't you go saying anything to him either."
Francesca walked behind the line and tapped Chef on the shoulder. She pointed at her belly, then signed. "I'm pregnant."

"No, congratulations, Fran, I know how much you wanted this. If there's anything you need, let me know."

"Aw sweet, love." Kate patted his back and smiled.

"Actually, there is something." Francesca came back out from behind the line. "You can help get me out a situation. Before you say no, it's for a good cause."

Aidan braced himself. "What is it, Fran?"

"My new school, Cherry Tree Lodge has an end of year, a sit-down meal and award presentation for the leavers. The normal venue's cancelled on my head teacher-"

"And you want to use my restaurant for forty snotty kids running around the place?" He puffed his chest out, narrowed his eyes, and tried to appear fierce, almost hearing a gasp from Francesca. "Go on, then. Why not? They're deaf, though, right?"

Francesca jumped up and down, excitement taking over. "Oh, thank you so much. And there's only twenty, not forty."
She cuddled him so tight, he didn't know she had that much strength. "Thank you! I thought you would put up a fight."

"They'll be well-behaved, right? I don't want them running all over the place."

"They'll be models of good behaviour; I promise. Plus, they'll be chaperoned by the staff, so you don't need to worry. I'll sort everything out with Kate. Oh, and I'll sort out a pre-order. There's going to be about sixty-five people in total. It's still okay, right?"

Going back behind the line, Aidan opened an oven, sliding out a single dish of shepherd's pie. "The more the merrier. Try and get them to order starters or desserts too, or both even. We can sort out some sort of meal deal for them. I'll leave it with Kate."

"They'll get a discount too?" Francesca's face lit up even more. "Where's the real Aidan?"

"Oi, cheeky," he said with a smile. "Tell your teacher, if it's a success, she can use us every year. You never know, it could be the start of a tradition." Francesca and Kate stood in the doorway; their mouths hung open. "What? Get out of here before I change my mind."

Francesca laughed, then left the kitchen.

Kate stepped up to the service counter. "Thank you! I was expecting to argue with you over this. With that many kids, I was sure you would say no, and given what we found out this morning, I wouldn't blame you either."

"Hey, we'll get through this, we always do. Even if we relocate, Marble's Marvels will survive." He put the hotplate light on and slid the shepherd's pie under it. "Now, though, we need to focus on the business, and we can't throw away a party of sixty-five diners, can we?

47

Elio Capelli smiled as he stacked and picked up three large dirty plates from table twenty-two. "I'll bring you our dessert menu over."

Carrying them through to the kitchen, the first thing he noticed was how many staff he had on. The reason he noticed them: they didn't have enough to do. "Put your phones away, please. You know the rule."

His pot wash, a local lad of seventeen years took the dirty plates from him and dunked them in the water.

Worried about the wage bill eating into his profits, Elio thought about sending one of his chefs' home, or maybe one of his waiters. It was still early lunchtime, and Saturday. He thought better of it. Some Saturdays were slow starters.

Martin, his assistant manager stood staring out of the window. "There must be thirty people in there. I don't know where they're all coming from."

Joining his assistant, Elio watched an elderly couple open Marble's Marvels' front door. He shook his head, knowing word was getting round about their new deaf, mute chef. The rumours were eating into his profits. "I'm going to take a poke around. Do we need anything I can go over and ask for?" He whispered, making sure none of his customers heard him.

"We need some change, for sure. Pound coins and fifties." Martin headed for the till behind the bar.

Elio followed him. "If you give me a hundred, I'll go scrounge some." He took the money in twenty-pound notes, folded them, and put them in his trouser pocket. "I'll see you in a minute. Oh, and if it stays like this, send someone home, please."

He smiled at a couple of customers as he walked back through the dining room. Once out on the street, Elio waited for a couple of cars to pass before he walked across the road, spotting another couple studying the menu in the window. "Afternoon, Mr Jarvis. Mrs Jarvis." He opened the door, holding it for the elderly couple. "Are you coming in?"

Mr Jarvis seemed nervous. "It's fine, if you want to try out Chef's food, you know. I won't hold it against you." He laughed, to put them at ease. "Come on inside. I heard the toad in the hole here is excellent."

Why he was encouraging them to dine at Marble's Marvels even he couldn't say. Elio held the door open long enough for them to saunter in. Mr Jarvis thanked him. "You're welcome!" He was met at the entrance by Kate. "Afternoon."

"Good afternoon, Mr Capelli," Kate said with a slight bow. "What can we do for you this fine afternoon?" She was putting on heirs and graces on purpose.

Elio stood. "Change, if you may, Mrs Marble." Said in his finest Queen's accent. "We are in need of pound coins and fifties, if you please."

Kate dropped her graces. "Course you can." She studied the room. "Fran's okay on the floor. Come up to the office, Elio, I'll see what I can help you with."

Following her upstairs to the tiny office, Elio stood in the doorway, leaning on the frame, while Kate took the long silver key out of her bag, and opened the safe. "Business is certainly picking up, I see."

"Like you wouldn't believe. I tell you, Chef's a Godsend, literally." Kate opened the safe door. Taking out bags of pound coins and fifties, she set them down on the desk. "How much do you need?"

"Say twenty in fifties, and eighty in pounds." He reached into his pocket, pulling out the notes. In his wallet, he had another hundred. "On second thought, make it a hundred and sixty in pounds and forty in fifties?"

"We can accommodate you on that. How're things over the road?"

"Oh, you know, busy, busy." He didn't want her to know how much Marble's Marvels' good fortune had impacted on his business.

Handing him the bags of coins, Kate smiled. "Hey, I was so sorry to hear about your wife leaving. How are you coping?"

"Oh, you know, day by day. She's divorcing me and wants half of everything I worked for. Our solicitors are busy hashing out a deal that we can both live with."

"And that includes the restaurant?" Her eyes were sorrowful.

"She thinks she's owed at least half for putting up with my obsession, as she puts it. So, it looks like I'll have to sell the property soon to pay her share."

"I'm so sorry, Elio." Kate put her hand on his shoulder. "Listen. If there's anything I can do to help, please let me know."

"Thanks, but you have your own problems to deal with, or so I hear." He didn't want to be the only one with dramas. "Rumour has it a new restaurant's opening up here soon. Where are you guys moving to?"

Kate's eyes narrowed. "How do you know about that? We only received the letter this morning. I only got back from visiting the estate agents a little while ago."

Elio put his hands up. "A couple of guys were heard talking about it yesterday afternoon at my place. Martin told me last night. He asked them what was going on, and the chef told him outright that he was opening a restaurant here. I'm sorry! I should've warned you, shouldn't I?"

"Oh? I don't suppose you remember what they look like, do you?" Kate's tone, and narrowed eyes were suspicious.

Shaking his head, Elio swallowed. "No, I'm afraid not. But Martin will know."

"Let's take a walk over to your place, shall we? I want to hear this for myself." She ushered him down the stairs, out of the building and across the road.

Holding the door for Kate, still carrying the pound coins, Elio walked briskly behind the bar, and deposited the bags of coins on the counter. "I'll be with you in a sec, Kate."

With the coins in the till, and the corresponding notes taken out of the drawer, Elio folded them and put them in his pocket. "Let's ask Martin."

He found his assistant talking to the chefs in the kitchen. "Martin, come here, will you?" Elio noticed how apprehensive he seemed. "It's okay, you're not in trouble."

Moving the conversation out back, in the glass wash area, Elio leaned on the silver machine. "Tell Kate what you told me last night, about the new restaurant opening up."

"Yeah, two guys, bold as you like, talked quite loud about opening a restaurant here in November. They didn't hide the fact they were talking about your place, Kate. They seemed to be enjoying it if you ask me."

"And who were they? What did they look like?" Kate stood with her arms folded.

"One of them identified himself as the head chef." Martin's eyes looked skyward, like he was trying to remember. "The other one, the quieter guy, I don't know. He didn't say much at all. They were both good-looking guys. The chef was in his forties, maybe; the taller one, he was in his early to mid-fifties."

"Is there CCTV footage I can take a peek at, Elio?"

"Ah, that's a problem, I'm afraid, Kate." Martin looked down at the floor. "Where they were sat doesn't show up on camera, I'm sorry. It's a black spot, or something."

"A black spot?" Kate turned away from him, her hands-on top of her head. "Just what I need, a chef with a big mouth." She spun round to face Martin. "Were there many locals in the restaurant at the time? Any blabbermouths?"

Elio had to force Martin's hand. "Come on, out with it!"

"The chef guy ended up talking to Mrs Price about it."

Poor Kate! Elio thanked Martin for his candour and walked her back through the dining room. Outside, he told her how sorry he was about her predicament, before leaving her to cross the road. He started off feeling sorry for himself but ended up pitying Kate and Aidan more.

On his way back to the bar, Elio's phone rang in his trouser pocket. When he took it out, he cursed. His wife. Taking himself away from the diners and his staff, he answered it in the safety of his office.

48

"So, this chef's been blabbing about opening his restaurant here to anyone who'll listen," Kate told Aidan, who was busy plating up a table of four. She stood out of the way when Francesca came in and picked up all four plates. She waited all lunch to tell Aidan what happened over the road.

"Mrs Price? He couldn't have picked a worse woman to talk to about it if he tried. Or for his purpose, a better person. This will be halfway across the village by now. I'm surprised the captain hasn't been on the phone." Aidan finished plating up.

"He has, love, I'm sorry. I had to tell him." Shortly after she returned from Elio's, she received the call from Aidan's dad. "He's already talking about us suing the estate agents. You might need to phone him and calm him down."

"Terrific! This is all I need." Aidan snatched the last ticket from the rack. He scrunched the paper up and launched it across the room.

"Take Chef with you to their house. He'll calm the captain down, no problem," she said, half joking. "I knew I would forget why I came in here. I'm taking a couple of meals over to Chris and Amy. Write them in your wastage book, would you? I thought I would take a couple of shepherd's pies."

"No problem take whatever you need," he told her, cursing at splitting his lip again.

Kate opened the fridge, taking out two separate bowls of pies, and placed them on the counter. "You'll lock up, right? I won't be coming back until we open tonight."

"I hope they enjoy it." Aidan said, as she walked out of the kitchen.

"I do, too." With the shepherd's pies in a plastic carrier bag, Kate walked into the dining room, where Francesca was clearing away the second to last table. "You're alright cashing up, yes? I appreciate it, Fran."

"Sure, no bother." Francesca carried four dirty bowls through the swing door.

It took Kate fifteen minutes to reach her car and drive over to Chris Ashcroft's small farm-turned-garage. She pulled up in front of the farmhouse, taking a moment to gather her thoughts. "Hold it together," she told herself, taking a deep breath.

"Kate!" Amy appeared in the doorway. "Come in, please."

Carrying the dishes in the plastic bag, Kate joined Amy in the kitchen. She kissed Amy on both cheeks, as was customary for them. "Here! I brought you both a shepherd's pie each." Looking around, Kate stood by the sink. "Where's your dad?"

"Out in the barn, where else?" Amy took the bowls out of the carrier and placed one in the microwave. "I'll call Dad inside. He hasn't had lunch yet. Thanks for this. We appreciate it. I've heard big things about your new chef, by the way."

"Oh thanks, yeah, he's a bit of a genius in the kitchen." She sat on a chair at the kitchen table, while Amy heated up her dad's food. "How are you doing?"

Taking the shepherd's pie out and giving it a mix, Amy placed it back in the microwave. "I'm fine." Her reply had no heart to it.

"I know how hard this must be for you. Mourning your mum while looking after your dad. You're a brave girl, Amy, but you can't do it all by yourself. I need you to know I'm here for you. And if I'm not in the vicinity, I'm only a phone call away."

"Thanks, I know that. You and Mum were like sisters." Amy took out the bowl using a tea towel, placing it on the table.

Kate waited while Amy went to the front door, yelling at her dad that lunch was ready. She asked herself if she should leave them to it. Before she could reply to her question, Amy came back in. Kate stood and walked over to the sink. She stared out of the window.

Chris emerged from the barn in greasy overalls. He stumbled. "Has your dad been drinking?" Chris stopped, checked no one was watching, and continued towards the house.

Amy joined her at the sink, watching her dad out of the window. "What? No way! He promised me he would stop. Only this morning. I watched him pour his whisky away."

"Ames! Why is Kate's car-" Chris entered the kitchen, stopping when he saw her. "Oh! You're here." He sat at the table, picking up a fork. "What is this?"

"Shepherd's pie." Kate joined him at the table. "Trust me, Chris, you'll love it. Cooked by our new sous chef. Villagers are going nuts for his food."

Kate waited while Chris prodded his food a few times. "Are you going to eat it, or play with it?" She received no reply from him.

"Dad! Eat it!" Amy crossed her arms, hovering over him. "Please? For me?"

"Fine!" Chris scooped a mouthful on to his fork. Popping it into his mouth, he glared up at Amy. "There! Happy now?" He put the fork back on the table, got up and walked out.

Embarrassed for Amy, Kate stood. "Let me talk to him, okay? I'm sure I can get him to eat." She got a nod of approval from Amy, who looked like she needed a good cry. "Leave it to me, honey."

Unsure of how to proceed, Kate left the kitchen, went outside, and walked slowly towards the big old barn that Chris had transformed into a garage. He was working on two cars, it seemed, both of which were on blocks.

Bracing herself for a blazing row, she poked her head inside the barn, to find Chris sat on a chair in front of his desk, a bottle of whisky in his hand. "Knock, knock!"

Chris lurched forwards, hiding the bottle under his desk. He turned in his chair, his eyes narrowing when he saw her. "You? Why are you still here?"

She could hear the slurred words. "I told Edie I would look out for you, and from what I can see, it looks like you need it."

With no warning, Chris got up from his swivel chair, pointing at the door. "Get out! I don't care what you promised Edie. I don't want you on my property, got it?"

He marched over to her, grabbed Kate's shoulders, and whirled her round.

Frogmarching her out to her car, Chris stopped in front of her MG. "Now get in your motor and leave."

Kate took the keys out of her pocket, unlocked the door, and sat in the driver's seat. "I'll be back soon to see how Amy's getting on." He waved her away.

49

The restaurant was half-full by eight o'clock. Kate checked the bookings folder to find that there were still a further three tables to arrive. They were set up, ready to receive their guests. She glanced over at the front doors to find Graham stood waiting to be greeted. "Table ten's ready to be cleared, Fran. I'm showing Graham to his table now."

She felt guilty leaving Amy with Chris earlier, but she couldn't interfere. Kate told Edie she would keep an eye out for them, yet there was not much she could do for her friend's husband and daughter. They were grieving.

Kate greeted Graham and his three friends, all guys in their fifties. "I'm thrilled you could join us tonight. If you'll follow me, I'll show you to your table." She turned and led them through the busy dining room. "Here. If you'll take your seats, I'll leave you with menus for a couple of minutes. Unless you know what drinks you would like to start with?" She reached into her apron for a pad of paper and a pen.

Graham wore mid-blue jeans and a white T shirt, which showed off his tanned arms. The rest of his dinner guests were lovely-looking, too. Having taken their drinks order, Kate walked back to the bar.

"Who are they?" Francesca signalled Graham's table.

Taking a bottle of red down from the racking, Kate started pouring two large glasses. "I know. I was thinking exactly that myself." Being a married woman, she shouldn't be looking, Kate told herself, and yet here she found herself ogling Graham in his tight T shirt. "We need to be professional about this, Fran. They're customers."

"Oh, give me a break," Francesca scoffed. "He's your ex-boyfriend, for Chri...Crying out loud. You know you're allowed to look, Kate. In fact, it's normal."

"Whatever! They're still customers." She continued gathering the drinks until she had a tray with two glasses of red and two pints of lager in the centre. "Here we go!" She lifted it easily, being careful to centre the tray.

Back at Graham's table, Kate placed the drinks in front of their respective owners. Keeping the tray wedged under her arm, she had her pen poised to take their orders. "Or if you need more time, I can come back in a couple of minutes?"

"No, I think you can take our orders now, Kate, thanks." Graham winked at her before taking a sip of his wine. He asked for a steak and ale pie with mash, peas, and sweetcorn.

Kate went around the table taking orders. The fourth guy caught her eye for a second.

"You don't remember me, do you, Kate?" He smiled up at her.

It took an extra five seconds for the coin to drop. "No! No way! It can't be. Stephen Unwin?" After a couple of seconds, she closed her mouth. "I'm so sorry, I shouldn't be so surprised to see you with Graham. Best friends at school. Why wouldn't you be as adults? Wow! Talk about blast from the past."

"It's great to see you again, Kate." Stephen, with his greying hair and trim face, glanced up at her. "I was sorry to hear the tragic news. I was thinking of you."

"Lovely of you to say, Steve, thank you!" It was all she could say, feeling a lump in her throat. She tried swallowing. When she couldn't, she made her excuses and left their table. Graham and the rest of the guests had a go at Stephen for bringing it up.

At the bar, Kate put the order through the till. When she finished, she made sure Francesca and Benjamin were covered on the floor, then walked through to the kitchen, where Aidan and Chef were busy. "That last one to come through was Graham's, okay? I want it to come out perfect. Aidan, do you hear me?"

"Yeah, I hear you."

"What was that? I can't hear if you're going to mumble." Not that she had to hear. "Please, Aidan, make sure it's the best. One of my old school friends is with him. I haven't seen him since I left secondary school. Don't embarrass me."

"We're working on it, Kate, okay? You can see we're slammed. I'll make sure it's the best damned food he's ever eaten, yeah? But please, take this order out to table eight for me." He stared at her with an intensity she had not seen in him for years. "Thank you!"

Taking the four plates out to her expectant diners, Kate placed each plate in front of their recipients. "I hope you enjoy your meals. If you need anything else, please let me or one of my staff know. Thank you!" She bowed, turned, and headed for the bar, where Francesca was pouring a round of drinks. "How's it going?"

"Fine. Fixing eighteen a round of drinks." Francesca unscrewed the top of a bottle of white wine, pouring two large glasses. "How's it going with Graham?"

"What?" She tried not to sound irritable. "Why did you say it like that? He's a friend, okay? You sound as suspicious as Aidan."

"What?" Francesca smiled, winding her up. "I was asking how his table are doing?"

"Yeah, not how it sounded, Fran." She faced the till, made a note of the drinks Francesca poured, and added them to the reservation's tab. "They're added." When the bell rang, Benjamin nodded at her from across the dining room, heading for the kitchen.

Kate loved the bustle of a busy night in the restaurant. With only three tables vacant, and food coming rapidly out of the kitchen, everyone loving their meals, she was happy for the first time since Vinnie's death. And it was all down to Chef.

In the distance, the mayor's wife held up her glass, attracting Kate's attention. Nodding at Harriet Gaines, Kate meandered over to her table, checking on other diners as she went. "Harriet, how is everything?" She stood to the side of the mayor's wife.

"Stunning as always, Kate." Harriet motioned for Kate to come closer. "I'll tell you now, before it becomes public news. Kendall's being investigated for embezzlement."

With a gasp, Kate put her arm around Harriet. "Oh my! How dreadful. I'm so sorry!"

The mayor's wife laughed first, followed by her three lady companions. "Don't be sorry, my dear. I'm not. We're not, are we, ladies? He deserves everything he gets."

"It's so weird, isn't it, girls? We've all either come into luck recently, or our husbands or exes have come into misfortune." One of Harriet's friends glanced at the others in turn. "Kendall's being investigated for embezzling money; my bastard of a husband's yacht sank in Portsmouth harbour. Janine's won a holiday to the Bahamas."

"Yeah, we class this place as our lucky charm now, don't we, ladies?" Harriet raised her glass to her friends for the second time. "To Marble's Marvels!"

Kate waited for the ladies to finish their toast. "Wait! What are you talking about? How can it have anything to do with my restaurant?"

"Relax, Kate, it doesn't." Harriet reassured her. "We were joking."

"It's a coincidence, but all our lives have changed for the better since we started coming here. In the last couple of months Harriet's changed the most. Kendall doesn't control her anymore. I came into a windfall recently, too."

"We've all had good luck," the woman Kate took to be Janine added.

"Your chef's serving up more than just food here, Kate." Harriet held her wine glass up for another round of toasts. "To Chef!"

They all toasted her sous chef. Kate smiled on the surface; inwardly, she was squirming. She didn't think they were too far from the truth, except- "I so wish that were true, Harriet. If everyone had luck on their side, you would think it might extend to us."

Harriet's joyful expression disappeared. "Oh? Why? What's happened, Kate? Tell us! We'll see what we can do to help."

Kate glanced around her, checking there were no eavesdroppers nearby. "You'll know this, being married to the mayor, but we're being evicted. We need to be out of here by the end of September."

"No! That won't do. What happened?" Harriet looked up at her with a mixture of pity and anger.

"You mean you don't know?" The mayor's wife shook her head. "I thought Kendall would have told you. The estate agent who holds the lease for this place on behalf of the owners decided not to renew our lease. Some privately owned company is taking it over and moving a new restaurant in here in November."

The ladies stared at one another, their shocked faces turning angry. "There must be something we can do to help, Harriet," Janine said, to nods from the others.

"I could use your help finding out who it is, if you don't mind?" Kate waited for Harriet to respond. "You couldn't have a spy around Kendall's office, could you?"

"Well, I suppose everything does go through Kendall, and straight into his back pocket." Harriet accepted a round of laughter from her friends. "Kate, I shouldn't laugh. It's no joking matter. Of course, I will try and find out for you. And if I do, I'll poke around some more, see what I can find out about the company owners."

Kate bent over and half-hugged Harriet from behind. "Thank you so much. Any help will be greatly appreciated. And thank you, too, ladies. If you need anything else, let me know, won't you!" She released Harriet, turned, and walked away with a smile.

Back in the kitchen, Francesca was preparing to take Graham's table's food out. Kate stood in front of the counter, tea towels ready to protect her arms from the heat. "You go and bring some dirties in, Fran. I'll handle this!"

"One steak and ale pie, mash, peas and sweetcorn; one gammon steak, eggs, chips and mushy peas; one liver and bacon, mash, peas, carrots and broccoli; and one sausage casserole, with due care and attention."

"Thank you so much, love." She stacked two on her left arm first, then carefully placed the third on her right forearm, and picked up the fourth plate. "Coming through."

Francesca held the door open for her.

Out in the dining room, she had to avoid a diner on his way to the lavatories. Cursing him under her breath while wearing a smile, Kate reached Graham's table. "Here we go!" She placed the steak and ale pe in front of Graham first, before unloading the rest in front of their owners. "Can I get you anything else?"

Stephen asked for a new fork, as he dropped his. Kate took his dirty one and headed for the kitchen. When she arrived at the swing door, Aidan and Chef were staring back at her through the window. She forced her way in. "What's going on?"

"They're watching to see if Graham likes his food." Francesca confessed.

"What? Of course, he'll like it. It smells divine, as usual." Kate grabbed a fork.

"Aidan has a theory, don't you?" Francesca giggled when Aidan waved her away. "He thinks horrible people won't like Chef's food, like the mayor didn't a few weeks ago. And he doesn't think much of Graham, so he thinks your friend will spit the food out."

"I'm not the only one," Aidan said, turning to her. "Chef thinks so, too. The guy's an arsehole, Kate. I'm sorry! I know he's an old flame and all that. You should've seen him in here yesterday lunchtime. Smarmy bastard!"

"Don't be so ridiculous!" She pushed him out of the way. "Just when I thought you were changing; you go and pull this. Maybe my sister was right about you."

"No, but I'm right about this, Kate. He's not what you think he is." Aidan called after her, closing the swing door behind her.

At the table, Kate handed Stephen the fork. She stood next to Graham, waiting for him to try his first mouthful. It was her favourite part. The closing of the eyes, the smile while eating, the pure joy of tastebuds pulsing in the mouth.

Graham put the fork in his mouth, sliding it out, empty, and chewing. He didn't close his eyes; he didn't smile at first. His eyes grew wide, as he frowned.

"Is everything alright, Graham?" She bent over, observing his reaction. "Don't you like it?" Her worst fears were coming true.

Graham nodded, forcing a smile. He put his thumb up. "It's lovely, thanks."

"Oh my God! This is revolting!" Graham's taller friend spat his food into a napkin, making the biggest fuss in front of all her customers. "I've never tasted anything that bad before in my life. What the hell are you trying to do to me here, huh?"

Kate caught diners around them staring. She smiled, embarrassed. "Oh! I'm so sorry! I don't know what's happened. Let me fetch you another." She took Graham's friend's plate, noticing Stephen salivating over his. "How's yours, Steve?"

"Out of this world, believe me."

She caught Graham washing his food down with his drink. He smiled at her, as she left for the kitchen. Once there, she found Aidan and Chef at the door again. "There's no need to be so smug. Graham's enjoying his." She hated lying to him, but she didn't want Aidan thinking he was right.

"Damn it!" Aidan threw a tea towel at the sink. "I was so sure. We both were."

"I don't know what you're talking about. Can I get a new one, please?" Kate set the plate by the sink, about to throw the gammon steak away.

"It won't help." Aidan handed her a fork. "Taste it for yourself. It's succulent, tasty. Cooking this guy a new piece of gammon won't work. Whatever he's given, he'll say it's disgusting, like Kendall did, and we all know what a prize-winning toad he is."

Kate cut herself a piece of the meat, popped it in her mouth. As Aidan predicted, the juices in the meat made her tongue salivate. "Beautiful."

"See? Do you understand now? Graham's mate's a tosser; he doesn't deserve our food." Aidan cut himself a piece of the meat. "I'm sorry, love, but you'll need to refund him. He won't like anything on the menu."

Turning to Chef, she stepped up to him. "What am I supposed to do now? I can't turn him away." Francesca signed her question. "I have to offer him something. There must be something you can do."

Chef shrugged. He started signing to Francesca. *'You don't want to serve horrible people here. This food is for good people, not bad people.'*

Kate put her hands through her hair in frustration. "This is silly, it can't be happening. Cook him a new gammon steak, would you, please?"

"He won't like it, so there's no point." Francesca said for Chef.

"So, you're telling me that the only people we can serve in this village are kind, good-hearted people?" Chef nodded, not apologising. "So, that's half the village gone then."

"Hang on! It doesn't matter, Kate. That guy's leaving, I think. He's arguing with your friend. Yep. He's walked out." Francesca blew out, relieved.

Not knowing what to say, Kate left the kitchen, and strolled back to Graham's table. "I'm so sorry about this, Graham. Is everything okay with your meals?"

Having smoothed them over, Kate's mind kept replaying Graham's reaction to his first mouthful. He hated it. Her ex-boyfriend lied to her, maybe to protect her feelings, but even still, what did it mean? What did it say about him?

50

Francesca stood in front of the till, adding drinks to a tab. With Kate carrying food out to a table, and Benjamin in the kitchen preparing a desserts order, it was up to her to prepare the coffees. The coffee machine sat next to the bar. The bane of her life, making hot beverages was her least liked task.

Moving over to the professional coffee machine, she unscrewed the meal holder, put fresh coffee grounds in it and screwed it back in place. Using a metal jug, she steamed milk, making it frothy before she pushed the latte button on the machine.

When she found she didn't have any teaspoons, Francesca walked to the bar, taking a peek at Kate's friend's table. She stopped, watching Graham spit his food into a napkin. By his face, he didn't like it. "Oh my God! He's faking it!"

Wanting to run in the kitchen and tell Aidan, she still had to make the hot drinks. "Oh bums!" After picking up four teaspoons, she hurried making the drinks, placing them on a tray and carrying it over to table three. "Here we go! Two lattes, one cappuccino, and one Americano. Enjoy." She carried the tray back to the bar.

Kate returned to the bar.

With chatter in the background, Francesca leaned in close to her boss' ear. "Aidan's right about your friend, by the way. That Graham bloke hates the food. I saw him spit it out and put it in his napkin."

"What? No, he didn't." Kate looked over there. "He's loving it."

"Sure, because he knows you're watching. He'll wait until your back's turned, and then he'll spit it out. Wait! Turn around."

Doing as she was told; Kate faced the wine bottles behind the bar.

"I told you! He spat it out." Francesca smiled when Kate whirled round to find Graham with a napkin full of food on his lap. "He's been playing you along this whole time, Kate. The guy's an arsehole, like Aidan said."

"You changed your tune pretty quick." Kate seemed angry. "It was only a while ago you were all but encouraging me to go out with him. Since when were you on Aidan's side anyway? Between you and my sister, I don't know which way to turn."

"Hey! I've never disliked Aidan. He's been through a lot. But this guy; there's something off about him. Seriously, Kate, ditch him as soon as you can."

"I keep telling you, he's a friend!" Kate's angry voice crept in. "You sound like you're suggesting I dump him. What for? Asking how I am?"

Francesca knew when not to push it. "Okay, enough said."

Kate was about to say something to her when the front doors opened. Francesca's mouth hung open when her husband and three members of his band walked in carrying guitars and a set of bongos. "What the-?"

Her husband stepped inside, standing in front of table four, his band members flanking him. He cleared his throat loudly. "Can I have your attention, please?"

"What is all this?" Kate asked from behind Francesca.

Unable to hear her boss, Francesca was too busy adoring Paul in his suit, the same suit he wore to every gig he played. Being a ska band, Paul wore black trousers an inch too short, showing white socks inside shiny black shoes. He had on red suspenders over a crisp white shirt topped with a black blazer. The funny hat crowned the look. "Oh my God!"

"I'm afraid I've been a bad boy. So, I'm here to grovel for forgiveness from my gorgeous, wonderful wife, Fran."
He stared through her. "Baby, this one's for you."

Her husband began singing Elton John's 'Sorry Seems to be the Hardest Word', in a ska tone. Francesca stood glued to the spot, the tables of customers drifting away the longer she stared at her gorgeous husband. He was singing to her, for her.

"Oh no, you don't," Kate said behind her.

While Paul was singing, Kate spun Francesca round. "He cheated on you, Fran. He went with that twenty-year-old, remember? What are you thinking?"

Francesca craned her neck to find Paul still singing for her. "I never could resist him in that suit. Isn't he a dream? What was I thinking not fighting for him?"

"I don't believe you!"

She didn't want to turn away from Paul, leaving Kate stood behind her. The customers were as mesmerised by him as Francesca was. "Plus, he's the father of my baby." Francesca looked around her for Kate. "Rude!"

At the end of the song, Paul stood there, not reacting to the rapturous applause. Francesca made the first move, not blinking, moving towards him.

"Baby, I meant every word. I'm so sorry! I'll spend the rest of my life making it up to you, I promise." He took a couple of steps towards her.

With the diners watching, Francesca could have heard a pin drop. "You're an arsehole." She took a step closer. "But you're my arsehole."

When he went to put his hands on her waist, Francesca pointed at him. "But if you cheat on me ever again, as God and these customers are my witnesses, I'll cut it off, do you understand?"

She received a round of laughter from her customers. "Come here, you!"

Pulling him in for the deepest and longest kiss of their lives, their lips only separated for the need of oxygen. The customers gave them 'aws'.

Francesca pulled his ear close to her mouth. "I was going to tell you soon, but I'm pregnant. And before you ask, it is yours."

She expected a reaction, but nothing like this. He bent down, putting his arms around her bum, picking her up and spinning her around.

"We're having a baby!"

Francesca had never felt this happy before. She was having a baby with her gorgeous husband. It was in complete contrast to how she felt a couple of months earlier. Maybe the rumour about Chef's food was true after all?

FRIDAY,
JULY 19TH

51

"I'm really sorry, Mrs Marble, but it's your credit history. That's your problem. Apart from the increase over the past four months, the last two years is our biggest indicator of the direction your business is going in." The estate agent, a round man with horn-rimmed glasses and a sweaty upper lip leaned forward. "Look, if it were my choice, I'd bet on you guys. I've been to your restaurant, albeit about five years ago, but I had a great time. Unfortunately, it's not up to me. I'm afraid the owner has made his mind up."

Kate glanced over at Aidan; whose deep scowl matched her own. "I would understand your decision if we were looking to mortgage the place, but we're only after a short-term lease for the moment. It can't be this hard to find business premises, surely? We've been to eight other estate agents in the past two months."

Aidan picked up his folder. "Look at last month's takings, damn it! That's the indicator you should be considering, not the past couple of years. Or hell, take the last seventeen years as a whole into account. You know why the past couple of years have been so tough for us, so why are you sweating us about it? We have a terrific chef now. He's amazing."

The estate agent sat back. "And therein lies your problem. You can't expect us to say yes when you're basing your new-found success on one chef. The industry has such a huge turnover of staff, it's ridiculous. What happens when he leaves? The place takes a nose-dive again, that's what. I'm afraid I've said all I'm going to on the matter, Mr Marble."

"Yeah, well, thanks for nothing." Kate stood and stared down at the portly man. "Come on, Aidan. We're not getting anywhere here."

"I am sorry, by the way. I love your food."

Kate walked to the door with her husband. "Yeah, I bet you do," she mumbled.

"Idiot." Aidan opened the door for her.

Checking her watch, Kate saw it was time to get back to the restaurant. They had Cherry Tree Lodge coming for lunch. With sixty-five guests, she'd shut the dining room off to other guests for lunch with a big note on the door apologising for any inconvenience. "You're sure everything's in hand for this afternoon? You have the pre-order sorted?" She closed the door to the estate agents. "This has to go smoothly, Aidan."

Aidan reached their four-by-four in the car park reserved for customers, unlocked it, and regarded her over the roof. "Chef's on it. We have everything covered, love." He opened up and got in. "Come on, get in."

Sitting in the passenger seat, Kate strapped herself in. She didn't bother questioning him, knowing he was on top of it. The Range Rover backed out of the space, turning into Winchester Road. Driving back from Basingstoke, she stared out of her window. "What are we going to do? No one's giving us the time of day. We're near the end of July. We need to be out in little over two months."

"I don't know, honey," Aidan replied, accelerating. "I'm sure something will come up. Chef doesn't seem to be worried, at all. I even told him why we are, and not a sausage. He keeps saying to have faith."

"If only it were that easy."

"Spoken like a true Christian." Aidan grinned at her.

"Hey, I'm a Christian, not an idiot. We can't just expect a divine intervention to give us new premises, can we? And stop taking the mickey. It's just so unfair that they're only looking at our business' recent credit history. That place in town would have been perfect, too. Oh, this is so frustrating."

They drove the rest of the way in silence, Kate not knowing what to say. The past couple of months had been eventful, yet they were no closer to finding out who signed their lease than they were eight weeks earlier. "I can't believe Harriet hasn't found anything incriminating in Kendall's office. This whole thing smacks of a back hander," she said as Aidan pulled into the restaurant car park.

Her husband pulled up the handbrake. "She did say she hasn't been inside his office, though, didn't she? I mean, who's ever heard of a husband locking his wife out of a room? Who does that? It's prehistoric if you ask me."

"Can you imagine the carnage if you tried that with me?" She smiled over at him.

"The chance would be a fine thing." Aidan huffed, opened his door, and got out.

Still on a break from one another, Kate could feel him slipping away from her. She opened her door, sighed, and got out, joining Aidan in walking round to the front door. Keeping behind him, Kate walked inside the restaurant, where Bonnie was putting the finishing touches to Cherry Tree Lodge's leaving presentation event. "It looks lovely, Bonnie. Well done!" She clapped her hands in excitement.

Bonnie, her black eye long gone, handed Kate the post. "Thanks. I thought I'd make an effort. Oh, and this was dropped off an hour ago."

"Bill, bill, special offer." She put the bills on the bar. A white envelope caught her attention. Tearing the top, Kate slid out a single piece of A4 paper out. "What's this?"

At the top of the paper, she read the name of the company: Food and Culture. It was a letter from her favourite industry-related magazine. She frowned, wondering why they were contacting her. Scanning the words, Kate gasped at the name: Gaynor Crane. Her hands started shaking. "Gaynor's coming to our restaurant."

Reading on, she gasped again. "Tomorrow evening."

Panic consumed her. Kate was nauseous. "Oh my! Gaynor Crane's coming tomorrow night. What am I going to do?"

"Wait! Who's Gaynor Crane?" Bonnie tried to stop her hyperventilating.

"Who's Gaynor Crane? Don't you watch Masterchef, or any food programmes on the BBC?" Bonnie shook her head. "She's only the most famous food critic in the country. Her opinions make or break restaurateurs' dreams. A bad review from Gaynor can destroy a business, but on the flip side, a positive one can lift a restaurant into the stratosphere. She's on the BBC, ITV, Sky, you name it."

Bonnie shook her head. "Nope. Can't say I do. I find those kinds of programmes quite boring. But I do like the Great British Bake-off, if that helps?"

"How did I ever give you a job here, Bonnie? You're not even a foodie, are you?" Kate, only half-joking, continued reading the letter. "Apparently someone at the magazine heard about Chef's food. They thought it would be good to send Gaynor over to see if the rumours were true." Their luck could be changing for the better, finally.

Thinking back to a couple of months earlier, Kate recalled Harriet and her friends saying how they'd all received good luck since becoming regulars at her restaurant. Kate poo-pooed it as ludicrous at first, but now, with this, and with Chef being so confident that everything would work out well for them, maybe she'd been too quick to dismiss it.

Reading on, the letter kept on giving. "Oh, my Lord, they're sending a food writer with Gaynor to do a two-page spread on this place as well." She noted Bonnie's lack of enthusiasm. "Food and Culture's the leading industry magazine. Thousands of people will read the piece. This could really put Marble's Marvels on the map again. Honestly, Bonnie, you could try and act a little excited."

"Oh, I am excited, Kate." Bonnie fiddled with the layout of one of the tables. "I'm going to be here for it, remember? I have a table reserved for tomorrow night. I'll be here for it." She stood back and observed her handiwork.

"Oh yeah, I forgot. How is Tate anyway? Has he found a job yet?" Kate hadn't asked after her husband in a while. Bonnie seemed good in herself, after he punched her in the face during a blazing row. Since then, her waitress seemed calmer, more in control. Thinking back, Chef had shaken Tate's hand, too. And he'd smiled broadly. "Has he had any luck on that front?"

"How did you know? We haven't told anyone yet." Bonnie eyed her with suspicion.

"You haven't told anyone what, honey? Has he landed himself a job?"

Bonnie nodded. "Last week he received a call from the CEO of a huge building contractor in London, one of the big six apparently. He's been headhunted. Tate went for an interview on Monday, and he was offered the job last night. He starts on Monday."

"Oh my! That's such wonderful news." Kate hugged Bonnie as tight as she could, pleased for her and Tate. "So, you're here celebrating tomorrow night?"

"I'll say! His salary will be three times what he made at his last place."

What with Harriet and her friends receiving good fortune, Bonnie, and Tate, too, and now this letter, Kate's mind whirred. What if the ladies were right? What if Chef was responsible for this spate of good luck? What did she really know about Chef?

"Aren't you going to show that to Aidan? I'm sure he'd want to know."

Bonnie's question brought her out of her daydream. "Hmm? Oh, right, yeah. I'll go and show him the letter now."

52

"Thanks for giving me a hand, Declan, I appreciate it." Chris bent down and put his fingers underneath the washing machine. With his neighbour on the other side, he counted down from three, then, with effort, lifted it into Declan's pick-up. "You're a good neighbour. And my wife loved you to bits."

"It's not a problem, Chris. Anytime you need a hand around here, let me know."

"Thanks, I might do just that." He walked round to the passenger door, got in and waited for Declan to sit behind the wheel. His head hurt from playing pool last night; well, from the six, or maybe seven pints he drank, more like. Attempting to hide it, and his breath, he stared out of his side window.

Declan started the engine. "Ready?" His neighbour glanced over at him.

"Dad, wait!" Amy appeared from the house. She ran over to his window.

"What is it, honey? We're just on our way to the tip." He tried to point his face away from her. If his daughter caught a whiff of alcohol on his breath, he would be in the doghouse. He switched to vodka recently, instead of whisky, to avoid Amy's wrath. So far, it had worked. "Can't it wait until I'm back?"

Amy passed him a letter through the open window. "A letter came through earlier. Here. I know it's from the bank."

He took the document from her, dropping it in his lap. "Great! Thanks. I'll take a look at it when I get back. Thanks, honey. See you in half an hour or so."

Chris nodded at Declan. "Let's get this over with." He needed help to get the old washing machine up to the tip in Basingstoke, on Wade Road. There was no way he could move the heavy machine by himself. He couldn't very well ask Amy to help.

For the first five minutes, Chris sat next to Declan in silence. He listened to a couple of songs on the radio, when the DJ would put one on, instead of talking. The problem, he found with today's DJs: they loved the sound of their own voices too much.

"How's things in the garage these days? Are you still busy?"

"More than I can handle myself, yeah." He glanced over at his driver. "Why? Are you after work? I thought you were choca yourself?"

"Just curious, Chris. I'm snowed under with orders. Don't forget, a single cabinet can take me a week to finish. Three orders came in yesterday alone."

"Then what are you doing giving me a ride to the dump? You should've told me you were busy. Now I feel like a right arsehole." He wished people would be straight with him, instead of treading on eggshells.

"This is what neighbours are for mate. It's fine. I'm still ahead. Don't worry about it."

Before losing Liam, he could hold a conversation. For the past couple of years, he found it harder and harder, even with a great guy like Declan. Instead of making small talk, Chris stared out of his side window again, hoping his neighbour didn't ask him anything else. All he wanted was to get to the tip, ditch the washing machine, get home.

"Is Amy still talking about leaving uni?" Declan indicated left on Faraday Road to join the roundabout and come off it straight away to enter Wade Road.

"She'll be going back next year," he stressed. "I've already spoken to the university. They're letting her stay in the same year. Fortunately, it's her first year, so she won't have missed too much."

"Ah good! She was talking about dropping out altogether."

Chris turned away; glad he'd thrown Declan off the scent. In truth, he'd not spoken to anyone at Amy's university regarded her studies. Too busy wallowing in self-pity and drowning himself in vodka to take an interest. He vowed to make it up to her when he arrived home. "Here we are. Not as busy as I thought it would be."

He helped Declan locate the domestic appliances zone. After his neighbour pulled into a bay in front of the huge container, Chris got out and pulled the washing machine to the back of the truck. "Again, on three. One, two, three."

The machine was heavy and cumbersome. It took one of the recycle centre's staff to help by opening the gate for them, before they dropped it in the massive skip. Chris wiped his hands on his oily jeans before heading back for the truck. "Thanks again, mate."

On their way back, he stuck on a country radio station, after Declan gave him permission. Sitting back, listening to 'Get Along' by Kenny Chesney, Chris tapped his foot to the music. Country was his only escape route, the only thing that took him out of himself. Friends and family members scoffed, but it didn't matter. He wasn't after their validation.

"That piece of shit!" Declan slowed to a stop in the middle of a residential street on the outskirts of Basingstoke.

Broken from his reverie, Chris frowned. “What’s the matter with you?” He checked to his left and right. They were surrounded by houses, some semi-detached, others terraced. It wasn’t a bad area. “Why’ve we stopped?”

“He’s cheating on her again.” Declan reverse parked in front of a Peugeot, and behind a Citroen Saxo. “After he made that play for her at Marble’s Marvels as well, the lying piece of shit.” He slammed his fists on the steering wheel. “And she fell for it.”

“Who? Who fell for it? What are you talking about?” Looking past Declan, all Chris saw were a couple of houses with three cars outside.

“Fran.” Declan stared over at him, his dark eyes intense. “Her dickhead of a husband’s cheating on her again. She’s having his baby, for crying out loud.”

“How do you know Paul’s here?” Chris couldn’t see any sign of him.

“Check out the numberplate on that Porsche.”

With a nod, Chris understood, and he’d seen Paul driving through Bishops Drake in his personalised Porsche. “Darby1. I always thought he was a bit of an idiot, to be honest. But why are you getting so bent out of shape, unless-”

“Unless what?” Declan shot him a stare.

“Unless you like her. Of course, why didn’t I see it before?” He grinned. “I don’t blame you, mate. Fran’s a looker, but she’s very taken. Come on, let’s go. If he’s in there, he could be hours.” When Declan dug his heels in, Chris folded his arms.

53

Aidan finished slicing the lettuce. He picked up the chopping board and slid the pieces into the stainless-steel pot. While Chef was busy prepping the main courses as much as he could without actually cooking them, he put himself on salad duty. He attracted Chef's attention. "Why are you so excited?"

He didn't need to read sign language. Chef shrugged, while smiling and continuing to place his shepherd's pie into single pots. "Fine. Be weird."

Once the salad bar was filled, Aidan took his knife and chopping board over to the sink, washed them, and placed them in the dishwasher. On the way back to the line, he walked up to the swing door, looking out to the dining room. "No one here yet. Oh, wait."

Three teenagers walked past the door. He thought they looked so young still, but maybe that was his old eyes. This was a leaving ceremony, so they had to be sixteen, if they were taking their GCSEs. "Here they come."

Behind him, Chef placed the covered individual pots of pie in the stand-up fridge. He wandered over to the door and joined Aidan in watching the students arrive with their parents.

'*Do you want to meet them?*' Chef signed.

It amazed Aidan that he could understand Chef's signing. "Meet them? Why?"

Chef pushed open the door without waiting for him.

"Wait! We're not supposed to go outside. We're back of house." Why was he talking to himself? Chef couldn't hear him. Aidan sighed, not wanting to show his face.

He was here to cook the food, not mingle with the diners. Aidan stepped into the dining room, the safety of the kitchen behind him. The guests were arriving en masse, like they'd met outside in a big group. It was a free-for-all.

One of the teenagers' faces lit up when he saw Chef. She rushed over to him, hugging him so tight, Aidan thought Chef's oxygen supply might be affected.

Catching Kate's attention, Aidan shrugged.

He waited for the teenager to relinquish his chef. "Wait! You know her?"

'*We've known each other for a long time.*'

In the distance, he caught sight of Francesca walking in with her students, signing to them as they went. Aidan put his hand up, waving for her attention. "Hey Fran, can you translate for me?" When she nodded, he started.

"How do you know her?" Francesca signed to Chef, then Chef to her.

Aidan could understand certain signs, about a third.

"Chef!"

Aidan turned to find a woman behind him, her shaking hand over her mouth.

"I thought I'd never see you again." She signed at the same time as speaking.

Not needing to be psychic, it was clear to Aidan that the woman knew Chef, intimately. He stood out of the way, as the woman stepped up to Chef, hugging him for dear life. Aidan thought he saw sorrow in Chef's eyes. He knew not to say a word during their reunion.

"Mrs Redmond? How do you know Chef?" Francesca stood next to him, her face as confused as his. "And how do the kids know him?"

Another teenager's face lit up, as he rushed over to Chef, hugging him tight. Aidan's sous chef put his arms around the two teenagers, his smile lighting up the room.

"Why, he used to work in the kitchen at the Lodge. Chef was a valued member of the team." She put her palm on his cheek. "And I thought I'd never see you again. I still can't believe you left me like that."

Mrs Redmond's face crumpled. She turned and rushed in the direction of the toilets, Francesca following her. Chef showed signs of regret.

"Does someone want to explain to me what's going on?" Aidan didn't know what he was a part of, how the kids seemed to know Chef, or anything.

Kate stood next to him. "I think we know where Chef was before we found him, love. He worked in the kitchen at Cherry Tree Lodge."

Still confused, Aidan stared at Chef. "Why didn't you tell us? I've asked about your background on numerous occasions. You could've given Francesca's headmistress as a reference."

"Aidan, it's headteacher now. No one says headmaster or mistress anymore."

Even more teenagers noticed Chef being harassed by their peers. They all rushed over, taking it in turns to hug him. Aidan stood back. Even the parents of the pupils seemed to know him, hugging him, or shaking his hand. They all loved him.

Aidan felt something hold his hand. He glanced down to find Kate's fingers wrapped around his. Looking up, she smiled at him for the first time in weeks. He smiled back, turning his attention to Chef once more. "Are you ready to cook sixty-odd meals now?"

His sous chef nodded, prying the teenagers from him. He pointed at the kitchen door.

Lifting Kate's hand, he kissed her knuckles. "It's time to go to work."

When she smiled again, he left, heading for the door.

Before he reached the door, he felt a tugging at his chef's trousers. Stopping and looking down, a kid with two hearing aids stared up at him. "Hello there," he said, mouthing the words clearly.

The little boy with ginger hair signed his name: Isaac.

"Hi there, Isaac," he replied, signing. "My name is Aidan. I'm your chef. I will be cooking your lunch today. I'm sorry, but I have to leave now. Can we talk later?"

Isaac nodded, smiled, turned, and ran back to his mum, who waved at him.

The morning had been eventful. Not only was he about to cook for what could become their biggest repeat account, Kate had informed him earlier of Gaynor Crane's imminent arrival tomorrow. Added to that his exchange with Kate, he had a lot to be thankful for.

54

"Come off it, Declan, I'm bored out of my brain." Chris stared across at his driver, who in turn stared out of his side window at the front door of the house with the Porsche on the driveway. "He could be hours in there."

"No, he'll be out soon, I know it." His driver twisted the key in the ignition, allowing the radio to come on. "Why don't you listen to the radio for a bit."

"You know, he could be meeting anyone in there. It could be his parents' house, or his sister's. How can you be so sure he's cheating on Fran?" Not that he cared; he only wanted to get back home, where he could listen to his music, instead of whatever station Declan had on. "This is ridiculous, mate. Let's go!"

Declan glared at him. "No one's stopping you. But if you want a lift home, you'll have to wait until I find out who he's with in there."

"Like I said, probably his parents or sister."

"Nope. They all live in Brighton," Declan confessed. "His entire family lives in Sussex. His sister in Lewes, and brother in Chichester."

With a frown, Chris was confused. "How do you know so much about him anyway?"

"From Fran, and being a good listener. She told me how she met this idiot at one of his gigs in Brighton. After his show they went to the same bar, where a mutual friend introduced them, and the rest is history."

"Maybe the sister's moved? Have you ever thought of that?" Agitated, Chris thought about getting out of the car, and walking home. He could phone Amy for a lift, although he had no idea where he was. He didn't have a smartphone. "Fine! You want to stay here and stalk Paul Darby, be my guest. Don't expect me to help you."

He pulled the release handle on the door, as it opened.

"Wait! Here they come. The door's opening." Declan shuffled in his seat excited at the prospect of catching Paul Darby cheating on Francesca.

Chris closed his door, turning his attention to Paul Darby emerging from the house they were spying on. Paul stepped onto the driveway, turned, and met a woman at the door. She had long blonde hair, a slender body, and long shapely legs. He thought she might still be his sister, until she bent down, and kissed Paul on the lips. "Right, I think we've cleared that up. We can leave now."

Opening his door, Declan glanced at Chris briefly, murder in his stare.

"Get back in here, and close that door." Chris yanked Declan back into his seat. Once the door was shut, he let rip at his neighbour. "What were you going to do, huh? Were you going to waltz on over there and beat him up? Don't be daft; you're not in school now."

Declan yanked his way clear of Chris' grasp. "Get off me! He's not going to just get away with cheating on Fran. Not this time, he's not."

In the distance, Chris noted the blonde woman staring at him. She pointed in his direction, as Paul turned and glared at him. "Great! He's seen us now, you idiot. Put your foot down, would you? Let's get out of here."

His neighbour went to step out of the car, but Chris had a better plan. He reached over and switched the engine on. Paul started walking towards Declan's pick-up. "Only bad things will happen from here, mate. Let's go!"

"Oh shit!" Declan put his foot down, releasing the handbrake at the same time, as the truck left the safety of its parking bay. He wound down his window. "You cheating scumbag. Fran deserves so much better than you."

As Paul ran at the car, or more specifically, Declan, Chris turned in his seat. Paul ran after the truck until they were well out of range.

Staring out of the windscreen again, he could have punched Declan for almost getting into a fight. "That was well done, mate. Bravo! What good could have come from that, huh? None. If you'd clobbered that idiot one in the street, what then? The police won't stand for it; they'll have you in the cell before you know what's hit you."

"Hey! I offered to help you this morning, Chris. I didn't ask for a lecture, especially not from an alcoholic burn-out like you. Do you think people can't tell you've been drinking? You stink, and you look like shit."

Shocked at Declan's outburst, Chris' mouth hung open. Normally so placid and unassuming, he couldn't recall ever having had words with his nearest neighbour before. He didn't have anything to come back with. "Why don't you tell me what you really think!"

Declan sighed, hard. "Look, I'm sorry, okay? I didn't mean it to come out like that, but that arsehole shouldn't be allowed to get away with it. He pisses me off! He's got a stunning wife, and yet he treats her like a piece of shit on his shoe. And he's having a baby with her soon, too. What kind of lowlife cheats on his pregnant wife like that?"

"I can't answer that. I never once cheated on Edie. I couldn't live with myself if I did."

"Right! Because you're a good guy, Chris." Declan paused while turning right onto a main road. "I'm sorry about back there. I didn't mean it."

"Bullshit! You meant every word, but it's fine. You're right. I've been a selfish arsehole, drinking and feeling sorry for myself."

"Which you have every right to do. You've just lost your wife."

"I know, but I still have a daughter to take care of, and I haven't been. If anything, Ames has been looking after me. But it stops here. I'm going to knock the booze on the head, you watch. I'm going to be there for Amy now, like a real dad should be."

Declan nodded. "Good. That's good. Music to my ears, mate. If you ever need anything, you know I'm only a phone call away, right? I can be round yours in five minutes, easy." He paused briefly, glancing over at Chris. "I know you don't think it, but you're a good man."

Nothing made him shut up quite like a compliment. Chris sat in silence the rest of the way home. Pulling up outside his house, Declan dropped him off, reminding him that he was only a call away. "Thanks, Dec. I appreciate it."

Carrying the letter into the barn-turned garage, Chris left it on his desk, opening the drawer and taking out his last two bottles of Smirnoff vodka. He went to the sink and unscrewed the caps, tilting them, as the liquid drained away, making gargling noises as it left the glass bottles. "I'm doing this for you, my love," he whispered into the ether.

55

Kate found Francesca comforting Mrs Redmond at the sink. "Hi! I'm really sorry about this, but you're needed outside, Fran. The parents are asking for you." She held the door for Francesca. "I'll look after Mrs Redmond, don't worry. Thanks."

Her waitress nodded her understanding, apologised to Mrs Redmond, and left.

Approaching the headteacher, Kate pretended she needed to wash her hands. Awkward, never knowing what to say in these circumstances, she glanced over at Mrs Redmond. "Your mascara's run, by the way."

Mrs Redmond observed her reflection in the mirror above the sink. "This is silly. I'm a grown woman acting like a lovesick teenager. I'm so sorry for making a scene like that."

"Nonsense. No one thinks you made a scene." She was a better liar than she thought she would be. Her words sounded genuine. "Can I ask how long it's been since you saw Chef?" Keeping the water running, Kate washed her hands still.

"Let's see. We opened the Lodge six years ago. He was with us for two years. Wow! It's been four years, I'd say. Where has that time gone?"

After washing her hands, Kate switched the taps off, walked over to the towel dispenser and wiped her hands on three sheets of paper. "Four years? That is a long time. Can I ask what happened?"

Staring at her through the reflection, Mrs Redmond stood up straight. "He was a Godsend. I mean, a real angel. We had a bad start to the school opening, you see. There were legal wranglings going on in the background, which could have meant we had to close the Lodge down. And then Chef arrived. During his first year with us the Lodge went from strength to strength. The legal barriers lifted, and it was all systems go."

Kate threw the paper towels in the bin. "I'm not sure I understand. You make it sound like Chef's responsible for your legal troubles disappearing."

Suspicion crept into Mrs Redmond's eyes. "Do I? I don't really mean that. Of course, he couldn't be responsible; he's just a chef."

The headteacher seemed to shut down, like she wanted to tell Kate a story, and then decided not to. "Strange things keep happening around here. Since we took Chef on, things have occurred." She wanted to make it intriguing.

Averting her gaze, Francesca's headteacher took out her mascara. "Oh? What kind of things?" She started applying the makeup, like she wasn't interested.

"Luck mainly." Kate wanted to confess all to her. "The odd little things. The regulars here, our diners, I've noticed most have come into good fortune. And the food. Everyone who eats it either thinks it's heavenly, or thinks it tastes like rotting meat. And-"

"And bad people don't like the food, am I right?" With knowing eyes, Mrs Redmond studied her. "So, what do you want to hear from me?"

Kate leaned against a wall. "I suppose I'd like to know more about him. I need to know who he is, where he's been. When he came to us, he said he didn't have any references. And now we learn of Cherry Tree Lodge. You would have given him a reference, right?"

"Not a chance. Not after he deserted us." Mrs Redmond's frown showed Kate all she needed to know. "Not after he left me."

"I'm sorry for asking, and forgive me for being rude, but were you two," she thought about how to ask her question.

"You want to ask if I was sleeping with him, don't you?" Mrs Redmond finished applying her mascara, turned to Kate, and regarded her. "Chef doesn't do intimate, not in that way anyway, but I was as close to it as anyone could get. I fell for him, hard. He broke my heart when he just disappeared from our lives as suddenly as he came into them. I can't tell you how broken the students were when they found out he left us."

"This must be very hard for you, seeing him again. For what it's worth, I'm sorry. I'm sure Chef had a reason for leaving."

"Oh, he did. He doesn't possess a bad bone in his body." Mrs Redmond took out a lipstick, put it on while watching Kate. "I got too close to him, I think. He bolts if he thinks people rely on him too much. That's his modus operandi if you like."

"Really? He doesn't seem the type to just up and leave without word." Kate at least hoped he wasn't.

"Give it time, you'll see. He'll leave you when you least expect it, too. It's what he does. I met one of his previous employers, who warned me that he would leave when he thought everything was on the up."

"On the up? What do you mean by that?"

Pressing her lips together, the headteacher turned to her. "Were you having troubles when Chef arrived?" She waited for a reply. "Financial worries? Anything like that?"

Kate didn't want to admit it. "Yes! Why would you ask that?"

"The previous employer I was talking about was about to fold her company. She had bailiffs practically at her door, until Chef came along. Of course, she didn't know him as Chef; he called himself Rider back then. She owned a horse farm, you see."

"And Chef, or Rider, helped this woman out of her financial crisis?"

"Uh-huh! And then one day, he just upped and walked away without so much as a goodbye, or farewell, just like he did with me and the students. Let me ask you something: are you coming out of your financial crisis?"

Kate neither nodded, nor shook her head. "Kind of, I guess you could say. We've got a food critic coming here tomorrow night with a food journalist writing a piece on the food. If she loves it, this place will be put back on the map again."

"And it will happen, you'll see. Before you know it, your restaurant will be thriving, and Chef will disappear one day. You mark my words."

"It's not that simple, though." Kate examined herself in the mirror. "If we can't find new premises by the thirtieth of September, this place closes, for good." She saw Mrs Redmond's face drop.

"Oh! I see! I'm sorry to hear that." She touched her permed hair. "Well, you do have luck on your side. If Chef's here, he won't let anything bad happen. You have nothing to worry about."

"Are you a religious woman, Mrs Redmond?" Kate wasn't sure why she asked the question. The headteacher's eyes narrowed.

"No, why do you ask?"

"No reason. Don't worry."

Mrs Redmond nodded. "Very well. For a minute there, I thought you were going to ask me if he's an angel." She laughed, hard.

Kate joined in with the laughter, only not with as much conviction. After it subsided, she opened the door to the dining room for Mrs Redmond. "After you. Let's get this show on the road."

She had so much to tell Aidan about Chef. As she strode towards the bar, the restaurant phone rang. Bonnie and Benjamin were busy helping the guests settle in their seats. Francesca was with her students, helping them find their places. Picking up the landline phone, Kate covered her other ear with her free hand. "Hello?"

“Oh great, it’s you. Harriet here, Kate. I tried your mobile just now, but I couldn’t get through. I have some news for you regarding the company taking over your lease.”

Kate gasped. “You found something?”

“Just the name of the company, and the CEO, that’s all,” Harriet replied. “Kendall did know about this all along. I found a file in his desk drawer.”

“How did you get into his office? I thought only he has a key?”

“I had a spare key cut yesterday. He knows nothing about it, the sad little man.” Harriet paused for a moment. “Anyway, here it is the company’s called Winston, Granger and Pope. Apparently, they’re an acquisitions firm, meaning they buy companies, help get them up and running to their highest value, and sell them at a vast profit.”

“Did you say Winston?” Alarm bells rang.

“Yes, the CEO’s a John Winston. The company operates out of California, but they have off-shoots of the company all over the world. Why, does that mean something to you?”

“You could say that.” Anger swelled in her gut, as Harriet went on to tell her the address of the company. John Winston was Graham’s father. She’d met him numerous times when she and Graham were dating in school and college. “Thank you so much for your help, Harriet. You don’t know how much this means to me.”

When she hung up, Kate decided she needed more evidence.

56

Feeling the need for a drink, Chris bashed away beneath a Range Rover. He didn’t think he was so dependent on alcohol. This morning was just the wakeup call he needed, and he had Declan to thank for it. He rolled himself out from under the four-by-four.

“Hey Dad, it’s lunchtime. Come and eat something.” Amy begged him to come with her. “I’ve made your favourite: Lasagne. And there’s garlic bread.”

He wiped his hands on a towel. “Coming, honey. You go on in, I’ll be there in a sec.”

As Amy walked back to the house, Chris threw the towel on his desk chair.

A speeding car tore up the road leading to his and Declan’s farms.

Stepping outside his garage, Chris cursed when a Porsche shot past the turning to his land. “Oh no! Ames, I’ve got to go up to Declan’s for a minute. Keep the food warm, would you! Sorry, honey.” He picked up his truck’s keys, ran to it and got in.

Faster than he thought possible, Chris reversed out of his driveway onto the lane leading to Declan's. "You stupid bastard. I told you not to bait him." He drove far too fast for the narrow lane, almost ditching it twice, until he stopped behind Paul's Porsche, its driver's door open. "Oh shit!"

When he exited his truck, he couldn't see Declan or Paul, but he could hear them. Shouting drifted over from behind the farmhouse. Chris ran past the house, towards the barn out back. "Declan!" He ran at full pace until they came into view.

Francesca's husband had Declan pinned up against the right wall of the barn. Chris could see Declan playing possum. "Paul! Get your hands off him, now!"

Paul kept his fists on the scruff of Declan's shirt, sneering at Chris. "You stay out of this, old man. I don't have anything against you, but you saw this arsehole earlier. He's going to go running to Fran, and I can't have that."

Declan kept his arms out. "You need to get your hands off me, right now." He pushed Paul back, putting his hands on his attacker's and prying them from his shirt.

Chris stepped between the pair. "Back off, mate. I'm warning you!"

Francesca's husband relented, letting go of Declan's shirt finally. "Surprise, surprise! I knew you'd take his side. It's always the same with these shitty little villages. Locals stick together, is that it?"

"I think you have me wrong. You're the arsehole here, not Declan."

He sneered at Paul. "Get back in that poser's motor and piss off, yeah?"

"And let this guy grass on me? You've got to be kidding! I'm not going anywhere." Paul folded his arms.

"I'm no grass," Declan objected. "How you treat your wife is none of my business, but I'll tell you this much, she deserves a lot better than you. Plus, she's having your baby. Doesn't that mean anything to you?"

"I don't need to explain myself to you. You've been sniffing around my missus since you came back. Do you think I haven't noticed?"

"I don't know what you're talking about. I've hardly seen her since I got back."

Chris pushed Paul. "Just go, would you! You're not welcome here. Dec's said he won't say anything, but he's right, you do need to start treating Fran better. If you don't, I'll come after you, do you hear me?"

"Oh, like I'm scared of the resident bum. What're you going to do, breathe over me?"

When Chris started walking towards Francesca's husband, Paul turned and walked away. He strutted in the direction of his Porsche, stopping, and turning back. "If you say a word to Fran, I'll come back here with the lads, *do you hear me*?" He got in his car, revved the engine in a show of bravado, reversed out and drove away.

"Hey, thanks for the backup, I appreciate it." Declan put his hand on Chris' shoulder.

"You're welcome." Chris opened his Range Rover's door. "I doubt you'd have needed my help, but I thought I'd give it. If you get any trouble from him again, I'm never far away."

56

"Let's see you wiggle your way out of this one." Kate stared at Graham's house in the suburbs of Basingstoke. It wasn't anything to look at, a semi-detached home with a square front lawn surrounded by a little white fence.

When she first started talking to him, he told her that he was only staying in the UK for a short time, helping a friend out with his business. What he hadn't told her was that the guy he agreed to help was the chef she was going to show around the restaurant.

Clenching her fists at the thought of the two of them laughing behind her back, the thought of Graham getting all friendly all the while knowing he was whipping the rug out from under her feet made her open the door of her MG. "What excuse can you possibly have?" She closed the door, anger bubbling inside her.

After waiting for a car to drive past, Kate walked across the street, her eyes fixed on Graham's white PVC door. Tense, her hands still clenched into fists, she strolled along the driveway, up to his door. "You'd better be in." She used the knocker.

It took a minute for Graham to open up for her. "Oh hi, Kate. This is unexpected. Come in, please. You'll have to excuse the mess; I'm no cleaner."

Kate smiled as sweetly as she could given the circumstances, stepping inside, and waiting for him to show her to the living room.

He offered her a drink, asking if she wanted a tea or coffee.

With a shake of her head, she signalled her wants.

"Is something wrong? You seem tense."

With her fists clenched, Kate stepped up to him. "Winston, Granger and Pope."

Graham swallowed, clearly worried. "Where did you hear that name?"

"Do you have something to confess, Graham? Huh?" A red mist shrouded her peripheral vision. All she could see was his treacherous face.

Before she realised it, her fists had unclenched, and the palm of her hand slapped his face so hard, Graham's head snapped sideways. "Tell me why you did it! Why come after my restaurant?"

"I didn't." Graham rubbed his cheek. "You started the ball rolling when you set up a viewing with the chef. You knew he was looking at your premises; you invited him to take a look around. And when you bumped him off, he went and put in an offer on your future lease. This is all your doing, Kate, not mine."

"So, why get involved yourself? You know me, we have a history. Why make a play if you know you're going to be destroying my restaurant?" She wanted to slap him again. "You'd better come clean, or so help me God, I'm going to keep slapping you."

"I run the restaurant division of the company, okay? When the chef came to me with this, and I saw your name crop up, I knew I had to see you again." He stepped towards her. "I wanted to see what you'd made of your life, Kate. I heard rumours that you'd fallen on hard times, and I was trying to find a way to help you."

"Help me? And you decided the best way is to destroy my place? Where does that kind of logic come from?"

"You were going to fold anyway, let's be honest," Graham replied. "I had my people look into Marble's Marvels. And up until a few months ago, you had hardly anyone visiting your restaurant."

Kate stepped back. "Sure, up until a few months ago, you're right, but we're on the up now. Chef has our customers coming back again and again. That's what my restaurant needs, repeat custom. Our finances are on the up, and we're turning over a profit."

"You can't expect one man to turn your fortunes around, Kate, be serious. What will happen when Chef leaves? Your place will hit the shitter again, Aidan will see to that. From what I hear, he's not exactly flavour of the month in Bishops Drake."

Graham talking about her husband? She poked her finger at him. "Don't you talk about Aidan. He's twice the man you'll ever be, you treacherous little snake. When Chef leaves, Aidan will be more than capable of keeping his kitchen in order."

"Yeah, right, it still doesn't alter the fact that you're going out of business, does it?"

"Not if tomorrow night goes smoothly. If we impress Gaynor Crane, she'll raise our profile ten-fold. The phone won't stop ringing for reservations after the magazine prints their double-page spread about us." As she shouted those words at him, she regretted it.

"Magazine? What magazine?" Graham stood in front of her, stunned.

"Food and Culture. Gaynor's a world-renowned food critic, and she's heard lots of rave reviews about Marble's Marvels. If we get a good recommendation from Gaynor, we're laughing. So, you can take your 'help' and shove it."

A long pause stood between them.

Graham glared at her. "It doesn't change a thing. You've still got to find new premises, Kate, and from what I hear, no one wants to touch you with a barge pole. Who can blame them? You've run your restaurant into the ground."

She'd said too much already. In the space of a morning, she went from considering Graham a friend, to hating him. "I can't believe you've done this to me. Doesn't our history mean anything to you? You were my first real love. What happened to you?"

Having had enough, Kate turned and marched out of the living room, through the hallway to the front door. Graham followed her.

"Kate, don't go like this, please." He went to grab her arm.

Feeling his touch, she whipped her arm away. "Don't touch me!"

"Don't be a fool, Kate. You don't want to make an enemy out of me."

She stopped walking, her back to him. Turning slowly, she couldn't believe the nerve of this guy she once knew. "It's a bit late for that, Graham. I tell you what, you go ahead and open your little restaurant. I'm going to make it my mission in life to destroy it, do you hear me? Your chef doesn't have a history in Bishops Drake. He won't last five minutes."

Graham scoffed. "Good luck finding an estate agent who'll take you, Kate."

"Arsehole!" Kate walked over the road, to her MG. She hated swearing, and seldom couldn't find a better way of expressing herself. There were plenty of other expletives she could have used, but 'arsehole' felt apt.

57

By nine o'clock, Elio knew he wouldn't be having a busy night. His eight reservations were already seated, with most on their main courses. They'd had half a dozen walk-ins as well, yet it wasn't enough to half-fill the restaurant. There were too many staff on.

"They're really busy over the road." Martin took a bottle of red down from the rack for table fifteen. He poured two large glasses. "We've got to do something about it, Elio, they're killing us here."

Standing behind the bar, next to his assistant, Elio nodded. "Yeah, I know, but what? They've found an excellent chef. What can we do?" He liked Kate and Aidan, especially Kate. He didn't want to do anything underhanded.

"What about the chef?" Martin whispered in his ear. "He's foreign, right? Has he got the right to even be here?"

"Are you suggesting we shop him to immigration?" Elio liked the sound of Martin's plan, except it was shady, deplorable behaviour. "No! We can't do that. I won't stoop so low, Martin. We need to fight fair, or we give up."

"In case you haven't noticed, we can't compete with them." Taking the tray of drinks over to the table, Martin walked back and stood beside him. "We sell pre-cooked food, Elio. We can't compete with their homecooked fare, so we need to find another way."

"And your way would see us snitching on their chef?" It left a bad taste in his mouth. "No! That's not how we're going to handle it. Go and clear table twelve, would you."

Having chastised his assistant for trying to help him, Elio, guilt laden, started clearing table six of their starter plates. Martin was only trying to help. He was right about one thing: he had to do something to limit the damage Marble's Marvels were causing.

Across the road, another group of eight entered Kate and Aidan's establishment.

With plates in hand, Elio walked to the kitchen.

58

"I'm off up to bed." Francesca used her elbows to hoist herself from the couch. Then she got to her feet, her belly more rounded than it had ever been. "Are you coming? Or are you stopping down for a bit? I know it's early."

Since they reunited in Marble's Marvels, Paul had been so attentive, their relationship was solid again. Even back in the early days he'd not been this loving. She held her hand out for him. "Come on. I'll make it worth your while."

Paul didn't need asking twice; he took her hand and walked upstairs with her. On the landing, he went to the bedroom while Francesca went to the bathroom, preening herself.

Her husband stood in the doorway. "When we broke up, did you get together with Declan?" He waited for an explanation.

Spitting out toothpaste, Francesca frowned. "What? No! Of course we didn't. Why would you ask that? We're just friends, Paul. He's like a brother."

"Oh! It's just that everywhere I go I see him, like he's watching me or something." He stepped inside, took his toothbrush out of the cup and applied paste.

"I'm sure you're just being paranoid. This is a village; you're bound to bump into him from time to time." She replaced her brush. "Did you think we were together then?"

He couldn't answer with his mouth full of paste. He spat it out after a minute, rinsing his brush under the water. "No, not really. I knew he was after you, though. He has been for ages. Since he came back, he's been following you around."

"Really?" She asked while drying her face on a towel. "You never said anything about him before. Why the sudden interest in Declan now?"

Paul seemed surprised by her question. "Because I don't trust the guy. I know you think he's a friend of yours, and I wouldn't ask you to choose me over a friend-"

"So don't!" Her voice came out stern, strong. "Look, we're good at the moment. Let us not spoil it by giving each other ultimatums. And besides, you're in no position to go making demands on me, okay? You have making up to do. I'm still smarting about Tegan, you know." She noticed the bravado drop from his expression.

He stepped up to her, lifted her top and dropped it on the bathroom floor, leaving her in just her bra and jeans. "Let me start making it up to you now." He unclipped her bra and took it off, staring at her, devouring her. "You're so sexy pregnant."

And she felt it. Francesca took his hand, following his lead as they went to the bedroom. Paul enticed her onto their bed, patting the duvet. When comfortable, she felt his strong hand over her belly, and between her legs, as she gasped.

59

"Can you believe it? Gaynor Crane, no less, over at Marble's Marvels tomorrow night."

Elio paused for a moment. He hovered between the two gentlemen dining. Had he heard that correct? "I'm so sorry, forgive me for eavesdropping, but did you just say Gaynor Crane's eating over the road tomorrow night?"

The taller of the two gentlemen eyed him with suspicion. "So I heard, yeah. Apparently, some magazine's doing a piece on the restaurant. Not that I know why, it'll be gone in a couple of months anyway."

"The Gaynor Crane? You mean the food critic? She's coming to Bishops Drake?" Elio had a hard time processing the information.

Dark haired gentleman nodded. "Uh-huh! Apparently so. Are you okay, buddy? You look pale. Do you want a drink of water, or something?"

Without replying, Elio walked back to the safety of his bar, where he could breathe deep, and prevent himself from hyperventilating. He found the only chair and sat on it, his elbows on his knees. This could be a total disaster, he thought.

"Elio, are you alright?" Martin put his hand on his back. "Can I get you anything?"

"It's over, Martin. They've won. Kate and Aidan have won." He put his hands over his face, imagining life without his restaurant. His assistant fussed around him. "Don't you get it? It's over. When Gaynor Crane starts raving about a place, they get sent to the stratosphere. What do you think happens to us when everyone wants to eat over there? We go bust, that's what. I don't believe it! How did this happen? We were doing so well."

Confusion etched in his furrowed brow; Martin shook his head. "What do you mean? I don't understand. Who's Gaynor Crane? Why are you so upset?"

Rolling his eyes, Elio glared up at his number two. "The food critic, for crying out loud. Keep up, will you! Those two chaps on table sixteen told me just now."

"Wait! Those two?" Martin pointed. "That shorter one's the chef taking over their lease. I don't know who the taller bloke is, but he came in with him the night they told us who the chef was. Don't you remember? Oh, no, you weren't here that night."

Elio stood from his seat, staring at his guests deep in conversation. There were only four tables left. "That can't be a coincidence, can it?" What were they playing at? He chided himself for getting worked up, although the demands his wife had given his solicitor only added to the weight he was carrying. "Let's find out what their deal is."

The other three tables were dotted around the dining room, away from table sixteen.

The pair of diners didn't look up at him at first, continuing their discussion, until he lingered. Elio regarded the chef first, followed by the taller, better-looking diner.

"Can I help you?" The taller one said.

"My assistant tells me you're the chef opening a restaurant across the road in a couple of months. Is this true?" He focused on the chef.

"Yeah, so? You're not going to kick us out, are you?"

"Of course not. I was just wondering why you'd tell me about the food critic visiting Marble's Marvels?" He stared at chef first, then taller guy.

"As it happens, we didn't tell you anything. You overheard us talking and apologised for eavesdropping, remember?" The chef's smirk screamed smug.

He could have hit himself for being so stupid. Elio nodded. "Oh! Right."

"But while we're on the subject, it can only be a bad thing for this place, right?" The taller guy pulled one of the chairs out, patted it. "Join us for a bit, won't you?"

Feeling like he was being tempted by the devil, Elio sat reluctantly. "Martin, look after the other tables, please." He received a nod from his assistant, turning his attention to his guests. "I'm listening."

Chef leaned forwards. "Seems to me that it will be in all our best interests if the new chef over there disappeared for the day. What do you say?"

Elio agreed. "It would. How do you imagine you would get him away from the restaurant? Martin was talking about shopping him to immigration, but I'm not doing anything underhanded." What was he doing? Why was even talking to these unscrupulous people? "On second thoughts, I don't think I will sit down."

When he stood, both diners grinned up at him. "Kate and Aidan might be my competition, but they're also friends. I won't do anything that hurts them."

"They're hurting you, right now."

Instead of giving into chef's assessment, Elio walked away. He went behind the bar, helped pay off the remaining guests' bills, including table sixteen's, and took the till drawer upstairs to the office. He left Martin and the two other waiters to tidy up.

While cashing up, he thought about what they said. If they could get Chef away from Aidan's kitchen, throw Aidan off kilter, they might destroy Marble's Marvels' chances of impressing Gaynor. Counting the takings depressed him. He was down by sixty percent on this time last year.

In the CCTV monitor Elio caught Martin talking to the guys on table sixteen. He shrugged, opened the safe door, and slid the till drawer inside. After locking the safe, he wandered back down to the dining room, where Martin suspiciously balked from table sixteen, like he was doing something forbidden.

The two diners, the last to leave, put their jackets on, and said goodbye. Elio followed them to the front door, waited for them to step out into the night, and closed it, turning the sign from 'Open' to 'Closed' in the window. "What are you up to?"

Martin shrugged. "Nothing. We were just talking."

With a knowing smile, Elio carried table sixteen's coffee cups to the kitchen, where his chefs were preparing to go. Leaving the cups in the sink, he walked back into the restaurant to find Martin leaning against the bar on his mobile. "Are you all done?"

The waiters nodded, said cheerio, and left. He shook Martin's hand. "I don't know what you were talking to those guys about, but they're bad news, I can tell. Please stay away from them. I don't want you getting into trouble, okay? Promise me?"

"I promise. And they weren't talking about anything bad, Elio, honest."

He wished he could believe his second in command.

SATURDAY, JULY 20TH

60

Aidan sat in his Range Rover outside the home of Wyatt Newall, the only survivor of the crash. Being wheelchair bound, Wyatt's home had been adapted to accommodation his disabilities, with a ramp leading up to his front door.

Across the road, Wyatt's father left his house, closing the front door, before getting in his BMW and driving away, seemingly oblivious to Aidan's presence.

Sitting up straight, Aidan opened his door and got out. With his only barrier gone, Aidan felt confident Mrs Newall would let him see her son.

He regretted the fight he'd had with Mr Newall after Wyatt came out of his coma telling everyone Vinnie swerved into Liam. At the time, Liam's blood alcohol content had only just been released; the thought that his son had caused the crash seemed unfathomable.

By his watch, Aidan had little over an hour to kill before he had to be at the restaurant for what was arguably the most important day of his life. They had the biggest VIP dining with them they'd ever had. Chef was on hand to see that everything went smoothly. He only hoped Gaynor Crane was a good person, or Kate's dream of a positive spread in Food and Culture magazine would be short-lived.

The walk across the road seemed to take forever, the dread from his inevitable conversation with Wyatt filling his boots. When he reached the front door, he paused before ringing the bell. Someone was in; he could hear movement.

Mrs Newall opened the door a crack. "Oh! It's you. I can't say I'm surprised." She opened up, standing to the side in her dressing gown and slippers, her dark hair tied back in a ponytail. "I guess you're ready to listen now. You'd better come inside; I've just put the kettle on."

Having a newly disabled son had taken its toll on her. Aidan thought she seemed tired by the bags under her eyes, and the exhausted way she walked him through to the lounge.

"Wait here while I go and talk to Wyatt. I'm not sure if he'll want to talk to you."

Sitting on the left cushion, Aidan leaned on the arm of the settee. Was he doing the right thing coming here? Was he ready to listen to Wyatt's side? He couldn't hear the words, but he heard Mrs Newall's voice in the distance. Why was he even here?

Footsteps preceded Mrs Newall entering. "He says he's up for visitors. I'll show you to his room." She glared at him. "But if you upset him in any way-"

"Relax! I'm not here to cause him any pain, I promise. I'm just after some answers."

Folding her arms, Mrs Newall nodded. "You know the truth already. The question is: are you ready to accept it?" She turned and walked into the hall.

Aidan didn't know if he was ready. Getting up, he followed her along the hall to the second room on the right. A small sign hung on the door: 'Wyatt's Room'.

Mrs Newall opened the door and stood aside to let him through. "I'll be right outside until you're done. If you put a foot wrong with my son, you're out of here so fast-"

"I get the picture." He couldn't blame her for being protective after the fight he'd had with her husband. They both landed a couple of blows before they were pulled apart from one another in the Kings Head.

Wyatt Newall sat in his wheelchair, his thin, withered legs on display. Mrs Newall had dressed him in khaki shorts, a white vest top that showed off his bulging biceps, and a black baseball cap.

In addition to his physical disabilities, Aidan had heard about Wyatt's mental state as well. Prone to nightmares, Wyatt underwent years of therapy to overcome his fears.

His son's friend sat in front of a computer on his desk. Wyatt didn't turn to greet him, or even say anything. He tapped away on his mouse, playing a game.

"I don't know if you remember me, Wyatt, but I'm Vinnie's dad, Aidan." His host carried on tapping the mouse. "I'm sorry it's taken so long to come. I don't think I was ready to hear your story until now. All this time I was sure Liam killed Vinnie and the others."

There was a long pause. Wyatt stopped tapping.

"Why now?" He stared at the wall in front of him.

"I don't know. I've been doing a lot of soul-searching recently, I guess. I need to know what happened. Please, Wyatt, tell me. Take me back to that evening in the car."

Wyatt turned himself round. Facing Aidan, he stared at him. "I don't like going back there. It's too painful, Mr Marble. I knew them all, Vin, Liam, all four of them."

"Please, Wyatt. I wouldn't ask if I didn't need to hear it." He didn't want to hear it, believing he knew what would come. He heard it often enough from the likes of Chris Ashcroft, and his buddies.

In his wheelchair, Wyatt nodded. "How can I refuse that?" With his eyes closed, head tilted back slightly, Wyatt started. "He was agitated before I even got in the car." Wyatt shuddered, like he was having a seizure. "Vinnie yelled at me to hurry up, to get in. I could tell something happened. When I got in, he took off. I remember feeling pinned to the back seat. He scared me, his driving was so aggressive I put my seatbelt on, which I didn't normally do in the back."

"What was he agitated about?" Aidan didn't want to hear the answer.

"He said he had a row with you about him leaving university and going travelling."

His worst fears were confirmed. With his head down, Aidan listened.

"He kept taking his eyes off the road, turning to look at me when I disagreed with him. I told him I thought he should finish uni, then take time out to travel. So did Yosef. We both did. He wouldn't have any of it; he was so angry. And the angrier he got, the more aggressive his driving became. And he kept turning to look at me. 'Keep your eyes on the road,' I kept telling him. Yosef had to put his hand on the steering wheel."

How could Vinnie have done this? His son had a temper on him; he knew, had been on the receiving end a number of times, but his son was a good boy. "Go on!" He kept his head down, not looking at Wyatt. "What happened next."

"Vinnie had a go at me, saying he knew how to drive. But he wouldn't turn back, kept looking away from the windscreen. The more I protested, the more he did the opposite. And that's when I saw it, the car approaching, and it felt like we were steering towards it. By the time I warned Vin and Yosef, it was too late."

Aidan stared at Wyatt, who sat in his wheelchair, his closed eyes darting left and right, like he was observing the scene in his head. "Wait! You don't have to-"

"Shh! Wait!" Wyatt put his hand up. "Vinnie hit the corner of Liam's car. The sound, the noise, it deafened me, as we went into a mad spin. I remember thinking 'this is it'. I mean physically thinking those exact words. And then we hit the tree. The only thing I remember about it was feeling my legs caught under the back seat. The front of the car came in and caught Vinnie and Yosef. They were both awake, crying, when I came round."

"The next half an hour is still a blur, but I can recall sparks flying everywhere. I could hear the saws going. I tried to comfort

Vinnie and Yosef, but after a time their sobs stopped. Vin's body went limp in the driver's seat. A short time after, so did Yosef's."

Tears raced down Aidan's cheeks, hearing his son's final minutes recounted. While Vinnie was being cut out of the car, he and Kate were having a record-breaking shift. "And all this time I blamed Liam for being over the limit."

"I'm sorry! If I could give you better news I would. I don't like telling you these things. He was always a hot-head, Vinnie. He should never have driven in that kind of mood." He paused for a second or two. "I know you blame yourself, but you shouldn't. Vinnie was a grown adult. You had nothing to do with the crash, Mr Marble."

Hearing enough, Aidan wiped his eyes, swallowed hard and rose. "Thank you for being honest with me, Wyatt, I appreciate it." His voice strained; Aidan cleared his throat. "I'm so sorry this happened to you. I'm going to make it up to you, I promise."

Before Wyatt could object, Aidan stepped into the hallway, where Mrs Newall stood waiting. "I'm sorry! I didn't know. I'll make it up to him, to you, to all of you."

Back in his Range Rover, Aidan drove slowly to Chris Ashworth's property. Sat at the entrance to Chris' driveway, he pondered whether to go in or not. After five minutes, he put the four-by-four in gear and accelerated further along the narrow country lane, towards Declan's. He found a suitable place to turn. He wasn't ready to confront Chris, yet.

61

Francesca had barely slept. Being seven months pregnant had its drawbacks. She found it hard rolling out of bed each morning, needing help from Paul, who was there for her when needed, especially getting in and out of the bath.

Drawbacks mentioned, she enjoyed being pregnant, apart from the morning sickness.

Everyone said how radiant she was, positively glowing, most said.

Wearing her specially made waitressing dress, she got to her feet, her back aching. Her hands seemed to be permanently placed there.

A loud bang made her jump, like something had hit her front window.

Curious, she waddled up to the bedroom window.

A blonde woman stood facing the house, at the end of her drive. Behind the blonde was a black car. Francesca didn't recognise the woman.

Francesca frowned when Paul appeared on her driveway, walking towards the woman, who stepped up to him. She watched as they argued. The woman hitting him. Paul's demeanour worried her. Her husband knew the woman. "Not again! How could I be so stupid?" Anger rose through her belly.

Her husband kept pointing at her house while yelling at the blonde woman. When Francesca opened the small window, he stopped shouting and the woman slapped his face. She jumped in her car, revved the engine, and drove away. "Let's see what you have to say for yourself, shall we?"

Marching downstairs, or rather waddling, Francesca met Paul on the porch. Her first instinct seemed accurate. "Who was that honey?" She studied the lawn. A piece of a brick lay on the grass. "Did that woman throw a brick at my house?"

Paul held her shoulders. "That was no one important, okay? You don't need to worry about her. You won't be seeing her again."

"So? Who is she? Your latest bimbo, I presume?" She glared at him, daring him to lie to her. "How could you! I'm carrying your child, for crying out loud."

"It's not what you think, Fran, I promise." He held her stare. "She's an ex. She came back to ask me to come back with her, but I told her to leave. I told her I'm with you now and I'm about to become a dad. Please, Fran, it's ovcr."

"Even now, with everything that's happened, you're still trying to con me." She turned to walk back in the house, shutting him away from her life, when he grabbed her and span her round to him. "Hey!"

"You're it for me, honey, don't you see that?" He pulled her close. "You're the one I want to be with, not her. I was with that woman for a short time after Tegan and she wants me back, but she won't be bothering us again. I've made sure of it. Let's go back in, you can get ready for work."

Shrugging him off, Francesca turned and waddled back inside, the early morning clouds burning up, leaving the promise of a gorgeous, cloudless sky.

He followed her, trying to talk her round. The problem she had with Paul: his arguments were almost always convincing. That woman might be a nutter, stalking him. Or, and this was more likely, he was still sleeping with blondie, and the poor woman wanted him.

Francesca was under no illusion. "Do whatever you want, Paul, okay? I've had enough of your lying and cheating."

In the hallway, Paul pulled her into him for a second time. "I promise I'm telling the truth, Fran. She's old news. You won't see her here ever again. And if you do, then you have my permission to dump me. I'll dump myself even."

Always convincing. Forging ahead, Francesca walked into the kitchen. She had an hour to get ready for work. She wouldn't miss Kate and Aidan's big day. Later, she thought, she might be serving Gaynor Crane, famed food critic and podcaster.

"Why don't you call in sick today? Look at you! You should be on maternity leave. I hate the thought of you serving people like this."

Spinning round, she pointed at him. "You don't get to tell me what to do, or how to do it, ever again. This is my life; I decide what I do, not you."

62

"Please tell me everything's in order." Kate tried to get Aidan's attention. "Today has to be perfect, honey. Perfect! Are you listening to me?"

"Yes! Perfect, I heard you." He continued chopping the cucumber without looking up at her. "If you would stop flapping for one second, we'll be ready on time. Go out to the dining room, check the tables are set-up properly. You're making me nervous."

Gaynor Crane wasn't due until the evening. That didn't stop her nerves jangling. They had almost a full house for lunch, with only three tables vacant for walk-ins. Since arriving at nine, the phone had not stopped ringing. She'd taken ten bookings for the evening's service, making sure she left table twenty free for their special guest.

Leaving Aidan and Chef to it, Kate walked out to the restaurant, where Francesca, Bonnie and Benjamin were rushing around, putting the finishing touches to the reserved tables. "Looks fabulous, peeps." She checked each placing had starter, main and dessert cutlery, a wine glass and salt and pepper holders.

Francesca seemed quieter than usual. "Fran, come over to the bar, please." When her waitress joined her, she studied her. "Are you sure you're up for this? There's going to be a lot of rushing about this afternoon. Say now if you don't feel up to it."

"I'm fine, Kate, really." Francesca leaned on the bar.

"Then why the face? Is there something wrong?" She could tell not all was right by her face. Francesca was one of the happiest, most up-beat people she knew.

"Don't mind me; it's Paul. He's being a dick again. I'll pick it up later, you'll see. The customers won't see it."

"Do you want to talk about it?" She poured both of them a glass of water. "Here."

Kate listened to Francesca's tale from earlier, her blood boiling. "Honey, I'm so sorry." There was only one thing to do, play devil's advocate. "Is it possible he's telling the truth? Maybe she is old news?"

"I don't know. Maybe." Francesca shrugged. "Anyway, enough about my stupid love life. Are you excited about tonight? I can't wait to meet her. I started watching episodes of her BBC One programme back-to-back last night. She's really funny. Stern, but funny."

"I wouldn't say excited, as such." Kate took a sip of her water. "I'm petrified. What if she doesn't like the food? What then?"

"Chef's food? Don't be daft. She'll love it."

"Yeah, but what if..." Kate drifted, thinking back to Kendall Gaines.

"What if what?" Francesca waited.

"What if it's like the mayor? What if she hates it? This place is done for if she does."

"Honestly, Kate, I don't think you have to worry about it." She leaned over the bar as far as her belly would allow and whispered, "She's a good person. Relax!"

"You know about that? You believe it.

"Mrs Redmond told me some stories about Chef you wouldn't believe. There's something magical about him. He wouldn't leave you high and dry, Kate, trust me on this."

"I do hope you're right." Picking up her glass, Kate noted her hands shaking. By the clock on the wall, they still had half an hour until opening. She left the bar, walking to the kitchen, where she spotted a full bin.

With Chef and Aidan busy prepping, Kate went to lift the full black bin liner out of the red receptacle, when Chef rushed over, taking it from her. "Oh, a gentleman." She grinned at Aidan, who smiled back at her. She almost forgot how beautiful his smile was. "Why, thank you, Chef."

Chef took the bin bag out through the fire exit side door that led to the back garden.

The smell in the kitchen was amazing; it made her mouth water. Slinking behind the line, Kate wandered over to the cooker.

Finding a silver dessert spoon, Kate hovered over a pan of chicken tikka masala. She dipped her spoon in and tasted some. Turning to Aidan, she closed her eyes, a smile forming. "Mmm! Heaven."

63

Aidan bent down, opened the cooker door, and took out three trays of toad in the hole. They smelled amazing, making him want to try some. When they were laid out on the stainless-steel counter, he grabbed a knife, slicing them into equal sized portions, when he felt arms around his waist, and Kate's cheek on his back. "Is everything alright?"

"Uh-huh!" She remained attached to him.

"Oh! It's just that you haven't touched me in months. I mean, don't get me wrong, I'm not complaining. It's just unexpected is all." He held her hand.

"I know. I'm so sorry how things have been between us recently." She let go of him.

He turned to her. "What's going on?"

"I owe you an apology." Kate looked up at him, her eyes pleading. "You were right about Graham. His company's behind the chef who has our lease. His family's company bought up the chef's company." She squeezed his hand. "When you tried to warn me about him, I didn't listen. I'm sorry! I thought you were jealous, and you didn't need to be. It's you I love. It always has been, always will be."

His mouth hung open. If someone had said earlier that Kate would be telling him she loved him, he would have laughed them out of the building. "I love you, too, honey. You know that. There's no one I'd rather be with. I'm sorry for how I've been over the last couple of years. I'm trying to change, Kate, truly."

"I know you are. I've seen it."

His heart pounded in his chest. Kate was still the only woman who could make it gallop. "Does this mean-"

"Oh Aidan, it doesn't mean I'm ready to come back. Not yet. I'm sorry! I just wanted to tell you I still love you. When I'm ready, I'll let you know." Kate put her palm on his cheek, pulling him down to kiss him on the lips.

Aidan took the peck on the lips as a good sign. He had changed a lot since they broke up. Chef's influence had caused these changes, there was no other way to explain it. He loved cooking again; it found its way to his heart. Since Chef arrived, life felt worth living again. "Please do. You're all I want."

Kate reached up and linked her fingers behind his neck, hugging him tighter than she had in years. He wrapped his arms around her waist, squeezing her. "I love you so much."

“Sorry! Didn’t mean to interrupt.” Francesca’s head poked inside the kitchen door. “Kate, I’m opening up now. Thought I’d let you know.”

“What time is it?” Aidan glanced up at the clock on the wall. “It’s midday? Where’s Chef?” He scanned the room, letting Kate go. “We’ll talk later.”

“You need to find Chef.” Kate stood out of his way. “The last time I saw him, he was taking the rubbish out to the bin. That was ten minutes ago, though. He can’t still be out there.”

With the pans still boiling away on the hobs, Aidan headed out of the fire exit door, along the path separating the two sides of lawn, until he came to the open gate at the bottom of their garden. “Chef?”

He surveyed the car park.

There were only five cars, and two were his and Kate’s.

“Chef?” His calls grew in both volume and intensity.

At his feet sat the full bin liner of kitchen waste. The big wheelie bin’s lid was open, like Chef was about to throw the bag in when he was interrupted. But interrupted by what, or whom? “Chef?” He glanced at his watch again. A couple of minutes past midday. The first couple of orders would be coming through in a minute.

“Oh shit!” He ran back to the kitchen, checked the ticket machine hadn’t spat out any orders, and ran into the dining room, where guests were being seated by Francesca and Bonnie. He legged it to the stairs leading to the accommodation above.

Frantic, Aidan checked the flat for any sign of Chef. Nothing. At eight minutes past midday, he ran downstairs to the dining room, clocked Benjamin, grabbed him and pulled him into the kitchen. “I’m sorry to have to do this, Benjamin, but you’re in here with me this afternoon. Chef’s gone walkabout.”

64

Elio unbolted the front doors, top and bottom and fixed them in place using the hooks attached to the door frame. He stepped outside, looking up at the clear blue sky. The forecast was for a hot, sunny afternoon, which was why he'd opened all the bay windows in the restaurant. He inhaled deeply, spotting a group of eight approaching Marble's Marvels.

Their first booking wasn't due in until half twelve, by which time Aidan and Kate would probably have served ten to fifteen customers. They were killing him. Martin was right about one thing: they had to do something, or his restaurant would be dead on its feet in less than a year. "Where are you, Martin?"

Taking himself back inside, his waiters were busy making last minute preparations to their tables. Elio went behind his bar, scanning the bookings folder. Ten bookings at lunch. "It's nothing." He slammed the folder shut.

A postman walked up to the bar, delved into his bag, pulling out three letters, which he left on the bar top. "Morning, Elio. It's going to be bloody lovely today. Good job I'm off in half an hour, eh!"

Picking up the letters, Elio waved. "Have fun, while I'm stuck here, won't you!" He quickly dropped two of the letters. Bills. The third letter had the logo of his solicitors written in the top left-hand corner. "Let's see what you're after now."

Taking himself upstairs to his office, Elio shut the door and sat on his desk chair.

Sliding the letter out of the envelope, he read it.

His bitch of a wife wanted, no demanded, sixty percent of everything he had. Sixty percent for putting up with his neglect, for putting her in a loveless marriage. "Bitch!"

This was what he dreaded. His and her lawyers had gone back and forth countless times over several months, and this was the best offer they could arrive at. "I could've done better."

With anger biting, Elio picked up his desk phone. "Yeah, it's me. I just got your letter. Sixty's the best you can do?"

"Honestly, Elio, I'm surprised she relented. She was gunning for seventy-five only a week ago. I've got no idea what made her change her mind. But she's adamant."

"So, you're telling me I've got to sell the house, the cars and the business?" He wanted to cry when his solicitor confirmed it. "And there's nothing I can do? Nowhere to complain?"

"Look, if you want my advice, I'd run with it. You're not going to make her accept anything lower. If I go back to them with counteroffers, she might revoke this offer and go back to seventy-five. Please Elio, take it."

"Offer her the house and the cars. I get to keep the business." Elio hung up before his solicitor could argue the point. They pissed him off, so much. They said they were there to protect his interests, but he knew better.

"Hey Elio, have you got a minute?" Martin beckoned him to follow.

Elio thought it strange that his assistant would lead him out to the car park along the fire escape on the first floor. "Where are we going?"

In front of him, Martin rushed ahead. "You'll see."

In the restaurant's twenty-bay car park, which sat empty bar Martin's Nissan Micra, Elio frowned when he scanned the area. At the boot of Martin's car, Elio stood back, as his assistant slid the key in the lock and turned it.

"Before I show you this, remember I did it for you, for this restaurant." Martin opened the boot and stood to the side, a proud smile stretched across his face. "There's no way Aidan's going to impress that food critic without his new sous chef."

Not knowing how to react, Elio's mouth hung open. On the one hand he was angry that Martin had put this master chef in the boot of his little car; on the other, Martin cared so much about his restaurant that he was prepared to kidnap Chef to prevent Marble's Marvels from impressing the food critic. "What have you done?" He bit his knuckles.

"I'm helping, Elio. If this guy's not in the kitchen with Aidan, then that Crane woman won't get her amazing food, will she? I'm doing this to help you."

Chef, curled up inside the small space, stared up at Elio.

"Martin didn't hurt you, did he?" He went in to try and free Aidan's sous chef, who shook his head. "Hang on, he's not tied up, Martin." Elio scratched his head.

"Why would I tie him up? I'm no kidnapper. No, this guy just hopped in when I ordered him inside, no hassle, no talking back, nothing."

“He’s deaf and mute, you stupid boy.” Elio helped Chef out of the boot, brushing him down, his chef whites creased, dirty. “I’m so sorry for this, Chef. Please accept my sincerest apologies. My assistant’s not a bad man; he’s worried for his job, for this restaurant.”

Martin’s brow furrowed. “You’re giving him back? Just like that?”

To his own surprise, Elio held Chef’s arm and walked with him up the iron stairs to the first floor of the restaurant, where no member of the public was permitted. “Again, I’m so sorry. This is only until the food critic leaves, okay? When she’s gone, I’ll let you go.”

Deciding to shut him in his flat, Elio had the perfect place, the spare bathroom. He led their way up the stairs, making Chef follow him into the cramped washroom. “Martin, in the kitchen in the third drawer down nearest the main door you’ll find some thin rope. Go and get it, would you?”

After Martin rushed off, Elio suggested that Chef sit in front of the sink stem. “You understand, don’t you? You know why I’m doing this.”

Chef sat on the threadbare carpet. He nodded.

“Pease don’t think I’m a bad person, Chef. I’m not. Neither’s Martin. We’re desperate. My wife’s trying to take everything I’ve spent a lifetime building. You understand, don’t you?”

He stared at the floor, like shame forced him, when he felt Chef’s hand on his shoulder. “Why are you smiling? You know what I’m doing to you, right? You know I’m kidnapping you, don’t you?”

Chef nodded, a soft smile radiating around the small room.

Martin arrived carrying the rope. “Here! Why’s he smiling like that? Does he know what’s going on? He knows he’s being kidnapped, right?”

On his knees, Elio took the rope. ”Uh-huh! He knows.” He leaned forwards, wrapping the rope around the sink stem and around Chef’s waist. He tied Chef’s hands to the rope tied around his waist. When it was tight enough, he sat on the floor opposite Chef. “It won’t be for long, I promise.”

His mobile phone rang in his trouser pocket. “I have to take this.” He ordered Martin out. Elio stepped outside the toilet, closed the door, and locked it. He took the key out and put it in his pocket for safe keeping.

Waving Martin off, Elio stayed in his hallway, leaning against the wall. “And? What did they say? The house and cars are worth more than the restaurant.”

"I'm afraid not, Elio. She wants you to put the restaurant on the market with everything else. She's adamant she wants sixty percent of the asking price. But, she says that if you give her sixty percent of the value of the restaurant, you don't need to put it on the market, and that's her final offer. The house and cars have to go, as do the paintings in the house."

"Where the hell am I going to get that kind of money from? That's," he thought for a few seconds, "over a hundred and fifty thousand. More like a hundred and eighty."

"You tell me! I work for you, Elio. I do what you ask. Have you thought about asking a partner to help you out? They front the sixty percent; you give them a piece of the business? Or ask someone to loan it? You don't care about the house and cars as much as the business, am I right? So, sell the house, take your forty percent, and give it back to her, and ask someone to help out with the rest. Just an idea."

Elio dropped his arm down by his side, the phone still in his hand. He had to do something; his wife wanted blood. He put the phone to his ear again. "Tell that bitch I'm putting the house up. I'll sell the cars as well. But tell her I'm not selling the business yet. I'll find a way of getting her sixty percent of its value." He hung up before his solicitor could argue. "Bloodsucking vampire."

Where had he gone wrong with his wife? He'd done everything asked of him. Some women were never satisfied, although he conceded that he spent a lot of time downstairs in the restaurant. If he had neglected her, he didn't deserve to lose everything he had worked so hard for. He deserved better than this.

65

"I'll go check on progress for you." Kate bowed to her table of four, who were yet to receive their main courses. "My sincerest apologies."

"I should think so. We've been waiting forty-five minutes." The beady-eyed woman with pointy features stared intently at her. "After we heard such good things about this place, too. The food had better arrive soon, my dear, or I'll be submitting a review on Tripadvisor."

"I'm sure it'll be ready very soon." Turning to run to the kitchen, as Kate sped away an arm grabbed her wrist. She stood in front of a table of six diners, who were as keen on receiving their desserts as the previous table were on tucking into their mains. "I'm on my way to the kitchen now. I'll bring your desserts out in two shakes of a lamb's tail."

As she passed the table closest to the kitchen, Kate was stopped by an elderly couple who were yet to receive their starters. The lunch rush was killing them without Chef. "I'm so sorry! I'll have your prawn cocktails with you in a jiff."

Checking that Francesca was fine on the floor – she was taking an order for table twenty-six – Kate went into the kitchen to find Aidan plating up the mains for table sixteen, who had just complained. "Oh, thank heavens you're onto their order."

"Don't talk to me right now, Kate, you'll put me off my pace."

The last of the tickets were on the rack. Her husband had just about caught up. He had three tables left to cook for. "What do you need help with? Tell me what to do."

Aidan asked her to throw a bag of chips in the fryer. Kate went into the fridge for the chips, picked up a pair of scissors and cut a triangle off the edge. She poured them all in, as they hissed. "Now what?" She saw a tray full of chips under lights. "Tell me which plates need chips and I'll serve them up."

Flustered, Aidan checked the ticket. He pointed out the plates that required chips. "I'm going to kill Chef when he comes back."

"Of course he's coming back. Don't talk like that. As soon as I'm able, I'm going to go out looking for him. Until then, we have to muddle through." After loading the plates up with golden chips, Kate saw Benjamin getting the starters ready. "How are you doing over there, Benjamin?"

Their young saviour put one thumb up. "About to take them out."

"Good man. We couldn't have done this without you, I hope you know that."

"I've got this, Kate. Leave the girls to finish off. Go and find Chef. We have to have him for tonight. We've got a full house, plus you know who."

Doing as she was told, Kate waited until her complaining table's meals were ready, took them out to their owners, and checked they had everything they needed. "My waitresses will take care of you from now on, okay? If you need anything, let one of them know."

With her bag over her shoulder, Kate took her keys out, walked into the warm sunshine, through the back garden to the car park. As she sat behind the wheel of her MG, she wondered where Chef could be? Why had he left so abruptly?

After driving around the village a couple of times, hope of finding him vanished. She could go further afield, look as far as Basingstoke maybe, but what would be the point? If Chef didn't want to be found, he wouldn't be. What had Mrs Redmond told her? He would leave her eventually; it was inevitable. But why now? They needed Chef more than ever.

Coming to St John's Church for a third time, Kate pulled into the car park. She sat behind the steering wheel for a couple of minutes, wondering what she should be doing now. If they were going to find Chef, she needed help.

With her phone in hand, Kate dialled the familiar number. "Yeah, Harriet, it's Kate. I need your help with something. Chef's gone missing."

"It's a bad time right now, Kate, the police have turned up. They're arresting Kendall as we speak. But I'll tell you what I can do: I'll ring the girls, get them to go out looking. How's that? I'll join just as soon as I can."

Kate thanked Harriet, hung up and stared at the church doors. Whenever something bothered her, she felt comfort from the old building. Getting out, she put her bag over her shoulder and walked inside the church.

She found a pew and sat three rows from the front, the only person there.

Clasping her hands together, her fingers interlocking, Kate bowed her head, her lips almost touching the tops of her digits. *Please, Lord, help us find Chef. We need him. Why present him before us if You are going to take him away in the hour of our greatest need?*

"Kate?"

The vicar's voice made her open her eyes. When she glanced to her left, her hands still together, Reverend Ingram sat next to her in his clerical uniform with the white collar, and black trousers. He was a wily man with a little moustache and oval glasses. "Oh hello, Reverend Ingram."

"You look pensive. Is there something on your mind? Anything I can help you with?"

"Where do I start?" Kate stared at the back of the pew in front, with its pouch full of programmes and hymn sheets. "We've lost Chef."

"Chef? Is this the new guy everyone's been raving about?"

"Yeah, he's a Godsend." She felt like crying. "We were on the verge of closing the doors of Marble's Marvels for good, you know. We were a month away from it when he walks in and asks for a job. Aidan and I, we were like, 'We don't have any vacancies.' And he gives us an ultimatum: let me prepare you a meal, if you don't love it, I will leave, but if you think it is the best thing you have ever eaten, give me a job as sous chef."

"And he blew you away, I know. You've told me this story." He smiled sweetly.

"Blew me away doesn't do it justice, Reverend. And ever since he's come into our lives business has picked up, to the point where we're paying off our debts and starting to turn a profit. He's helped us in so many ways I couldn't even tell you."

"And now he's gone?"

"That's just it; it's like he disappeared into thin air. He was taking out the rubbish one minute, and gone the next, the bin bag on the ground waiting to be thrown in the wheelie bin, like someone snatched him, or something."

Her mind fired in a thousand varying scenarios, as she sat next to Reverend Ingram. "Oh no! Why didn't I see it before?" Kate stood, thanked the Reverend, and waited for him to scooch over, so that she could leave.

"I hope I helped!" The vicar shouted after her.

Back in her MG, Kate started the engine, reversed out of her space, and sped off towards Basingstoke. She swore at herself; she should have thought of this before. Driving angry, Kate arrived outside Graham's house, and pulled up behind a Honda Civic. "Let's see what you're hiding, you little weasel."

Without thinking of her own safety, Kate climbed out of her car, slammed the door, and stormed over the road, her legs confident, not afraid. “Graham! Open up!” She banged on the front door with her fists to show her rage.

The door swung open. “What the bloody hell-”

Kate barged past Graham, knocking him to the side, using her full force to gain access to his home. “Where is he? I know you’re behind it. This is just your kind of underhanded trickery.” She reached the stairs and started climbing. “Tell me where he is!”

“Tell you where who is, you lunatic?” Graham climbed the stairs after her. “You don’t just barge into my house like this, Kate. If you touch anything, I’m calling the police.”

Kate ignored him, going from room to room searching for Chef. “I know he’s around here somewhere. Just tell me where he is.”

“Where who is? I don’t know what you’re on about.” He stood behind her.

Coming out of the main bedroom, Kate stopped and glared at him. “Chef! I know you grabbed him when he was throwing out the rubbish. We need him back, where is he?”

“I don’t have the first clue where he is. Why would I kidnap your chef?”

She pointed at him. “You know full well why. You’re the only person who’ll benefit from Chef not being in the kitchen tonight.”

“Me? How will I benefit? Our restaurant’s not even open yet. If you want to accuse someone, try that Italian chap across the road from yours. Elio, or whatever his name is. His place has been suffering since you took on Chef. He’s more likely to have taken Chef than me.” He walked her downstairs to the hallway.

Kate had not even thought about Elio or given him a moment’s thought. Had his restaurant been suffering recently?

66

Chris gently eased the pick-up truck's bonnet down, leaning on it to help close it properly. In his oily overalls, he went and sat behind the steering wheel, making sure he put down a towel beforehand. "Time to check you out." He inserted the key, twisted it, and tried to start the engine.

It whined a couple of times, before it turned over, smoke billowing out from the exhaust. "Got you." He kept the engine running for five minutes, listening to her roll over, before he killed the motor. *Another job done*, he thought, glancing over at his desk drawer.

Before he knew what he was doing, he had all three drawers out, hunting for a bottle of vodka. Nothing. "Shit!" He left the mess on the ground, choosing to hunt the barn for opened bottles of whisky. He used to hide bottles around the place from Edie and Amy. In little hidey holes, nooks, and crannies.

Locating half a bottle of Scotch hidden behind an old toolbox, he unscrewed the cap, and tipped a mouthful in, feeling it burn his mouth, throat, and chest. He had not touched a drop in what felt like days.

It wasn't enough. Chris fetched his keys from the house, yelled to Amy that he was going to the petrol station on the way to Basingstoke, and left before she asked to come with.

He took his own pick-up out for a spin, navigating the roads like the expert he had become. Ten minutes later he pulled up by a petrol dispenser, got out, and filled up his tank with diesel. Inside the shop, he checked there were no customers behind him. "Number four, please, and three bottles of Smirnoff Red." He said it quietly, almost under his breath.

The clerk fetched his vodka without so much as a cursory glance. He told Chris the price, with the petrol on top and held the card terminal out for him.

Placing his bank card over the terminal, Chris waited for the bleep, then picked up his three bottles of Smirnoff, and left, putting two of them under his armpits, trying to hide them as much as he could. There were shops closer to home, but he knew the owners.

He raced back home, pulling up outside the barn. With the bottles hidden in front of him, Chris hid each of them in turn. He wished he had lockable drawers on his desk. He would, except Amy might get suspicious, especially now.

Filling up a hip flask with vodka, Chris hid the rest of the bottle. He went and sat at his desk, skimming through his jobs folder. The pick-up he just fixed was his last job. "Oh shit!" In over four years, he'd not been without a tinkering job.

After taking a big swig of neat vodka, he screwed the cap back on the hip flask, hiding it in the bottom desk drawer. He was in trouble. If he didn't get some more jobs coming in soon, he would be in real trouble. His bank had given him a three-month payment holiday already, but he needed work coming in all the time to make ends meet.

In the top drawer of his desk, he found an old pack of cigarettes with five left. "What the hell." He lit one, drew in the smoke, and slowly exhaled, letting it work its magic.

"Dad! Are you smoking?" Amy stood in the doorway, glaring at him.

"It's just the one, sweetie, and besides, I've given up drinking, haven't I?" He turned in his chair. "You can't expect me to give up everything at once. I'm only human."

His daughter's expression softened. "I suppose so. Smoking's so disgusting, but I guess it's better than you drinking yourself to death."

"I'm glad I have your approval." He took in another lungful. "Did you want something, Ames? You must have come here for a reason?"

"Oh, yeah, I was hoping to stay over at Oaklyn's tonight. Is that alright with you?"

Chris smiled. "Fine, princess. You go and have fun. I'll see you tomorrow at some point. Ring if you need a ride home, okay? I'll come pick you up." He knew Oaklyn lived in Basingstoke, so it wasn't a chore picking her up.

Thinking about work, Chris opened his phone book, looked up his mate, and dialled the number. If anyone could throw work his way, this guy could. "Yeah, it's me." He gave his friend small talk for a couple of minutes, before getting down to business.

"Ah mate, I would, you know it, but we've died a death, too. I'm looking at possibly laying a couple of guys off myself. Sorry!"

"Great!" After a brief conversation, Chris hung up.

67

Elio surveyed the tables, going around the dining room checking the layouts were all present and correct, with enough cutlery, place mats and salt and pepper shakers for service. They had seventeen bookings guaranteed, which was down heavily on the same time last year, when several tables had to be re-set. He sighed.

His staff, including Martin stood by the bar waiting for his confirmation that they could open up. They were all professionals, each knowing their jobs. He only made them wait for him to teach them respect. "Go ahead, open up."

There were no early diners at six o'clock. Elio stepped outside, stood on the pavement outside his restaurant. He glanced left and right. Not one person ventured towards him.

Over the road, Elio spotted a group of six heading for Marble's Marvels. It made him so angry that their new chef had made such an impact at Kate and Aidan's business. He grinned, thinking of Aidan sweating in the kitchen, dreading Gaynor Crane's arrival. As soon as he felt the grin, he forced it to drop, knowing what he'd done was wrong.

Across the road, Kate emerged from the restaurant. She welcomed her guests, spoke to them briefly before heading over the street towards him.

"Kate?" He feigned concern. "Is everything alright?"

She stood in front of him, concern furrowing her brow. "You're my last hope, Elio. We've lost Chef. One minute he was taking out the rubbish, the next he's gone. He left the bin lid open, and the full bin bag on the floor."

"Oh my God! Kate, I'm so sorry! Here, come in." He walked her into the restaurant, guilt enveloping him. He hoped she couldn't read him. "Let me get you a glass of water."

"You haven't seen him, have you?" She accepted his drink, holding it.

"No, I'm afraid I haven't. I had a woman in her sixties drop by this afternoon asking about him. I just assumed you'd found him."

"That must have been one of Harriet's friends. She's mobilized a search party. I thought you might have seen him in passing. Thanks anyway." Kate placed the glass on the bar, excused herself, and left the building, crossing the road to her own restaurant.

"Too close, Elio," Martin whispered.

“I know. I feel awful.” He told his assistant to take over the floor, while he disappeared upstairs for a while. Martin assured him they were doing the right thing for the restaurant.

Outside the bathroom, Elio dived into his trouser pocket, took out the key, and opened the door to find Chef still sat on the carpet, tied to the basin stem. He stepped inside, crouching down in front of his ‘captive’. “You have lots of friends, by the way. Kate’s got the whole village out looking for you.”

Chef nodded, a little smile forming.

“What’s the right thing to do here, Chef, huh?” He folded his arms. “I wish I knew. I mean, I know what the right thing to do is for Aidan and Kate. If I let you go, you’ll dazzle that food critic, won’t you? But that isn’t what’s best for me; it’s not best for my restaurant. If Gaynor Crane praises Marble’s Marvels, Elio’s is history, do you understand that?”

With a shake of his head, Chef confused him. The tied sous chef used his hand to ask for pen and paper.

Elio retrieved the writing materials from his lounge, going back to the bathroom, and placing the pad to Chef’s right, the pen in his captive’s hand.

‘*You do what you think is best, of course. You’re a good man, Elio. You have a good heart. I don’t blame you for this.*’

Chef couldn’t have made him feel any worse if he tried. “Great! Now I’m a good guy, am I?” He stood and turned away from Chef. “I’m sorry! I can’t let you go until it’s over, Chef. I have to think of my place now. I can’t let Kate and Aidan steal any more customers from me. I hope you understand, but if not, it’s too bad.”

Stooping down, Elio took the pen and paper away from Chef, stepped into the hall, and closed the bathroom door, locking it, guilt circling him again.

68

"Do you have any idea when she's coming?" Bonnie sat with a menu in her hands.

Kate shook her head, a pad of paper in her hands, pen poised. "No, the letter didn't say a time, just that she's coming tonight. I have our best table reserved for her, though." She smiled at Tate, who wore a smart suit to dinner. "Are you still deciding? I can come back in a minute? We're so busy, Aidan's finding it hard to cope."

"We'll order now if that's okay with you? Tell Aidan there's no rush. We're here for the duration, and to see Gaynor Crane in the flesh."

"I didn't think you followed her?" Kate grinned, knowing Bonnie would have binge watched episodes of Gaynor's BBC programme. "Oh no, she's gone fan girl on us, Tate." She winked at him.

Bonnie chuckled, then relayed her food choices. Kate wrote both orders down on her pad, and walked with speed up to the till, where she input their choices on a tab. At half eight, nerves were starting to show in her shaky hands, as she poured Bonnie and Tate's wine.

Francesca came back with an order. "There she is, Kate. She's waiting to be seated. Do you want to greet her, or shall I?"

"No, I'll do it. Leave Gaynor's table to me, Fran." She carried the two glasses of wine, and the jug of water with two empty high balls over to Bonnie and Tate. Once she'd carried the tray back to the bar, she headed in the direction of Gaynor Crane and her photographer.

"Miss Crane, welcome to Marble's Marvels." She stood in front of the celebrity, smiled, and stood to the side. "I have a table reserved for you, if you'd like to follow me?"

The food critic was even prettier in real life than on TV, with long wavy dark hair, high cheekbones and full lips that were obviously filled, but in a tasteful, sensual way rather than giving her the dreaded trout pout. "It's lovely and warm in here, inviting even. I approve."

"Why thank you. We've been here for seventeen years now." She headed for the reserved table of two near the fireplace. Kate thought it the best table in the house, with a clear view of the dining room. "If you'd like to make yourselves comfortable, here are the menus. Now, let me start you with some drinks."

After a bit of chit-chat about her wine selection, Gaynor ordered a bottle of Chianti for the table. Her photographer, a black woman with big hair, and a stylish choice in outfit ordered herself a glass of lemonade, on account of being pregnant. "Congratulations! Francesca, who will be serving you later, she's also expecting. When's it due?"

Listening, nervous, Kate made all the right comments and sounds, until she left for the bar, her heartrate souring. "This is so stupid. Why am I so nervous?"

After pouring the orders, Kate asked Francesca to carry the tray of drinks over to Gaynor's table, fearful she might drop it herself. "Gaynor's guest is pregnant. It'll be a good way of starting a conversation. Get their order, too, please. You're serving them now."

With Aidan backed up in the kitchen, Chef's disappearance couldn't have come at a worse time. Braving it, leaving Francesca out front, Kate rushed to the kitchen, where the tickets queue was long. Both her husband and Benjamin were hard at work. "She's in the house, love. As soon as her starters come in, I want you on them, Benjamin, understood?"

"While you're here, Kate, you might as well take these mains out to twenty-six, please." Aidan stepped over to the chip tray and scooped three lots onto three plates. "That's twenty-six to go. Thank you." He whipped their ticket down and handed it to her.

"You're both doing so well," she said, checking the meals against the docket. "Everyone's loving the food, as much as when Chef's here. Thought you'd like to know."

Picking up four large dishes, Kate walked them out to the dining room, through the maze of tables until she arrived at an eager family. "My sincerest apologies on the wait." She went and placed the meals in front of their respective owners. "If there's anything else you need, don't hesitate in calling me over. Enjoy your meals!"

"Thank you so much. It smells like it'll be worth the wait." The father said, rubbing his hands together, like he couldn't wait to tuck in.

Kate met Francesca behind the bar. "Do you have it?" She took the pad from her waitress, studying the orders. "Four starters, and four mains." She input Gaynor's choices into the till, praying that the food critic loved it.

69

The screeching ticket machine spat out Gaynor Crane's choices. Aidan tugged on the paper, checking the contents of the order. "You're up, Benjamin. These are Gaynor's starters." He tore the docket in half, handing the eighteen-year-old the ticket with the appetisers.

Prawn cocktail, Tomato and basil soup, stuffed mushrooms, and cheesy garlic bread. Aidan helped Benjamin by heating up the soup in a pan. "You've got the rest, right?"

While his helper made himself busy in the starter area, Aidan had more than enough to be getting on with, He had the mains for five tables to start. Hot in the kitchen, he used his sweatband around his wrist to wipe the sweat from his temples and forehead.

After putting three steaks and two chicken breasts on the grill, Aidan went to the stand-up fridge and took out the rest of his next two tables' main courses to be heated up in separate dishes. He opened the cooker's door and slid them inside.

With all twelve meals on the go, he had to fetch chips from the freezer in the dry store.

Wiping his forehead with his wristband again, Aidan lifted the freezer lid, pulled out two bags of chips, and rushed out.

He stopped, dead on his feet. "Chef?"

Thinking his desperate eyes were deceiving him, his sous chef stood behind the main counter, fetching empty plates from the shelves above like nothing had happened. Chef noticed him, smiled. Aidan walked behind the cooking line and stood in front of him. "Where the hell did you come from?"

'*It's a long story*'. Chef signed.

"I don't care how long it is." Aidan said it as well as signed.

'*I had to help a friend. I'm sorry! It won't happen again. I'm here now.*'

"Aidan, these starters are ready. Shall I ring the bell, or take them out myself?" Benjamin pointed at the four starters for Gaynor Crane.

Pulling himself out of a daydream, Aidan picked up a bag of chips. "Ring the bell. Fran will take them out. We've got cooking to do."

Francesca stopped walking when she saw Chef. "Where did you come from?"

Aidan poured half a bag of chips in the fryer. "That's exactly what I said. He had to help a friend apparently. We're going to have words later, Chef, you know that. You can't just ditch us mid-session." He couldn't help but smile. He had Chef back.

"I'm on my way with these. Wish me luck." Francesca took all four starters out.

"Right, if you take over these two tickets, I'll make a start on Gaynor's mains." He pointed at the two dockets, so Chef knew what he was doing. "These four, here, have to be perfect when they leave the kitchen, okay? These are for the food critic."

70

Elio had too many staff on. He was wasted behind the bar making drinks for his diners; most of them wanted bottled beer and wine anyway. All night he kept a vigil on Marble's Marvels, watching their customers come and go. Even from this far back he could see how busy they were, with a full restaurant.

The only thing that kept him going was the knowledge that Aidan had to be pulling his hair out by now, serving a full house. Having Chef upstairs meant his rivals had a good chance of disappointing Gaynor Crane. "Take over for me, Martin."

"Sure thing, where are you off to?" Martin took his place behind the bar.

"I'm going to see how they're getting on over the road."

Stopping to chat to a couple of locals, Elio went outside, crossed the road, and stood outside Kate and Aidan's place, hoping to see mayhem inside.

When he peered through the window, all he saw were happy diners. "I don't believe it! This can't be happening."

Everywhere he looked he saw customers laughing, eating, drinking, having a good time. Without Chef, the floor staff, particularly Kate, should have been running around, flipping their arms, and chasing their own tails. "How is he doing it?"

Angry that Aidan could be satisfying this many diners singe-handed, Elio opened the door and stepped inside. Laughter, the din of voices.

At the bar, he leaned on the counter, attracting Kate's attention. "It's quiet over the road. I thought I'd come and see if you needed a hand. Being neighbourly and everything." He turned and surveyed the busy room.

Every table either had starters, mains, or dessert plates on them. Elio scratched his head, wondering how one man could cook this many meals, keeping this many customers happy. It defied all logic.

"Thanks for the offer, Elio, but we're good, thanks. Chef came back an hour ago."

Elio froze. He spun round. "He did?" Had he heard her right? How could Chef be in the kitchen, if he was tied up and locked in his bathroom?

Kate smiled. "Sure. Go see for yourself. And not a minute too soon, I have to say. Aidan was pulling his hair out, trying to keep up when Gaynor arrived. She's loving the food, the service, the atmosphere. Francesca's been keeping her amused."

Forcing a smile, Elio's mind fired in a thousand different directions. "That's great, Kate. I'm really happy for you." He checked her response. Had Chef told her of his behaviour? She didn't seem to know, or maybe she was hiding the fact she knew. "I don't suppose he said where he went?"

"He's being cagey about it, but I'll get it out of him." Kate moved to the till, printing off a bill. "He says he was helping a friend, but I don't believe him. He'll fold under my questioning, believe me."

Not knowing if Kate was joking, or being honest, Elio walked slowly towards the kitchen door. He stood to the side of it, as Francesca came flying out of it carrying four large mains plates.

As the door swung back and forth, Elio caught Chef behind the counter.

"Are you coming in to say hi, or staying out here, Elio?" Francesca was behind him with dirty dessert dishes. "Come and say hi to Aidan and Chef."

"Oh no, I couldn't, Fran. They're still so busy." He backed away, not wanting Chef to see him. Or Aidan. "I have to be getting back to my place."

He walked out of Marble's Marvels with as much speed as his old legs would allow, leaving the mocking laugher behind him. How could Chef be in that kitchen? He was tied up in his bathroom. None of it made sense.

So deep in thought he was that he didn't see a car coming.

He received the biggest shock of his life when the car screeched to a halt, the owner punching his horn. "Sorry! My fault." He bowed to the driver.

Inside his restaurant, Elio grabbed Martin, put one of the other waiters in charge, and pulled his assistant upstairs. Martin objected to being man-handled. "He's gone!"

"What do you mean? He can't be." Martin frowned.

"Well, he is. He's in the kitchen with Aidan, large as life." He reached the bathroom in his flat, stopped outside the door and retrieved the key. Sliding the key in the hole, Elio twisted it and opened the door.

Martin stepped inside, his mouth open, shocked. "But...How?"

All that remained of their mad, crazy morning's antics was the rope they used to tie Chef with. The knots were still holding; it wasn't like Chef had untied himself. "You're right, how? How did he get out of that rope, and out of this locked room? You tied it tight."

Scared, Martin crouched and picked up the rope. “He couldn’t have freed himself from this. Could he?” Staring up at him, Martin dropped the rope. “And that door hasn’t been touched, has it? It’s like the guy upped and vanished.”

Damage control. Elio had to come clean with Kate and Aidan, explain himself before Chef told them what he and Martin had done. He had to beg forgiveness.

“Wait! Where are you going?” Martin ran after him.

“To clean up your mess.” He ran down the stairs to the first floor, passing the office, and flew down the stairs to the dining room, where his waiters were making themselves appear busy. “I’ll be back later,” he shouted to them, flying out of the door.

When he reached Marble’s Marvels, he stopped, asking himself what he was going to say to Kate and Aidan? Should he confess? What if Chef didn’t say anything? Elio stopped outside the main window, his back to it, contemplating his next move.

71

"Here's your bill, Gaynor." Kate presented her guest with the docket on a small dish. "I wish you would let me treat you. It's been lovely having you here."

"Nonsense, Kate, the pleasure is mine." She glanced around the all-but empty dining room. "This has been one of the best nights I've had in quite a while, and we've been to some swanky outlets, haven't we, darling?" The photographer agreed. "And besides, the magazine picks up my bill."

"I'm so grateful to hear you say that." She stacked and picked up the four dessert plates. "Would you like to join us for a drink after? It would mean the world to Aidan to meet you. Oh, please say yes."

"Who can refuse an offer like that?" Gaynor picked up her bottle of Chianti. "I've got another glass in there. I'd love to meet your husband, the gourmet chef."

"Excuse me, Ms Crane, sorry to bother you, but could I ask for an autograph?"

Kate stood to the side, giving the woman in her early twenties the space to hand Gaynor a notepad and pen. To her surprise, Gaynor smiled warmly, took the pad, and signed it, asking the young woman her name and what she did for a living. The woman was at the University of Southampton studying journalism.

Leaving her guests to it, Kate joined the others in the kitchen. Benjamin was washing up while Aidan and Chef wiped down the rest of the kitchen, after a brutal shift. She handed the four dessert plates to Benjamin. "She wants to meet you, Aidan. And you, too, Chef."

"Chef says he'll be there." Francesca left the kitchen.

Following her pregnant waitress, Kate helped her wipe down tables, laying new white cloths over them, and setting them up for lunch service the next day. The diners had staggered leaving, giving her and Francesca the time to relay tables as they went.

"I keep seeing Elio hanging about outside." Francesca whispered in her ear. "Should we invite him in for a drink?"

Happy, ecstatic even, Kate told Francesca not to worry about it, that she would speak to Elio. With only two tables of customers left to leave, she met her neighbour and rival outside on the pavement. "Are you alright, Elio? Would you like to come in? Join us for a drink."

He seemed agitated. "I'll come in, but not for a drink. I don't deserve it."

Confused, Kate ushered him inside, took him to the bar, where she made him a large gin and tonic. "Here. Looks like you could use this."

Before she could give him time to start talking, she went and helped tidy the dining room, saying cheerio to her last remaining customers. The clock on the wall said it was quarter to midnight. "Please don't forget to tell your friends about us."

Bolting the doors top and bottom, Kate locked them all in. "Who would like a drink?"

Aidan and Chef emerged from the kitchen wearing their whites, closely followed by Benjamin in his waiter uniform that needed a wash. Kate took their orders for drinks, Aidan and Chef taking a pint of ale each, to Benjamin's glass of Coca-Cola.

At the back of the restaurant, Aidan and Benjamin joined three tables together, giving them room to relax and unwind. Kate carried the tray of drinks over to them. While everyone except Elio took a seat, Kate stood in front of everyone. "To friends, new and old!"

Everyone took a sip after joining in her toast. "I just want to say thank you so much to Gaynor and Simone for joining us tonight. It's been a pleasure serving you."

While Gaynor was thanking everyone, Kate's attention turned to Elio still stood in front of the bar, the odd one out. She walked over to join him, sitting on a stool next to him. "You're acting strange tonight. What's the matter?"

"I need to confess something."

Kate raised her eyebrows, interested. "Oh yeah? I'm listening."

"Come and join us, guys." Aidan waved her over. The rest of the group, including Gaynor and Simone joined in. "Who can argue? Come on, Elio, join us. We'll talk later."

She interrupted him, as he was about to spill his secret. Taking him by the hand, Kate dragged Elio over to their tables, found him a chair next to hers and sat him down. "There! This is better."

Conversation and laughter strong, Gaynor was badgered into telling everyone her worst experiences of being a food critic. Kate noticed Elio not laughing. He was normally the picture of joviality. Trying to ignore it, she joined in, laughing at Gaynor's amusing stories.

"I can't do this, I'm sorry!" Elio jumped up from his seat. "I've done something terrible, and I can't pretend otherwise. I shouldn't be here drinking with you when I haven't been a friend. Please forgive me!"

“Whoa! Hold on, Elio, relax.” Kate stood to meet him, but Elio balked.

Chef stood, approached Elio, and put his arm around the Italian’s shoulder.

“I’m the reason Chef wasn’t around today.”

Kate’s eyes narrowed. “You? How?”

Next to Elio, Chef flapped his arms, waving at Francesca to translate.

“Go on, Chef. I’ll relay it for you.” Francesca held her bump, focusing on the hand gestures. “It’s true. I went to help Elio, I’m sorry. I should have told you where I was going.”

Confused, Kate studied an equally confused Elio. “I’m listening, Chef. Elaborate.”

“He’s lying for me.” Elio broke away from Chef’s embrace, stepped back. “We kidnapped him. I held him in my bathroom, tied him to my sink, and locked him in. I’m so sorry! I don’t know what came over me, a moment of madness, I guess.”

Smiling, Kate regarded her neighbour, then Chef. “You what? You kidnapped him? How? You’re not exactly big, Elio.” She almost laughed. “Good gag. Very funny.”

“Obviously, I didn’t kidnap him. Martin brought him to me. He cornered Chef while he was throwing out the rubbish. I was shocked when Martin opened the boot of his car, and I saw Chef lying there. I wanted to let him go, I really did, but I knew you had this big shot with Ms Crane coming here tonight. I had to stop you impressing her. I have to stop you ruining my business. When it came to crunch time, I made Chef walk up the stairs. I tied him up with rope, and locked him in my bathroom, until tonight was over. Please forgive me.”

Her face dropped when Chef gave her sad eyes. “You’re not kidding, are you?” Kate sat on her chair, her mouth open. “But why, Elio? I don’t understand. We’re friends. I mean, we’re rivals, too, sure, but above all we’re friends.”

“Why you sneaky little-” Aidan stood up.

“Aidan! Sit down!” She glared at him. “This isn’t helping. Let Elio explain himself.”

“The restaurant’s all I have left. You’re killing it here, and my customers are coming to you. In two months, I have seen a forty percent drop in trade. I can’t compete with your home cooked food, even with meal deals. The locals are flocking back here.”

“That’s no reason to go sabotaging us, Elio.” Aidan’s eyes grew dark.

"I know, and I'm sorry! My wife's divorcing me. She wants sixty percent of everything, including the restaurant. So, I have to put my baby on the market because she wants to punish me by making me give her up. She doesn't care that she could earn good money by letting me keep her open. All she's interested in is the lump sum she'll receive from selling her outright."

The room fell silent, listening to Elio gently sob.

"We had no idea things were so bad, Elio." Aidan's face softened. "You should've said something."

"And said what? Should I have asked you to stop trading?" Elio wiped his face. "We're in competition, Aidan. When you guys weren't doing well, and I was, you didn't come begging me, did you? No, this is all my fault. I worried Martin. He only approached Chef because I made him fear for his job."

Chef kept his head down, his eyes on the floor, Kate noticed. "I'm so sorry, Elio. I didn't know you were having such a hard time."

After a lengthy silence, Kate got up and walked behind the bar.

She poured another round of drinks.

Gaynor and Simone made a point of consoling Elio.

"Here, have another gin and tonic, Elio." Kate left it in front of him.

The group divided into smaller pockets. Gaynor and Simone talked to Francesca, while she tried to console Elio, and Benjamin spoke to Aidan and Chef about training to become a chef. "It'll be alright. You'll see. We've all got problems. Aidan and I are still looking for premises, but we can't catch a break with the estate agents. They keep looking at the last two years' takings, not the past couple of months."

Chef rose from his chair, stretched, and wandered behind Elio.

Kate watched as Chef touched Elio's shoulder, before he walked to the toilets.

"I've got it!" Elio jumped up, like he'd had a Eureka moment.

Staring up at him, Kate frowned. "You've got what?"

"The solution to all our problems." He stood in front of the whole group, minus Chef. "I have to sell my building, right? You need premises to move to, yes?"

"Yeah," Kate replied, confused as to where he was going with it.

"Don't you see? You give me a hundred and eighty-five thousand and move into my restaurant. You'll never have to worry about landlords or paying rent again. It's perfect! I'm planning on retiring anyway. You pay me the money I need to get my wife off my back, and I'll take a third of your takings, leaving you with two thirds. I can't say fairer than that."

Kate gauged Aidan's response. Her husband had a glazed expression. She shrugged. Moving across the road, while not ideal, would be preferable to moving away. "What do you think, honey?" Aidan shrugged.

"It's the perfect solution, Kate. The restaurant's exactly the same size as here. All your furniture will fit in over there. It will be your own place, I won't interfere. I'll be your silent partner. And as a sweetener, I'll even pay for the refurbishment before the grand opening. How about that? What do you say?"

"Whoa! Hold it, I think you're forgetting something, Elio." Aidan stood up. "The money. The reason we're not buying a place outright is because we don't have the money. All we have right now is a restaurant capable of earning us the money over a long period."

Chef came out of the toilets. '*What did I miss?*'

"Kate and Aidan are moving this place across the road." Francesca signed for him.

"No, Fran, we're not because we can't afford to." Aidan sat down, deflated.

When Chef put two thumbs up, alarm bells rang for Kate. "You think this is a good idea, Chef? Why? We don't have the money."

"Not now, you don't, but I'm confident you'll get it." Francesca smiled, signing for Chef. "There are so many ways to draw funding."

"I'll help however I can, Kate." Gaynor smiled. "Come on, we can do this."

SUNDAY,
SEPTEMBER 29TH

72

"Now you're cooking." Aidan opened the cooker door for Philippa to slide the first of three trays inside. "And that's how you make toad in the hole. Easy peasy. The trick is not to overcook it, so we put on the timer, and make sure you're near the oven when it goes off."

Including himself, he had five kitchen staff. Elio suggested training a couple of his chefs in his kitchen, so that when they moved across the road, they already had trained staff who could show the untrained employees how everything was done.

Over the past six weeks, Aidan was pretty impressed with them. "Right, I'm going upstairs to see how Kate's getting on."

He left Benjamin and Bonnie on the floor setting the tables up. Last night they were slammed with a full house, and a huge party of thirty who wouldn't leave, so Kate told the waitresses to leave it for the morning. "We've only got half an hour, peeps."

"We're nearly done, Aidan." Bonnie continued laying table seventeen. "How are we doing on the Go Fund Me campaign, by the way?"

"That's what I'm about to find out." He ran upstairs to the first floor, where Kate was sat in the pokey office with her back to the door on the PC.

He stood behind her, put his hands on her shoulders and rubbed them, Kate tilting her head back, enjoying it. "Dare I ask where we're up to?"

Kate opened her eyes. "Well, we're not there, if that's what you mean." Staring at the monitor again, she clicked on her mouse a couple of times. "There. A hundred and thirty-five thousand, give or take. We need fifty thousand by close of play today or all bets are off."

"Elio's wife's such a bitch. She could give him the extra day." He sighed, knowing how unlikely it was that they would manage to get their hands on the fifty thousand. Their lease ended in less than forty-eight hours. "You never know, the piece their doing in The Sunday Express might help. You gave them our campaign details, didn't you?"

"You know I did. You were there, remember?" Kate sat back, massaging her temples with her fingers. "I'm not relying on readers of The Daily Express to get us through this. We need to be thinking bigger. Damn it! How hard is it to raise a hundred and eighty thousand?"

Aidan rubbed her shoulders again. "It's a lot of money, love. It's not like asking for twenty quid off a mate, is it? A hundred and eighty grand is something else."

Breaking from his grip, Kate sat forwards, and turned in her seat to look at him. "You know, we could always ask your parents again? Their offer's still there as far as I know."

With his hands up, palms splayed in a placating manner, Aidan took a step back. "Oh no! We're not back to this again. Forget it! If we get enough money, Elio will be into us for thirty-three percent. Do you want Dad to have his twenty-five on top of that? Don't forget his help doesn't come free. He'll own us."

Working the math out, Kate sat back again. "Yeah, I suppose you're right. That will only leave us with forty-two percent. There must be something we haven't thought of."

"What about Harriet? She's asking her U3A lot this afternoon, right? You never know, they might be feeling generous." He doubted it but wanted to Keep Kate's spirits up.

"I forgot to ask her what U3A stands for. And let's hope they are."

"University of the Third Age. They're some retirement club. A lot of what they do revolves around golf, I think. Or at least it does for Harriet." He didn't know; he'd never Googled it before. "Let's keep our fingers crossed."

Kate clicked off the campaign page and shut down the computer. "It's a shame we've got a full house today; I could've used this afternoon to go online." She stood with her back to him, hiding her face.

"Honey?" He turned her round, as her eyes glazed over.

"I don't want to leave here." She put her arms around his waist, her cheek in his neck. "This is home. It's not fair!" She bucked in his arms.

"No, you're right, it's not." He held her tighter than he had in months, perhaps since before Vinnie died. When her sobs subsided, she stared up at him with teary eyes. He held her cheeks in his palms. "We'll get through this, I promise."

Their eyes locked.

Aidan leaned in towards her, her eyes closing the nearer he leaned.

"Kate, we need you downstairs." Bonnie poked her head inside. "Oops! I'm so sorry. I didn't expect you both to be...The till's gone down again. Sorry!" She pulled an apology face and backed out of the office.

"Yeah, thanks." Aidan sighed, as Kate withdrew. It was the closest he'd come to kissing her since they split up. "Don't worry! I'll sort the till out."

Over the last two months he and Kate had grown closer. Every time he thought they were getting somewhere, she retracted. As he walked downstairs to the dining room, he cursed to himself. If Bonnie had not interrupted them, he might have kissed her.

"Oh Aidan, I'm so sorry. I honestly didn't expect you to be-" Bonnie walked with him to the bar. Instead of going behind it, she leaned on it from the front. "It was on one minute, and off the next. Kate usually turns it off and back on again."

"I've got it, don't worry." He bent down and pressed the power button once. The computer terminal closed down, and he pressed the button again. Standing straight, the till monitor came to life. "It should stay on now. And don't worry about it, Bonnie. If we're meant to get back together, we will."

"I have my fingers crossed, Aidan. You two are so sweet together."

A knock on the front doors caught Aidan's attention. He groaned when Graham's face appeared in the window. "Oh not today, you arsehole." With effort, he wandered over to the entrance. "What do you want?" Like he didn't know.

"My guys need to do a last-minute measure up," Graham shouted through the glass.

He put his hand to his ear, mouthing, 'I can't hear you.'

"Just let them in, Aidan." Kate appeared at the bottom stair, her face flushed. She went to the doors, unbolted them. "Just get it over with, Graham. I'm not in the mood for your crap today, so get your measurements and go. I don't want to see you until tomorrow night."

"Even that's too soon." Aidan stood behind his wife, as Graham stepped inside.

Graham didn't say a word; he didn't have to, His smirk was enough to enrage Aidan.

"You smug git. If I didn't think you'd set the police on me-" He let it trail off.

"I'm so scared." Graham ordered his guys into the kitchen with their tape measures. "It's a glorious, crisp morning out there. Why, you both look so glum. Cheer up, it might never happen." His smile broadened. "Ooh, but wait, actually it is happening. Tomorrow when you close these doors for the last time."

Aidan felt Kate's fingers around his wrist, pulling him back. He wanted to launch himself at the bastard. And by how tight his wife held him, she wanted him to.

The two builders came out with their measures. "Did you get what you need?" Graham ushered them out, turned and headed outside. He turned back to them. "I'm looking forward to tomorrow night. Have a lovely day, won't you!"

After closing the doors, Aidan found Kate staring at the floor. "Like I said, we'll sort it. We'll get the money from somewhere, I promise."

He wrapped his arms around her.

"What did I ever see in that monster?" Her voice was low, soft.

"Everyone has exes they regret going out with." Or rather most did; he met Kate at college, so he didn't have many ex-girlfriends. "But Graham is a prize-winning arsehole, I'll give him that. Come on, honey, let's get set up."

Aidan walked his fragile wife over to the bar, where Bonnie and Benjamin were sat waiting to open the doors. "We've got two days left, guys. Two full houses. Let's make them the best services ever. Let's go out with a bang."

73

Chris rolled onto Edie's pillow, inhaling it for the fiftieth time. It still smelled of her. Sometimes he opened her wardrobe, and took out her dresses, giving them a good sniff. He never wanted it to fade, but it was.

Rolling onto his back, he reached over to the bedside cabinet, picking up his packet of cigarettes. He slid one out, lit it, and sat up. His chest hurt. Coughing, he got up, pulled his jeans up, and walked out to the bathroom.

Relieving himself, while trying to avoid smoke in his eyes, Chris put his hand on the centre of his chest. It felt tight. Throwing the cigarette in the toilet bowl, he wheezed. "Right, that's enough smoking." He coughed, his chest still tight.

"Dad! Are you getting up today, or what? It's almost lunchtime."

"I'm coming, honey! I'll be down in a sec." He dressed in a white T shirt and dark blue jumper; the last item of clothing Edie bought for him. Before he went downstairs, he slid his cigarette packet back in his jeans pocket.

In the kitchen, Amy placed a plate of scrambled eggs on toast down. "I made your favourite. Happy birthday, Daddy. I wish I could stay for longer."

"Thank you, beautiful." He kissed her on the cheek, before sitting in front of the scrambled eggs. "As much as I'd love you to stick around to look after me, you have your own life to live up in Manchester now. Your Mum wouldn't forgive me if I let you drop out."

"Still, maybe I should go back tomorrow afternoon instead?" She sat opposite him, watching him eat. "How are they? I made sure they're not too rubbery."

"Mmm, lovely. Your Mum couldn't have made them better." He smiled at Amy, the tightness in his chest getting worse. Trying not to show it, Chris carried on eating for Amy's sake, although it was the last thing he wanted to do.

He tried not to let his shaky hands notice, so he talked to his daughter while he ate. Although Amy let him drink at the restaurant last night, he came home and added half a bottle of vodka to the mix out in the barn. "What time are you heading off anyway?"

"I'll set off at four, I think. I've got to pop round Violet's before I go. I promised her I'd stop and have a chat. You don't mind, do you?"

"Of course not!" He had one las mouthful of eggs and toast, then put his knife and fork together. "Delicious, honey. Thank you!"

Amy took his plate, washed it under the tap and placed it in the airer. She left the kitchen, returning a minute later holding a wrapped box. "You didn't think I'd forgotten, did you? Here's your real present. Happy birthday!"

After coughing, Chris took the long box from her. He genuinely had no idea what it could be. Amy had not asked him what he wanted. "You shouldn't be wasting your money on me, Ames. I told you not to bother." He checked his tone, softened his face. "But thank you."

Tearing at the paper, eager to get out of Edie's kitchen, Chris revealed a velvety oblong box. Opening it, he smiled. A brand-new watch. Not an expensive one, a newer copy of the time piece he had on. "Oh, thank you, honey. I love it."

Amy kissed and hugged him. "I'm dashing off for a couple of hours, but I'll be back to say goodbye. Are you sure you don't mind?"

"You go on. I'm going to be in the barn fixing Mrs Stringer's car."

When Amy left the house, Chris sat at the table, his fist on his chest. So tight, he could barely breathe. "It's a panic attack, that's all. You've had them before."

Scraping the chair feet along the floor, Chris bent over, his head between his knees, just like Edie taught him last year, after his first debilitating panic attack. He could be having withdrawal symptoms, he thought, lifting his head.

After three minutes with his head between his knees, Chris got up. He felt like death warmed up. Only one thing would cure him. As much as it pained him to do, he wandered over to the barn, where Mrs Stringer's BMW sat on blocks waiting for him to finish mending her. Over the past couple of months, Chris had mended maybe a handful of motors.

The dry spell couldn't have come at a worse time. His bank had already given him a three-month payment holiday, and he'd not paid last month's mortgage bill. On Friday he received a letter threatening repossession if he didn't pay two months' worth by the seventh of October.

Feeling light-headed, giddy, he made it to his desk, where he sat, reached for his bottom drawer, and took out a full bottle of cheap Asda vodka. After unscrewing the cap, he took a large swig, feeling it burning is throat and chest. “That’s more like it,” he said, relaxing back into his chair.

74

Francesca was due the next day, September the thirtieth. Her midwife warned her that a lot of first time Mums were late giving birth, that she might not go into labour for a week or so after the due date. She didn't want to spend another day pregnant, much less a week. "Help me up, please, honey." She held her hands out.

Paul got up from the armchair, held her hands and pulled her to her feet. "Where are you going? I've told you; I can get whatever you need."

"You can't go to the loo for me, can you?" With her hands supporting her back, Francesca walked out of the lounge, as Paul's mobile rang. "It's fine, Paul, take your call. I'll make it to the toilet, don't worry."

Out in the hallway, a letter caught her eye, half-in and half-out of her letterbox. She'd just missed the sender, whose shadow was walking away from her house.

When she reached the door, she yanked on the letter. A hand-written name was scrawled across the envelope, in female writing. Without thinking, Francesca opened the door. "Son of a-" A blonde woman at the top of her drive ducked behind a bush.

Instead of giving chase in her heavily pregnant state, Francesca tore open the envelope, and slid out the single piece of paper. Reading it made her blood boil.

Blondie wanted to know what she had done wrong. When he ran out on her a month earlier, he had not let her explain. Her rantings went on to explain that she was now ten weeks pregnant. They needed to discuss their options. "Of all the cowardly...Paul!"

In the doorway, Francesca had no option but to empathise with the woman. Blondie, or rather Reese, was a victim of his womanising as well. "Get your arse out here, Paul. Now!"

When he surfaced from the lounge, he had his phone to his ear. "Oh shit!" He tried ducking back inside the lounge.

"It's too late for that. I've read the letter she posted through our door."

Paul's head popped out from behind the doorframe. "It's not what you think. I don't know what she's put in that, but it's all lies, I promise. She's a bunny boiler, a nut job." He stepped into the hallway. "You have to believe me, she's a stalker."

“Yeah, a pregnant stalker at that.” Francesca screwed the letter into a ball and threw it at him. It hit his chest, and he caught it as it fell. “Go on, read it! You bastard! You’ve been seeing her all this time, haven’t you? Whenever you said you were going to a meeting. God! I need my head examining letting you move back in here. You won’t ever change, will you?”

Along with the volume of her voice, her blood pressure increased. Incensed at being made a fool of again, Francesca wanted to fly at him. Instead, she closed her eyes, trying to control her breathing before it harmed her baby.

”Yeah, don’t get angry, or you’ll hurt our baby. Please, Fran, I haven’t been near her in weeks.” He drew closer to her, the phone still in his hand.

“How can you say that? You’ve been cheating on me this whole time. I’m carrying your baby, Paul. How can you treat me like this?”

Trying to ignore the intrusion, Francesca continued her breathing exercises the midwife had shown her. Her eyes closed, she felt a draught, as Paul walked past her, out onto the drive. Seizing her chance, Francesca slammed the door on him, locking it.

She let out a long breath, as tears escaped and she slid down the door until she was on her bum, her back against the wood.

“Fran! Open up, honey. Come on, she’s lying. She’s mental.”

Not knowing what to think, or how to feel, except humiliated, Francesca forced herself onto her feet. She waddled into the lounge, falling onto the couch.

How could she have been so stupid? Leopards and their spots. What made her think Paul would change? Once a cheat, always a cheat.

She needed someone to talk to. The first name she came across on her mobile: Aidan. No, she couldn’t use him, not after the way she treated him, could she? Francesca missed his handsome face, his lovely manners, and sense of humour.

75

If Kate had to explain the restaurant's position to one more customer she might explode, she thought, producing the bill for table twenty-five, who enjoyed their lunches immensely. Running it over to them, she thanked them, and headed back for the bar.

On her way back, table fifteen accosted her. "Mrs Osbourne, what can I do for you? Is everything to your liking with the Ploughmans?"

"Oh, yes, dear. It's delicious." The elderly woman accepted an envelope from her husband and handed it to Kate. "We heard about your campaign to save the restaurant. Here's our little contribution to it. We do so hope you succeed. We've enjoyed coming here since you opened. I can even remember our first visit all those years ago."

Kate took the fat envelope from her, tears welling up. Wiping her face, her chin crumpling, she tore it open. Without counting, it appeared to be a thousand pounds in twenties. "I don't know what to say." Kate glanced at the money for a second time. "What am I saying? Of course I do. Thank you so much!"

She bent over and hugged Mrs Osbourne tight. After wiping her tears away, she gave Mr Osbourne a hug as well. "Thank you both so much. This is beyond generous."

"Like I said, we have fond memories of this restaurant; we don't want to see it close."

"This site is definitely closing," she confessed. "The estate agents gave our lease to some Michelin starred chef. But we're hoping to move across the road to Elio's."

"I didn't wish to speak out of turn. I heard a rumour. I think it's a great idea; you never know, you might give the new restaurant a run for its money. Anyway, you're busy. I'll let you get on. Good luck with the campaign."

"A hundred and thirty-six thousand." Kate showed the cash to Bonnie, who squeezed her shoulder. "Only forty-nine to go. And one dinner service left to pull it off."

76

"Are you going to be alright in here?" Aidan checked for confirmation from Chef, who still had Philippa and Lucia to help him clear down the kitchen. He'd just sent the last table's lunches out with Bonnie.

'*Where are you going?*' Chef asked him in sign.

'*Nowhere special. I have someone I need to see.*' His signing was getting better by the day. Before Francesca went on maternity leave, they started signing to one another as practise. He'd learned so much in a relatively short space of time.

'*Can I come?*' Chef pleaded with him.

'*No, this is something I need to do alone. Sorry!*' He made sure the girls were good with him leaving. "I'll see you all here at six."

In the dining room, Aidan found Kate behind the bar, printing off a bill for table twenty-one. She showed him the envelope of money from Mr and Mrs Osbourne. "That's so generous of them." He handed back the cash.

"Where are you going anyway? It's not like you to disappear this early." She looked up from the till monitor, her eyebrows raised.

"Nowhere special. A man can have some secrets, can't he?"

"Uh-huh! I suppose." Kate went back to the till screen, tapping on it.

On his way out, he shook Mr Osbourne's hand, and hugged Mrs Osbourne in thanks for the donation to their campaign. "That is so generous. I can't thank you enough."

"We only hope it helps," Mrs Osbourne told him.

After changing back into a jumper, jeans and jacket in the office, Aidan left the restaurant, walked round the back to the car park and jumped in his Range Rover.

Before he started the engine, he sat staring at the fence ahead.

Was he doing the right thing?

The five-minute journey to Chris Ashcroft's small holding took ten, due to a lorry causing a traffic backlog on the village high street. Instead of yelling at the driver, like he would normally, Aidan sat in silence, dreading the inevitable conflict to come.

"What are you doing?" He asked himself, pulling up outside the driveway leading to the Ashcroft farmhouse. Aidan took a deep breath, and took a right, following the drive.

Stopping behind Chris' pick-up truck, Aidan switched off the engine, wanting to reverse and drive away. He had not spoken to

Chris in months, or rather years, in fact. How would Liam's angry dad react to his turning up unannounced?

"Come on, Aidan, pull yourself together." Opening his door, he exited his Rover, a song playing in the distance. Amy's car was in front of Chris' truck.

Walking up to the house, Aidan banged on the wooden door with his knuckles, and stood back, expecting Chris to fly at him. Nothing. Music blared out of the barn out back.

After knocking two more times, he gave up.

Aidan walked with caution round the side of the house.

The music grew louder. "Chris? It's me! Aidan Marble."

Following the music, he passed Amy's car, approaching the barn, where a BMW was on blocks. It was the same colour as Mrs Stringer's. "Chris?"

Nothing. No reply. Aidan kept walking towards the barn-turned-garage.

At the rear of the barn, Chris Ashcroft sat in a chair in front of his desk, his back to the entrance. Throwing his head back, the mechanic took a swig of vodka.

Aidan stopped walking. He didn't know Chris smoked. "Hey, Chris! It's me. Aidan."

Disturbed, Chris tried hiding the bottle of vodka. He remained with his back to Aidan. Reaching for the radio in front of him, Chris turned off the music. "What do you want?"

Too late to turn back, Aidan stepped inside the barn. "I've come to apologise."

Placing the vodka in the bottom drawer, Chris stubbed out his cigarette. He stood and faced Aidan, his hands balled into fists. "You've come to apologise? Don't make me laugh. Aidan Marble doesn't admit he's in the wrong, ever."

As Chris approached him, he gripped his left arm with his right hand.

"You're right. I never have before. I wasn't ready to face the truth." He didn't like Chris' demeanour, the way he held his arm, or the way he slurred his words.

"You've got some nerve coming here." Chris kept pacing towards him. "After the shit you put us through. Edie's dead because of you."

With his hands up, placating his angry host, Aidan stepped backwards. "Hey, come on now. I had nothing to do with Edie's passing. You know that. You're just angry at the world." He matched Chris' steps back until he bumped into the side of Chris' pick-up.

"Stress killed my wife, Marble. Stress you caused."

Drunk, Chris lunged at him.

Foreseeing the assault, Aidan ducked out of the way with ease, jumping back, getting himself in a defensive position. "I don't want this. I only want to say I'm sorry. I'm sorry for blaming Liam for the crash. I know what happened now. Wyatt told me how Vinnie lost control of his car; he told me my son took his eye off the road."

Chris stood with his fists up, ready to attack. "Do you think I care how sorry you are? You ruined my life. Now I'm going to ruin yours."

Knocking out a drunk Chris would have been too easy. A year earlier, maybe Aidan might have enjoyed it. "Please stop this, mate. I don't want to hurt you. I've missed you."

Chris was beyond reasoning with. His eyes were glazed over. "I'll come back when you've had less to drink."

"You won't come back here, ever."

Aidan had to jump out of the way for a second time. Chris tried punching him, but his fist hit the pick-up's window instead. His would-be attacker hurt his hand. "Please stop. I don't want to hurt you. Look, I'm leaving."

Before Chris hurt himself even more, Aidan turned and walked back to his Range Rover, leaving Chris to nurse his wounds. He jumped in and turned the key in the ignition. Instead of reversing out of the drive, he stared at the back of Chris' truck.

77

Francesca heard Reese's car drive away. She assumed Paul was with her, as he wasn't banging on her door anymore. She sat up, managed to pull herself to her feet, and waddled over to the front window. The car was gone.

The clock on the wall said it was 15:22. Sat listening to Paul pleading to be let back in made her miss lunch. She couldn't have eaten anything had she tried; her stomach was tied up in knots. How could she be back to square one?

With her hands bracing her back, Francesca walked through to the kitchen, where she leaned against the counter. Visions of Paul in bed with Reese, laughing behind her back at stupid old Fran made her clench her fists.

Uncontrollable rage forced her to reach for the plates in the drier. She picked them up one at a time, and threw them at the cupboards, the clatter loud, hostile, as they smashed into pieces on the wooden floor.

Feeling stupid, humiliated, anger made her open the cupboards, and launch glasses at the floor. Fortunately for Francesca, she was wearing trainers. She stepped over the broken crockery and glass, into the dining room, where she broke down in tears.

How could Paul do this to her? Didn't he love her?

Leaning on the dining room table, her rage evaporated, replaced with fear.

Something wasn't right.

A stabbing pain in the centre of her belly made her pitch forwards.

The pain was excruciating, unlike anything she had felt previously. Francesca recalled her appendix bursting three years earlier; that pain was insignificant by comparison.

Careful to fall on her back without hurting herself, Francesca lay on the soft new carpet hugging herself, her face sweaty. Until the pain stopped.

"Oh my God!" She was in labour! And she had no way of getting to the hospital.

The first person who sprung to mind was her mum. Crawling on her side, careful of the baby inside her, she reached the sofa in her lounge. Her mobile was on the cushion.

With her back against the settee, she dialled her parents' home number. Straight to voicemail. Francesca cursed under her breath. Next she tried her mum's mobile. Four rings, then an answerphone. "Mummy, I need you!" Sweat dripped down her cheeks. "I'm in labour...I need you to come get me...Paul walked out."

Desperate to get to the hospital, the fear of giving birth in her house with no assistance ever-present, Francesca phoned her dad. Voicemail again. She screamed at him before leaving him an urgent message.

Another stabbing pain made her writhe on the carpet, clutching at her round belly, her hair damp with sweat. When it passed, she picked up her phone.

The only other person she could rely on sprang to mind: Declan. Her situation too serious to start thinking about etiquette, Francesca dialled his number, the pain threatening to return any second. "Declan, hi! It's Fran. I'm in trouble; I need your help."

After explaining her situation, Declan took over. "The contractions, Fran, how far apart are they?" She told him eight to ten minutes. "Great! We have some time. Have your waters broken yet?" She told him, "No." He told her not to bother phoning for an ambulance, that they would take longer to reach her than he would.

Declan told her he was jumping in his truck, that he would be with her before she knew it. Francesca hung up, waiting for the crippling pain to return. Before it did, she crawled out to the hallway. Managing to unlock the front door, she leaned against the wall waiting for him. "Please hurry, Declan. I need you. We need you."

78

Yanking on the bottom drawer, Chris took out the almost empty bottle of vodka. His heart racing, he unscrewed the cap, tilted the bottle, and swallowed the remaining liquid.

Who the hell did Marble think he was? He couldn't come here, apologise for causing his family such heartache and anguish, and expect to be forgiven. Maybe he could. Chris would never forgive him.

After noticing the bottle was empty, he threw it at the wall.

It smashed with a satisfying noise. "Damn you, Marble!"

He paced the same tracks back and forth, differing scenarios playing in his mind.

He imagined clobbering Marble out there on his drive, pictured himself punching him time and again. There was nothing he wanted more.

Edie made an appearance, telling him to calm down, not to hate. How could she ask him such a thing? The stress Marble had caused her, he contributed to her cancer, Chris knew. Dr Bryson never confirmed it, but he knew.

His life was over without Edie. Tears welled up. He didn't want to die, didn't want to leave Amy alone in this God-awful world. A sob escaped him. Despair enveloped him. It took on a physical presence in his heart; he could feel it racing.

The tightening in his chest intensified. Chris held on to his desk, his knuckles white. A second later his bones seized up. He fell backwards, his heartrate so fast it almost felt like one long beat. Calling out for help, no noise came out.

On the ground, he reached out for help, trying to call Aidan's name.

The stabbing pain in his chest hurt like nothing before it. His fists were like rock, as he writhed on the ground in agony, still no noise escaping. Someone had just speared his heart. And now they were twisting it, yanking on it. Marble! He tried shouting out.

79

Aidan turned the engine off. He couldn't leave Chris in this state; the guy was drowning in vodka. He could do himself an injury, he thought, pulling on the handle, and opening his door. "This could be a mistake," he said, hauling himself out of his seat.

Walking towards the barn, Aidan hoped Chris wasn't drinking more. "Chris! We need to talk, mate." No reply, no ranting. "Chris?"

When he reached the barn, Chris lay on the floor unconscious. On the other side of the room, shattered glass littered the ground. "Chris!" Aidan ran over to his ex-friend, got on his knees. He tapped Chris lightly on the cheek. "Come on, wake up."

The main problem he had was ascertaining if Chris was drunk and unconscious, or if he was suffering something more insidious. Aidan thought Chris looked like a heart attack waiting to happen. He put his ear to Chris' chest. "Come on, Chris. Please breathe."

When he put his ear to Chris' mouth, he knew his old friend was in trouble.

His mind went into panic mode; he didn't know what to do.

"Help! Somebody help me, please!"

He got up, scanned the room. The desk was cluttered with bits and bobs. Was there a telephone around? He spotted a landline phone amongst the clatter. The first thing he had to do was phone for help. "Don't worry, Chris, I'll get you help."

At the desk, he picked up the receiver, and dialled triple nine.

There was no dialling tone.

Not believing it, he pressed the plastic connection buttons.

"Shit! Why aren't you wired up?"

As he put the receiver on its dock, he noticed a letter.

The letter read, 'Final Notice' in big bold type.

His mobile was in his Range Rover. "So stupid!" What should he do? Start CPR, or run for his phone? He couldn't think straight.

On his knees again, Aidan tilted Chris' head back, put his finger in his mouth to check for an obstruction. So scared he thought he might pass out, he glanced around for help. He had not been on a first aid course in about four years.

"Help!" He yelled one final time before having to act.

About to start compressions, a pair of blue and white checked trousers appeared in front of him. Aidan followed the trousers up, becoming chef whites. "Chef?" He could have jumped up and down for joy. "What are you doing here?"

'*I followed you.*' Chef signed.

Relief flooded him. "I need your help, buddy. Chris isn't breathing. I need you to start compressions while I phone for an ambulance. Do you know what to do?" He leaned over Chris, one hand on top of the other, mimicking the act. "Do you think you can do that?"

Chef nodded, waiting for him to move.

Getting to his feet, Aidan sprinted to his Range Rover, opened the driver's door, and leaned inside. He grabbed his mobile from the passenger seat. "Oh shit!" He didn't know the exact address of Chris' farmhouse.

Back inside the barn, he passed Chef, who seemed to be doing compressions, and stopped at the desk, where he picked up the letter from the bank. He dialled triple nine.

Talking to the emergency line woman took an age.

She asked to stay on the line with him, but he needed to help Chef.

"What are you doing, Chef?" No reply.

He switched his mobile to speakerphone. He waved at Chef to get his attention. "That's not how you do compressions. I showed you how just now." All he could think of was how long Chris had not been breathing for. It had to be a couple of minutes or more.

When he went to push Chef out of the way, his cook put his hand up, telling him to back off. Aidan stopped moving, somehow knowing not to approach his employee. "What are you doing?" Chef had his left hand on Chris' chest.

The woman's voice rang around the barn, as Aidan watched, transfixed on Chef, whose eyes were closed. He breathed in and out deeply with Chef.

All panic drained away, leaving Aidan calm.

Chris' body came alive. He sat up, his mouth open, as he sucked in a lungful of air, and let it out in a long stream, his eyes fixed on Chef's.

Aidan's mouth hung open at Chris' resurrection, which was the most apt word he could think of. Ashcroft should be dead after so long not breathing.

Chef lay Chris back down. He leaned over his patient, placing his hand on Chris' forehead. With a hand on Chris' chest, Chef closed his eyes once more.

Checking for signs of life on Chris, Aidan noted his eyelids moving. Chef had resuscitated Chris. What Chef was doing now, he could only guess. "What are you?"

When Chef opened his eyes, Aidan felt nothing but serenity.

In the distance, an ambulance wailed.

"We need to put him in the recovery position until the ambulance gets here." Aidan went to move Chris, when Chef put his hand up, and shook his head.

'*He is full of anger. I must help him.*'

Wondering if he'd read Chef's signs correctly, Aidan sat back, as his sous chef went back to Chris, one hand on his chest, the other on his forehead, his eyes closed, breathing deeply. What was he supposed to do, argue? Aidan didn't know what Chef was.

The siren grew louder, until it stopped.

Getting to his feet, Aidan met the emergency workers at the entrance to the barn.

They took over from Chef, checking vital signs. One of them gave him a thumbs-up, telling him they'd done a good job.

Chris had strong vitals, but they needed to take him to the Basingstoke and North Hampshire Hospital, the nearest facility with accident and emergency department facilities.

With the letter in hand, after ten minutes, Aidan climbed in the back of the ambulance with Chris on the gurney hooked up to an oxygen mask, and heart monitor that bleeped.

80

Another stabbing pain shot through her belly, as she lay on the carpet. Francesca looked up as the door opened. Declan entered, getting down on his knees next to her. "I'm so sorry! The way I treated you before. I should-" The pain was almost unbearable. "I should never have got back together with him."

"Don't worry about that now, Fran." Declan felt her forehead. "We need to get you to the hospital. Once this contraction has passed, we'll get you to my truck, got it?"

She nodded, sweat trickling down her face. "Please, I need to say this. I love you, Dec. I always have." She closed her eyes, wishing the pain to go away.

"Yeah, I love you, too. You're a good friend." He stared at her like she was mad.

"It's easing." Francesca relaxed her muscles, the pain dissipating.

He took her arm and put it round his neck. "Right, are you ready?"

"Uh-huh!" Francesca nodded. She groaned when he helps her to her feet. "I mean it, I love you. I've loved you since primary school, but I was always too scared to tell you. I'm sorry!" She walked with him along her driveway to his truck half on the pavement.

"I love you, too, but this isn't the time, sweetheart," he said, opening the passenger door, and helping her into the seat. He tilted the back rest, so that she was practically horizontal. "Lie back. I'll get us there."

Declan jumped behind the wheel, started the engine, and began their journey to Basingstoke and North Hampshire Hospital. "Keep talking through the contractions, Fran. Tell me what you've been up to recently."

Lying next to him, gripping her huge belly in her loose-fitting dress, Francesca couldn't think about anything but Declan. She didn't want to think about Paul, or the myriad of women he'd been sleeping with. Reaching out to him, Francesca wanted to touch him. "You're the one I want."

Declan put his hand on her bare knee. "And I want you, too, baby."

“You’re just saying that now. When we get to the hospital, you’ll leave, and we’ll go back to how we were before.” She felt like crying.

Another wave of pain swept over her like a hot breeze filled with daggers. She screamed, her eyes closed, wishing it away.

“Hold on, sweetheart, we’re nearly there.” Declan put his hand on her sweaty leg, squeezed it. “Remember your breathing exercises. Inhale, hold, exhale, in and out, nice long breaths. Come on, Fran, you can do it!”

She felt like screaming at him. It was easy enough for him to say; he wasn’t the one with a baby inside his belly. He wasn’t about to go through the most excruciating pain he had ever known. Francesca wanted her baby out, now. The pain had to stop.

Even lying back, she could tell how fast they were going.

Declan was steering in and out of gaps between cars.

“If we go much faster, we’ll go back in time.”

“You focus on your breathing; leave the driving to me, okay?” He glanced down at her, smiled. “I’ll get you there in one piece, don’t you worry.”

In spite of the pain, the journey to Basingstoke and North Hampshire Hospital on Aldermaston Road seemed to take no time at all, thanks to Declan’s speed-limit breaking driving. She smiled at him through the pain, as he stopped the engine. “Quick! Help me out.”

As he ran round to her side, Francesca felt warm liquid dribbling down her legs, onto Declan’s poor seat. With wide eyes, she stared up at him. “My waters broke. I’m so sorry!” Tears rolled down her cheeks. “I’m sorry!”

“Don’t be silly, it’s fine.” He put his palm on her cheek, leaned in, and kissed her on her lips. “Let’s get you out of here, yeah?”

Declan helped her into the wheelchair, where a male nurse, a kind looking man in his mid-forties began wheeling her inside the main foyer of the hospital. “Wait! Where’s Declan?”

“I’m right here, honey. I need to park the car.”

“Your husband will be with you soon.” The male nurse patted her shoulder.

81

Parking, even on a Sunday at Basingstoke and North Hampshire Hospital was a nightmare. It took Kate ten minutes to find a space. She asked a receptionist where the waiting room was, and then followed her instructions.

"Kate! Over here." Aidan stood, the waiting room busy.

Relieved to see him, Kate wandered over and sat next to him, smiling at a rotund lady next to her. The room was quiet despite the amount of people there. "Have you heard anything? How is he?" Aidan didn't have the chance to tell her over the phone.

"He was unconscious in the ambulance." He leaned forwards, elbows on knees.

Rubbing his back, she smiled. "I can't believe you got to use your CPR training. I told you it would come in handy one day, didn't I?" He didn't respond. "I'm so proud of you, love." A lump rose in her throat.

Aidan sat back. "Don't be. I really didn't do much." His voice became a whisper. "I was totally out of my depth, Kate. I didn't know what the hell I was doing. I couldn't remember what I was supposed to do, and when. I couldn't even remember if I was supposed to call for help first or start CPR."

A frown forming, Kate regarded her husband. "Well, you got him here, didn't you?"

"Chef got him here, not me," he confessed.

Shocked, Kate had to physically shut her own mouth. "Chef? What does he have to do with this? You left the restaurant by yourself. Chef was cleaning down when I left way after you." The more stories she heard about Chef, the more her suspicions grew.

"He just turned up at Chris' place. He found me about to start CPR, and I tell you I've never been so pleased to anyone in my life. He's the hero today, not me. If he hadn't turned up, I'd still be trying to resuscitate Chris now."

Two nurses called for their next patients. The large woman sat next to Kate stood and followed one of the nurses out. There were two seats free to Kate's left and Aidan's right. "Why were you there anyway? It's the last place I expected you to be."

He leaned into her. "I went to speak with Wyatt Newall a while ago now. He put me straight on what happened. All this time I've been blaming Liam when I should have been questioning Vinnie's part in the crash." He welled up. "So I went to apologise to Chris."

"And you found him unconscious?" She was puzzled.

"Not at first, no. He tried to fight me; he was blind drunk, so I put my hands up and left before I hurt him." He paused for a moment. "Don't ask me why, but I didn't leave. I went back to the barn to try and reason with him when I found him on the ground unconscious."

"You were looking out for him, like a good friend does," she whispered. "You wouldn't have left him in that state." Kate put her hand out, picking his up, interlocking their fingers. "I know you, Aidan. You're a good person. I've learned that over the past few months. You're so much better than other people I could mention." Lifting the back of his hand to her lips, she kissed it. "Thank you!"

"You haven't asked about my visit with Wyatt Newall."

"No, I don't need to. I already know what happened. I visited him a few weeks after he came out of hospital." The shock on his face caused a frown. "What? How would you have reacted back then, hmm? You had to reach the decision to see him by yourself. I was ready to face the ugly truth before you; no one could force you."

"And how do you feel now you know the truth?" He asked, still holding her hand.

"It hurts. Of course it does, but we can't keep our lives on hold like this, Aidan. We need to move on. Vinnie would want us to, don't you think? He wouldn't want us to break up over it, would he?" She wanted Aidan back, had for weeks, but something in the back of her mind prevented her from committing.

"Are you saying what I think you're saying? You want to come back?" His face lit up.

"It's all I've ever wanted, silly. And seeing how far you've come over the past few months lights up my heart." She squeezed his hand, wanting to kiss him. The people in the waiting room with them made her decide not to.

Aidan lifted her hand, kissed it. "You don't know how much I've wanted to hear those words. I'm so ashamed of how I behaved; I'll make it up to you, I promise."

"I know you will." She leaned into him, her head on his shoulder. She glanced down at his other hand. "What have you got there?" He held a folded sheet of A4 paper.

"Oh this?" He unfolded it, handed it to her. "I needed his full address when talking to the emergency operator and found this on his desk. I don't know why I brought it here."

Lifting her head from his shoulder, Kate read the letter. "It's a final notice of payment on his mortgage." She read the full page, the bank's request for two months of mortgage payments, or they will request the full amount of ninety-eight thousand, or repossess the farmhouse, and all land included in the purchase. "Poor guy. Like he hasn't been through enough already. Now he has the bailiffs knocking on his door?" She handed him back the letter. "If only there was a way of helping him out."

Aidan took the letter and sighed.

"If only we didn't have our own problems, we might be able to help him." Nothing would give her greater pleasure than to be able to help Chris out by paying off his mortgage. They would soon lose their lease to the restaurant.

"Chef was so confident everything would work out for us." Aidan put his arm around her, pulling her into him. "I guess even Chef can be wrong sometimes."

"What did Chef do earlier anyhow? How did he get to Chris' place?" Her suspicions made her stare straight ahead, not wanting to alert him to them.

"He must have hailed a taxi? I don't know. But he didn't resuscitate him."

She looked over at him, confused. "You said you didn't resuscitate him."

"I didn't either. Chef just put his hand on Chris' chest. One minute he wasn't breathing, the next Chris sat bolt upright gasping for air. I swear, honey, it was the strangest and calmest experience of my life. By rights, Chris should be dead now. And after Chef resurrected him, he started talking about Chris being full of anger, and taking it back."

Chef wasn't some stray off the street they'd taken in. Kate didn't have the first idea what Chef was, or rather she did, but didn't want to say it out loud. Somehow saying it made it real, a thing. How could she expect Aidan to believe her suspicions that Chef was in their lives for a reason? He'd been sent by a higher power to help them in their time of need.

"There she is!" Aidan stood. "Amy, over here."

Kate stood to greet a distraught Amy Ashcroft. She hugged her, kissed her on the cheek. "I thought you would make it here before me."

"Parking here is a nightmare. It took me twenty minutes to find the right spot, and I stopped off to grab a sandwich. How is he?" Amy hugged Aidan.

“I’m not going to lie to you, it was touch and go, but when the ambulance arrived, they said he had strong vitals. Plus, your old man’s a fighter, don’t forget that.” Aidan let go of her. “He’ll pull through this, no problem, you’ll see.”

Kate checked her watch again. “I really need to get a move on. I know Bonnie hates opening the restaurant by herself.”

“Both of you can go, honestly. The Singhs are on their way over, so they’ll be here very soon. I know you have a busy night ahead of you. When I hear more, I’ll ring you, Kate. And Aidan, thank you so much for being there when Dad needed you. I won’t ever forget it, and I’ll make sure he doesn’t.”

“Amy, are you sure? I can leave Aidan here with you for a while?” She wanted, no, needed Aidan tonight, but Kate wanted someone to stay with Amy.

“Go! Please! Now I know he’s going to be alright, it’s fine.”

She kissed Amy goodbye, and walked towards the entrance holding Aidan’s hand, like they were teenagers again. She had to face facts: unless by some miracle they came into fifty-thousand pounds over the course of the evening, Marble’s Marvels would cease to be, and Elio would be putting his place up for sale.

82

Aidan rang the bell for service. They had a full dining room of thirty tables of paying guests. With only four in the kitchen, and Benjamin as a go-between, they were fortunate the tables were mostly twos and fours. They had a party of eight in, but they had their mains an hour earlier. "Keep it going, peeps. We're doing great."

Kate rushed in carrying dirty plates, stacked them by the sink, and met him in front of the line. "Table sixteen. Four gammon steaks, two with eggs and two with pineapple. Got it."

"Thanks, honey." He wiped down the stainless-steel counter ready for the next round of meals. "Next up, number eighteen. One steak and kidney pudding, one liver and bacon, and two sausage casseroles. How are we doing on those, Philippa?"

"The casserole's in the oven now. I'm taking it out." Philippa bent over and slid the large bowl out. "The steak and kidney pudding is in, too. The liver and bacon are right at the back."

"Well done. All we need now is the chips, mash and veg."

Sliding the steak and kidney pudding bowl out of the oven, Aidan carried it over to the line, where Chef started dishing out the mash and chips. "*Thank you, Chef.*" He signed. He placed the individual bowl on the plate.

"Aidan, there's someone to see you out here." Kate's voice carried through the kitchen.

'*You're in charge for a minute*,' he signed to Chef, who nodded. "You're doing brilliantly, though, guys. Keep it going. I'll be right back." He left his tea towel on the side, and strode out of the kitchen, into the dining room.

Just outside the door, he stopped when Kate beckoned him over. She was talking to Flo, the florist from next door. "Flo, this is unexpected. I can't remember the last time you came here. What can we do for you?" He smiled at the lovely lady.

"I wanted to wait until I had both of you here." Flo dug into her handbag, retrieving an envelope, which she handed to Kate. "It's not much. If I could afford more, I would gladly donate to help save this lovely place. I was so sad when I heard your lease was taken over. Marble's Marvels has been here for a long time."

Kate handed him the envelope. "There's a thousand pounds in here, Flo." He touched her arm. "This is no small amount. We can't thank you enough."

"I do so hope you manage to raise the money you need. We need you across the road to see the new lot off, don't we?" Her frown marks spoke volumes.

"Why do you say that Flo? Have you met the new people?" Kate caught his eye.

Stepping closer, leaning in, Flo scanned those around her. "Oh yes, dear. Two of them, a taller man, and the shorter chef. They came in and started measuring my shop. When I asked them what they were doing, they went all quiet."

"You're kidding!" There were no lows these guys wouldn't sink to.

"Bold as you like. They were talking about knocking through to mine, like I wasn't there. They seem to think extending will be easy." Flo's voice changed in tone, the hostility palpable. "I hope you open Elio's and show those two what for. They've already rubbed a lot of locals up the wrong way. One thing's for sure, they'll need out-of-towners to keep them going. I've spoken to so many Drakers of late; they've all said the same."

"Already making friends and influencing people, huh?" Aidan handed the envelope back to Kate to keep in the office. "Again, thank you so much, Flo. This is so generous, and if we do manage to stay open across the road, you'll be our VIP guest. Plus, we'll give you and other sponsors regular discounts."

"That sounds lovely, Aidan. Thank you!"

"You'll have to start eating here regularly, though, Flo," Kate joked with a wink.

"Oh, I shall, don't you worry. I'm moving back here next month."

Aidan thanked her once more before making his excuses. As he went to return to the kitchen, four ladies walked through the main doors, the leader being Harriet Gaines, who waved him over. He checked that Kate had seen, gestured for her to join him.

Finding a quiet-ish spot to the right of the restaurant, they stood in a circle, Aidan next to Kate, opposite Harriet and her three friends. They made small talk for the first couple of minutes, all the while Aidan kept checking that food was coming out of the kitchen.

"Anyway, that's all water under the bridge." Harriet reached into her bag and pulled out a fat envelope, that clearly contained cash. "So, we all had a little whip around at the U3A meeting this afternoon. It's amazing how many members have eaten here; they had nothing but positive things to say."

Kate took it. "Do you know how much is in here?"

"There's two thousand in the envelope, and another thirteen thousand went on your campaign app, whatever it's called. Getting some of these ladies to use technology is no mean feat, I can tell you. Anyway, there's a grand total of fifteen thousand eight hundred towards your target."

Excitement caught Aidan off-guard. He encouraged Kate to look it up on her mobile. Judging by her solemn expression, the added money didn't meet their needs. "And? Are we there? Did we make it?" If she said no, it was pretty much over. They had two and a half hours left to reach their target.

Kate shook her head. "Afraid not. We're twelve thousand shy, give or take."

He wanted to kick or punch something, anger rising up through his gut. "It's not fair! We can't close. If only there was someone we could ask for a loan, or something."

"Honestly, you know how much I love you two." Harriet put her arms out to both of them. "If I could donate, or loan you the money I would. We all would, wouldn't we?"

The three friends all nodded.

"Thanks, Harriet. We appreciate it, but you've done more than enough for us. We'd have fifteen thousand more to look for without you." Kate hugged the mayor's wife.

"So, Kendall's been advised to plead guilty at his trial." Harriet smiled at him. "And he's going to do it. They're going to ask for two years at Ford Open Prison."

"Harriet, I'm so sorry." Kate looked confused.

The ladies all laughed. "Oh, don't be, Kate. He deserves it. And I get peace and quiet for a couple of years. It's a win-win. I still think this place has brought me good luck."

"And Kendall terrible fortune," one of the friends cackled.

Their voices dimmed, as Aidan thought of a way out of their predicament.

83

"That's it for now." Kate placed the stack of smaller dessert plates next to the sink for Benjamin to soak before he slid the tray of dishes in the machine.

The atmosphere in the kitchen couldn't have been any more sombre, with Aidan wiping down the surfaces, while Chef and the two new recruits finished getting the last four mains out.

Instead of trying to buoy their spirits, Kate strolled into the dining room, where over half their guests had left. Most of them offered her their well wishes; some left larger than normal tips, like they were contributing to her campaign.

Attitudes out front were no cheerier. Bonnie worked hard, rushing back and forth with plates full of food, then back to the kitchen with dirty dishes. Kate appreciated her hard work. Losing her and Francesca would be the toughest part of closing the restaurant. She always said people made a company.

"Have a look now, Kate." Benjamin pushed her mobile across the bar, having scurried out from the kitchen.

Kate was afraid to. At quarter to eleven, if the money was short now, it was over. Trying not to look scared, she picked up her phone.

The fundraising app took a few seconds to open.

Before she checked, she took a deep breath, praying for it to say the magic figure.

"Well? What does it say?" Bonnie looked over her shoulder.

With the shake of her head, Kate said all she needed to. "I'm sorry! I wish it were different. I don't want to close her doors tomorrow night." She fought the lump in her throat. When Elio walked in the lump grew bigger.

Bonnie put her arm around Kate's shoulder. "We know you want to keep this place open, Kate. You have nothing to apologise for."

"How much are we short, Kate? My parents might help." Benjamin's wide eyes made Kate want to cry more. He was such a sweet kid.

"Just shy of ten grand, Benjamin." She clicked off her campaign, placing her mobile on the bar again, as Elio approached.

Before he reached the bar, she saw a table that had plates in need of collecting. "Be right back," she told him on her way past.

The diners thanked her for clearing away their dessert plates. Kate offered them hot beverages, but they declined, opting for their bill. "It'll be right with you. Thank you so much for choosing Marble's Marvels."

"I'm not kidding, that was the best meal I've ever had. The sausage casserole was off the charts tasty. Thank you so much." The husband and father smiled.

"You're so welcome." Before she teared up, Kate carried the plates through to the kitchen, where the whole team were busy scrubbing, wiping, and washing up. She left the plates by Chef, whose shoulder she squeezed.

He enquired about the campaign without using words. Kate shook her head, like she had to Benjamin. Chef's head hung. She'd never seen him glum in the time she'd known him; it scared her seeing him so downhearted. "You never know, some miracle might happen."

"Kate, I think you should come out here," Bonnie shouted through the door.

"I'll be there in a sec." She put her arms around Chef's waist, cuddled him.

"No, now, Kate. And you as well, Aidan." Her waitress' tone had an urgency to it that piqued her interest.

Leaving Chef to the washing up, Kate followed her husband out to the dining room, where a group of walk-ins stood inside the main entrance.

The mob was headed by Mr and Mrs Singh, who were supposed to be with Amy and Chris at the hospital. She poked her head back in the kitchen. "Everyone come out, please."

Excited, her heart doing somersaults, Kate turned back to the gang.

She held Aidan's hand, as she approached them.

Looking at the group, they were mostly Chris Ashcroft's friends, regulars at The Red Lion, who had boycotted their restaurant. "Hi! How can we help you? Mrs Singh, is everything alright? How's Chris? Please tell me he's okay."

"Relax, Kate, he's fine." Mrs Singh stepped forward. "In fact, the doctors seem to think with a decent diet and exercise he'll make a full recovery. They're calling this a warning."

Kate exhaled. "Oh, thank the Lord! For a minute there, I thought."

"No, we're all here for a different reason."

Mrs Singh asked for 'The Bag'.

One of the mob passed it forward until she held it in her hand. "Amy told us what Aidan did for Chris. She told us how he went and resuscitated our friend-"

"Well, that's not entirely-"

Kate kicked Aidan in the shin. "Let Mrs Singh speak, honey. Sorry! He can be so rude, please do continue." She needed to see what was in the bag so badly. Without viewing their faces, she could tell the kitchen staff were keen to find out as well.

"Because you were there today, Aidan, Chris is alive." Mrs Singh swallowed. "So, my husband and I did a whip around with Chris' friends. None of us want this place to close; it has history within the village. We've all had wonderful times here, albeit not recently, but we hope that will change now."

Kate interlocked her fingers with Aidan's. He was choked up; she could tell. "I don't know what to say, except thank you?"

"Here!" Mrs Singh handed her the bag. "Everyone's been running around like mad things trying to get to their banks on time. Others have written cheques."

"I don't suppose you know how much there is in total?" Peering inside the plastic carrier, it was a lot.

"How much do you need to clear your target?"

"Nine thousand, eight-hundred and eighty," she answered.

"Somewhere in the region of fifteen thousand."

Closing the bag, Kate glanced up at Aidan, who was welling up.

A brief silence befell the whole room, everyone trying to register the information.

Aidan erupted, grabbing her by the waist, then pulling her in and lifting her off the floor, whirling her around.

Kate was flying for the briefest of moments, weightless, the magnitude of Mrs Singh's words filling her with merriment. The joy!

Back on her feet, Kate turned and hugged Chef as tight as she could.

They'd just saved Marble's Marvels, thanks in no small way to him.

Pulling back, she stared into his eyes. "Thank you so much, Chef." She spoke clearly and concisely. "I know this is somehow your doing. You're our guardian angel."

Chef smiled, then slunk back, letting the kitchen staff congratulate her.

Right after them, she hugged Elio, letting him know she would either hand over, or transfer the required money to him in the morning, if he would contact his wife, and let her know. "Thank you so much for giving us this opportunity, silent partner. You don't know how much this means to us. You're a good man, Elio Capelli, I hope you know that."

Having hugged and kissed everyone present, including the leftover diners, Kate grabbed Aidan's hands. "I love you, Aidan Marble. I always have, always will."

Wolf whistles and comments about getting a room followed, as she pulled him down to kiss her. She had goosebumps on her arms.

With so much love in the room, Kate felt like she was home, where she truly belonged.

Pulling away from their kiss, she stared up at him.

"Does this mean you're coming home?"

"You are my home, so yes, please. If you'll have me?"

Bonnie brought her mobile phone over from the bar. Kate took it, looking at the caller ID. "Hello?" It was Francesca's mum calling from outside the hospital. "Uh-huh! Oh my!" She put her hand over her mouth. "Really? That's wonderful news. Thank you so much for letting me know."

She couldn't stop smiling. The best day ever!

"Kate? What is it?" Aidan waited for her to stop grinning and talk.

"That was Fran's mum. She's just had her baby, a healthy seven-pound girl."

A chorus of gasps followed by cheers and clapping preceded a night of celebratory drinking and laughing. Electric. Buzzing. The only two words she could use to describe the evening they enjoyed.

MONDAY,
OCTOBER 7TH

84

"Are you sure about this?" Kate glanced over at Aidan's parents' house.

"No!" He stared past her at his dad's red double garage door. "I never know what he's going to ask me to do when I ask for a favour. You remember the last time? He took me deep-sea fishing on that tiny trawler."

Kate laughed. He would, too, had he not almost died of hypothermia from wearing the wrong kind of clothing. "I can still remember my teeth chattering so hard I thought they would shatter."

"How could I forget?" She slid the key in the ignition of her MG. "Say the word, and we're out of here. I've got a ton of publicity to do before the re-opening." Turning the key, the engine started. "What's it going to be, love?"

Aidan stared down at the letter he'd taken from Chris' garage. "Let's do this!"

When she switched off the engine, Kate opened her door.

"Just promise me that if he suggests us going fishing again you'll come up with a reason why I can't." His wife nodded her agreement. "This could be a huge mistake."

Pulling himself out of Kate's MG seemed to be getting harder each time. Aidan took a deep breath. He had not set foot inside his parents' house in months. Even now he didn't want to see his dad, 'The Captain.'

"Thought I heard a car pulling up." His mum appeared in the doorway. She pretended she was there accidentally, but Aidan knew his mum would have been excited to see him and stood waiting by the door. "Come in, both of you, please. You have great timing; I've just put the kettle on for your dad's morning tea."

Stepping up to the door, Aidan kissed his mum on the cheek, giving her a little hug before going through to the kitchen, where, true to her word, the kettle had steam rising out of the spout. Kate followed him and they were both flanked by Celia Marble.

"Sit, please. I'll pour us all a nice cup of tea, and we'll eat a scone each, how's that?" Celia fussed about in her good-natured way. "Joe, tea's ready. Look who's come to visit!"

Unsure why, Aidan was nervous. His hands were clammy, and his belly was doing cartwheels. He lied to himself, though, he did know why. The last time he met with his dad, they had a massive argument, and neither had apologised since.

Captain Joseph 'Joe' Marble entered the kitchen in his customary dark trousers and rugby style sweater. His face showed no emotion when he sat at the table. No hello, no hug or kiss for Kate. "It's been a while, Aidan." His dad did the honours, pouring them their drinks.

"Yeah, we've been busy with the restaurant. My apologies." His dad always made him feel like a little kid, and worse, a failure.

"I hear things have picked up now. That's good. They couldn't have got any worse, could they?" His dad took a sip of his tea, while eyeing him.

"We had a blip, yes, but we're over it now. We're back on track." Forever the voice of reason, Kate massaged his leg with her foot under the table. "We're opening the new restaurant on Friday the first of November, and we would love for you to join us as our special guests."

"Oh, we'd love to come, wouldn't we, darling?" Celia encouraged her husband with a smile, and flick of the head. "You said only last week how we haven't been to the restaurant in ages, didn't you?"

"We can't on the first, Kate, sorry. We've a prior engagement we can't get out of."

"Oh, well, we're running specials the whole opening weekend. Maybe you could make the Saturday or Sunday?" Her voice grew small, like a child's.

"I wouldn't waste your breath, Kate," Aidan whispered, taking a sip of tea.

"We'll try and make it at some point over the weekend, I'm sure." Captain Joe Marble's eyes narrowed. "Why are you both here anyway? We don't see you for months, and you suddenly pop over out of the blue like this? To what do we owe the pleasure?"

Aidan smiled. "What? Can't a son and daughter-in-law just come and visit?" His smile was coy, telling his dad he had an ulterior motive. "We were nearby, thought we'd pop in and say hello."

"Uh-huh!" His dad's eyes narrowed further. "I'm sure."

The four of them sat around the table, taking the occasional sip, taking little bites out of their cheese scones that Celia made with love.

"These are lovely scones, Celia. Really cheesy." Kate kicked him under the table.

"Look, Dad, I'll be honest with you. We do have an ulterior motive for coming over here, okay? Do you mind if we go into your study and talk?" Aidan breathed out in relief when his dad stood, beckoning him to follow.

Carrying his mug of tea, Aidan followed his dad through the house to the study at the front, next door to the huge lounge. The study, the smallest room in the house, was larger than most people's sitting rooms, with a massive mahogany desk in the centre. His dad looked tiny behind it, but maybe that was the Great Captain Joseph Marble shrinking with old age? Aidan sat on a chair opposite his dad, staring at him across the desk.

"Why don't you start by telling me what this all about, huh? I don't like ulterior motives, Aidan, you know this." His dad sat back in his high-backed chair regarding him.

Aidan passed his dad the letter. "Here! This will explain most of it."

He kept staring at his dad, waiting for him to look up from the page.

"I had no idea Christian was in such a dire situation." His dad folded the letter and handed it him back. "It's not like the poor man hasn't been through the mill already, and now they're trying to repossess his home?" His eyes were full of sorrow. "But I'm not sure why you're showing me that, son. There's nothing I can do about it."

Aidan slid the letter back inside his jacket pocket. "That's not entirely true."

"What? That's a hundred grand you're talking about, Aidan. If you've come here to ask me for a hundred thousand, forget it. You must think I'm loaded, or something. I can't just give you that kind of money, even if it is for a good cause."

"You won't be giving it away." Aidan leaned forwards. "With the restaurant opening next month, I'll put in a repayment plan. If Marble's is as popular as we think it'll be, you'll have your money back in no time. So, consider it a loan."

His dad showed his suspicion. "And what if it's not popular at all? What if you take it back to being a tomb? Or what if that new chef of yours leaves, hmm? What happens to the repayment plan then? Can you even tell me?"

"No, because it won't happen. Chef's happy here with us, and I'm over my slump now, Dad, don't you see? Can't you see the difference in me? I have my mojo back."

His dad tutted. "Your mojo. What nonsense."

"Fine, a poor choice of words. A new lease of life, how about that? I enjoy cooking again, Dad. Chef brought me out of the rut I was stuck in for so long. He showed me how to live life again. I won't let the restaurant slip back downhill again, I promise." Why he had to placate his old man, he didn't know. "So, you see, I'll be in a position to pay you back in monthly instalments."

"Look, it's not that I don't want to help Christian out, because I do, but this is a huge sum of money you're asking for here, Aidan." His dad pulled out a drawer of his desk, picked up two cigars and offered him one.

"No, you're good, thanks." He waited for his dad to light it. "I'll clear it with Chris, so he has to help pay you back, too, how about that? And if, God forbid something unforeseen happens with the restaurant, and I physically can't pay you back, it can be my inheritance?"

Suspicion grew in his dad's eyes. "You'd risk your inheritance on Christian Ashcroft?"

"He's an old friend, sure." He surprised himself with his own revelation. "So, how about it? You know Mrs Singh already; she's Chris' accountant. I spoke to her yesterday about paying off Chris' mortgage, so she'll be expecting your call."

"Did something happen? I thought you both hated each other. At least that's what I was led to believe. You blamed him for Vinnie's death for so long, why this? Why now?"

Aidan looked past his dad, avoiding eye contact altogether. "Because I was wrong, okay? Is that what you want to hear? I was wrong all this time. If Wyatt's testimony is any indication, it looks like Vinnie caused the crash." He paused, thinking about Wyatt's confession. "I went to visit Chris to apologise to him, and he got really mad at me. He tried to throw me off his property, and that's when he had his heart attack."

"So, you feel guilty, and think you need to pay his house off for him? That's a hell of a leap, Aidan." His dad leaned back again. "But it's bloody selfless, putting yourself in that much debt to say sorry to someone."

Aidan heard the softness in his dad's voice. "We can't see Chris and Amy on the street, can we?"

His dad continued mulling it over.

"Well? Come on, Captain. You know it's the right thing to do. Chris deserves peace of mind, knowing his house is paid for. Imagine the relief."

"I have to say I like this change in you. Putting someone else first like this should be commended." He rose from his desk chair. "I will have a little chat with Mrs Singh in the morning, how's that? If she can get it done, I'll cover the cost of the mortgage on the proviso that both you and Christian start paying it back."

Aidan joined his dad on his feet. "Oh, thank you, Captain. You won't reg-"

"I haven't finished yet, son." His dad sat back down, the fingers tips of both hands touching their opposites. "You and Christian will pay it back until your mum and I pass on, at which time the remainder of the money will form part of your inheritance, is that clear? We'll reach a mutually agreeable sum of repayment, nothing that will put you or Chris out of pocket. Should you wish to increase the amount to repay your debt more expediently, I won't argue with you."

Waiting for a punchline, Aidan leaned forwards. "Really? That's it?"

His dad nodded.

Aidan got to his feet, extending his hand. "Thank you so much, Da...Captain. This means so much to me and Kate. What can I do? How can I repay you?"

"You can come fishing with me if you want?" His dad shook his hand.

Wanting to pull his hand away, Aidan refrained. "On that rickety trawler?" He continued shaking the Captain's hand.

"The very same." His dad smiled, more grinned. "Why? Do you not like deep sea fishing on the trawler? It's real fishing, for real men, not this puny pond fishing I see everywhere. Battling the sea and the wind is the fun part."

After taking his hand back, Aidan swallowed. "Exactly. Real fishing, in the middle of the ocean, on a boat that looks about ready to sink. How could I not want to?"

"Great! It's settled. I'll speak to Mrs Singh tomorrow morning, and we'll set sail next week sometime. Oh, and don't forget to wear warm clothing. You looked chilly last time."

Aidan knew when to quit. He joined his dad back in the kitchen.

When Kate enquired with a look, he nodded with a barely noticeable smile.

85

Francesca pulled up outside Declan's farmhouse. She switched off the engine and turned in her seat to find little Wren staring up at her with big brown curious eyes. "You've been such a good girl for mummy, haven't you?" She cooed over her daughter for a couple of minutes, getting out, and pulling the front seat of her Mini Cooper forwards.

"How about we go and visit Uncle Declan, huh? Would you like that? Oh yes, you would. Let's get you unclipped, shall we?" Francesca pressed the button, clearing the belt from the carrier, freeing her beautiful girl. "You're so pretty, yes you are."

Making a fuss over Wren took her mind away from her nerves. She had not seen Declan since he dropped her off at the hospital. Her mum and dad rushed there when they heard her voicemails, making it to the maternity ward before Declan managed to find a space.

"Need a hand?" Declan asked from behind her.

"Oh hi!" Francesca held the carrier handle, and as delicately as she could backed out of her car. She tried to come across as calm, cool, and collected. "I was trying to surprise you, but it's kind of hard with this little one."

Declan bent over, cooing over her daughter. "Ah Fran, she's beautiful. She has your big brown eyes. What's her name?"

"Wren, spelled like the bird." She held her daughter up for Declan to take a closer look.

"That's a beautiful name; it suits her." He smiled at her daughter. "Almost as beautiful as her mummy, aren't you?" He said without looking up at her. "Yes, you are."

Francesca smiled at the compliment, not that Declan saw.

He was too busy taking the carrier from her and walking it into the house to notice.

"Thanks. It can get heavy."

While Declan fussed about making her a cup of tea, and warming up a bottle of milk for Wren, Francesca sat at the kitchen table. For a whole week she'd felt guilty about her mum taking over at the hospital and excluding him.

"I just came to thank you for driving me to the hospital. I'm so sorry my mum made you stay in the waiting room. I should've been more forceful, and asked her to leave, for all the good she did." She laughed.

He stopped and leaned against the sink. "That good, huh?"

"She was terrible. I was calming her down, making her breathe." She chuckled at the memory of her mum almost fainting at the sight of her Wren crowning. "The nurses almost gave her oxygen. You would have been far calmer than mum, so I'm sorry she pushed you out. Do you forgive me?"

Declan put his palms out in a placating manner. "Hey, it doesn't matter to me, Fran. The only thing I cared about was getting you two to the hospital. And I did that. I almost sent us back in time in the process, but you got there in one piece."

After an awkward silence, Declan handed her the warm bottle of milk. "May I?"

Francesca was taken by surprise. Most guys would run a mile when offered a baby to feed. "Really? You want to feed her?"

His eyes apologised. "What? Is it too weird? I'm sorry!"

"No! Don't be silly. Of course it's not weird. I just didn't expect you to ask." She got up from her chair, took Wren out of the carrier and waited for Declan to get comfortable on his chair. She handed him her most prized position, her daughter. "Make sure you support-"

"Fran, I know how to look after a baby."

She put her hands up. "You're right, I'll back off."

Declan managed to get the teat in Wren's tiny mouth, as she suckled on it. "Mummy's a little protective, isn't she, gorgeous?" He looked up and winked at her. "You'd be forgiven for thinking I don't have experience with kids, but I do. I looked after my cousins when they were small. And I had loads of friends with babies when I lived in the city."

Feeling calm, Francesca sat down next to him. "You're so good with her. She's staring up at you. Probably wondering who this handsome stranger is. I know I would be thinking that if I was her." When his eyes met hers, she looked away.

An awkward silence fell over them.

All Francesca could hear was the gentle suckling sound. Her daughter's eyes started drooping. She couldn't help but smile at him holding Wren, and her daughter falling in love with him. "I meant what I said in my hallway, you know."

"Hmm?" He glanced up at her, smiling himself. "Sorry! What was that?"

"I said, I meant what I said in my hallway the other day."

Declan had a blank expression. “You might have to elaborate on that.”

Francesca knew he was teasing by the coy smile. “Really? This is how you want it?” She shook her head. “Okay, when I said I love you. I meant it. There! Are you happy now you dragged it out of me?”

She was expecting him to shy away. After all, she’d just given birth to a child who wasn’t his. Why would he want her now? Only she couldn’t let him go without at least trying to win his hand. “I can’t believe I just said that out loud.”

With Wren resting on his knees, Declan used his free hand to reach out for Francesca. He grabbed her blouse, and pulled her towards him, his lips meeting hers.

On her knees, she massaged his tongue with hers, making sure Wren wasn’t crushed.

On the drive over she’d dreamed of something like this happening. Reality was far sexier than even her dreams. She pulled back, staring into his dreamy eyes. “Does this mean?” She left a pause.

“I love you, too.” Declan made sure Wren was comfortable on his lap. “I always have. Every girl I ever went out with could never compete with you. Why else do you think I’ve never stuck with any of them? They were mostly lovely women, but they weren’t you.”

Francesca sat on her knees, her mouth open in shock. “You’re kidding! But I’ve always fancied you. Oh my God! This is too much. You mean to tell me we’ve liked each other since secondary school, and we’ve only just now found out?”

“Since primary.” He fussed over Wren, playing with her tiny hands.

Confused, Francesca stood and stared out of the window at his barn. “So, why didn’t you ever ask me out? I thought you fancied Zoe. You made me help you ask her out, for Heaven’s sake. All these years we’ve wasted.”

“Hey, you can’t blame me for that; I was a dumb kid back then.”

He was right. She sat back down on the chair next to him. “I’m sorry! I didn’t mean to get angry. It’s just that you won’t want me now, will you? It’s not fair!”

Declan put his hand on her knee. “Why wouldn’t I want you?” He looked back down at little Wren, her hands in the air begging to be touched. “What, because of this little one?”

Francesca nodded, welling up at the thought of losing him. Why would he want her?”

He picked her daughter up, raised her in the air and smiled. "Wren only makes you more attractive, Fran." He put her daughter back on his lap. "I've never seen you looking more beautiful than you do right now."

"Really?" She checked herself. There might have been a bit of sick on her blouse. "You find this attractive?"

"Immensely." He reached out for her.

Francesca went on her knees beside his chair.

He put his palm on her cheek. "I'm all yours, if you'll have me."

Francesca's lips met Declan's for the second time. Squealing inside, she enjoyed the moment with her tiny little family. Was he for real? Only time would tell. One thing was for certain: she would enjoy finding out.

FRIDAY,
NOVEMBER 1ST

86

"And that's it. The last ticket." Aidan speared the paper, checking out the orders on the metal spike. "You see this, peeps? These are all from tonight." He wiped his forehead of sweat that had built up over the stove. "How are you doing over there on desserts?"

"We're on the last two tickets, Aidan," Philippa answered.

Stepping back from the line after switching the heater light off, Aidan surveyed his kitchen. They'd successfully cooked for a hundred and twenty-six diners, with several tables turning over twice. The place looked like a bomb hit it. "Well done, Chef. Couldn't have done it without you." He signed, then shook Chef's hand.

'*Yes you could. This is all you,*' Chef signed, patting him on the back.

"That's lovely of you to say, but you're the reason everyone comes here," he argued, happy that his restaurant was packed to the rafters again. Also happy that he and Kate were back together. He took in a deep breath, smiled. "Right, let's get on with those dishes; they won't wash themselves."

Kate walked in carrying another stack of plates that she left next to the rest. "The fire alarm went off over the road again. That's the third time tonight. You should see Graham. He's fuming."

Aidan chuckled to himself. "That's funny. We never had any trouble with the alarms over there, did we?" He caught Chef's attention. "You wouldn't have anything to do with the fire alarms over the road, would you?"

With a 'who, me?' shrug, Chef put on his marigolds, filling up the sink.

"Have we heard how the food is over the road yet?" Aidan opened the dishwasher and slid the tray of clean plates out. "Fire alarms aren't going to put people off going there."

"We've had to turn their guests away. We've had about twelve of their diners come by asking if we have space because the food over there was so rubbish." Kate went on tiptoes and kissed his cheek. "Let's hope the food critics they invited thought the same, huh!"

Their opening night couldn't have gone any better had they tried. Elio's team of fitters did a fantastic job decorating the place to replicate their old restaurant over the road. He and Kate decided to stick with the same décor. The bar was located on the other side of the dining room, but apart from that, the restaurant was identical.

Even the kitchen was identical in size. Aidan wanted the cookers and stoves, grills to be in the same place, so the transition was seamless. It felt weird going to the window, looming out and seeing their old place, looking out and seeing Flo's next door.

Benjamin stuck his head inside. "You're both needed outside. Some guy's going off his nut at the diners. Sorry!"

Tapping Chef on his shoulder, Aidan beckoned for him to follow. "I might need your help." He waited for Chef to peel off his marigolds.

Out in the dining room the diners were quiet.

Aidan greeted one table of locals with a smile and a nod.

In the centre of the restaurant, Graham stood glaring at Francesca and Bonnie, who they'd asked to help on opening night.

"Here he is!" Graham held his arms out like he wanted to hug him. "I know you're responsible for the alarms over there."

Aidan stood in front of Kate's ex-boyfriend. "I don't know what you're talking about, mate. We never had any trouble with the alarms over there, did we, Kate?" His wife agreed with him from a safe distance behind Chef. "Are you having a tough opening night, Graham, is that it? And you thought you'd come over here blaming us for it?"

Taking two steps towards him, Graham curled his hands into fists. "I don't know how you've done it, but our diners are walking away saying the food's crap. He has two Michelin stars to his name. He doesn't know how to cook bad food."

With his fists clenched, Aidan grinned. "Maybe he's learned."

Graham went to pull his fist back.

Some of the diners gasped, until Chef shot in the middle of them, his hand on Graham and Aidan's chests.

"Do yourself a favour, Graham, and go back over there. We've just had the best night, and we're in the mood for celebrating. Everyone happy with their meals tonight?"

The guests confirmed with a chorus of yeses.

Aidan wanted to laugh when Graham turned and walked out with his tail firmly between his legs. He refrained until the snake had gone. "Fran, put the music back on. Let's celebrate the re-opening of Marble's Marvels."

Cheering with him, the room full of guests went back to enjoying themselves.

While Francesca, Bonnie and Kate went around each table taking drinks orders, Aidan made himself busy pouring the drinks. "This is table two's order, Fran. Thank you!"

Electric. Like the Marble's Marvels of old, back when they had a full dining room every night of the week, and when they used to turn tables over twice, sometimes three times on Friday and Saturday nights.

"*Marble!*" An angry cry came from the doors.

Aidan stopped pouring a pint of lager, spotting Chris Ashcroft sporting a walking stick.

Kate stood in front of the bar. She touched his arm.

"I'll deal with this." Kate went to walk away, but Aidan stopped her.

"No, this is on me, love. I'll deal with Chris." He swallowed, then stepped out from behind the bar. He thought Chris looked awful.

Chris came with company, some of his friends from The Red Lion, locals who all knew of their affairs. Three of his four friends had come with Mrs Singh to hand Kate and he the money to keep their restaurant open. Why were they with Chris now?

Time seemed to slow as he approached Chris in the middle of the room. "Chris! This is a surprise." He noted how out of breath his ex-friend appeared. "Can I get you something?"

Taking out a letter, Chris pushed it into Aidan's chest. "Here! Are you responsible?"

The letter came from Chris' mortgage lender, telling him that the total amount of the mortgage was paid. "I am."

"We are." Kate stood next to him.

All chatting voices ceased. The guests stayed still, not knowing what to expect.

Chris' face screwed up, like he was snarling, Aidan prepared himself for the assault, although he wouldn't fight back. It wouldn't be fair on Chris. "I can explain."

Before he had the chance to blink, Chris' face changed, the sneer turning to a smile.

Chris extended his hand. "What I really came here to say is, thanks."

Gripping his hand, Chris shook it. "Thank you so much, for everything."

Aidan tried to swallow the lump in his throat. "Um, you're welcome."

Kate put her arm around his waist.

"I'm going to come up with a way of paying you back the money, mate, I promise. Consider it a loan. I always pay my debts off."

"Sure thing, we'll sort something out."

In the distance, Chef smiled at him.

Aidan was puzzled by the strange smile Chef wore, like he was surveying his handiwork with pride. Aidan waved him over, but Chef declined, walking back into the kitchen.

The waiters finished clearing away the last of the plates and cutlery, leaving only glasses on the tables. Half an hour later, the kitchen staff came out and joined them at the bar. Most of the customers left, having tipped them all well.

"Now that is what I call a successful night," Aidan said, chinking Kate's glass.

"There's Declan." Francesca skipped over to meet her boyfriend.

Aidan couldn't think back to a time he'd been happier. He enjoyed the company of his family and the finest friends a man could ask for. Feeling emotional, he poured Declan a drink, said cheers. "You're a big step up from Paul."

"Oh don't, we still have to see Paul on a weekly basis." Francesca chimed, rolling her eyes. "He has Wren tomorrow and Sunday daytime. This will be the first time I've been away from her overnight. I don't know if I can take it."

"I'll be with you." Declan kissed her cheek.

Aidan saw the time: quarter past twelve. "Where is he?"

Picking up his pint of lager, Aidan left the throng of diners stood at the bar, wondering where Chef had got to. "Chef?" He peered inside the kitchen. Nothing. He tried the dry store. Nothing there. "That's odd."

Kate joined him. "What is it? What's wrong?"

"I can't find Chef. Have you seen him?" He double checked every nook and cranny in the kitchen, taking his drink out to the dining room. "Well, he can't be upstairs. Elio lives there. He won't have walked back to the house without me, would he? Not without saying something, surely?"

Kate regarded him with sad eyes. "He's gone, Aidan."

He shook his head. "What? No, he's taking the rubbish out or something."

Taking Kate's hand, Aidan walked with her through the kitchen and out of the fire exit door onto the back patio. No sign of him. He scratched his head.

"I spoke to that headteacher, do you remember? Fran's boss, the one who hired Chef at Cherry Tree Lodge." She held his hand. "She told me that he just disappeared one day. Like he waited until he knew the Lodge was sorted and decided to up and vanish."

Aidan shook his head, fighting the lump. "No! Chef wouldn't leave me, not now. We need him. It's his food that brings people here."

Back inside the kitchen, he closed the emergency exit, and stood by the dessert station,

Kate in front of him holding his hand, it dawned on him. "He's gone, hasn't he?"

When Kate's face crumpled, he couldn't hold it in any longer, pulling her in for a cuddle. Why would Chef desert him like this? They needed him now more than ever.

A gust of wind blew Kate's hair.

Aidan felt something hit his back. When he let go of Kate, an A4 pieced of paper hit his leg and landed on the floor. "Where did that come from?" He stooped, picked it up and opened the folded paper.

"*Dear Kate and Aidan,*" he read out loud. "*The time has come for me to leave. I told you when we first met that I'll be here as long as I'm needed. Well, I'm not needed anymore. You have everything you require to continue your fruitful and rewarding lives.*"

With a sniff, Aidan went back to the pretty cursive. "*Kate, you have come to realise how much Aidan means to you, how much you love him. This is all I wanted for you. You are both so much better together than you would ever be apart. You belong together.*"

"*Aidan, you now know the truth about your son's tragic accident. You've accepted it, and now you may move on with your life, one day at a time. You have your love of cooking back, which is all you need to keep your lovely diners coming back time and again. If you ever doubt yourself, just remember to season with love. I have left my pepper grinder here; it won't steer you wrong.*"

"*I have had the best time meeting you and your colourful group of friends, family, and colleagues. They are the best bunch of people I've ever met. Please don't feel I'm deserting you. I have many more people I need to help. Yours forever, Chef.*"

A tear fell on the letter. Aidan wiped his eyes, folded the piece of paper, and hugged Kate once more. "He's gone? Just like that? What are we going to do now?"

Kate pulled away, her palms on his cheeks. "Take his advice. Live life one day at a time. It's all we can do, honey. Come on, let's go and join our friends and family for a drink. Tomorrow's another day."

WEDNESDAY, DECEMBER 25TH

87

The sound of breaking glass at the front of the farmhouse woke Morris Hackett with a start. He turned on his light, noting the time: 03:46. The sound of laughter followed by a truck driving away at high speed told him all he needed to know. “Damn it! Not again.”

Morris flung back the warm duvet and sat up, his legs dangling over the bed. His wife, Yvette joined him on her feet getting dressed.

“On Christmas morning, Morris? This has got to stop. We need to either take them up on their offer, or you need to sort this.”

She wasn’t wrong. The construction company buying up farms surrounding them meant business. There were only two properties preventing them from starting their project, his and his next door neighbour’s. “I’ll sort it, I told you.”

The bedroom door opened. Their seven-year-old daughter, Una stood in the doorway, rubbing her eyes. “What’s all the noise, Daddy? Was that Santa Claus?”

He glanced over at his wife for support. “I don’t know, pet. It might have been, although I think it’s still too early. We’re one of Santa’s last stops.”

Pulling on his jeans, a jumper, socks, he took her by the hand. “Come on, let’s get you back to bed. We don’t want you awake when he gets here, do we?”

Out on the landing, Una looked up at him. “Can we go and see Shepherd?”

“No, pet, we need to get you back to sleep, or he won’t come and leave you presents.” Morris tried leading her to her bedroom next door to his.

“Shepherd!” Una struggled free of his grasp when his hired help opened his door.

She rushed over to the deaf, mute man with white hair, wrapping herself around him. Shepherd hugged her in return.

With gentle encouragement from himself and Shepherd, Morris managed to get Una tucked up in bed. After reading her the fifth story of the night, he switched her light off and left her door open a crack, the way she liked.

Fully dressed for outdoors, Shepherd asked him what happened.

His helper couldn’t have heard the breaking window, so how did he know he was needed? There were so many unanswered questions about Shepherd. “They broke a window downstairs. Help me board it up. We’ll have to wait until the New Year now, I reckon.”

Whenever he tried to broach Shepherd's previous history, the guy wouldn't let on. When he'd just appeared on his farm looking for work one day, at first Morris had fobbed him off saying he couldn't afford him, until Shepherd told him he would work for room and board. Whoever heard of that in this day and age? According to Shepherd, he didn't need money; he had a vastly wealthy family.

In the lounge, Morris switched on the light to find two small panes of glass broken by medium sized rocks. Still single glazed, it wasn't hard to smash his windows. "Let's find a piece of hardboard to cover it up with.

Terrific start to the festive season! He found the wood, held it in place while Shepherd hammered the nails in place. "Let's give the outside a once over as well."

After putting boots on, he and Shepherd stepped outside. He quickly noticed how quiet it was. His sheep were nowhere to be seen. "God damn it!" He wanted to punch something. "That's the third time in two weeks. When are these arseholes going to get it through their thick heads, I'm not bloody selling?"

Shepherd wrote that he'll go and get them back on a pad of paper he kept handy.

"Would you? You're a lifesaver." Morris put two fingers in his mouth and whistled.

Two border collies came bounding towards him.

Getting Shepherd's attention, he pointed at the dogs. "Take them with you, okay? They'll herd them up. Good luck."

Morris thanked his lucky stars that Shepherd turned up on his doorstep. He couldn't put his finger on it, but strange things were afoot on his farm. In the past month, his livelihood had taken a turn for the better. Only in November he thought he would be selling his parents' old farm. Not now, though. Not after hiring Shepherd.

As Shepherd disappeared into the darkness with his two-best sheepdog, Morris told himself that his new helper was a star, a real Godsend.

The End

Acknowledgements:

Katie (and I) would like to thank, first and foremost, you, the reader, for taking a chance on reading my book. Without you picking up and reading it, there would be no need for me writing it, or the publisher releasing it. So, thank you. If you enjoyed Marble's Marvels, please consider leaving a review. And if you'd like some behind the scenes information, please follow me on Instagram: @dcbrockwell or my Facebook page: DCBrockwell Author. In addition to writing, I like gardening and making cocktails, so you'll find quite a mixed bag on my Instagram account.

I decided to write Marble's Marvels under a pseudonym to differentiate it from my grittier crime and psychological thrillers. My wife, Beks and I chose the name together. At first it was going to be Kitty Simpkins, but we both thought Kitty a bit too cutesy, and I didn't know anyone called Kitty, so we went with Katie instead. My first book written under Katie Simpkins was The Southern Belles, a feelgood, heart-warming romance novel set-in sunny Brighton, East Sussex.

In addition to you readers, I would also like to thank Donna Morfett at Fusion Press Publishing for taking a punt on my story. Thank you so much for this opportunity to showcase my work; it's more appreciated than you know. Donna is also my editor, marketer and all-round cheerleader. Thank you for your contributions in every form; you are superwoman. I hope I don't let you down. There are others who have contributed to the release of Marble's Marvels; Lesley Lloyd and Lynda Checkley, my two main beta readers. They pull me up on certain issues, so thank you so much.

And I can't sign off without thanking all my arc readers, who give up their time to read my ramblings and review them on Amazon and Goodreads. You're an amazing group of people and I feel lucky to have you on side. Brockwell's Betas is a fabulous group.

DC Brockwell can be found here:

Instagram: @dcbrockwell
Facebook Page: DCBrockwell Author
Twitter: DCBrockwell

Printed in Great Britain
by Amazon

58844979R00167